Escape
From the Past

The Kid
(Book 2)

ANNETTE OPPENLANDER

First published by Annette Oppenlander 2019
Second Edition
www.annetteoppenlander.com
Text copyright: Annette Oppenlander 2019
ISBN: 978-3-948100-04-9 eBook
ISBN: 978-3-948100-05-6 Paperback
The Library of Congress has cataloged the hardcover
edition as follows:
ISBN: 978 1 78535 213 3

Library of Congress Control Number: 2015946052

Design: Akira007/Fiverr

WHAT OTHERS ARE SAYING

"… a gripping YA historical novel. There's something about the essence of Western drama that makes exciting, wonderful reading. Max is fortunate enough to participate in the gritty, courageous kind of living that was once a day-to-day challenge. This is a great historical fantasy read that will make you want to read the first book in this series!"
–Historical Novel Society

"What a fun summer read! The Kid is an artful combination of science fiction and historical fiction that come together in a fantasy that is believable enough that the suspension of disbelief is possible and make the reading truly enjoyable. The contrast between Max's present-day gamer lifestyle and the historical setting that he finds himself in offer a glimpse of the past and make history relevant for young people who may find historical connections difficult to make. What a wonderful way to bring history to life, re-imagine the past, and imagine the future all at the same time!"
–Patrice W. Hallock, Ph.D., Associate Professor of Education, Chair, Educator Preparation & Psych-Child Life, Utica College

"Escape from the Past: The Kid is a magical fictional mystery interwoven with historical facts and exciting adventures. The reader experiences the twists and turns of the story while gaining a greater appreciation of the challenges of life in the Wild West during the late 1800's.
Max, a typical teenager of today, is thrown into a series of arduous challenges he must overcome in order to return to his former humdrum life. Along the way, he and we gain valuable insights and appreciation of the hardships encountered by the new western settlers and the Native American people amongst outlaws and the formidable desert

climate of the New Mexico area. It's a thoroughly enjoyable experience you will not want to miss."
–Richard Rafes, Ph.D., J.D., President of East Central University

"As an English teacher of 43 years and as a life-long student of the Wild West and Native Americans, I found Annette Oppenlander's, The Kid, to be an accurate, well-researched and thoroughly entertaining novel for young readers. The portrait of Max, the adventurous and risk-taking protagonist, is spot on;he has the language of young men his age and all the angst, dreams and longings that are hallmarks of a typical 17 year-old adolescent male. Ms. Oppenlander has a keen eye for detail, and her ability to create cliffhanging situations of high suspense makes for a great read. I strongly recommend this novel for any imaginative young reader who likes to have one foot in fantasy and one in reality."
–Bill Hays, English AP/Honors Teacher, Retired, Bloomington North High School

ALSO BY ANNETTE OPPENLANDER

A Different Truth *(Historical Mystery – Vietnam War Era)*
Escape From the Past: The Duke's Wrath(Book 1)
Escape From the Past: At Witches' End (Book 3)
47 Days: How Two Teen Boys Defied the Third Reich *(Historical Novelette)*
Surviving the Fatherland: A True Coming-of-age Love Story Set in WWII
(Historical Biographical Fiction)
Everything We Lose: A Civil War Novel of Hope, Courage and Redemption *(Historical Fiction)*
Where the Night Never Ends: A Prohibition Era Novel *(Historical Fiction)*
When They Made Us Leave *(WWII)*
A Lightness in My Soul: Inspired by a True Story *(WWII Novella)*
Boys No More (Short Story/Novella Collection)

GERMAN
Vaterland, wo bist Du?: Roman nach einer wahren Geschichte
Erzwungene Wege
47 Tage: Wie zwei Jungen Hitlers letztem Befehl trotzten
Immer der Fremdling: Die Rache des Grafen

"When I was young I walked all over this country, east and west, and saw no other people than the Apaches. After many summers I walked again and found another race of people had come to take it."
—Chief Cochise, Chiricahua Apache

For my children, Brian, Ethan and Nicole

CHAPTER ONE

"I thought you wanted the new Xbox for your birthday." My father's eyebrows knitted into a frown. "You've been talking about nothing else all year."

We were sitting in the pizza parlor in *Heiligenstadt*, Italian music playing in the background. We meet every two weeks as outlined in the divorce decree and as usual, my father sounded irritated.

"*I* thought you'd be glad I didn't want more gaming stuff." I stared at my father who had the same blue-green eyes I had. At one point he'd had the same dark brown hair. Now, he was mostly gray with a bald spot on top.

"But horseback riding? You've never wanted to be near anything larger than a dog. What's this new interest? Or will you change your mind next week?"

I shook my head and threw the tired crust of the last pizza slice back on the plate. "I already went a few times this spring. I can ride my bike there and if I help with the stalls, they charge only half."

"All right," my father said. "I'll cover the first four months. After that we'll see if you're still interested."

"Great. Thanks, Dad."

"So what else are you not telling me?"

"What do you mean?"

"Your mother called. She's really concerned."

"Because I want to spend time with her?" *And not you.*

"No, only your general behavior, studying history like a maniac. The books in your room about the Middle Ages, the new interest in herbs and natural medicine. Your visits to the Hanstein ruins, the sword practice in the yard. Isn't that a bit excessive?"

I shrugged. "It's interesting to learn about this stuff. I never realized it until now."

"I see."

But it was obvious that my father didn't see. He kept staring at me, several times opening his mouth as if to comment, then clamping tight. The silence between us grew.

"I'm meeting Jimmy at the movies," I said.

"Of course." My father waved at the waiter. He seemed relieved to put an end to our visit. "There is one more thing."

"Yeah?"

My father hesitated and cleared his throat which should've clued me in right there. As a captain in the U.S. Army my father is used to calling the shots. "I'm getting married again."

"What?" My stomach knotted angrily around the half-digested pizza. "You mean that chick who looks like a college student and giggles like a halfwit."

"She isn't a college student and she's certainly no halfwit," my father snapped. "She's doing her residency at the hospital." He bit his lip, obviously unsure how to continue.

"You can't be serious." Scenes from long ago flashed by. My parents holding hands, the three of us on a beach in Cancun. Truth is, I always expected they'd get back together. Now my dream had popped like an overinflated soap bubble, leaving a bad taste in my mouth.

"Maybe one day you'll understand—"

Swallowing a nasty comment, I abruptly straightened and hurried outside. If my father did call after me I didn't hear it.

A perfect summer sun mocked me as I stormed up and down the shopping street. I still had an hour before meeting Jimmy, but I'd rather hang out by myself than spend one more minute with a guy who was robbing the cradle. It was so gross, it was nauseating.

I'd considered telling him about the game. How I'd been transported to the year 1471, chased by lords and spent weeks with Knight Werner at Castle Hanstein. I'd almost died in a dungeon and fallen for a girl. Impossible. My father would have me committed before he believed one word.

But I couldn't help thinking about it.

Every day since I'd returned I thought about the mess I'd left behind and that I wanted to go back and straighten things out. Talk to Juliana, dive into her brown eyes again, stick my nose into her hair. Kiss her… I sighed again. I wanted to explain to her how I was from a different time and that you didn't get married as a teenager. That I was finishing high school and planned to go to college.

And there was Bero. My friend. He was a squire now and probably practicing sword fighting with Enders right this minute. He'd be jumping around in that squirrel-like way, shouting with glee when he got the best of Enders.

And Knight Werner? You didn't cross a mighty lord and just disappear after he'd offered to make you his squire. Werner was probably mad and would kick me from the castle if I showed my face again.

A rattled breath escaped me. It was best to move on. I was comfortable at home and school. I had a few friends, even if they weren't super cool, I felt reasonably happy. My parents were another story, but soon I'd move out on my own. So, why couldn't I just forget the darn game and enjoy the stuff I'd been doing before? Like playing *normal* computer games, like hanging out with Jimmy and watching the girls from my class at the movies and the ice cream parlor afterwards. Hanging out at parties, hoping for a piece of warm skin next to mine.

School was a drag, but it wasn't *that* bad. Especially when compared to the lousy lives Juliana and Bero led before they moved to the castle. At least they were safe now. Until the next battle when Bero would be forced to help protect Werner's right hand, Konrad. Maybe Bero was dead already.

Of course, he was dead. Almost six-hundred years had passed. The game was messing with my head.

"Max?"

I spun around. Jimmy was standing in front of me.

"Oh, hi."

"You were a million miles away," Jimmy said with a grin. "Got here early, drove the GTI." When I didn't answer, he said, "Something wrong? You aren't still thinking of playing the game again?"

I shrugged. "Haven't decided."

"Didn't you hear what Father said? What if you don't return at all or they cut off your arm or leg in a battle? Or you get the Plague or something…"

"I don't want to talk about it."

"Fine."

"Let's watch the movie," I said, eager to change the subject. Jimmy was right, of course. There were thousands of unknowns and even if I studied for ten years, I'd not be prepared for the dangers lurking in fifteenth century Bornhagen.

In my mind the voice continued to whisper. I'd carry a few things in my pockets. I knew more about treating illnesses with plants. Luanda, the healer could help, too. I'd prepare my clothes, wear different shoes. I knew the place.

My chances had to be way better, even if I didn't know what the missions would be. Maybe I had to brew some more herbs, meet new people.

I wondered if anyone else had ever played the game. Jimmy's father had said some things that sounded suspicious. That it was dangerous and they couldn't control the parameters of the game. How would he have known that unless someone else had played? But it was useless to ask him again. Jimmy's father wasn't talking.

"Are you going to get the new Xbox?" Jimmy said as the lights dimmed and we settled into our seats. "We could do a tournament at my house. Stay up all night, eat junk food."

Of course, Jimmy already had the new Xbox. Just like he had the newest iPhone and Mac.

"I don't think I'll get one," I said. I wasn't really in the mood to explain why I wanted to ride horses instead. Let Jimmy think that my father was too cheap.

The theatre went dark.

"What do you mean, we aren't going," I yelled panting with anger.

My mother leaned against the stove, holding a ladle in midair. "I'm sorry, Max. The promotion is finally happening and my new boss—he…we're attending a seminar in Munich all week." Her hand sank and the spoon dropped into the soup. "Maybe we can get away during fall break."

"You mean that creep, Parker, don't you? He's been drooling over you for over a year. I've seen him!" My voice was reaching new heights. I coughed to clear my throat.

"Herr Parker is a good manager. And I'm quite old enough to take care of myself." My mother straightened, though she only reached to my collarbone.

I saw how he ogled you at the Christmas party. The man's eyeballs were practically glued to my mother's cleavage. Disgusting.

"Can't you tell him you have plans?" I said aloud. "We booked months ago."

"It doesn't work that way," my mother said. "We'll be able to afford more trips in the future. And we'll start saving for a car for you."

"Yeah, right." I ran down the hall and threw shut the door to my room. I fell on the bed, ignoring the pressure in my throat. It was stupid to cry, a girl thing. Angrily I swiped an arm across my face.

This had to be the lousiest weekend ever. First my father, now my mother. I'd been so happy about going to Crete. Two weeks of swimming and hanging out at the beach, riding scooters across the island and looking at old stuff.

I shook my head as if the movement could make the memory of my joyful anticipation vanish. Jimmy was going away for the entire summer break. First to some place in southern France, then to an adventure camp. And I would be stuck in Bornhagen for six weeks with the highlight being the public pool in Heiligenstadt.

If I thought about it, Jimmy was a jerk the way he kept rubbing his wealth in my face. He knew perfectly well, my mom and I were struggling. And he of all people still had both his parents. A perfect little family.

Truth was I was completely alone. Nobody cared what I did, not even my so-called best friend.

I wiped away a tear and sat up.

I'd had it.

There was only one way I'd get my mind off things. I'd been undecided for months, but it was obvious nobody gave a damn about me anyway. If I returned, I'd rest through the summer. If not, well…I'd see about that.

I listened for movement from the kitchen. My mother would leave me alone to cool off. Now was as good a time as ever.

Digging into my closet, I pulled out several items. The window stood open, curtains billowing in the breeze. With a sigh I changed and slumped in front of the computer. The air smelled of mowed grass and my mother's yellow roses...of promised vacations and broken dreams.

I inserted the disk and grabbed the half-empty soda can. There wouldn't be any soda where I was going.

The can hovered in midair. I had to be insane. Hadn't I almost died last time? But the memory of my stupid parents returned and I drank quickly, my gulps loud in the stillness of the early evening. To heck with them. I needed to forget.

I took mental inventory of my outfit, the items I'd prepped and stuck into my pants pocket.

On the monitor the globe appeared and began to spin. I slid backwards until my spine rested firmly against the chair. This time I'd pay attention to the way it felt when my room dissolved. Maybe it wouldn't happen at all. Maybe I'd just play a game and remain in stupid Bornhagen.

I aimed the mouse, trying to remember what had happened last time. The globe was supposed to stop and show an entrance door. I waited, but the earth kept rotating.

The start button flashed, "Enter now."

I sighed with relief and clicked.

The screen turned dark, almost black. I leaned closer. Had the monitor quit? But then the faint outlines of something bulky materialized in the distance, the sky above peppered with a million stars. I grinned. The skies in the Middle Ages were breathtaking. No pollution, no artificial lights.

The screen kept zooming through the darkness. A second shadow of something tall appeared ahead. I remembered the thick forests, oak trees soaring a hundred and fifty feet. Somebody whistled or was it the wind whispering. The screen kept moving slowly, yet remained dark. It was definitely nighttime.

The ancient parchment unrolled from the bottom, its corners torn and burned as if it had escaped fire: the menu.

Level Two
Expert
Pause
Exit

Upgrade to expert now blinked below.

My mouse finger trembled, in fact my entire arm shook. I was about to enter the most dangerous place I'd ever been to. Why couldn't I just put up with my life even if it sucked?

You are going to do this.

I was prepared. I knew what to expect, had even gotten clothes that looked more medieval, a long-sleeved shirt with wide arms, leftover from Carnival, a hooded oversized sweater that would have to double as a coat.

I'm doing it.

Now.

As soon as I clicked, my chest began to throb, then tighten. Had it been this painful last time? Ten months had passed since I'd last played. I smiled despite the ache. I couldn't wait to sneak up on Bero. Hug Juliana. The pressure on my body increased. She'd be mad, of course, but then she'd kiss me. Maybe we could sneak into the barn tonight.

The weight on my lungs grew further. Breathing stopped, my vision filled with the red haze of oxygen deprivation. I tried to gulp, but my ribs were glued to my sides. I was stuck…and terrified. The fog turned gray…then black. Like last time, I managed to stand, but my legs and feet stood rooted like the giant oaks in Hanstein's forest.

My heart pounded in my neck, the only sign I was still alive. The fog deepened. Why was this taking so long? Still the pressure held as if I'd been thrown under a boulder. I was dying.

I'd made a huge mistake.

It's easy to forget fear. Stuff happens and you get distracted. After a while all you remember are the good things. Now that I was unable to move, unable to do anything, I remembered the way I'd felt the first time I'd landed in the game. I'd felt terror.

And terror was back now in full force, squeezing my middle and poking at my heart. As the pressure lifted and the fog cleared, the sense of impending doom gripped me with such force that I fell forward.

I'd made a horrible mistake.

Stumbling, I stubbed my toes and suppressed a shout. In the near darkness, a rock or cliff rose wide as a house and three stories high. I only saw its outline, a black edge against the starry sky above.

The whistling I'd heard earlier definitely came from between the giant rocks. The air was filled with the scent of grasses, grit, and something like sage. Had I returned in the summer?

Behind me the area appeared more open. Maybe I was down near the river and Luanda's house. Should I move in the dark or wait? I'd get lost, wandering off in the wrong direction.

A cold wind dug under my shirt and nipped at my skin. I tugged my sweater closer around me when I saw something glowing on the ground like a huge red eye.

"Not a move, boy," the voice hissed. "Or I'll blow a hole through your gut."

CHAPTER TWO

The voice was deep and cold as the wind. Something hard and unyielding dug into my back. Maybe it was one of Werner's men or had I run into Schwarzburg's guards? But something felt wrong, something I couldn't put my finger on.

Before I knew what to do, the ground shifted as several shadows rose around me.

"Wade, what is it?"

"Found us an intruder," Wade said. "Showed up like a stray coyote." For emphasis he shoved at my ribs. I suppressed a yelp as the pain spread to my stomach.

"You sleeping, Wade? Let someone walk in here like that." This voice was scratchy as a cheese grater with an Irish-sounding twang.

A sudden light stung my eyes. One of the shadows had lit a match not five inches from my nose.

"Look at that. What *is* that?" the man with the Irish voice said. "It's a kid."

I caught a glimpse of a reddish beard, a grimy bandana on the neck below and a leather vest. Definitely not Duke Schwarzburg or Werner.

Wait a minute.

I gulped as new panic sucked away my air and turned my stomach. These men spoke English. I was nowhere near Hanstein. Though they spoke a weird dialect, I understood them clearly.

I shook my head. It had to be the game. I'd been able to

communicate with Bero and Juliana even though they spoke some kind of medieval German. What if they were speaking some other language entirely and it was all an illusion? What had Jimmy's father done?

"Damn, Wade, can't you shoot 'em?" a voice drifted up from the ground.

"Kill 'em and let us sleep," someone else grumbled.

I trembled as I realized that the poking thing in my right kidney was a gun. Any second now the guy could pull the trigger. And unlike last time when I'd gone to medieval Germany, this time I knew with certainty that I'd really die, that these were the stakes of the game.

I felt my knees wobble as I tried to think of a way out. But running was suicide. These guys would shoot me in the back.

"Let him talk," the short Irish man said. "Almost time to leave anyway." The horizon was growing the faintest bit of gray. "You got a name, boy? Speak."

Wade shoved at my back. The sharp pain made me gasp and I crumpled to the ground, inches from the fire pit. "Open your pie hole or we're going to put you out of your misery. You're costing us sleep."

"I'm Max."

"Max what? You got a name. What're you hiding?" the Irish said.

I hesitated. Was I still Max Nerds? It had been fitting at Hanstein.

"I'll split you in half," Wade said, shoving his rifle into my side once more. I winced as pain shot up my spine.

"Damn, Wade, he's a kid. Let him talk." Another guy, his head resting on a saddle, had spoken. Even in the morning gloom I knew his nose was broken and bent sideways.

"Max Nerds," I gasped as I struggled to kneel without falling into the coals. My back was on fire from the vicious blow and I wondered if I'd cracked a rib. "Dude, I got lost out here."

"You're speaking a strange tongue? Where's your parents?"

"Don't have any." Better to make stuff up than try to explain. These men looked like they had the patience of a gnat. "I'm looking for a job."

"He's looking for work in the desert? On foot?" Broken Nose guffawed. "He's lying," Wade said. "Look at his clothes. That shirt." The guy spit. "He's dressed like a girl. Way too clean, too."

"Where's your horse, laddy?" the Irish said.

"It died." I tried looking like I did when my mom asked about late night gaming.

"You got no bags, no gun, no horse and no family," Wade sneered. "The guy is a nobody. Let's finish him off. Nobody will miss 'em."

"Yeah, let's get us more sleep," someone mumbled.

"Not so fast." The Irish tugged at the filthy cloth with a blackish stain on his neck. I wondered if he'd been shot. "He may come in handy. Horse or errand boy… or bait." He opened his mouth as if to add something, but then seemed to think better of it. "Let's keep him for now." The Irish spit, his projectile hitting the dirt an inch from my boots—fur-lined leather hiking shoes, I'd bought on sale in Heiligenstadt.

"We can't trust him," Wade said, moving to face me. His forefinger twitched on the rifle he pointed at my belly.

"He'll do for now," the Irish said. "Go back to your post." He waved at me. "Sit and no wrong moves."

I nodded, watching Wade walk off. He wore a short leather coat, the spikes on his boots clinking with every step. I sank next to the fire and wrapped my arms around my knees, trying to look relaxed. I was freezing despite the thick sweater.

Despite my icy cheeks and my fingers stiff with cold, my brain was doing overtime. I had to know where I was and more importantly, when. But if I asked these thugs, I'd be dead faster than you could say Max. The scene looked as if it'd been taken right from an old western. I was definitely somewhere in the American Wild West and these men were some kind of gang. Cold dread clogged my throat. Something felt totally wrong about them. About this…this place.

I shook my head in frustration. Broken nose got to his feet, spitting and scratching his back, then rummaging among the cast-iron cooking pots. The Irish leaned against his saddle, taking a drink from a flask.

A pale strip of light edged across the horizon and illuminated the ground in front of me, littered with reddish gravel, rocks, and clumps of thick grass. Larger boulders lay strewn near the men, forming a natural outdoor arena. In the distance towered rock formations the size of apartment buildings. They looked reddish, too, though I couldn't be sure. I licked my lips. Already, they felt dry and stretched painfully. And I was unbearably thirsty.

Broken Nose rekindled the fire and was cooking something. I sniffed. It smelled strange, but definitely like food. I thought of home where my mother would soon fix dinner.

You aren't home, so quit thinking about it.

A sunray pierced the landscape like a giant laser. I blinked at the sudden brilliance and inspected the ground again. It was definitely red, fine dust now clinging to my pants, turning them almost pink. Some of it had made it to my mouth like gritty toothpaste.

As the light steadily grew, I remained seated, too afraid to move. I watched the sun's beam edge along the towering rocks behind me. With every minute the air grew hotter. And dryer.

I had no weapons, but it was apparent these men each packed several, revolvers on each hip and plenty of bullets on leather belts draped across their chests, assorted rifles at their feet.

What was I supposed to do now? How far was it to the next town? Even if I escaped, without water I'd be dead soon. The sun was turning into a viciously burning sphere, blowing superheated air like a hairdryer on maximum setting. My back throbbed. Sweat trickled down my chest, so I peeled off my sweater and stuffed it under my legs. I was going to boil alive.

The men didn't seem to care. Judging by their sweat-stained, hats, shirts and pants, they were used to it.

They stumbled behind the rocks relieving themselves, lit stinky brown cigars, and shoved down the primitive stew with beans and jerky. My mouth was filled with grit, my lips burning as I stared longingly at the water skins lying next to the men's saddles. A cast iron jug sat on the fire, emanating the faint smell of coffee. Outdoor camping at its finest.

I grimaced.

Here I'd expected to visit the Middle Ages and instead I'd landed in another country altogether, most likely the U.S.… *Home*, I thought bitterly. Not the home I'd loved and lost near Seattle. The man had said we were in some kind of desert. That left several places in the southwest: Arizona, Texas, maybe California.

I peeked sideways. The man they called Wade was perched on a rock, but his eyes were still on me, his mouth curled into an evil grin.

I looked away and inwardly shuddered. That man would kill me like a rattlesnake. With a sigh I rested my head on my knees. If I wanted to live I'd have to find out where I was. And I'd stay close to the short Irish guy who seemed to run the show—at least for now.

I dozed, the dehydration making me groggy and slow. Around me the men ate, the only change was Wade joining the group and Broken Nose taking his spot.

The sun blazed full strength now, the men shading their faces with hats and saddles. I had nothing to cover my head. I'd contemplated wearing a hat into the game, but had worried about raising suspicion, just as my *Nikes* had last time.

My eyes stung from the sun's intensity, reflecting off rocks and sand. My forehead pounded. I imagined my kidneys shriveling, my body turning into a mummy.

"Could I have some water?" I croaked finally. Nobody had paid attention to me, except to kick me here and there as if by accident. Wade had been most vicious, ramming his pointy boot into my thigh.

"Give the boy some water," the Irish guy ordered.

"But Boss, we're short already." The man who'd spoken had a scar on his jaw wide as a pink ribbon. "If he's stupid enough to wander around the desert without water, he should pay for it."

The Irish shot Scarface a look and I found myself with a thin pouch of water.

"Make it last," Scarface barked.

I drank carefully, remembering my stint in Schwarzburg's dungeon. I'd been so dehydrated and weak that I almost died. The jury was still out on my fate here, but it sure didn't look good. After a short meal accompanied by grumbles, the men saddled their horses. I landed on a gray donkey with a severe overbite, the beast trying to take a chunk out of my forearm.

"He bites," someone snickered as I yanked the reins and mounted. Despite having been doled the biter, I was glad to have a small animal. The few riding lessons I'd paid for myself in the spring by no means equipped me to control some half-wild beast. The men would immediately know I wasn't a rider. At least the donkey was slower and seemed in no mood to exert itself anymore than it had to.

We headed west, me third in the row of men, wishing for the

sun to stop blazing and scorching my neck. The landscape stretched in front of us, red rocks, a few wind-bent bushes, grass hard and sharp as blades and lots of gravelly sand. I kept my head low, my insides churning with terror.

I was utterly lost.

CHAPTER THREE

My attention shifted to my butt. My riding lessons had lasted a half hour tops. Now each step pounded my muscles, the saddle digging into the bruises, sweat pouring from my thighs, drenching my pants and sending sharp jolts of pain to my lower back. I wanted to pull up my legs, away from the unforgiving leather that was tearing up my skin, but the prospect of walking in the unrelenting heat was worse.

The men didn't seem to care. They lived on their horses, eyes hidden in the shadow of their hats. They hawked wads of tobacco, spit once in a while or muttered a few words.

I kept my lids low to reduce the glare and often closed my eyes altogether. I'd read a story on snow blindness and worried about my corneas. My water pouch was shrinking fast, but no matter how often I drank, the thirst remained, my lips breaking open and bleeding. Whenever I squinted around, nothing changed except for the size of the rock formations and the shape of the low-rising hills.

By the time we stopped in the shadow of a humungous boulder I was ready to collapse. My butt was hamburger meat and my head had turned into an aching balloon void of thought. All I wanted was to lie in the shade and drink a gallon of water. Make that two. By the lean feel of my water skin, I had a few drops left. By tomorrow I'd be completely dehydrated. The day after I'd be dead.

The men dozed, alternatively chewing jerky and tobacco.

Scarface threw a piece of jerky at me. On closer inspection it looked like shoe leather from my grandfather's boot. Besides, I refused to chew something that took moisture to swallow. I stuck it into my pocket.

Whenever I looked up, Wade stared at me. He seemed to wait for me to trip up. The Irish guy with the raspy voice was definitely in charge, the men keeping their distance. Even Wade didn't seem willing to provoke him.

Getting back on the donkey was the hardest thing I'd ever done. By the way the sun hung lower, it had to be midafternoon. I was bone-tired and so hot that my light shirt was dark with sweat. Once in a while I scanned the horizon, wishing for clouds, wishing for something to change and get me out of my misery. Of course, there was no such thing. The relentless blazing continued, the sky huge and intensively blue. My muscles screamed with every step and the insides of my thighs burned raw.

"Hey Kid." The voice sounded muffled as I awoke from a daze. The Irish had pulled his horse next to donkey biter, watching me with clear green eyes.

"What?" I croaked.

"You don't look so good. Where do you say you come from?"

I swallowed, but there was nothing but grit in my mouth and my mind was blank. I finally waved my chin toward my right shoulder. "East."

"You a city boy." It wasn't a question. "Going to make your fortune in the west? Get some gold?"

I nodded and threw a sideward glance at the man, my eyes aching from the scorching brightness sinking low in the sky. I had to ask. "Where're we going?"

The Irish threw me a quick look. "Santa Fe. Isn't that where you were heading?"

I managed another nod. That was in New Mexico if I remembered right. "How far?"

"Boss, look." Wade yanked around his horse. I saw nothing, but Scarface next to him raised an arm. Everyone stopped. I was glad my donkey got his cues from the other horses or I would've walked on.

"Looks like settlers," Broken Nose said. "Are we going to take them?"

"Don't be stupid," the Irish said. "They have nothing we

want."

We moved on and as the setting sun turned everything red as blood, I finally saw them. My back and legs were on fire and I felt miserable, but the two families in front of us appeared much worse.

Four oxen each pulled two cloth-covered wagons. By the looks of them, the animals were close to collapse, their heads drooping, bony hips nearly sticking through the coarse gray skin. Two men, their faces hidden behind months-old beards walked alongside, followed by three women, their skirts covered in reddish dust, their cheek bones sharp in their hollowed faces. On top of the wagon, two small grimy faces seemed equally starved. The group walked so slowly, they looked like sleepwalkers.

Despite their obvious exhaustion, both men raised their rifles when they saw us.

"Top of the evening," the Irish called, sounding as fresh as if he were strolling in a park.

"And to you," the older of the two men said with a courteous nod. I noticed him throwing an anxious glance at the women. One of them was a girl my age. She looked as if she were acting in some old western, her dress long and brown, a hat squashed low over her forehead, hiding most of the blonde braid. She was leaning against one of the wagons, wiping her forehead with a bony arm. Our eyes met. I nodded, but the girl immediately glanced down.

"Heading to Santa Fe?" The Irish asked.

The older man shook his head. "Left the Santa Fe trail for the Sunnyside settlement." His rifle swung seemingly casual across the ground.

"Should be close, maybe another two days."

"Good."

"You got any water?" The Irish nodded toward us. "We're thirsty."

The older man began to shake his head when the second man chimed in. "Maybe a sip. It's been a hard journey and we're low. But if you say we're close, we'll be happy to share." He nodded at the women who scrambled toward the back of the first wagon. The gang climbed off their horses with ease. Too tired to move, I followed them with my eyes.

The older of the two women returned with a wooden pale. Her blonde hair and brown eyes reminded me of my mother.

Except that this woman looked twenty years older—and thirty pounds lighter.

I cringed. Even from atop my donkey I could tell the water in the pale was brown as weak coffee and emitted a foul smell. The Irish seemed to think the same and tipped his hat.

"Thank you, Ma'am, you better keep it for yourselves and your oxen. Safe travels." He nodded at Wade and Scarface and walked toward his horse. The men slowly followed as if they were disappointed not to engage in a fight.

With a sigh I straightened my aching back.

And froze.

From my higher vantage point I noticed a dust cloud growing rapidly larger. And from it grew an apparition of terror, the likes I'd never seen.

Two-dozen Native Americans galloped toward us, fanned out like the tip of an arrow. They rode bareback, their faces painted black, red and white, their long oiled hair flowing behind them. They wore leather pants with loin clothes and nothing but beads and feathers around their necks.

"Indians," I mumbled. I hadn't even realized I said something except that Wade whipped around and followed my gaze.

"Injuns, Boss," he shouted, "looks like Comanches." He ripped his gun from its holster on the saddle, the other men following suit.

The next moments were a blur. I felt myself slide off the donkey and race to the wagons for cover. The settlers were scrambling underneath, getting in position. The girl raced to grab the two little kids and shove them under the wagon.

I watched in fascination. As if time had slowed to a crawl, the Indians, shrouded in a dust cloud, drew near. Their faces looked hideous with war paint, but their cries were what made me tremble with dread. It sounded like something out of this world, eerie whoops that curdled my blood.

I had no weapons. Even if I'd had any, my body was stiff with panic. Apparently, I wasn't the only one. The girl stood motionless, her eyes wide with fear, her mouth open in a silent scream. I dashed to her. There was no more room underneath the wagon. Besides, it wasn't really a hiding place anyway. The gang had joined the settlers except for the Irish and Wade who hid behind the tarp on either side.

I grabbed the girl's hand and turned the other way. Gunshots exploded behind us as we rushed past the horses toward the towering rocks. Any second, the Indians would be able to see around the wagons. I wanted to run faster, but the girl whose skinny wrist I held onto, was dragging behind.

Shouts rang out and more shots were fired, the Indians' whooping so loud that my ears rang. In-between I heard the swish-swish of arrows. Then a scream.

We slipped behind the rocks as the Indians began to circle the wagons. I pulled the girl with me, hoping nobody had seen us.

The ground was uneven here, the rocks stacked, leaving huge holes for a foot to get wedged or an ankle to turn. I looked frantically for a hiding place. These Indians would hunt us down. The whooping continued while the blasts thinned out.

Horses neighed, followed by braying.

They had my donkey. Another scream, the high pitched shriek of a woman in agony.

Trying to make my shaking legs move, I inspected the rocks towering above us. We had to get off the ground. Fast. The boulders appeared set on top of each other, huge chunks of red stone each as tall as a truck. Some had split apart, gravelly debris spilling like a stony carpet from above. They'd slide and throw up dust, a perfect trail for the Indians.

Better to climb the actual rock instead. I grabbed hold of a boulder and pulled up, willing my fingers to be strong enough to carry my weight. Nothing mattered except that we had to get out of sight. I found a toehold and straining against the rock, grabbed the girl's wrist.

To my relief she was completely silent, her face drained of color, her mouth trembling. *You're too slow*, my mind screamed. The rock wall was steep, the crumbling reddish gravel still so superheated from the day's blaze that my fingers burned. I kept climbing and dragging the girl.

Rocks scattered below us. I worried about the Indians hearing us move. There were no more shots, only horse clatter and snorts. Then the air filled with shouts, deep and guttural and full of satisfaction.

I kept pulling myself up, forcing my aching muscles to move. Higher, higher. At last I landed on a narrow ledge, above me nothing but sheer walls. My arms had turned to pudding, my thighs ached with fatigue. I lay flat and squeezed against the rock that burned easily through my shirt, yanking the girl toward me.

The clip clop of horses drew near. I quickly scooted sideways, away from the edge, coming to rest against the vertical rock face, drawing the girl next to me, my forearm across her chest. There was no place to go, no caves or holes. Only solid, unyielding stone. I felt her breathing and trembling at the same time. The view up here would've been amazing, had it not been for the setting dusk and the lethal threat below.

Who cared? I didn't give a possum's ass.

Not bad, I sounded like some wild cowboy already. All I hoped was that they hadn't seen us and didn't know how many people had been there.

We waited, the horses below quiet. On the other side voices jabbered and yipped something unintelligible. Though I knew little about Indians, I knew what this meant: victory.

A woman screamed. And grew silent.

The girl's body vibrated in response. Still she made no sound.

My mind summersaulted. What if the Indians were climbing up here? I'd read terrible things about scalping and rape, Indians torturing their prisoners. Without any weapon I couldn't even kill myself.

We lay absolutely still—only my forefinger rubbed the girl's thumb. Below us the horses resumed their stroll. Slowly the sound faded. The last light disappeared and the air turned immediately cold. I didn't feel it.

Sandwiched between the sun-scorched boulder and the girl, I looked at the sky where a million stars twinkled uncaring. My heart ached with longing for home... for my safe, boring room.

I'd entered a new kind of hell and worst of all I'd done it willingly. Once again the game had screwed me...Jimmy's father had screwed me. I wasn't in the Middle Ages and I certainly wasn't in Germany. The realization that I once again had to play at something I knew nothing about and likely would lose my life hit me. This time I was the one vibrating and I was thankful the girl remained silent.

I must've nodded off when somebody shoved me. Fighting the daze, I noticed the girl sitting on the ledge. The memory of the attack came crashing back and I hastily sat up.

"Are they gone?" I whispered. I had no idea how much time

had passed.

"I think so," the girl said, her voice surprisingly deep.

"You sure."

I could tell she was nodding.

"I'm Max," I said, moving next to her.

"Grace."

"I better investigate. You wait up here. Just in case." I slid off the ledge, for once glad for my thick boots. I'd cursed them all day in the terrible heat, but now they helped cushion the rocks.

"No," came from above. To my annoyance, the girl followed, her movements slower and more cautious.

I had to feel my way down, the bluish light of the half-moon creating more shadows than light. One false step and I'd break my neck. I hadn't realized how far up we'd climbed and how steep some of the rocks were. It took forever.

When I felt firm ground, I let out a sigh. For a second my knees wanted to buckle. *Keep it together!*

Leaning against the stone, I listened to her slow descent. Somewhere high the wind whistled. I shivered. I remembered my sweater that I'd left hanging on the donkey. What if it was gone? According to what I understood of the game, I needed all my stuff to return to present day. Either way, I was light-years from home. Grace climbed off the last rock and crumpled next to me.

"You want to wait here?" I whispered, trying to adjust my girl-communication tactics.

Grace pulled herself up. "No."

Stubborn idiot. But then I was dreading what was on the other side of the rocks. And these people were her family. I took hold of her arm and together we snuck around the huge rock. Above us the wind shrieked a lonely song.

Despite the semi-darkness, I will never forget the scene that awaited us.

First I noticed that our horses were gone. Except for donkey biter I'd loathed. It lay on its side in a gray heap of crusted fur and blood, half a dozen arrows in its side. I was surprised that I felt sad. The animal had been mean, but it hadn't done anything to deserve this.

I kneeled and fumbled around the ground, where a lukewarm mass of blood was congealing in the sand. My sweater, its sleeves sticky, lay next to it. When I got up I didn't see the girl. I only noticed the sickening stench of blood, loosened bowels and an eerie silence: the smells and sounds of death.

I wandered toward the bulking shadows of what was left of the caravan. The two wagons had been upturned, their contents strewn around. Even in the gloom it was clear they were modest household goods: a mattress, a few pillows, some pots and pans, wooden pails broken, suitcases torn open and clothes spread around.

That's when I heard it. A terrible sobbing sound, so lonely and so desperate that I shivered. I ran toward it.

Grace kneeled on the ground, cradling her mother's head in her lap, seemingly unaware that the woman's scalp was missing. The bare patch looked grotesque in what was left of the blonde hair, a pale bloody hole showing the bony skull beneath. I looked away, my stomach ready to erupt.

That's when I noticed the others. The two settler men had been stripped, shot and scalped. Next to them lay what was left of Broken Nose and Scarface. Three more men from the gang whose names I'd never learned lay crumpled nearby. The oxen, still in their harnesses, had been slaughtered: eight big heaps of bones and meat, soon to be devoured by whatever was hungry out here.

Ignoring the bile in my throat, I staggered among the dead. I didn't see the Irish or Wade. Maybe they'd been dragged farther away or taken prisoners.

We'd escaped an Indian raid. And everything I'd read or studied in school had been true. I returned to the girl, who still sat on the ground, her wail reduced to whimpering.

"We should go. It's not safe." I forced myself to sound convincing. Grace didn't seem to hear and I put a hand on her shoulder. I thought of my own mother and how I'd feel if she were dead.

Impossible to imagine.

"Come on. They may return." I scanned around the emptiness, the silence of death. The slowness of the girl was annoying.

At last Grace looked up, her eyes mysterious pools in the darkness. She gently took a necklace off her mother's throat and covered the woman's bony thighs. I remembered the screams and knew what the Indians had done.

"Do you know what direction we have to go?" I asked. I

looked at the stars wishing I'd learned to read astrological signs.

Grace stared at the night sky. "That way." Without another word she began to walk.

I scrambled after her. Chances were great she'd get us lost. "How do you know?"

She didn't answer.

"Come on, Grace. I don't want to wander around in the desert. We'll die for sure."

"I wish I'd died," she suddenly cried. "I wish they'd killed me, too. Why did you take me away?"

I struggled to say something. Nothing sounded right. I'd saved her, but that was obviously not appreciated. Finally I took her hand. "I can't imagine what you're going through right now. But we're still alive and we need to get going. All I'm asking right now is that you figure out a general western direction. Cause we need to find Santa Fe."

That's when it occurred to me that I had no idea why the Irish and his gang had been headed there. Even if I knew now it meant nothing. I was lost in this vast country in this vast game with no idea where to turn.

"Weren't you going to some settlement?" I managed.

"Sunnyside."

"You know the way?"

Grace stifled another sob and wiped her face with a grimy sleeve. "The North Star is always north. See." She pointed into the night. "That one low in the sky. If we keep it to our right, we'll go west."

With a sigh I bound the bloody sweater around my waist. In less than twenty-four hours I'd been captured by some gang and attacked by Indians. How could I've been so gullible to play the game a second time?

I hated Jimmy's father. But I hated myself more for being so stupid, for underestimating the game. I'd not had a clue how it worked and I'd assumed...

Now I was trapped in some Wild West nightmare where it was even easier to get killed than in the Middle Ages.

"In that case, let's go," I said aloud.

CHAPTER FOUR

The ground was an obstacle course. I hadn't realized how easy I'd had it on the donkey. We stumbled across grasses, bushes with thorns the size of daggers, and rocks and more rocks. Crevices opened without warning, hills stretched across the horizon in unending procession.

We climbed left and right, up and down. Some holes opened into canyons the size of entire neighborhoods. After a while I knew nothing... Not where we'd come from nor where we were going.

I tried remembering a map of New Mexico, but drew a blank. All I knew was that we were somewhere east of Santa Fe and not too far from this settlement of Sunnyside.

Which left another huge question: what year was it?

My mind was going in circles, the lack of water making me groggy and slow. My body felt like I'd been beaten, my throat was raw with thirst. The water skins had disappeared. The wind was picking up, tugging at us. I was thankful for my warm boots, but the shirt was way too thin, and my eyes and cheeks burned from the dry cold air.

The girl stumbled along beside me. She hadn't said a word since we left. I longed for rest, but I'd be damned if I said anything first. I kept my eyes trained on the horizon, every once in a while checking the low-rising star to our right.

The wind was gaining speed. Near the vast rocks, the air was alive with eerie sounds, a whistling and shrieking that reminded me of ghosts. I wasn't really afraid of the noise, but when a pack of coyotes joined in, the girl grabbed my arm.

"Did you hear that?" she said.

"Yep. Nothing we can do. They won't attack us unless…"

"Unless what?" The girl's voice trembled.

"We bleed or they think we're weak."

The girl fell back into silence. We continued walking while I kept my eyes peeled on the horizon. The Irish had said *a day or two till the settlement* but what did it mean? Was it by horse or on foot? Straight ahead, south or north? What if we walked right past it in the dark and disappeared somewhere into the wilderness?

In a few years somebody would come across a couple skeletons. I imagined shreds of fabric fluttering across bleached ribs. Anonymous casualties of the desert. At home nobody would know where I'd gone. My mother would cry and cry. Put up ads for lost children.

I sighed. "Maybe we should stop and wait till daylight."

"What about the coyotes? They'll come for us." As if to confirm her point, howls echoed to our left, then more from behind.

We were screwed if we stopped and screwed if we continued. The sun would get us during the day. I forced my legs to move on.

"Where are you from, Grace?" I asked to distract myself.

"Pennsylvania."

"It's a long way." Duh, I was making really smart conversation. "I mean how long have you been traveling?"

"We left last year. But we stopped in Oklahoma to see my uncle to wait out the winter. He's got a homestead."

Now was my chance. Even if I sounded like an idiot. "So what year did you leave?"

The girl hesitated. "What do you mean?"

"What I said. What year did you leave Pennsylvania?"

"Obviously 1880. We only stayed one winter." Grace sounded exasperated. She clearly hadn't expected to have the company of an imbecile. "Where did *you* come from?"

But I was in no shape to answer, my mind a tornado. The game had tossed me into the past all right. But instead of returning to medieval Germany, to Bero and Juliana, I was on an entirely different continent—my old home. Except I was in a different century.

"Hey, did you hear me?" Grace's voice had an edge.

"What?"

"What's the matter with you?"

"Nothing, had to think for a minute." *Come on brain, ask her something else, something to distract her from being in the company of an idiot.* "Have you got any brothers and sisters?"

A weird sound came from the girl and when I looked over I saw she was crying. Well done, Max. Another stupid thing to say.

"They were on the wagon. They're dead..." the rest of the girl's words went under in a moan.

I thought of the carnage. The kids hadn't been there. "I read the Indians take children with them. They're often found later. Alive."

"Where did you hear that?" the girl said, her voice a mix of suspicion and hope.

I shrugged. "Onli— in books."

"You read? I finished fourth grade, but then I had to help with the fields. I—"

"What's that noise?" I grabbed the girl's forearm. The coyote howling had stopped, but in its place roared something much fiercer. It sounded like a train was running us down—except there were no trains in the middle of this desert.

The girl shrieked in fright. "A Norther." She took off running and I followed, slipping and staggering after her.

"Wait," I shouted. "What *is* that?"

The girl stopped, her voice vibrating with fear and impatience. "Don't you know anything? It's a storm. We must find shelter or we'll die." Somewhere my subconscious registered her hand reclaiming my arm.

It made me feel better for a second because when I looked up I could hardly make out her face and the wind had turned up three notches in intensity. The sky, where a second ago the North Star flickered, was black. The girl's hand on my forearm clawed painfully as we hurried on.

"Faster," I yelled, but my voice was snuffed out immediately. *Where to.*

"Norther...dangerous...cover..." the girl shouted.

I looked straight ahead, but there was no more light. Not even a pinprick or a glimmer. Nothing. My eyes began to burn and my face hurt as if a thousand needles pelted it. Even though I kept my mouth tightly shut, grit scraped across my teeth and coated my tongue.

I felt the girl tug on my arm. I had trouble breathing, not the kind of pressure on my lungs the game began with, but a choking thick paste clogged my nose. Like inhaling spoonfuls of sand.

In my panic I fell to my knees and started to crawl. I had to do something. The girl held on as we crept forward. Or was it in a circle. I had no idea.

Move. I kept my face down, but my ears were filling with sand. The shrieking sounds of the wind sounded muffled. The sand hit my head, crawled into my hair and neck. My skin ached from the sharp sand pebbles exploding around me.

I pulled up my shirt across my nose to filter out the worst.

I wanted to ask Grace if we should wait, but couldn't open my mouth. I was in a vacuum, a cocoon of thick, burning and spinning sand. Still I crawled, the girl on my right arm, pulling along.

Crawling…choking…crawling. How much time had passed? How much did we have left before being buried alive?

When my knee hit something solid, I extended an arm: stone. Turning right, I crept along, one hand touching the rock like a blind man. The wind had reached insanity level, howling like a freight train. I couldn't hear my own breath. My hand felt an indentation, some kind of recess. I dragged the girl now, beyond caring. We had to get away or we'd die. I inched forward, the air around us boiling sand. The recess deepened and I kept edging into it.

If some wild animal had the same idea, we'd know soon enough. I hit my head and crouched lower. The rock formed some sort of overhang, a ceiling that was sloping down to no more than two feet. I got on my stomach, eyes blind with sand and darkness. It was terrifying not to be able to see.

Even in Schwarzburg's dungeon I'd had some light, however weak. I'd known the size of the room. I'd been able to stand upright and breathe, albeit the worst stinking air of all times.

Here I didn't even have that. I choked because the air was solid with particles.

Still I crawled, low to the ground, scooting on knees and elbows, fighting for breath underneath my shirt. The roaring lessened to a low growl. The pelting stopped. I swung my arm up and let go of the girl. The stone ceiling was gone and I carefully opened my eyes.

"Grace?" My voice sounded hollow. I wiped my face with my t-shirt and took a breath. The air was cool and slightly musty. I coughed to get some of the grit out of my mouth, rubbing caked sand from my ears.

"Yes?" Grace's voice was nearby though I couldn't see her. It was like sitting in ink.

"You okay? I think we're in a cave."

"I can't see anything."

"What was that thing out there?"

I heard the girl crawling around mumbling. "He doesn't know anything…I wish I could see."

"I'm such an idiot." I groped through my pocket until my fingers came upon a small box. I'd been carrying matches the entire time. It had been a last addition before I entered the game. If the game required me to return all the matches I'd be in trouble. I hoped that as long as I burned them and then returned with the box, I'd be okay.

Outside, in the wind they were useless, but right now I'd at least be able to inspect our place. I pulled out a match, patting the box in search of the porous surface, the roar outside a mumble as I struck.

Grace screamed in fright as the flame turned the air orange. Shadows danced along the walls and lost themselves in darkness beyond. I looked up where pockmarked sandstone had been hollowed out and formed a roundish ceiling seven feet high. I stood up and walked around, my feet and pants unrecognizable from the reddish soil.

"Look for wood, something to burn," I said as the tips of my forefinger and thumb grew hot. Another second. "Anything?"

Grace had been crawling away from me. The light went out and she shrieked, "Light another."

I fiddled for the tiny box. My hands shook and the match slipped away into the darkness. I caught myself before the curse came out. I imagined Grace shaking her head with that disapproving twist of the neck. The light was blinding when the sulphur exploded in my hand.

"Here, here, look," Grace shouted. She held up some branches and a clump of tumbleweeds. "This will burn."

I hurried over, but before I reached her, it grew dark again. I lit another match and the tumbleweed caught as if it had been dipped in kerosene. The cave turned bright, shadows dancing around us. I added the wood. "See if you find more stuff to burn."

Grace rushed around the space. "There is nothing. Just an old snake skin." She held up some parchment-like remains nearly six feet long. I shuddered. I hated snakes. They didn't really have any in Seattle where I'd grown up and Germany's snakes were harmless if there were any at all. That was fine with me.

"Maybe we should sleep," Grace said, scraping the ground with her boot.

"How long do these storms last?"

She shrugged. "Not long. But we won't be able to see any stars for a while."

I sagged down and rested my back against the stonewall. My eyes felt scratchy from the sand and my throat was so parched that I was unable to swallow. Still, I loved watching the fire. For a moment I forgot my misery.

Then I passed out.

CHAPTER FIVE

Something was pressing against my cheek—hard—making me open my eyes. Inches in front of me I saw pebbles: tiny ones, larger ones, oval and round ones. They were digging into my skin. I remembered last night and was surprised I could see. The cave was only semi-dark. I sat up and twisted to have a look.

Grace wasn't there. Behind me, a portion of the ground was brightly lit. Like fingers, sunrays were crawled through the cave's entrance.

Just then I noticed movement, a shadow falling over the opening. Instantly afraid, I jumped up quickly to scan the ground. I had nothing to attack with, not even a stick. The coals from last night's meager fire had gone out long ago, leaving behind a pile of charred dust.

I breathed deeply when I recognized the dark hair of the girl. She had smudges below her eyes and I knew she'd been crying.

"We better go," she said without looking at me. "It's hot already. We have to hurry and find water. The settlement can't be far.

"I'm ready as soon as I take a leak," I said.

"What?"

I shrugged, remembering my problems in the Middle Ages. I was only a hundred some years back, but communication was still an issue. "I've got to piss. There. Is that better?"

Turning pink around the nose, Grace looked away. I immediately regretted my words, but instead of apologizing, I scooted outside.

The landscape was unchanged, the low-sitting sun already hot, turning rocks and ground red. I discovered the girl's tracks in the fresh cover the sandstorm had left and walked the other way to relieve myself. I barely had any pee and the bit I produced was dark. I needed water badly. I swallowed a few times, grit crunching between my teeth. My lips were still swollen.

I rushed back and hollered into the cave. "Ready? Let's go."

Grace appeared looking sullen. Without making eye contact she turned east, her head low against the already blazing sun. I followed. As we emerged from the rocks, I kept scanning the landscape, more and more worried. The sky above us was huge, a universe of the darkest blue with an occasional puff of white.

I expected to see the settlement the Irish guy had mentioned. But every time we passed another rise and climbed across, we saw nothing but sand, rocks and more sky. The sun rose slowly higher and with every minute the air turned hotter until it felt as if we were walking inside an oven turned on high.

I carried my sweater, switching back and forth between hands. Even the little bit of fabric was too hot and too heavy. Besides it was stiff with the donkey's blood and reeked.

By afternoon, my knees started to have a mind of their own, especially when the ground was uneven which was all the time. The place was getting on my nerve with its vastness, its unending skies and gravelly traps.

I kept stumbling, each time catching myself. Soon I wouldn't be able to manage that. Grace seemed much tougher and I resented that. Just because she'd grown up with hardship didn't mean she was supposed to be stronger than me. Stupid girls.

Modern life was so much easier and I was way too soft for this place. You were thirsty? No big deal. You went to the fridge or stopped by the gas station to get a nice cold can of soda. Or water. I licked my lips again. I had to stop thinking about water.

I was just contemplating what the girl's legs looked like below the checkered skirt when she shouted something. I was walking behind her, no longer caring to be the leader.

"Look! Over there." She pointed at something in the distance.

I squinted at the wobbling shapes far away. The air moved and swayed. "Probably a fata morgana."

She turned to me with the same angry face. "What's that? You speak in riddles again."

"A fata morgana is a mirage, a fake something. Heck, I don't have a clue. But it's not real."

Grace vehemently shook her head. "No, it's a town…probably Sunnyside."

"A town? In your dreams." I stared, ignoring the stinging in my eyeballs. I needed sunglasses. The Irish guy had mentioned a settlement whatever that meant. But then who was I to argue. I had no clue what was out here.

What did it matter if we died in one spot over another? "I guess we can walk toward it and see if it disappears."

The girl marched off. By the way she held her head and jutted out her jaw, I knew she was mad at me again as if I had anything to do with the stinking situation we were in. To my annoyance her anger seemed to give her extra energy. I struggled to keep up.

Now that we had something to walk toward, I felt a shred of strength return. And to my amazement, the gray globs grew larger. But what had appeared pretty close turned out to be much farther. And with every step I grew more desperate. My legs didn't want to cooperate any longer. My usual stride of three feet had shrunk to the shuffling of an old man in a nursing home.

The girl kept going. And I had to admit she was right which didn't help because that made me angry all over again. But stopping meant to burn alive. By the time I was able to make out the individual buildings—adobes with pink or mustard-brown plaster, one-stories with wooden planks, weathered silvery gray—I wanted to collapse. My face was no longer my own. My nose burned and my lips were numb.

"I told you it was real," Grace said with a touch of smugness. Had I not been so tired I would've rolled my eyes. Girls, no matter *when* they lived, always had to shove it to you.

We passed a sort of warehouse with few windows that stretched nearly a hundred feet. Ahead, I noticed a modest church, a few houses, followed by a scattering of official-looking dwellings: a general store and a sheriff's office and in the distance more one-story buildings made of brick and wood.

It had to be afternoon but we saw no one. Half a dozen horses, their rumps twitching with flies, were tied in front of the saloon. *Beaver Smith's Saloon and Gambling House* it said. I wondered if they had rooms to rent and I imagined a hot shower. Then I remembered that I didn't have any money. Since I'd expected to go back to the Middle Ages and Castle Hanstein I'd not even considered taking money along. Worse, I was in no shape to lift as much as an arm.

"What are we…" I began when I watched Grace heading for the saloon. "Hey, wait," I croaked, hauling myself after her. "Do you have dollars?"

She looked at me with that same deprecating expression. "What do you think?"

"Excuse *me*," I hurried. "How am I supposed to know you've got cash?"

"It was Mother's," she said, pushing open the swiveling doors. Feeling guilty for reminding her of her dead family, I followed her into the gloom.

I'd stepped into the middle of a western. Any second, Clint Eastwood would join us dressed in his brown carpet poncho, a glass of whiskey in one hand and brown cigar stub in the other. He'd squint and say something cool.

My smirk disappeared when I recognized myself in the mirror across the room. I looked like a sick copy of myself, forehead and nose aflame with sunburn, hair pinkish with dust and my clothes coated with grime—a scarecrow dipped in sand. I quickly looked away.

The place had a long bar across the back wall, oil lamps illuminating bottles and glasses. A man with wisps of gray hair above his ears and a matching grayish apron was staring at us. That had to be Beaver Smith. I hardly had time to look around when I saw the girl already at the counter.

"We need water and something to eat," she said a bit too loud. "How much is a room?"

Smith lowered his head to peek above tiny gold-rimmed spectacles. "Twenty cents for the meal including water. Five cents for a beer. A room is three dollars for the month if you share or five for two rooms." Grace swallowed. Surely, by the looks of her parents and the squalid wagons, she couldn't have much money.

"We'll take the meal with water for now," she said, her voice less certain.

Smith seemed to struggle for an answer. "Miss, better show me you can pay."

Sliding her belt upwards, Grace rummaged through a hidden

pouch inside her skirt's waistband. She held up a couple of crumpled dollar bills. I sighed. She was going to pay for us. Not exactly gallant of me, but I had no energy to care. All I wanted was water and food. I'd feel guilty about it later.

Smith had given her change and was walking toward the rear.

"Excuse me, could we have the water now?" I said at his back.

Smith ignored me and kept going.

"Hey Beaver, why don't you give the kid a drink?" someone called from the shadows.

I turned around. In the back corner a few men sat playing cards. I'd not even seen them in the gloom. One of them was now strolling toward me. To my surprise the barkeeper turned around and grabbed two glasses.

I licked my lips when I felt a hand on my shoulder. "Long trek, eh?"

The man who'd spoken was a few inches shorter than I and not much older. He wore a whitish shirt, neckerchief, leather vest, and chaps over pants so faded, they had no color. He leaned onto the counter and shot me a sideward glance. His eyes were blue. Not the burning blue of Werner von Hanstein, but the blue of a hazy morning sky.

"What's the matter, the sun got your tongue?" he smirked.

I didn't feel like smiling. "Didn't have any water for a couple days." My gaze returned to the glass that had appeared in front of me. Ignoring the stranger, I sipped slowly. The fire in my throat eased instantly.

"You want to put something on that face or your nose may fall off," the man said. "It's a bad burn. Desert is no place for greenhorns?"

"Hey Kid, you done gallivanting? Game isn't finished," one of the men yelled from the table in the corner.

My head swiveled toward the murky back, but I didn't know any of them.

"They're talking to me," the young man said. "Take it slow with the water or you'll throw up."

I nodded and watched as the man returned to his buddies. He wore two heavy colts and a second belt with bullets. Though he had narrow shoulders like a girl, his gait clearly said: *don't mess with me.*

"You ready to eat?" Grace said as she plunked into a seat.

I nodded. The barkeeper refilled our glasses and I slumped down across from her. Somehow between coming in and sitting down she'd managed to wipe her face. I noticed how deeply tanned she was. She had none of the burns that made my skin throb.

"He's right, you know," she said, wiggling a forefinger in my direction. "You'll get scars."

I touched my nose and shrank back. It hurt as if I had no skin at all. I thought of the lotions in my bathroom, the drug stores and pharmacies. But I had neither money nor access to a doctor. I'd get skin cancer and grow moles like a toad.

"Dinner," the barkeeper said, placing two tin plates on the table. I sniffed. It smelled like food, but the stuff was mostly brown and I began sifting through in search of something to identify. There were baked beans, some kind of soggy bacon and a piece of roast with a side of cornbread. After a few tentative bites I wolfed down the rest. During my last adventure in the Middle Ages, the food had been too spicy. This was gross on another level, but I no longer cared.

The barkeeper kept refilling our glasses and I began to feel human again. Except the pain on my face and neck got worse by the minute.

"You want to rent a room?" The girl eyed me carefully.

"I don't have any money. I'll have to find a way to earn some." I looked around to distract myself because I had no idea how one earned money in 1881. Several men entered. They looked Mexican, their skin dark as chocolate.

"Here's a whiskey from the Kid." Smith placed a couple of shot glasses on the table.

I straightened my aching back and nodded toward the corner. "Thanks." The young man waved.

I lifted the glass to my lips, the alcohol painfully sharp in my nostrils. I really didn't want booze, though it might help digest the shoe leather meat.

"That was nice of him," the girl said as she nipped from the drink. She wrinkled her nose and put the glass back down.

"I'd want to pay you back, of course," I said. "For the room, I mean."

"I only have ten dollars," the girl said. "If we get a room, you must promise to stay decent." Her cheeks turned a shade of pink.

I nodded, trying to appear cool. Since my face already burned and was undoubtedly the shade of a tomato, at least she couldn't see me blush. "Promise."

After the girl paid, we followed the barkeeper upstairs. "Here you go."

The room reminded me of a hot shoebox, the bed no wider than a twin. How were we supposed to fit on that? I looked for a second door, a sign of a bathroom, but there was none—only a flowered porcelain pitcher and basin on a dresser.

"I'm in the wild west," I mumbled before rushing to the window and opening it all the way. There was no relief, the air outside as hot as the inside.

"What?"

"Nothing."

"Why don't you talk right? Like a normal person?" Grace was pouring water into the bowl.

"Tell me, what is a normal person?" I suddenly yelled. I'd reached my limit. I couldn't breathe in the airless room and I sure as heck wasn't going to sleep on a cot fit for a child. Not to mention that I was grossed out by my own sand-covered, stinking body. And my face felt like it wanted to peel off my skull.

The girl whipped around. "You sound so…odd."

This time I rolled my eyes. I was sick of hearing it.

"And you're rude and thankless."

"What?" I shouted. "I'm rude and thankless when you're the one who's having an attitude and pouting the entire time."

I stomped off, throwing the door shut behind me. My throat was tight with fury and discomfort. Without looking at anyone, I dashed through the saloon and headed down the street.

CHAPTER SIX

The dust-covered road, the buildings and sky glowed like fire. Even while the sun was setting, the air sizzled. An Indian in tattered leathers hollered something unintelligible as he stumbled toward the saloon, his fist cramped around a whiskey bottle. A woman in linen skirts, her face hidden beneath a straw hat, was tending her garden. Two men with sweat-stained sombreros passed me, one singing in Spanish.

I marched on as my anger moved toward despair. Things were even worse than last time at Hanstein. While I wasn't stuck in a dungeon, this felt like I'd stepped into a different torture. What was I supposed to do? Despite playing the game once before, I had no idea about its missions. Everything was utterly different.

Jimmy's father had been tightlipped while I hadn't thought about asking the right questions. And Jimmy? Stupid idiot didn't do anything to help. All he did was play around on his Mac and his iPhone. He was probably lazing in some exclusive camp right now, drinking fancy cocktails.

Worst of all I really missed my mom, regretted my anger. So what she had to go to a conference. So what we had to postpone vacation. I could've been lounging at the pool right now watching girls.

And the joy I'd felt anticipating my reunion with Bero and Juliana? I was stuck in this hellhole of superheated earth with a bunch of gunslingers and an orphaned girl. I was broke, my body ached and my face was peeling with second-degree burns. I swallowed because the lump in my throat was growing again. Angrily I wiped my eyes and looked around.

I was at the outskirts of town with nothing but desert for company: rocks, sand, cacti and prickly plants. Wait a minute.

My head swiveled back around. I knew the ones that looked like green sword blades: *Aloe Vera*. My mother always kept a plant or two in our house.

Without hesitation I groped for my father's knife. It had been a risk to take it into the game. I'd lost it when I traded fabric at Hanstein. I was sure you needed everything you took into the game to leave again.

Never mind that now. I had to take care of my face. I cut off several of the thick leaves. A gooey clear liquid oozed out. I squeezed one of the leaves until my palm was covered and dabbed my nose. Suppressing a scream I grimaced, but kept going until my face and neck were covered with goop.

As if the aloe had given me new strength I straightened. Time to clean up and sleep. Tomorrow I'd make plans. Wandering back into town, I wished I didn't have to go back and accept Grace's charity.

Lights lit up windows and more people were outside in the streets. They watched me with guarded yet curious expressions, but nobody said anything. The saloon was in full swing with every table occupied. Twenty or more men crowded the bar, the air heavy with alcohol vapors and cigar smoke. Somewhere in back, a man plunked a slow tune on a piano.

I was halfway up the stairs when I had an idea and turned around. The men who'd played poker earlier were still in the shadowy corner. So was the young guy who'd bought us whiskey. "You ready for some cards," he said, removing a narrow-brimmed hat from the chair next to him.

To my surprise I shook my head. I'd played online poker a thousand times and was pretty good at it. Why couldn't I relax for five minutes and play cards like a cool dude? But I had no money and the thought of being beaten or shot for non-payment didn't seem appealing just now.

"Actually I wanted to ask if there is a place to wash."

"Sure is," the guy said. "Across the street. Left of the barber shop." He turned his attention back to the cards and pile of dimes, quarters and wrinkly dollar bills on the table. I noticed how white his forehead was against the tanned lower part of his face.

"One more thing," I said. "What's the name of this town?"

Now all the men at the table stared at me. And broke into raucous laughter.

The young guy carefully covered his cards and leaned back. "You mean to tell us that you don't know where you are?"

I nodded. I wanted nothing more than to get out of here. Go home and burn the stupid game.

"We got lost and there was this storm…"

The men continued laughing and banging the table with their fists.

"By the looks of it, you brought the *Norther* with you." One of the players threw back a whiskey and laughed some more.

"Look…what is your name?" the young guy said.

"Max."

"Max," he said, trying to keep a straight face. "We're in Fort Sumner. This here is Pete Maxwell, these two are Jesus and Francisco. I'm Billy Bonnie. Everyone calls me the Kid."

I nodded to each man in turn when a bell began ringing in my foggy brain.

Right in front of me sat Billy the Kid, one of the most famous outlaws of all time. Supposedly The Kid had killed twenty people. I'd read about him in school and seen a bunch of movies. But this dude looked nothing like the photo on the Internet. He was attractive and friendly.

"You're Billy the Kid?"

The Kid quickly glanced around the room. Then he nodded, his eyes dancing.

I swallowed, a vision of Jimmy's father talking about the ultimate history game dancing in my head. I'd stepped into history all right.

"What's that on your face?" the Kid asked.

I was so shocked about who I'd met, I'd completely forgotten about the aloe. "It's from this plant." I raised a hand with the remaining stalks as new laughter broke out around the table. The piano playing stopped and most of the saloon guests now gawked at me. "Eh, it's aloe."

"You smear that prickly bush over your skin?" someone shouted. "No wonder you look like raw meat." The room exploded with renewed amusement, reminding me of standing in front of

Knight Werner, being laughed at by everyone in Hanstein's great hall.

For a second I wanted to yell back. But then I smiled. "Yep, it'll heal the burns." I turned to the Kid. "Thanks for your help."

In response Billy whistled a low tune and a girl about my age with black hair rolled into a bun approached the table. She wore a dark blue dress with bits of lace along the collar. "Paulita, will you show Max here where the bathhouse is?"

She nodded as her dark-brown eyes met Billy's.

Somebody shouted near the bar. The drunken Indian who I'd seen on the street earlier was staggering through the crowd in an attempt to reach the counter. He still clutched the bottle which was now empty. The single feather in the leather band of his hair drooped over one ear. His eyes were bloodshot.

"Whiskey," he slurred. Most men near the bar were making room though some laughed and pointed.

"You've had enough," Beaver Smith said.

"I can pay."

"Come back tomorrow."

The Indian stood waiting, obviously at a loss of what to do next when a coarse-looking thug with a stained hat and a month's beard kicked him in the knees. The Indian crashed to the ground.

"Oops," the thug laughed, reminding me of the gang I'd met in the desert. Their kind was obviously all over the place. Meanwhile the Indian was making an attempt to right himself, but every time he got to his knees, the thug kicked him again, each blow accompanied by the cheers of his two friends. When the Indian crawled off toward the door I looked away. Cruelty never seemed to go out of style.

Just then I noticed Pete Maxwell's mouth, almost hidden under the mustache, twist into a sneer. To my surprise he wasn't looking at the thugs or the Indian, but at Billy. I tried remembering the details of the Billy the Kid story, but my mind had quit for the night. By the time I got outside, the Indian leaned against a post staring into space.

Paulita ignored me and rushed down the street. For once I was glad the girl was silent. She pointed at a building and disappeared into the night. What I'd witnessed in the saloon didn't make much sense, but then nothing did in this crazy game. First things first—I had to clean up.

To call it the shack a building was an overstatement. It reminded me of Bero's hut with slightly fewer holes in the siding. Despite the heat, a stove simmered in the corner, a cast-iron pot of laundry steaming on top. To my right, three narrow doors opened into closet-sized *private* baths.

"Ten cents for the bath and another ten to wash your clothes," the girl behind the counter said. Like Paulita she had black hair tied with a ribbon and brown eyes, her skin dark as molasses. But where Paulita looked Hispanic, this girl's high cheekbones looked Native American. With a pang I remembered that I didn't have any money. Not even five cents. It was laughable. In today's dollars these prices were dirt-cheap. And yet, here I was with nothing more than…I looked at my fist that still held the aloe.

"Would you be interested in a trade?" I asked.

The girl frowned. "If you can't pay you have to leave."

"Let me explain," I tried. "How about I give you something to fix your skin? You ever have cuts and bruises." I looked around the room, anxiety brewing at the back of my throat. I wanted a bath, bad. "Imagine you could sell the men ointment to treat rashes and sunburns and… saddle sores."

"I'm not allowed," the girl said. She seemed worried as her eyes darted between me and a curtain in the back.

"What's your name?"

"*Ela,*" the girl whispered. "They call me Antonia." Her gaze returned to the curtain.

"I'm Max. Look, Antonia, I'm in bad shape. But I can fix you some stuff and if you let me take a bath, I promise you won't regret it."

"I'll get beaten."

"What if you tell your boss how to make extra money?" I tried to sound convincing, but the girl was starvation thin and scared.

She put a forefinger on her lips and tiptoed towards the curtain. Then she sighed.

"He's gone. Hurry."

"If you get me some containers…jars with lids, I'll show you how to use it." My gaze fell on her hands. They were red and chapped, probably from spending all day in dirty wash water. "Here, let's fix your hands."

Apparently self-conscious, Antonia hid her arms behind her.

I smiled and raised my hand to show her the aloe. "Come on,

I've seen them already."

Antonia gasped in surprise and her eyes lodged on the plant. "The wand of heaven."

"What?"

She pointed at the leaves. "How do you know?"

"My mother taught me."

The girl slowly stretched out her arms. "My people use it for many things."

I cut a fresh piece of the aloe stalk. The girl's skin looked worse on close-up: reddish with puffy scratches where infection had set in. I squeezed some juice on the girl's fingers and carefully spread it across. "Leave this on and allow it to dry."

Antonia stared at her hand. "It takes away the pain." She offered me her other and I smiled. "My people use it. I never thought…"

She looked at me again, her eyes black in the gloom. "Are you a medicine man?"

I shook my head. "I'm just glad I found something that grows in this wasteland."

"Our land," she whispered. Before I could ask what she was doing in the bathhouse when she was clearly Indian, she rushed to the stove. "We must hurry, before he returns."

An hour later I reentered the saloon. My clothes were wet, but reasonably clean. Best of all I was free of sand. The bath had been nearly cold, the girl being afraid to use too much firewood without collecting payment, but it had been heaven to rinse off the filth.

The drunken Indian had disappeared and I wondered where he lived and how he'd gotten hooked on booze. My mother sometimes drank too much though she always managed to get to work and keep me safe. I sighed with sudden longing, which immediately switched to anger. If my father hadn't left, my mother wouldn't be drinking in the first place. It was all his fault. And now he was getting married. My stomach cramped as I remembered our meeting at the pizza parlor. The longing deepened. For something else, something long forgotten.

The saloon was quiet now, a few men slumping low along the bar, the table in the corner empty. I dragged myself upstairs and tiptoed into the bedroom. I was shivering, the sunburn making my head feel like a superheated balloon on top of a frozen body. In the near dark, I made out Grace lying on her side on top of the blanket. I hung my damp clothes except for my boxers on the bedpost and squeezed under the blanket next to her. The bed frame complained as if the mattress wanted to collapse in two. I stretched to spread out my weight and was instantly asleep.

Sometime in the night I heard Grace mumble and cry out. Her hand landed on my chest. Before I figured out what to do about it, I was out again.

CHAPTER SEVEN

I forced open my eyes. My right cheek was pressing against Grace's shoulder and I jerked backwards, the mattress swinging like a tidal wave on the ropes. Thankfully, she seemed to be asleep, so I jumped up and dipped a finger into the pitcher. Lukewarm. I wondered if it was drinking water. My throat ached and felt like sandpaper. In spite of my thirst I was ravenous. Not wanting the girl to see me half-naked, I yanked on my jeans.

Too late. When I looked up I found Grace staring at me.

"Where are you going?" she asked.

I zipped up my pants and shrugged. "Find a job."

Grace's eyes remained on my crotch. "What is that?"

I felt my cheeks warm. "What do you mean?"

"That thing," she asked, her forefinger pointing at my middle. The heat on my face intensified. "I've never seen anything like…it makes a sound."

I finally got it. She was talking about my zipper. "Just a way to close pants," I said clearing my throat.

"Oh."

"From the East Coast." Judging by her frown, she was suspicious once again.

She finally nodded, adjusting her blanket she had pulled to her neck. I'd caught a glimpse of some kind of full-body underwear earlier. Smirking, I abruptly turned away. They still had a while to go until they reached Victoria's Secret perfection. "They'll give us breakfast. It is part of the room."

"I'll wait downstairs."

An old-fashioned clock chimed eight times as I entered the saloon, empty except for the barman wiping tables and straightening chairs. The air was still thick with cigar smoke and vapors.

"Is your girl joining you?"

"What?"

"For breakfast." Beaver Smith had returned behind the counter.

She isn't *my* girl. But I felt in no mood to explain. "Yeah, thanks." I walked to the swinging door. Though they'd seemed corny, I'd always loved westerns. Now I'd landed in one. The earth outside glowed pink. Across the street a man in a white apron was sweeping the porch of the general store.

"You know where I'd find Billy," I asked turning back.

The barman's cloth hovered in mid-air. "Why do you want to know?"

I shrugged. "Maybe he can help me find a job."

"Doubt that," Smith mumbled and disappeared in the backroom.

Grace hurried down the stairs. She'd tied her hair into a ponytail and attempted a smile. "Wonder what we get. I'm hungry."

"Don't have a clue." I caught the frown on Grace's face and hurried, "I mean I don't know. You have any idea what you're going to do?"

The frown deepened as the girl's eyes grew shiny. "I'll have to make my way to San Francisco. I have an uncle there. The money won't be enough, though."

"How will you travel?"

"I'll need a horse. But it's not safe. Maybe a coach..." Her eyes were far away. "It'll be too expensive."

"Sounds like we should both find work," I said.

"Slapjacks and coffee," Smith announced, placing mugs and two plates with pancakes in front of us.

I dug in. At least the pancakes were better than last night's brown mush. It was hard to concentrate on the game and what I might need to accomplish to get home when I was starving and my face ached with sunburn. I'd have to find more aloe today.

"You want to go with me to look for work?" I asked between

bites.

She shook her head. "I'll go alone." She hesitated. "I think you might ruin my chances. I mean, when they see two people at once, they might say no," she hurried. I nodded. But I knew Grace had other reasons for not taking me with her.

I jumped up. Fine. Let her see how she got along. I'd find the Indian girl again. Ask her if she knew where Billy the Kid was staying. He'd been nice and maybe, just maybe he'd help again.

When the sun hit my face, pain shot through my nose and forehead. I needed a hat, something to shade my skin. I turned right toward the bathhouse when I saw the Native American girl, Antonia, rush into the alley behind the saloon. She hadn't seen me and on a whim I followed. By the way she walked with her head low and her shoulders hunched, she was on a secret mission.

I kept my distance as the girl disappeared behind the building. Afraid to lose sight of her, I broke into a run. Around the corner, outbuildings and rickety sheds spread in the dust. Chickens pecked at the sparse tufts of grass. I was momentarily reminded of medieval Bornhagen. A couple of horses nibbled from a trough in a corral. A carriage and wagon stood inside an open stall. I caught a glimpse of the girl's checkered skirt disappearing into the shadows beneath.

I slowed down, treading carefully. It was obvious Antonia was hiding something. I wondered where her master was and what she was doing out here. As I drew closer I heard low voices—foreign sounding voices.

I couldn't understand a word. Before I reached the entrance to the stall it became quiet. Maybe I should turn around and leave now. Who knew what I'd get myself into? But my legs remained stubbornly determined to move ahead.

When I peeked around the corner I noticed Antonia hastily straighten and walk toward me.

"What're you doing here?"

"I saw you. Eh, I wanted to ask you something." I detected movement in the deep shadows behind the carriage. Somebody else was there.

"Let's go and you can ask me your question." Antonia turned to leave but I remained, my eyes still fixed on the corner.

"What are you hiding?" I asked.

"Nothing, let's go."

I pushed past her instead. There in the corner next to a couple of straw bales lay the drunk Indian I'd seen in Beaver Smith's saloon last night. Even from here I saw his eyes were bloodshot.

"What are you doing?" Antonia cried. "Leave him alone." She was tugging at my arm now.

"What's wrong with him?" I said ignoring her. "Maybe I can help."

Antonia shook her head, her shoulders slumping as if all energy had left her body. "You'll tell on us. They'll beat him…and me."

I shook my head. "Your secret is safe with me." I stepped closer as the Indian on the ground tried to sit up, his broad cheekbones stretching tight above a strong mouth. He was hugging himself, shooting angry glances at me.

I thought of the Indian raid earlier and my narrow escape.

"He's my brother," Antonia said. "Narsimha. It means *Lion among Men.*"

Not much left of the lion. His hands were bony and brownish stains covered his leather shirt. He was even thinner than his sister.

"Hi," I said aloud, wondering if I should offer a handshake. In the movies, Indians always raised their hands to show open palms or smoked peace pipes. Neither seemed fitting so I bowed instead. Now that I was getting used to the shadows, I noticed the resemblance between the two. Narsimha's nose and forehead were shaped the same, though the fierceness I'd seen in the girl's eyes had been replaced with something sad. And very ill.

"Who is he?" Narsimha said in broken English. His voice was scratchy and full of suspicion. Then he coughed, a dry hacking sound like the yipping of a coyote.

"He came to the bathhouse yesterday," Antonia said. "He helped me with my hands." She lifted her arms, but Narsimha's eyes remained glued to my face.

"Send him away. Don't trust him."

Ignoring her brother, Antonia tugged at my arm and I let myself be pulled away. "I have to be back before he wakes up."

"Your master?"

She nodded.

"What happened to your brother?" I asked as we walked off.

Antonia shook her head. "I must hurry." She abruptly stopped and placed her hands on my chest. Her brown eyes bore into mine. "You mustn't tell."

I nodded. "I promise."

Before I managed to say another word, she took off down the alley, her head low, the checkered dress billowing around her lithe figure. Then she was gone.

With a sigh I headed toward the main street. Instead of getting answers I had more questions. I'd totally forgotten to ask about Billy.

Two women in long dresses, wicker baskets dangling from their arm, were leaving the general store. When I stepped onto the porch, they stared at me, one of them shaking her head, the other pursing her lips. I tried a smile, but my cheeks fired a warning shot of pain and I relaxed my jaw.

The store was exactly as I'd seen on old TV westerns: only dirtier and reeking of leather, caramel and stale air, with a layer of pinkish dust over everything. The counter along the left side served as storage for bales of fabric, candy jars, glass bottles with some amber liquid, boxes of jerky and leather whips. Behind it, shelves were loaded with assorted pots and boxes.

In search of the shop owner, I dodged barrels filled with onions and some kind of brownish root. The farther in I went, the darker it got. I barely avoided a stack of shovels leaning against wooden crates. There were gloves and hats, belts and nails. Fort Sumner's general store was a grocery, hardware and department store combined.

"Hello?" I called into the dark just as the man in the white apron appeared from the backroom.

"May I help you?"

"Eh, yes," I said and when the man stepped closer, I recognized him from last night. Billy the Kid had introduced him as Pete Maxwell.

"The Greenhorn," Pete said. "Are you lost again?"

"Yes, sort of. I wonder if you'd have a job for me. I'm pretty good at organizing." I swept an encompassing arm through the air.

"Are you?" By the way he asked it was obvious that he didn't feel any need for organization.

"Yes," I said. "I can inventory the place or stack shelves or whatever you need."

Pete shot me another look, his lips curling into the brown mustache that looked like an upside-down horseshoe. I didn't really like the guy, but I had little choice. There were few options in this town and I had neither money nor transportation to travel somewhere else.

"You read and write?"

I nodded. "I can do math and stuff, too. You won't regret it."

"Not very strong though." The mustache moved up and down as if contemplating while Pete Maxwell's eyes seemed to measure my biceps. "Come back this afternoon. You can help with a delivery."

I sighed. "Thanks." I hesitated. "How much…"

"Dollar a day. If you work hard."

I nodded again. Pathetic.

I'd work for next to nothing.

CHAPTER EIGHT

With a longing look at the hats and sombreros stacked on a shelf, I left the store. As the sun hit me again, I remembered the aloe. Turning left I scurried up the street. I might as well investigate the town some more.

I grimaced. Town was an overstatement. Other than the two-story saloon and a few adobe style homes, most were squat wooden buildings a strong wind would blow down.

In the distance I noticed a large house with assorted smaller buildings around it. They looked more solid and well taken care off. The ground was flat and barren except for a few shrubs here and there. Behind the house the land was covered in rows and rows of short trees. And as I drew closer I saw they were gnarled like old men, with thick silvery bark. And among the green I noticed… peaches. Not many, it was probably late in the harvest, but definitely an orchard. And I smelled the sweet, juicy aroma of the fruit.

I'd kill for a peach right now. Breakfast was long forgotten and the relentless heat kept me thirsty. What if I went straight to the front door and asked to pick a few? Dah. I still didn't have money. My feet turned the other way. To my left a band of green trees snaked along. Cottonwoods. I sniffed. The peach scent mingled with something foul like rotten leaves and mold.

Keeping my eyes on the orchard, I ambled along, for once glad I wore decent shoes—even if they kept my feet boiling hot. The reddish ground crumbled with every step, unleashing mini-avalanches of rocks. The brackish stink grew stronger and as I stepped into the shadows of the cottonwoods I knew why.

There was the Pecos River, the cowboy in the saloon had mentioned. Well it was more like a glorified creek because it couldn't be more than eight or ten feet wide. The water glittered, but the idyllic landscape was ruined by the brownish silt and rancid odor.

I remembered the River Werra near Bornhagen and the refreshing dips I'd taken. I'd not dip a toe into this mess. My feet might fall off.

I turned and approached the peaches, their silvery leaves rustling in the wind. There was nobody around and I quickly picked a couple from a low-hanging branch. Not wasting a second I bit into one. Juice exploded around my jaw and I closed my eyes to savor the aroma. I'd never tasted anything this good. The peach disappeared in lightning speed and I threw the pit into the trees where it bounced off a limb and disappeared in the grass below. Just as well not to leave any trace.

"If it isn't the Greenhorn," a voice said from deep within the swaying green. Feeling guilty about my theft, I froze and quickly stuck the remaining peach into my pocket. Wiping my chin, I attempted to look relaxed when a familiar face came into view.

"What you wandering around for?" Billy the Kid's eyes were hidden in the shadow of his hat. He only wore a beige shirt over long pants, but his guns were at his hips as usual.

I shook my head. "Investigating the area."

"Peaches are good, aren't they?" Billy picked one and took a bite. "Just don't let Mrs. Maxwell see you."

"I got a job with Pete," I said, stepping into the shade. "In the store."

"You going to stay around then?"

"For now. I have to make some money."

"Where're you from? You sound like nobody I know."

I pointed to what I thought was east. "Pennsylvania."

Billy nodded, his blue eyes still on my face. I knew he didn't believe a word.

"What are *you* doing out here?" I hurried to change the subject. "You working the orchard?"

Billy shrugged. "Not exactly. More like laying low."

Shreds of Billy the Kid history filtered into my brain. The Kid was wanted for murder. He'd tried to get pardoned by Governor Wallace several times, but had been turned down. And he'd been a patsy for a bunch of killings he didn't commit. At least that's what most historians said.

"You didn't get a pardon."

Billy's jaw tightened. "How do you know that?"

I opened my mouth but nothing came out. I knew because I'd seen movies and my middle school history book had a chapter on Billy the Kid, the famous outlaw. Alarmed, I watched Billy's right hand twitch near his revolver.

"Look, I read about it in some newspaper. I don't mean you any harm."

Billy nodded. "Guess not." But his eyes still carried doubt.

"Hey, you wouldn't know where I can find a hat?" I said, anxious to change the subject once again. "I'll earn money soon, but I really need something now."

A grin crept across Billy's face. The change was immediate like sunshine after a storm. I relaxed.

"Come with *me*."

We crossed through the trees, the aroma of peaches heady in my nose. At the edge of the orchard, Billy stopped. "Wait here."

I watched as Billy approached the garden behind the main house where a squat Indian woman was hanging laundry. Billy said something in rapid Spanish. Exclaiming words of surprise, the woman smiled and patted Billy's cheek. She was a foot shorter than he was, but seemed to have no fear. They talked some more in Spanish before the woman disappeared inside the house.

Billy nodded at me from afar when the Indian woman reappeared with a hat. More Spanish followed before Billy touched the woman's hand and leisurely walked back to me.

"Deluvina sends her regards." Billy held out a sweat-stained sombrero. "I'll see you around. Got a lunch *meeting*." There was the careless grin again.

I covered my head, trying to hide my disgust. The hat stank of stale sweat: the price to pay for getting to shade my nose. "Thanks a lot." The squat woman watched me from afar, her dark eyes suspicious. They reminded me of Antonia. I waved. With a nod she turned to resume hanging up clothes.

Billy disappeared between the trees, looking relaxed as if he were on a stroll in the park. He was cool—a little jumpy—but definitely cool. Certainly not the ruthless outlaw he was made out to be. Surprising that people wanted him dead.

As I entered the path, I noticed someone leaving the main house. Paulita. She hurried toward the orchard and didn't see me. I grinned. Billy had a meeting all right.

Somewhere in the back of my head, a voice whispered shreds of forgotten history. At some point Billy would be killed by a sheriff. And if I remembered correctly, Paulita would be pregnant with Billy's son. Or was she already? A cloud of doom seemed to sweep across the orchard and something cold traveled up my spine.

Shaking off the uneasiness I headed for town. Chewing my last peach, I found a few clumps of aloe along the way and cut a piece to lather my face. I thought of stopping to see Antonia and offer treatment, but decided against it. It had to be getting late. Time to score lunch before reporting to duty at the general store.

Grace sat alone at one of the tables, a half-finished plate of beans and cornbread in front of her.

"Where have you been?" she said with the familiar frown.

"Around. I got a job at the store." Despite the lousy pay, I felt good about the prospect of earning my keep and impressing Grace. "What about you? Did you have any luck?"

"I saw you," Grace said, her voice rising in anger. "With that…that Indian."

"What Indian?"

"The girl in the alley. She had her hands on you. Looking all cozy." Grace's voice grew steadily louder. "How could you? After what they did to my family." A sob crept into her voice.

I stared. I hadn't even thought about connecting the Indian raid with Antonia. She obviously had nothing to do with Grace's parents. Besides, the Indians were the ones losing everything and from what I remembered the Indians who'd slaughtered Grace's family were a different tribe. I wondered if Grace had seen who was hiding in the shadows of the shed. "She's a poor girl working at the bathhouse," I said aloud.

"Poor! Ha." Jumping up, Grace threw down her fork so hard that it bounced and hit the floor below. "She can die for all I care." With another sob she disappeared up the stairs.

I sagged into the chair. Great. Now she was even more pissed at me. I shook my head. Why were things always so complicated? I'd only been in the game a few days and nothing was going right.

Just like last time. At least then my love for Juliana and my friendship with Bero had made it tolerable. Suddenly I felt very alone.

With a sigh, I yanked Grace's half-eaten plate closer and began to eat.

"You want another serving?" Beaver Smith yelled across the empty space.

I nodded. Might as well fill my stomach while I had the chance.

"Could you tell me what day it is?" I asked when Smith placed another helping of beans and cornbread in front of me.

"Wednesday."

"Yeah, I mean what's the date?"

Smith wrinkled his forehead in concentration. "June first." He shot me a curious look over his gold-rimmed glasses. "Why wouldn't you know that?"

I shrugged. "Got confused when I was lost in the desert."

"More like scorched your brain." Smith grumbled something like *stupid* and *slow* as he shuffled off.

I took aim at the beans. *Let them think I'm an idiot. It isn't the first time.*

My stomach near bursting, I hurried across the street to the general store. Somebody had left the door ajar and I entered the murkiness within. The place was deserted. I wandered among the displays when I heard voices in the back. Weaving my way past displays and boxes I came to a stop next to a shelf with oil lamps. *...tell'em the Kid is at my place.* Pete Maxwell's voice was unmistaken. Somebody else said something, but his voice was too low to hear. *...Find John Poe...White Oaks...he'll know what to do...*

Without warning a shadow rushed past. I caught a glimpse of a guy with chaps, his hat pulled low across his forehead. I ducked and hurried to the opposite end of the counter. Something told me it wouldn't be a good idea to be caught eavesdropping.

"Hello," I yelled. "Anybody here?"

Pete emerged from the backroom, rubbing the back of his neck, his mustache twitching.

"Ah, yes, Max." His eyes flitted to the front door. "I didn't hear you come in."

Trying my best naive look, I said, "Oh, I just got here."

Instead of answering, Pete headed toward a side door hidden behind stacked wooden crates the cowboy had disappeared through. "What're you waiting for?"

I hurried after him.

"These bottles need to be unpacked and placed over there behind the counter. It's our best whiskey so don't break anything or you'll pay for it."

I nodded and went to work. An hour later my arms ached. Three hours later, I was drenched in sweat, my shoulders numb with exhaustion. Still Pete kept finding new projects. And each one of them was physical labor: carrying crates and sacks of dry beans, climbing on ladders and moving barrels, stacking saddles and sorting ropes.

When Pete finally ran out of things to do, I was ready to collapse. My arms shook with fatigue.

"Here is your pay." Pete dropped a few coins in my sweaty palm.

"Fifty cents?" I stared at the five dimes. "You said a dollar a day."

"That's for a whole day. You only worked a few hours." He dangled a key. "Hurry, I need to lock."

I swallowed hard. I wanted to scream slave driver, exploiter. Instead I set my jaw and walked off.

"You can come back tomorrow after lunch. I've got another delivery," Pete yelled after me.

I only nodded, too tired to answer, even too tired to be hungry. I felt sticky with sweat and the powdery dust coating my skin. I probably looked like a breaded chicken. I'd tried hard to drink water whenever I'd passed by the jug. At least Pete hadn't denied me that. But my throat was as dry as a bone in the desert.

Fifty cents. Lousy stinking five dimes. I shook my head. It'd take years to make enough to buy anything. In a daze I crossed the street to the saloon, but when the sounds of piano music and drunken shouts reached my ears I turned around. I had no stomach for that right now or seeing Grace for that matter. I needed a cool shower and an ice-cold soda, followed by a few leisurely hours of gaming. Very funny, Max.

The bathhouse was stifling. "Antonia?"

Two of the three rooms were occupied and I waited.

"You want a bath." The man approaching from behind the

curtain was short with the dark skin and eyes of a Mexican. He seemed irritated for having to take care of business.

"Eh, yes. I was looking for Antonia…"

"She's getting my dinner. Unless you're here for a bath, get the hell out."

"No, no, I need a bath for sure."

"This way," he said, grabbing a couple of pails. "I'll bring the hot water in a minute." I followed the man into the open compartment.

There was even less water in the zinc tub than last time. As I sat in the semi-darkness, rubbing down my body with remnants of soap, I remembered what I'd overheard at Pete's store. It didn't make much sense. Pete was Billy's friend, yet he wanted somebody, what was the name again, John Poe to know where Billy was staying. I frowned.

That name didn't sound familiar. What was the sheriff's name, the man who'd shot Billy the Kid? Garty or Garritt or something. I was confused and frustrated I hadn't paid better attention in school when we studied U.S. history.

CHAPTER NINE

I spent the night uneasy, waking up several times, always aware of Grace next to me, her anger like barbwire between us. She'd pretended to be asleep when I slid under the blanket beside her. I knew by the way she lay rigid, her breath catching in the stillness.

I'd eaten alone in the saloon while everyone around me had a good time. I hadn't seen Billy or the drunken Indian. The whiskey was tempting to help drown my sorrow, but after the bath I had forty cents to my name. I already owed Grace more than that, I needed to buy a hat and maybe a horse. My clothes needed washing, but that was another ten cents…which I might need for survival.

Amazing how low I'd sunk that even forty cents made a difference when before I hadn't thought twice about spending a few Euros on drinks and ice cream. I felt more and more depressed. I was broke and my body would wear out from the unrelenting heat and the hard work I wasn't used to. And like last time, the game gave no indication what I was supposed to do. I turned my back to the girl, exhaustion taking over.

In my dream Billy wielded his guns at me. Traitor, he said, his blue eyes squinting angrily. I turned to run, but Grace was on the ground holding my legs in place. Shoot him, she yelled, he loves Indians.

I woke with a start, drenched in sweat, the blanket twisted around my thighs. The room was aglow with the morning sun. Grace wasn't there. By the looks of the dirty water, she had washed while I'd snored like a dog next to her. I wondered if she had snooped through my things. I rummaged through my pockets, but the knife, matches and coins were still there.

Like the day before the saloon was empty. Eating another stack of pancakes I racked my brain for what to do. I could stay a while, remain uneasy roommates with Grace and earn a few dollars. Then what?

I had no idea. I obviously wasn't going to travel home from the game because whatever I had to do, I hadn't done yet. Working in a store for a dollar a day was hardly a mission. Nor was being supported by a girl.

I remembered the sweater I'd retrieved from the donkey. It needed washing and mending so I could wear it again in case the game was ready to send me home. Taking two steps at a time I went to retrieve the stinky thing from upstairs. It reeked of sweat and something worse, the blood crusted into hard brown stains.

The bathhouse stood silent as I approached. I hoped it was early enough to catch Antonia alone while the Mexican was still sleeping. I breathed easier when I saw her. She half-smiled at me when I entered, but then I noticed a fresh bruise under her eye. The skin had a one-inch cut, looking puffy and bluish.

"What happened?" I asked.

Antonia shrugged. "He is an angry drunk. He wants to make me his wife. I try to stay away."

I blushed, imagining the stout Mexican pushing himself on the skinny girl. Instead of giving an answer, I scanned the curtain in back.

"He's sleeping off the whiskey."

"Good." I held up my crusty sweater. "You think you can clean this? It's all stuck together with blood. I have to be able to wear it again."

Antonia wrinkled her nose. "What did you do?"

"It's donkey blood. The Indians killed…" I sighed.

Her dark brown eyes grew larger. "The white man takes our land, so we fight. Then he takes our people. And we fight some more. Until there is nobody left."

I nodded. She was right, of course. And there was nothing for me to do or say to make a speck of difference. For a moment, the room turned still. Only the stove crackled.

"I must check on my brother. I take him food every day."

By the looks of it, she was giving him most of her food allowance.

She hesitated. "Will you wait here and tend the store? It is never busy in the morning." She glanced at the curtain and whispered, "I'll wash your shirt for free."

"Sure."

"I won't be long." Antonia grabbed a cloth bundle and hurried off. I marveled how quietly she moved. I never heard her step.

The stove needed tending so I added a log and removed some of the ashes. I refilled two pails from a water barrel outside, walked around the space and inspected each room. The zinc tubs had been cleaned, the floors swept, waiting for customers.

I remembered my own bathroom. It had been ages since I'd taken a shower. I wondered how my mother was doing. How stupid. She was fine because at home time didn't pass. She was in the same place, probably watching TV in the living room, waiting for my anger to go away. Time happened only here in this forsaken game.

"Thank you," Antonia said.

I jumped. I hadn't heard her return. "No sweat, glad to help."

Our eyes met and I knew something was wrong. "What is it?"

"My brother is worse. He is losing weight."

"Is it the alcohol?"

She fervently shook her head. "The white man's disease. They call it consumption."

I took a step back. I was pretty sure that consumption was an old-fashioned word for *Tuberculosis*. "That's really contagious."

"What?" The alarm in Antonia's eyes intensified.

"It means you can get infected yourself. It's a bacteria…" I sighed. "Tiny organisms that live in the lungs. You must keep your distance."

Antonia looked at me as if I spoke Chinese. Maybe she hadn't understood me—even if her English seemed really good.

I was suddenly afraid for her. "Are you coughing?" I put a hand on her forehead and she flinched. "Just checking if you have a temperature." Her skin felt smooth and dry despite the heat.

Antonia's palm landed on my chest. "Do you have medicine power? My uncle had big medicine until the Mexicans shot him."

I shook my head, trying to remember when antibiotics had

been invented. I had no idea. Even if they existed, I had no way of getting any. Antonia's brother was going to die as sure as winter followed fall. I swallowed hard, not wanting to tell her that nothing would save her brother.

To give me something to do I grabbed Antonia's fingers. "Promise me not to touch him. Wash your hands really well afterwards. And you have to put something over your mouth and nose when you visit. I'll make it for you. You have any fabric. Anything?" I couldn't keep the urgency from my voice and Antonia began to tremble.

"What are you saying? I gave him my amulet, powerful medicine from our people. It will protect him."

Not able to meet her eyes, I turned to search for a piece of cloth. It was answer enough. When I finally looked at her, Antonia was crying. Silent tears rolled down her cheeks and dripped off her chin.

"What are you doing?" she asked. "You have seen Narsimha die in your dreams?"

"No, but you need a mask. Did any of your customers leave clothes behind?"

She nodded. Obviously glad for something to do, she disappeared behind the curtain and returned with a linen shirt and a leather vest. "I washed them."

"We'll use the shirt." I took out my knife and began cutting a patch. "Can you sew?"

Instead of answering she showed me a needle and thread she kept on a shelf. "We... my mother and aunts made all our clothes before...Beautiful beadwork, too." Her voice was heavy with sadness.

Glad for something to distract me, I ripped strips from the shirt, the tearing sound loud in the stillness. Antonia's eyes were still shiny, but the tears had stopped.

"Before?"

"Sometime I'll tell you a story."

"I'd love that." It was true. I really wanted to know what had happened to her. Why she was here in this white town with a dying brother. I wanted to ask about her people, how she'd ended up with the brute. But first I had work to do. "Here, take this patch and stitch a thin strip of cloth or leather to each corner to bind around your head. We'll make two masks so I can go with you."

"What is going on here?" The Mexican was leaning heavily against the doorway, his eyes dull and bloodshot. I wrinkled my nose as the stink of sweat and dirty skin wafted across. The man needed to be his own customer.

"You again? Taking another bath?" the Mexican sneered.

I shook my head, aware that I still held the pocketknife but was otherwise defenseless. The man's arms were twice the size of mine.

In a sweeping motion I collected the fabric patches and stuffed them into my pocket.

"You filthy red skin," the Mexican panted. "Wasting my time." In horror I watched him clamp down on Antonia's upper arm. It looked like he'd snap it in two. Still the girl didn't say anything. She just shook her head at me.

No sooner had I hidden the knife, I felt my fingers curl into fists.

"What? You're going to fight me over a redskin." The Mexican spit on the cleanly swept floor. "Come here, then." A vein throbbed on his temple, his face flushed. I hoped for a heart attack. With a vicious shove the Mexican rid himself of the girl. Antonia flew across the room and came crashing down near the front door.

I stepped back, keeping an eye on the man. I knew I was no match for a guy who obviously wanted blood. At least I didn't carry a weapon to provoke the man. As if he'd heard my thoughts the Mexican turned. "Where is my gun? I'll blow your brains out, you little sneak," he hissed.

"Hurry," Antonia whispered. "Get out before he kills you." I stared at the girl who leaned against the wall like a worn-out rag doll. I couldn't move. Surely I was supposed to help this girl, but in a few seconds the mad dog Mexican would shoot me. Game over.

But I stood frozen, my legs unwilling to leave the girl in the clutches of a tyrant. Something crashed to the ground in the backroom, followed by a flood of Spanish that had to be swearing. The sounds brought me to my senses and I rushed to the door.

Not a moment too soon. The Mexican shouted something and the doorframe next to me exploded. Splinters pierced my neck and right cheek as I flew around the corner. Thank goodness for running practice. I raced around another corner into the alley. The noise behind me quickly died into a low rumble. I crept to the corner and scanned the street. No sign of the crazy man.

Hurrying through another alley, I found myself facing the shed where the Indian was hiding. I carefully stepped underneath the overhang, picking bits of wood from my neck and face, trying to get my breath under control.

"Hello?"

A grungy blanket lay in a heap next to the straw. I noticed a tin plate with bits of scrambled egg, a few beans and an empty bottle. There was no sign of the Indian. I walked back the way I'd come, wondering where Narsimha spent his days.

The plaza sparkled in the midmorning heat. The Mexican was gone.

I hesitated. Antonia was in danger and instead of helping her I'd run off. I thought of going to the sheriff, but then they would probably laugh at me. Who cared about a poor Indian slave girl? I'd have to report to Pete after lunch. My arms still ached but I needed money, lots of money. If I wanted to help the girl, I needed supplies.

We'd have to run away. Soon.

During lunch I faced the saloon's front door. In case the Mexican was coming after me. Grace was nowhere in sight and I wondered what she was doing. Maybe she'd found a job and was working. Having nothing to do, I crossed the street to Pete's store. Later I'd figure out a way to see Antonia, make sure she was okay. And collect my sweater.

As I stocked shelves with canned beans, two girls entered the store. Despite their fancy outfits they looked like they were about my age. They giggled when they saw me which annoyed me because I was wearing a white apron like Pete Maxwell—except mine was already stained and hung limply like an old bed sheet around my neck.

"Pete isn't here," I offered.

The girls giggled again. I recognized Paulita, Billy's girlfriend. "When will my brother be back?" she said.

I shrugged. "Don't know."

"What's your name?" Paulita's friend asked.

"Max." Assuming my best customer service face, I asked, "Can I help you with something?"

Pete had shown me the book with long lists of goods and what they cost. The writing was orderly, but tiny and I longed for my laptop. Even the simplest excel sheet would have been an improvement.

"In that case..." the other girl said. Like Paulita she was dressed in a black skirt and white ruffled blouse. The girls looked very clean among the dusty goods, their black hair shiny and braided in back.

"I need new riding gloves," Paulita said. She wrinkled her nose in distaste, looking at the pair she held in her hands. They looked perfectly fine to me, the leather a bit worn, but otherwise intact and spotless.

"Let me show you what we have," I offered.

Paulita's friend giggled again. "I heard you got a shipment of lace."

I nodded. "Give me a minute." Rushing into the bowels of the store, I desperately tried to remember where Pete had stuck the lace. I'd seen gloves on some shelf, but it was hard to keep it all straight.

Sweating and confused, I rummaged through the newly arrived boxes. They had New York and Boston imprinted on them. In the background I heard the girls chatting. I didn't pay attention until Paulita's friend mentioned the Kid.

"Is Billy going to marry you?"

"Pete is against it. So is Mother," Paulita said in a low voice. I temporarily halted my search.

"But you're still seeing him, right?" the friend said.

Paulita let out a nervous laugh. "He's a wonderful dancer. So polite, too."

"What about his visits...you know?" the other girl said, followed by a nervous giggle.

"Shsh," Paulita said. She whispered something too low to hear.

I wasn't sure what I'd heard. Though the schoolbooks hadn't exactly said so, Billy was quite the womanizer. At least that's what the movies wanted you to believe. And if history had it right, Paulita was pregnant when Billy got killed by the sheriff.

Smiling innocently I returned to the counter, my arms filled with three types of riding gloves and rolls of black lace. "Here we go."

"How much is this lace?" the friend asked, pointing a dainty forefinger at one of the spools.

I dug into the lists, but there was no new entry for lace. I looked like a fool again. I was glad for the distraction when the door clanged and a Mexican man entered. For a second I feared it was the bathhouse owner, but this man was tall and much thinner.

"What are you doing here, Paulita, dear?" he asked.

"Hello Mr. Silva," Paulita said. "Picking out new gloves."

"Pete not here?" Silva said to no one in particular.

I shook my head.

"Max is helping us," the friend said as another bubble of mirth escaped her. I knew she was checking me out, her eyes following my every move. Annoying. These girls looked wealthy with not a care in the world.

"Well, I'll let you two shop," Silva said, turning to me. "Will you tell Pete I need to talk to him?"

I nodded, my attention on the two girls.

Paulita held up a pair of buckskin gloves. "I'll take these." I rifled through my lists, but again they made no sense to me. Were gloves categorized under clothes or equipment? Or maybe leather goods?

"Just tell him what I got. He'll fix it," Paulita said.

"Eh, can I ask you something?" I tried. "Do you have any use for your old gloves? I'd love to have them, if you don't mind."

Paulita raised an eyebrow. "Your hands are much too large." She glanced at my dirty fingernails.

"I know," I hurried. "I'd like to have them for a friend."

The other girl laughed again. "He has a girlfriend, Paulita. Look at him." I felt my cheeks grow hot. What was that supposed to mean? Stupid irritating girls.

"Why not." Paulita shoved her old gloves across the counter. "And hand me some of that jerky." She pointed at a glass jar.

"Is it for Billy?" the friend said with another chuckle. Paulita shot her a look and the smile vanished. "What about my lace? I'd like four yards."

"I'm sorry, Pete hasn't written down the new prices yet. Could you...come back later?" When the girl's face clouded into a frown, I stumbled, "I give it to you now as long as you promise to come back and pay."

"Oh, she will," Paulita said. "Let's go, it's too hot in here." She unfolded an ornate fan and waved it in front of her face.

I measured and cut the lace and rolled it into a piece of brown paper, nervous about my grimy hands leaving fingerprints. Only when they'd gone did I remember that I hadn't asked for the girl's name.

Great. I'd given some anonymous customer free stuff. What if she didn't return? I glanced at the spool of lace. It was clear there was a good length missing. Pete would say I'd stolen it.

"What are you doing dream walking behind my counter?" Pete had materialized in the back.

"Oh, I just helped your sister and her friend."

"Paulita was here?" Pete looked like he disapproved. "What did she want?"

"New riding gloves. And her friend bought lace. I…I didn't know what things cost. Paulita said to tell you."

"Who was with her?"

I stopped in midair, my arms filled with spools and gloves. "I forgot to ask. She took four yards of the Paris lace. I wrote it down on the paper."

For a moment, Pete remained quiet. "You mean to tell me you gave some girl my merchandise without collecting or noting her name?"

I stood frozen. "I didn't mean to…I'm sure Paulita can vouch for her. She said…"

Pete waved a dismissive arm. "You better stick to manual labor. Put that away and move the empty barrels outside."

I nodded. Inside I was fuming. How could I do a good job if they had such antiquated systems? I was sure Pete already knew who the girl was.

By evening when my arms had turned to jelly, Pete gave me sixty cents. Like yesterday I needed a bath badly. But the Mexican was ready to kill me. Which meant I potentially risked my neck to get clean.

Still, I'd have to check. At least I had to see if Antonia was okay. But when I approached the bathhouse, I heard the Mexican yelling inside. Unable to peek through the only window, blind with steam, I kept my head low and returned to the saloon.

It was more crowded tonight, patrons drinking and playing cards. Most were Mexican—a few looked like regular American cowboys. A woman in a corset and long skirt played the piano singing something in Spanish. The barkeeper rushed back and forth, serving beer and whiskey. To my surprise, Grace threaded her way through the crowd, arms loaded with empty plates. I slipped past her and found an empty seat near the back wall.

It was just as well. I didn't want to talk anyway.

"What do you want to drink?" Grace asked, appearing by my side and avoiding eye contact. She wore a different dress with a much lower neckline.

"Water…and a beer," I said. Maybe it would help me forget. "Wait, how much is that?"

"Five cents for the beer. I'll bring you your dinner."

I nodded.

"I see you found a job," I said, when she returned with my plate and two mugs.

Ignoring my comment, she slammed down my dishes and hurried off. I sighed. The game was getting on my nerve. Grace was a pain, Antonia was stuck with a maniac, my new boss was a slave driver and, generally speaking, life sucked. I'd earned the grand total of one dollar and ten cents in two days, wearing myself out in the process.

I longingly remembered Juliana and Bero. How they'd made life tolerable in the Middle Ages.

A woman's scream near the bar ripped me out of my misery. Two rough-looking characters shouted something before the entire throng began shifting apart. Unable to see anything, I straightened.

The piano music stopped as Narsimha wobbled away from the counter, a small bottle of brown liquid in his hand. His eyes shone brightly as he headed toward the door. Everyone made room, shoving at their neighbors. The Indian was taller than most everyone and at some point he must've been an impressive warrior. His shoulders were still broad, but his hair was matted while his leather breaches hung loose and his shirt was covered with brownish splotches.

TB. The Indian was coughing blood. Some customers were whispering and pointing while others stood and stared. Just when it looked as if the Indian had made it safely to the exit, he tripped.

I recognized the grungy cowboy from the other night who'd stuck out his boot. Narsimha crashed heavily, glass shattering and liquid spilling across the floor.

"Puihhh, smell that?" the cowboy slurred. "This is one drunken redskin."

Nobody said anything. In slow motion the Indian came to his

knees. His hands were bleeding and a piece of glass stuck in his forearm. He was moaning something unintelligible. Still everyone stood watching.

I'd had enough. I stomped to the bar where Beaver Smith was filling orders.

"Give me another bottle," I yelled.

"Fifty cents for a quart."

"I don't care." I felt the anger choke off my air and threw five dimes on the counter. "Now!"

Smith slid a new bottle across the counter and I shoved past the gawking crowd. Narsimha was still on his knees, staring in wonder at the puddle of whiskey evaporating through the floorboards and the glass in his arm.

I removed the shard and pulled the Indian upward. "Come on. I've got your drink."

"Injun lover," the thug jeered.

"Leave him alone. He's sick," I hissed back. Ignoring the mob, I put an arm under Narsimha's bicep and led him outside. I was worried about getting sick, the masks still in my pocket, useless without the strings. The Indian mumbled again as we wandered down the street. I led him around the corner and into the alley, past the corral to the straw bed.

When at last Narsimha sat down, he was shaking all over. His hand and arm were covered in blood where the gash was oozing. I kneeled and handed him the bottle.

"Here, take it slow." While the Indian took a deep gulp, I wrapped a couple of the strips leftover from the masks around the man's forearm. The bleeding had stopped and at least there wouldn't be dirt going into the wound.

Narsimha watched from dark eyes. Satisfied with my bandaging skills, I slumped down a few feet away, leaning against one of the shed's support posts. The Indian took another swig, his eyes fixed on me. The craziness had left and he looked almost normal. I imagined him on a horse with feathers in his hair. He must've been quite a sight.

Remembering the Indian's terrible illness, I took handfuls of sand and rubbed blood spots from my fingers.

"You Ela's friend."

I looked up. "Ela?"

"My sister."

I nodded. I was such an idiot. The poor girl had been renamed by the Mexican thug. I'd never call her Antonia again.

"She says you have medicine." Narsimha touched the two leather pouches hanging from his neck.

"I just know a few things."

The Indian took another drink. "Too late for Narsimha. I'll soon join *Ussen*," he said glancing upwards.

I wanted to say that it wasn't so, that things would improve. But when I looked into the other man's eyes I knew better. There was sadness there, knowledge of earth and sky…impending death. And something else. Acceptance. The white man had won another fight. My mouth tasted bitter. I was suddenly ashamed. And fuming.

"You should rest," I finally managed. "I'm sorry." I was trying to straighten when a hand clamped down on my arm.

"You must save Ela," the Indian panted. "Promise you will take her away…from this." I stared at the bony hand with remnants of dried blood squeezing my forearm. What if the Tuberculosis infected me, crept into my lungs. "Please," Narsimha wheezed. "I planned to do, but I can't. White man's sickness too strong."

"I'll try," I said. I knew I sounded unconvincing. How was I supposed to leave town when I had no clue where to go? Not to mention the minor detail of having forty-five cents to my name. I couldn't even take care of myself. How was I going to take care of a girl?

Yet, my insides twisted with worry for her. "It'll be a few weeks." *More like years.* "I have to save money so I can buy a horse and food."

The Indian mumbled something and let go of my arm. But instead of lying down, he yanked one of the leather pouches from his neck, contents spilling into the sand. A hawk feather, a bird's dried claw, a lock of black hair tied with a piece of leather, a tiny shoe with elaborate beadwork. Something rolled into the folds of the blanket, but before I managed to take a look, Narsimha had snatched it up and held out his palm.

"Here."

In his hand lay the largest gold nugget I'd ever seen. Years ago I'd been fascinated with gold when we'd gone pretend *panning* in South Dakota. This piece was nearly the size of a golf ball. "Buy horse and food. Head south and west into the mountains. Ela will know what to do. Find our people." Narsimha sagged into the straw, the last shred of energy gone. He took another swig and waved at me. "Go now. I'll watch for you from above." He tried a half-smile before his eyes fell shut.

I hurried into the alley. I didn't know I was crying.

CHAPTER TEN

Dusk settled into deep shadows, but I didn't pay attention. My mind whirled. I had to plan this right, get the dying Indian out of my mind. I needed horses and supplies. I had to see Ela and make an escape plan. The sooner we left the better.

Emerging from the alley I scanned the main street. The male residents of Fort Sumner were heading for the saloon. I pulled my sombrero low and casually walked toward the bathhouse. All was quiet, not even a light shone through the window. I remembered seeing an alcove inside, more like a glorified closet, where Ela slept. It had no windows to climb through. I decided against knocking on the door. The Mexican was liable to blow me off his doorstep.

I'd have to sneak in to find her. The doorknob didn't turn—either he'd locked her in or they were both in there.

A sigh escaped from my chest. In real life you wrote a quick text and things were arranged. Here, I didn't even have pen and paper for a note. Real life. Hah! This was as real as it got.

I'd start with item two on my list. Jogging across the plaza and past the general store, the nugget bounced in my pocket. In front of the saloon, horses waited for their masters. Drunken voices mixed with piano music. Beaver Smith was doing well tonight.

I remembered Grace. She was probably working. Despite her constant anger towards me, I felt guilty. I'd leave instead of helping her find a way to San Francisco.

A couple of oil lanterns burned on either side of the cavernous doors of the town stables. A dozen horses were tethered outside. More occupied the stalls. The concentrated stench of horse manure bit my nostrils. A million flies buzzed, having found a perfect place to raise families.

"Hello?" I stepped into the gloom, swatting myself.

A man with a brush in one hand and a lamp in the other appeared from one of the partitions. "Can I help you?"

"Yeah," I said. "Do you have horses for sale? I need two."

"What kind?"

I was confused. "The riding kind." I remembered the donkey. "Not too wild or biting."

The man chuckled. In the shine of the lantern, he looked like Santa with a white beard reaching to his chest. Only his eyes didn't quite match. They were a watery blue and hard to read.

"Let me show you what I have." He headed into the depth of the barn. "How about these two?" he said pointing into a corner. "Both mares, one about five, the other roughly ten. Shoed 'em myself."

The horses looked sleepily at me, their tails swishing at the annoying flies. I remembered how my father had test-driven a half dozen cars before settling on one.

"Can I ride them?"

"And head into the hills, never to be seen again? No, my friend. They're sixty dollars apiece." He paused, his white brows narrowing. "You don't look like you've got money. Aren't you the new kid working for Pete? You planning to steal from me, boy?"

"I do have money," I said, my confidence faltering. I neither knew what a good horse looked like nor what the nugget was worth.

"You get the hell out of here," the man said. "Before I call the sheriff."

I eyed the revolver on the man's hip. "I can pay, I promise."

Santa's hand inched to the holster. He was breathing heavily. "Now, listen boy, my patience is running thin. You work at Pete's for what, dollar a day? You don't even have money for a gun. And now you march in here wasting my time. Get out before I lose my patience."

"I can pay," I insisted, feeling my voice rise. "Can't you believe me?" It was probably easiest to show the gold, but remembering the guards in Schwarzburg's dungeon who'd stolen my coins, I hesitated. I didn't know this guy and by the looks of him or anyone else in this rotten town, I couldn't trust anyone. But then, maybe the gold wasn't worth that much.

The man turned to pick up a pitchfork. "Believe some dog-eared kid full of palaver?" Then he whistled and a grimy stable boy materialized from the gloom. "Get the sheriff." The boy nodded and raced off.

I started to sweat. What if the sheriff accused me of stealing and threw me in jail? Nobody would speak for me. They'd take the gold—Narsimha's escape money.

"Right here." I yanked the lump of gold from my pocket.

"Let me see that." The man's demeanor switched to greed and curiosity.

I held out a palm, but kept my distance. "It's real. You can be sure of it."

"Where did you get that?"

None of your damn business, I wanted to say. Judging by the way the man acted, the gold was plenty to pay for the horses. "It was a gift. I'll pick up the horses tomorrow evening. Have them ready."

"Calm yourself, Mister." The man sounded all slimy business. "I'll even throw in a bag of oats for you."

"Two bags," I shouted over my shoulder. "And don't screw me." I grimaced. Santa probably didn't know what I was talking about. But he was right about one thing. I needed a gun. *You've never shot a gun.* Even if I had one, I certainly wouldn't aim it at a human being.

Hurrying down the street I thought of what to buy for our journey. New saddles were forty dollars at Pete's store. We needed food, a rifle. I hoped Ela could shoot. If not, we'd at least have a weapon to threaten with.

I'd get the nugget exchanged for cash. Pete accepted gold dust at the store. Things were falling into place.

I whistled when I entered the saloon. Until the rest of my days I wondered why Grace didn't warn me about the new arrivals near the bar watching me climb upstairs.

CHAPTER ELEVEN

I awoke at first light. Grace was asleep and didn't stir while I got dressed. I felt stinky and hot, new welts, courtesy of my bedbug friends, itching my belly. The critters didn't care if I was sweaty and covered in filth.

I'd made lists in my head half the night, only falling into heavy sleep in the early hours. *Normal* hotel rooms had pen and paper. Here in the Wild West you had to organize everything yourself. The barroom was empty and I hardly noticed what I ate. Nor did I acknowledge Beaver Smith's curious gaze. Still chewing, I headed to the bathhouse.

To my relief the door opened. I quietly entered, ready for instant retreat. Ela was on her knees, scrubbing the floor in one of the rooms.

"Hey," I whispered.

She flinched, raising the brush over her head before she turned.

When she recognized me, her eyes grew larger still. "It isn't safe. You must leave." Her right forearm was dotted with bruises while the left bicep showed bluish outlines of the Mexican's fingers.

"I need to talk to you."

Ela put a finger on her lips and stepped to the door. Then she returned, leaning close. I noticed how dark her mouth was—like it was covered in lipstick.

"He's back there. Hurry."

"Your brother wants us to find your family. He gave me gold to buy horses and take you into the mountains. We must leave tonight."

Ela's eyes widened. Then she shook her head. "I'm not leaving my brother. He's too sick to know what he is saying."

"He wants you to escape before it's too late. The Mexican will kill you sooner or later." *Or rape you, if he hasn't already.*

"No."

Why on earth do all girls have to be stubborn? Still, I hesitated. I wanted to tell her that there was no hope for her brother. That he was as good as dead, but I couldn't make myself. "You go and see him now. He'll tell you. And tonight, after dark, I'll meet you at the stables. I'll have everything ready. Do you understand?"

Ela just looked at me with those brown eyes, the color of dark chocolate. They were like glimpses into pools of secrets. Secrets I didn't understand.

I grabbed her hands. "Ela, listen to me. Your brother made me promise to help you."

She shook her head again, but this time it was less forceful. "Will you go and talk to him?"

"I can't go now." She nodded toward the curtain. "He's awake. I'll meet you at my brother's hiding place at dinnertime. We'll talk to him and if…he asks me I'll do what he says."

"Antonia, get your skinny butt in here. I want coffee," the Mexican grumbled from the backroom.

Ela lifted her chin. "I'm coming."

"One more thing. I got you something for the ride." I stuffed Paulita's used gloves in Ela's hand. "Hide them till tonight."

"I don't have anything to give you," she whispered. "It is bad luck if I don't give you a present as well."

"You can do it later. I better go."

Ela opened her mouth. But then she nodded and hurried to the back.

I crept to the entrance and looked back. Our eyes met for the briefest moment. Then she disappeared behind the curtain.

Only when I stepped outside did I wonder what dinnertime meant. I'd seen people eat anytime through the evening hours. I'd keep my cover at Pete's, quit early, assemble supplies and then pick up horses. This was exciting, a real adventure going into the wilderness with an Indian girl. It had to be what the game wanted me to do.

The morning moved excruciatingly slowly. I strolled to the edge of town to collect more aloe. My skin was better, but still tight around nose and cheeks. I grinned. I'd finally buy myself a new hat and get rid of that stinky sombrero.

Still, it'd been nice of Billy the Kid to help out. I wondered what he was up to. Ever since the first day at the saloon and the visit in the orchard I hadn't seen him. It was pretty obvious Billy was lying low. Either that or he was on a trip.

I stopped in my tracks. What if I warned him? Prevent Billy from getting shot by that sheriff. Would the game allow the altering of history? I wasn't sure. Nothing in this second round of the game made sense. I shook my head to chase away the vision of my mother's face. I needed all my wits to pull this off. Avoid being scammed by Pete and the Santa lookalike.

When I reported to work, Pete was in his office writing in a ledger. He sent me to dust the glass counters. Whirling a cloth I was merely moving the dirt back and forth. But this did present a fine opportunity to check the scale. The sign on the wall said: *We pay twenty-one dollars per ounce.*

Making sure all was quiet, I lifted the nugget from my pocket and placed it on the scale. The tray smacked to the bottom and sat. Worried someone would enter while I was playing with the gold, I scanned the front door.

But my curiosity was too great. Different sized weights lined a wooden box next to the scale. Numbers were imprinted on each, ranging from quarter and half to one, five, ten and twenty ounces. I lifted the ten-ounce piece. Might as well see where I stood. The tray with the nugget remained glued to the counter. I grabbed a twenty. Nothing. Another twenty. The tray shot up. Too much. I removed the twenty and added a ten, then one...two. The scale quivered and moved upward, but still the nugget hovered an inch below the other side. Another half-ounce and I had it.

Holding my breath I counted. The nugget weighed forty-two and a half ounces. That was...I calculated... worth more than 890 dollars. I was rich!

When I heard footsteps I quickly straightened the scale and slid the gold in my pocket, quietly whistling and cleaning the shelves behind me.

"You asleep today," Pete said, eyeing me skeptically. "Laziness isn't paid around here."

"No, Sir. Doing what you told me." I smiled. Only a few more hours and I'd kiss this sorry job good-bye.

"Say, I need to deliver a few groceries to our family cook. You keep cleaning. I want this place sparkling when I return." Pete threw me another suspicious glance.

I nodded enthusiastically. Even better. I'd be able to check all the items and decide what I wanted to buy. It wasn't like a car you could stuff with supplies. We'd have to pack carefully. Considering how little fit on a horse, we'd have to be frugal, hope that we…Ela could hunt.

As soon as Pete left, I ripped a piece of brown packing paper from a roll and began to make notes. Two horses at sixty dollars, two saddles at forty dollars each. I found tins of biscuits, sacks of dry beans, salted pork and beef jerky. A Winchester rifle cost forty dollars. I also needed bullets. The list grew longer. A calculator would've been nice about now. I needed saddlebags and water skins. My brain churned.

Running back and forth, I piled the goods in a corner near the backdoor. I'd wait until close to quitting time to tell Pete unless he asked. The fewer people knew the better.

By the time Pete returned, I'd made little progress with the dust.

"Here are fifty cents," Pete said, handing me the coins. He scrutinized his gold pocket watch. "I'm heading to an early dinner in fifteen minutes. Finish folding the sacks and stack them in the storeroom for tomorrow."

I took a deep breath. It was time to come clean. "I'm buying some things before I leave tonight. I've made a list." I handed over the torn piece of packing paper.

Pete stepped near the window to read. Waving the paper impatiently, he said, "What is this? How are you going to buy all this? It's hundreds of dollars."

I opened my palm. "It was a gift. I've got to go somewhere."

Pete hurried closer. "You a thief? Let me see." He gasped. "Where did you find that?"

"Nowhere, as I said, it was given to me."

Pete stepped back to stare at me. "Who would give a mere kid a nugget like this?"

"It's true." I held Pete's gaze. "So can I get my stuff?"

For a moment, the room turned quiet and I expected Pete to refuse. But then he shrugged. "I can't make change for that big a piece. It's probably what, forty ounces?"

"Forty-two and a half."

Pete whistled. "I've got to go to the bank." He held out a hand. "After I weigh this."

Reluctantly I handed over the nugget. What if Pete kept it and pretended it was his? Who would believe a strange kid who worked for a few cents a day over an established businessman who was rich?

But Pete grabbed a magnifying glass and inspected the nugget. It sparkled even in the dull light of the store. Without comment he stepped behind the counter and quickly maneuvered the scale.

"Forty two and a half ounces." He whistled again and handed me the gold. "Better hide that well." Returning to my list, he mumbled, "Let's see, I'll withdraw five-hundred. With what I have here I can make change. Boy, you better not have stolen this. They'll hang you." Pete's mustache twitched.

"I swear, it's rightfully mine."

"We'll take care of it first thing in the morning."

"I've got to do it tonight."

Pete shook his head. "The bank is closed and I can't make change. Why didn't you tell me earlier?"

"Sorry, I didn't think about it." I considered leaving the money, but that meant Pete would keep several hundred dollars, a small fortune. Chances were great Ela and I would need it. And I'd give Grace the fare to travel to San Francisco.

Pete glanced at his watch again. "I'm going to be late for dinner. So, if you'll excuse me, I'd like to lock up." He headed for the door.

"I really *must* have it tonight," I shouted at Pete's back. "I can pay extra."

Pete turned to face me. "Boy, you're a sore excuse for a customer." He rubbed his mustache, probably trying to figure out how to maximize his profit. "Are you on the run? The sheriff will hunt you down."

"I swear it's mine. I just have to be somewhere…else."

Pete watched me. I stared back. I felt my heart pound in my neck.

"I tell you what," Pete finally said. "I'm going to dinner now and afterwards I'll find Mr. Tims from the bank. We'll meet back here, say in a couple of hours, and you'll get your money. I'll charge ten percent."

Ten percent of what, but I nodded instead, half relieved and half furious at myself. I'd had all day to plan. Why hadn't I thought of how much money I'd get back? New worry crept over me. Ela. She was probably waiting for me. It was dusk outside and the store was turning dark.

I grimaced. Instead of riding off she'd have to return to the bathhouse and hope to escape later. I'd just put her in more danger.

The alley was nearly dark as I hurried along. I saw nobody. The chickens had disappeared and the assembled sheds and stalls sat quietly in the gloom. Narsimha leaned against the straw bale. Even since yesterday he'd gone downhill, his nose more pronounced, competing with sharp cheekbones. Ela was squatting nearby watching her brother.

"I'm ready," she said, wiping a tear from her jaw as if she were swatting a fly.

I sighed. "Sorry, it'll have to be a bit later than I thought."

Ela turned to face me. "What do you mean?"

"I've got all the stuff, the horses are reserved, but I still need to pay. The shop owner couldn't make change. It was too much money. He's eating—"

"You said dinnertime," Ela's voice was sharp despite its low tone. "The Mexican will look for me. And if I go back now, I can't leave again—"

"You promised to take her," Narsimha mumbled. A coughing fit followed and I tried to hold my breath.

"I will. Everything is ready. Only a little later—"

"Doubt that," somebody said from the shadows.

I swiveled around but it was too late. Something sharp dug into my back.

"Having ourselves a little powwow? You a redskin now, boy?" The evil sneer of Wade's voice was unmistaken. "Told you, Boss, he's in cahoots with the Injuns. Raise your damn hands, boy."

I yanked up my arms, trying to control the shaking in my knees. Shreds of memory returned. Emerging among the nasty gang when I'd expected to land at Castle Hanstein to see Bero and Juliana. Wade making it a point to punish me with kicks and threats, almost shooting me on sight.

From the corner of my eye I noticed Ela getting up. Behind her, the Irish had materialized, drilling a rifle into the girl's back. So, they both had gotten away after the Indian raid. I thought about the carnage. I'd simply assumed the Comanches had dragged Wade and the Irish off or made them prisoners.

"Didn't think you had it in you, Max," the Irish said. "Last time I saw you, you were struggling in the desert, wanting us to think you were penniless. I took pity on you. Offered you a ride and water. Saved your life."

"Stinking right," Wade interjected.

"Let me do the talking," the Irish hissed. Even from my less than ideal position I saw that the Irish looked worse. He'd lost weight, his pants covered in dust, his shirt torn. "And now I hear you aren't all it seems. I hear you've got a claim?"

"Claim?" *What was the guy talking about?*

"Don't play me." Compared to our first meeting, the Irish was a lot less friendly. "You made me think you were just a kid, but it turns out you're holding out on us. Carrying around nuggets and pretending to be poor, living off my charity—all the while striking it rich behind our back."

I stared. The Irish knew about the gold. "I don't know what you're talking about." Out came my innocent face.

"What I can stand even less than poor sons of bitches are liars," the Irish said, ramming his rifle into Ela's back.

When she whimpered, I yelled, "I…it was a gift."

"Ha." The Irish hurled a glob of spit toward Narsimha who sat rigid and seemingly asleep.

"Gift my ass," Wade jeered.

"Whatever you say, boy. Fact is you're coming with us and you're going to show us where you found the gold."

I opened my mouth, but no words formed. "It was given to me," I stumbled, wishing my voice sounded forceful. Wishing even more I hadn't messed up again.

"Let's get the nugget, boss," Wade said behind my back. For emphasis, the rifle tip twisted harder.

"Empty your pockets." The Irish shoved Ela toward me. "Give it to her."

I stood rooted to the ground. My hands cramped with fear, but I couldn't make myself turn over the only treasure, Narsimha had kept hidden to save his sister.

Ela's eyes were black pools in the dusk.

"Hurry up," Wade growled. The rifle stabbed viciously and my fingers disappeared in my pockets. Why hadn't I bought a revolver? I'd been so stupid and naïve. This was the *Wild* West where people took what they wanted, where violence ruled. Ela held open her hands and I placed the nugget on her palm. I touched the knife and matches buried below, hoping the thugs wouldn't find them.

As if the Irish had picked up on my hesitancy, he waved his rifle. "Everything—unless you want a hole in your gut."

With shaking fingers I placed the knife and matchbox on Ela's hand.

"Let's see what we got. Bring it to me, lass," the Irish said. Ela stepped toward the man when several things happened at once.

With a hoarse cry, Narsimha hurled himself at the Irish. They collapsed in a whirl of arms, legs and grunts. I saw something flash. The gold, my knife and matches flew through the air. A shot rang out. For a second it looked as if Narsimha had killed the Irish.

"Damn, Wade, you almost shot me," the Irish cried instead as he crawled out from underneath the lifeless body of Narsimha who lay face down in the dust. "Stinking redskin had a knife hidden. Who knew, he looked half dead when we got here."

"He won't bother you again," Wade said, satisfaction swinging in his voice.

I wanted to punch him in the gut, my stomach twisting with hatred. Ela cried something and threw herself on her brother's back.

"Don't touch his front," I said, remembering Narsimha's terrible illness. Ela didn't move, but at least she didn't turn him over.

Wade picked up the nugget and knife. "Look at that, boss."

The Irish grabbed an oil lamp from the side of the stall and struck a match under his shoe. "Can't see a thing. Show me." In the flimsy light the gold glistened in Wade's fist. And something else sparkled. There was blood all over the Irish's face.

I knew what it meant. It had been Narsimha's last revenge. "Give it to me," the Irish said, his voice now thick with greed.

"Boss, what's that on your face?"

"Don't waste my time." The Irish touched his lips and inspected his red fingertips before wiping a grimy forearm across his face. "Not my blood," he mumbled as if it were nothing.

Wade handed over the nugget. "What is this thing?" He turned my pocketknife over in his hand.

"He can show you later," the Irish said as the nugget disappeared inside his vest. I watched my knife slide into Wade's pants. "Let's go. We'll find a lot more where that came from. Take the girl, too. She'll make herself useful."

Pretending to touch Ela's back, I bent low and swiped up the matchbox before Wade's rifle renewed contact with my kidneys.

"Time to go, lucky boy. And you, sweets."

I forced my legs forward. I was ready to kill someone and my fury made even walking a chore. I felt like a coil that had been stretched too far and would break any second. Chances were good, the Irish would die anyway: a nice slow and painful death of Tuberculosis. I grimaced in the dark. That left Wade. I'd have to get him somehow.

It was the only thought that kept me from screaming.

CHAPTER TWELVE

The next hours were a blur. One minute I wanted to attack my captors, the next I wanted to throw myself on the ground and die. Only the closeness of Ela kept me from making a move. We shared a saddle, the girl sitting in front, still and rigid as a dark porcelain doll. Her silence was worse than if she'd cried or made sounds of distress. Instead there was nothing. Not even when I whispered to her.

In *K-Pax*, one of my favorite movies, the main character played by Kevin Spacey ends up in a wheelchair and doesn't move. Nobody knows if anything goes on inside his brain. Ela looked like that.

Wade and the Irish had a third companion they called Fred, a shady-faced guy with a month's beard. That was about all I was able to see in the darkness as we rode out of Fort Sumner.

I had no idea what to do. Why couldn't Billy the Kid show up and stop them? He'd shoot the men down in a flash and help me and Ela escape. I forced my mind back to reality. They wanted me to show my claimed land, some place where I'd found the gold. So I'd told them the only thing I thought of, to go southwest toward the mountains. Narsimha had said that was where Ela's people lived.

Despite my anger and worry I finally dozed off, only to jolt awake as soon as I grew aware of the horse beneath me and the girl in front. The realization that I could've avoided the entire thing made me want to go back to sleep and forget. But sleep wouldn't return.

Even Ela slept by the way her head bent forward, her shoulders relaxed and her fingertips curled inward. My butt was getting sore from being squeezed in the saddle, but I was afraid to move and wake her.

Instead I went over the evening's events, wondering when things had unraveled and turned into a nightmare. How Wade and the Irish had found out about the gold. If Pete had been involved or the horse seller was to blame. Or someone in the shadows had gotten wind.

Whoever it had been, I'd screwed up big time and turned my one perfect chance of getting away into a pile of horse dung. By being stupid, I'd betrayed Narsimha and Ela. Which meant we were as good as dead because I had no claim and the only nugget I'd ever possessed—for one lousy day—was with the Irish.

Worse, Narsimha was dead. Even though he would've probably died soon, I felt guilty. I'd promised to help Ela get away. Instead I'd dragged her into the midst of ruthless criminals. Wade and the Irish were much worse than the Mexican. At least the Mexican had wanted to keep Ela for his shop. These guys thought nothing of killing people. Especially Indians. They'd probably rape her or make her do other nasty things. Bile rose in the back of my throat. I wanted to throw up, but my stomach was empty as a balloon.

Ela's shoulders trembled, but she didn't wake.

The night sky was clear, the air crisp. How far were the mountains of Ela's people? How could I get us out of this mess? Not to mention return home from the game. Wade had my knife. And the sweater was at the bathhouse.

We were heading into the wilderness without any way to defend ourselves. If our captors didn't kill us first, the Indians would. Maybe not Ela, but what reason did she have to shout a warning not to kill me when her Indian friends arrived. None.

In fact, she was probably glad to get rid of me. I'd screwed her out of the one chance for escape and, for good measure, had helped to have her brother killed.

And if by some miracle I did survive I wouldn't be able to get home ever again. My vision turned foggy as the hopelessness of my situation became clear. I'd die. Very soon.

A whistle interrupted my contemplations. The horses stopped.

It was too dark to see much as we made camp. Wade threw Ela and me a filthy blanket and once we were on the ground, kicked me for good measure. After making a fire, Fred, rifle at the ready, sat watch over horses and us prisoners while his friends slept.

The ground was hard, plain rock with a few patches of grass and prickly plants. My hips and shoulders ached with bruises.

"You okay?" I whispered after a while against the girl's back. "We need to talk."

Fred was nowhere in sight. I had to trust that the sounds of the wind concealed my words. Ela lay still as the rock beneath.

"I'll tell them to head toward the mountains, but I need your help. I have no idea where to go." Still nothing. "I know you're mad at me. I'm so mad at myself I can hardly breathe. But I want to help and at least try to get us a chance. And the only chance we have is to…," I leaned closer so that my lips touched her ear, "lead them near your people. With any luck we get rescued."

The girl didn't speak, but I thought she'd moved her head just the slightest bit. I could at least hope.

"Move your lazy bones," Wade said, following his words with a targeted kick to my stomach.

I doubled over as waves of nausea rose from my middle. By the time I found enough breath to sit up, everyone was assembled around the fire, eating some kind of bean mush from tin plates. Ela sat cross-legged, our eyes meeting for a brief moment.

"She's pretty sweet," Fred said, baring a mouthful of rotten teeth the color of chewing tobacco. "Wouldn't mind me a poke. Even if it's redskin." He spit. "Revenge for some of this." He pointed at his head. Now that the light was up, I saw that most of his hair was missing from the crown, the skin tight and pink. He'd been scalped and somehow escaped.

"You'll get your chance," the Irish said, hurling the drags of some brown liquid into the fire. "We've got to move." His gaze fell on me. "Tell us the way, gold boy."

I raised an arm. "That way. Into the mountains."

"What mountains?"

I opened my mouth. I didn't know. I'd never been particularly good in geography and memorizing the names of some mountain in New Mexico hadn't been exactly a priority in school.

The Irish stepped closer, his eyes narrowed. "Come on, boy.

You surely have a name for those mountains. If you have a claim, it was written down."

"I…don't—"

"Black Range," Ela said.

I closed my eyes to hide the relief flooding through me.

"Devil's Range," Fred whispered. "I don't know, Boss. That's Injun country."

The Irish shrugged. "Everything is Indian country." Then he stood squinting into the distance.

How right he was. Except that the white people were stealing it all away.

The land rose to the west, giving way to row after row of hazy mountain tops—jagged rock surfaces broken apart by eons of unrelenting sun and freezing nights, covered here and there with scraggly trees. In the valleys between, shrubby pines covered the ground. It was breathtakingly beautiful. And utterly wild.

"How exactly did you get your claim?" The Irish turned toward me, his green eyes squinting with suspicion. "I seem to remember you wandering in the desert much farther east. Without a horse. Without water."

Think, I scolded myself. What if I said I'd gotten it from the Indian? They wouldn't believe me. Not Narsimha, the town drunk who was obviously poor as dirt. And if they did believe it, they'd kill me right here and now. I had to buy time.

"It was given to me by my father. He died…out there and sent me—"

"You never *saw* the land claim?"

I shook my head.

"But you know where it is?"

"Yeah, I…memorized the map."

"Where *are* the map and your claim papers?"

"I lost them in the desert. There was this storm—"

A wad of tobacco juice hurled on my boot. "The desert again." The Irish stepped closer and though a half-foot shorter, he looked menacing, his eyes blazing green fire. I began to tremble. "How about I slit your throat? I don't believe you."

The tip of a blade cut into my throat. Something warm trickled down my neck. The pressure increased until pain shot like fiery arrows through my skull and down to my feet. I was going to die. I tried to think of something smart, some better explanation, but my brain didn't work well when I was that scared.

"I know how to find *oro-hay*…white man's gold." Ela's voice was low, but as clear as a church bell. "He showed me the map. It is where my ancestors lived."

"Oh, so now *you* know the way." The Irish had turned sideways. The pressure on my throat lessened. I took a deep breath, trying to look at Ela. Small but proud, her shoulders straight, her long hair shone in the morning sun. Despite the ugliness surrounding us, she stood rooted as the pines of her homeland. I couldn't help but admire her. She was beautiful.

"Didn't gold boy loose the map in the desert?" Wade interjected. He'd been watching, his mouth twisting into the familiar sneer.

"It is lost, yes. Max asked my help, but my master at the bathhouse took it from me when I was studying it."

"Hey, boss, you think, the Mexican is going after the gold?" Fred asked.

The Irish didn't speak. He was watching me and Ela, his gaze wandering between us, trying to gauge if we spoke the truth. At last, he kicked a rock, sending it into the fire.

"Break camp, we're leaving. And you," the Irish took hold of Ela's wrist. "Don't try anything or I'll split your skinny bones apart." His gaze fell on me. "That goes for you, too."

"Why don't we waste him, Boss?" Wade said. "He's of no use if the girl knows the way."

The Irish turned. "As far as I remember I'm the one to make the decisions."

"Yes, Boss." Wade ducked his head, but I could've sworn his eyes were filled with mutiny.

Perfect, let them fight each other. Maybe we could find a way to escape. Nights were best, of course, but it was too early. The Black Range sat brooding on the horizon.

The trail, if you could call it that, was steep and crumbling. Sometimes we had to get off our horses and walk, the path no wider than our shoulders, the edge falling away hundreds of feet below. One false step and both men and horses would be gone.

With every day, the mood of our three captors grew worse. Rations were low and the blistering heat was making everyone irritable. Clearly, the Irish hadn't expected to travel for days. In fact, I wondered if he'd thought any of this through. From what I knew of the gold rush he wasn't the first guy to go nuts over a nugget.

To add to our misery, gray clouds boiled above the mountaintops, rolling slowly into the valleys. Lightening storms sizzled in the air, unleashing torrents of rain that turned the ground into mud.

Despite the thunder and ear-numbing flashes, I welcomed the rain, a chance to fill the water pouch I shared with Ela, wipe down my skin sticky with sweat and dust. Though we were close, we barely spoke.

I didn't mind. I was too angry and loathing myself for being stupid.

I glared at Wade who'd stolen my knife. And the Irish who carried Narsimha's gold. As much as I hated them, I was more worried about endangering Ela. Despite it all, I found myself enjoying the feeling of her body in front of me. Last night I'd fought the urge to wrap an arm around her.

The fourth day we came across a mining camp, a miserable huddle of tents and a primitive blockhouse. It was late morning and the Irish was all smiles as he rode ahead, whistling a tune and shouting a greeting.

The miners were too busy to pay much attention, one group digging with shovels and pickaxes in the open ground, another working on the entrance of a mineshaft. They looked hot with feverish eyes that could already see the riches hiding below.

One of the men finally stopped. Wiping the sweat from his eyes he nodded, "Morning gents." I noticed they all were covered in muck and wore revolvers. Rifles lay within easy reach.

"Top of the morning," the Irish said, "You doing a good turn here?"

The miner grimaced. "For the most part. Some are luckier than others, but we're working teams so we share."

"Say, you wouldn't happen to have some food for sale? We're on our way to the Black Range and ran out."

The miner's eyes grew guarded. "We could spare a bit, but we still have four months until winter. So, it's going to be slim."

The Irish waved, "No worries, Laddy. We only need a bit to hold us over."

The miner squinted as he took in the visitors. "Town of

Chloride is maybe three days ride southwest from here, north of the Black Range. Huge silver mining camp going up there. They've got plenty of tools and food."

The miner nodded toward Ela. "Watch out for Apaches. Heard they raided the general store earlier this year."

The Irish threw a glance at Ela who hadn't moved a muscle. "Maybe we better stay away, eh?" he said with a wink.

The miner slowly nodded as if he wanted to make up his mind whether to turn us away. "Meet me over there. It's almost break time."

The main campsite was a hundred yards downhill, consisting of a smoldering cook fire and a few makeshift tents. Pots and pans, plates and mugs sat in the open, some clean, some half filled with indefinable leftovers. A lone woman was scrubbing a cast-iron pan with sand. Even she had a rifle next to her.

Break time arrived rather quickly as the miner and a few of his buddies hurried after us. They were obviously worried, their eyes nervously shifting between the Irish, Fred and Wade. I was glad they didn't pay much attention to me or Ela as we sat waiting by the fire. I didn't have the faintest doubt they'd blow each other away at the slightest provocation.

Chances were good Ela and I would be among the victims. I remembered Grace's family and how I'd worried the gang would shoot them.

But the Irish seemed to have other plans. Or maybe the number of rifles and revolvers opposing him were too numerous. He produced a few wilted bills and bought a small cache of beans, a sack of sugar and some coffee.

"Sorry," the miner said. "We don't have jerky. We hunt every few days and nothing is left over. Can't leave it out. Too many wolves." He grimaced.

I wondered if they'd found anything in their digs. The way they acted it was likely. Even the Irish knew not to press. We bid farewell within the hour and settled for camp at dusk. The ground had turned so treacherous that it made no sense to continue. In the arid air, rocks split and loosened the ground, creating a rolling carpet of gravel. Stone avalanches dusted the hills. It seemed even easier to get lost in the narrow canyons that twisted along the valley floors.

"How much farther, Boss?" Fred asked, though his eyes

remained glued to Ela's chest. He often stared at the girl, licking his lips with unchecked hunger. The man was twice her size and strong as a bull. Ela wouldn't have a chance.

"What do you say, Redskin?" The Irish threw down his saddle and pulled a cigar stub from his vest.

Ela, who arranged rocks for a fire pit, straightened and shaded her eyes against the western sun.

"Not far, maybe two days to the foot of the mountains. Then another day or two to find the claim."

The Irish nodded. "Let's eat and get some sleep."

As the fire died away, I crawled under the blanket. I felt self-conscious about the way I smelled. The rains helped cleanse my chest and head, but my lower parts were another story. The men scratched constantly. Apparently, they didn't care one bit. I at least tried to hide when I did it.

Ela laid quietly, her back to me. I moved closer until my nose touched her hair. It smelled earthy and mysterious, of sun and wind and rain. And despite my memories of Juliana, despite the nightmare I'd got us into, it made me unbearably excited.

I thought of her proud gait, the way she stood up against these nasty men, and to my horror I felt my body react. My breath was having a mind of its own. So did my other leg. I abruptly moved away to create space.

All was quiet when I turned on my back. I had to think of a solution. Some way to get us out of here, but my brain never worked right for more than a few seconds. My thoughts slid around without finding traction.

The stars looked cold and abundant as glitter. Time was running out. Once we reached the Black Range, I'd count down the hours. Ela seemed to know what she was doing, but I ached to talk to her alone. Find out her plans. So much for me helping. Like with Grace, I relied on Ela.

The old fury returned, festering like a nasty wound. The men's constant spitting, bickering and nearness were rubbing my nerves raw. But the knowledge that they had taken what was mine made it worse. It only emphasized how helpless I was.

Every day Juliana's and Bero's memory seemed more distant. I had trouble recollecting what Juliana looked like. Instead, Ela's face floated in front of me. Damn, this was no time to go after a girl. *Why not*, a voice snickered. *You may be dead tomorrow.*

With a sigh I turned my back to her.
Stupid life, stupid girls.

CHAPTER THIRTEEN

The next morning, breakfast was even more hurried as if the Irish could smell the gold waiting for him. I hastily gnawed on a piece of cold roast, the last of a young deer Fred had shot the morning before.

While I scrubbed my plate with sand, I saw Fred plant a paw on Ela's backside. She'd been rolling up blankets and without a word moved gracefully out of reach.

"Haha, you little devil," Fred chuckled, attempting to move his bulk after her. "Playing games. I'll get you—"

"Kill the fire and get on your horse," the Irish cut in with a cold voice.

Mumbling something, Fred turned and shoved sand and rocks on top of the coals. Across the smoke, I watched Ela. Now that Fred had turned away, the tension left her shoulders. She'd been ready for flight.

Our eyes met and I nodded gravely, wishing I were strong and had some way to protect her. I wondered what she thought of me and my helplessness, whether she despised me. Her eyes never gave anything away. With a sigh, I climbed behind her into the saddle. I wouldn't blame her a bit if she hated me.

The path opened into a long, downward slope. Our horses struggled to keep their footing in the shifting rock as we slowly descended. At last, the ground leveled into cottonwoods as tall as three-story houses, their twisted trunks and branches providing welcome shade.

"There is water ahead," Wade yelled. He'd been scouting whenever he had a chance, rifle resting in the crook of his elbow.

"The Rio Grande," the Irish said.

"But Boss, I can't swim," Fred's voice quivered. "Can we go around?"

"Stay on your horse." The Irish yanked his stallion to a stop. "We'll camp here for an hour. Then we cross."

I grinned. Maybe Fred would drown. I for one was looking forward to the river. I'd wash off the filth and it wouldn't hurt if the men got a good rinse—they reeked worse than a pig farm.

"Who goes there?" a deep voice said. "Identify yourselves."

I swiveled around. Half hidden by a shrub with pink feathery seeds stood a man in some sort of uniform, weathered dark blue jacket with brass buttons over gray pants. His black face, half concealed under a pouchy-looking hat, was slick with sweat. Curly hair covered his head and beard, reminding me of a wooly mammoth.

"Buffalo soldiers," Ela whispered.

When Wade adjusted his rifle toward the man, the Irish shot him a warning look.

"We are traveling west," the Irish said. "My name is O'Brian, they call me Irish." He smiled, his eyes casually scanning the black soldier's rifle. "This here is Fred Jackson, over there is Wade, and those two are Max Nerds and his Indian girlfriend."

The buffalo soldier squinted upward to look at Ela. "Indian? What kind of Indian?"

"No idea, Sergeant," the Irish said, twisting in the saddle to face Ela. "What kind are you?"

Straightening her back, Ela said, "My people are *Chíhéne Nde*."

"*Chiricahua* Apache." The soldier spit in the sand. "Thought so. I'm Sergeant Tate from the Ninth Cavalry. You better come with me. All of you." His tone left no doubt that he expected obedience.

I watched the Irish and Wade exchange glances. Right now I didn't know what I wanted. The fact, they were taking an interest in Ela was scary. If I remembered correctly, the U.S. Army had hunted Native Americans for decades. On the other hand if the Irish opened fire, and if we'd be able to get away, we'd all be fugitives and likely chased down quickly. I swallowed, finding no relief with my dry throat.

I was going to be dead either way.

The soldier whistled and within seconds a dozen men in uniform surrounded us.

"Off your horses," Tate said, waving his gun. Two-dozen dark eyes watched as the five of us marched toward the river. "Turn right, upriver."

We followed the Rio Grande until we came upon more guards. And beyond in the shade of five wind-battered cottonwoods spread the camp of the Ninth Cavalry. The buffalo soldiers were hanging out in the open, some men lounging, some sitting and playing cards in the sandy soil. Others were cleaning equipment: carbines, knives and assorted handguns. A cook fire smoked nearby, the man in charge stirring a cast-iron pot. Tied along a rope behind the encampment, horses and pack mules stood chewing on sparse grass.

What I saw here looked medieval. I smirked. Okay, not that old, but close.

The modern U.S. Army, their gear and high-tech fatigues, their first-class radio equipment, Humvees, tanks and machine guns were worlds better. My father had taken me on open-house tours at the base where I'd climbed inside a real Bradley tank, even an Apache helicopter.

Kind of sick how the military had named their equipment after an Indian tribe they'd destroyed in the first place.

I walked close to Ela when I noticed two Native American men whittling pieces of wood with curved-blade knives. They wore white-brimmed hats over long black hair, vests and light cotton pants. And with them was the only white man.

Watching us approach, he calmly drank from a tin cup as if he were sitting in a café in Heiligenstadt. He had brown curly hair cut short above his ears and reminded me of a young Tom Hanks.

Sergeant Tate abruptly stopped and saluted. "Found these men in the woods, Lieutenant."

The Indians stopped whittling and stared while the lieutenant calmly set down his cup. Then he straightened, his posture textbook-perfect.

"Lieutenant Guilfoyle. Identify yourselves."

The Irish repeated his introduction finishing with Ela.

"Sir, if I may," Sergeant Tate said. "The girl is Chíhéne. I thought it prudent to stop them."

"Well done, Sergeant. I'll take it from here," Guilfoyle said. "Our scout here will translate for the girl," he continued in the direction of the Irish. He waved at one of the Indians. "Find out where she's from?"

The Indian nodded and fired off a rapid salvo of what had to be Apachian. I watched and worried what Ela would say. Her eyes were glued to the Indian, an intense fevered stare. And for the first time, I saw her self-control disappear as her mouth turned into a hateful sneer.

"Wait," Guilfoyle interrupted. "Maybe we better start with you, Mr. O'Brian. Tell us what you're doing in these parts."

I watched in fascination as the Irish spun a story, an elaborate tail of us traveling west to join his Irish family who'd settled in California. How he'd taken pity on me and my girlfriend, offering us a place on his family's farm.

I bit my lip. If I came clean, they'd shoot me the first chance they got. What exactly did that mean? Was I supposed to tell the Lieutenant that I was actually playing a computer game in the twenty-first century and was time-travelling? Right. The Irish's story was as good as any. I'd play ball long enough to escape.

"How did you meet the Indian girl?" Guilfoyle interrupted my worries.

I threw a glance at Ela, but she still glared at the Indian scouts.

"I met Ela at Fort Sumner. She was working for a very cruel man who beat her every chance he got. We became friends and when Mr. O'Brian offered to help, we went along."

"Where are you from?"

I tried to remember what I'd told the Irish. "Eh, East Coast."

"I see," said Guilfoyle through pursed lips. "Where exactly on the East Coast?"

I forced my eyes to remain on the lieutenant. The guy would sense my lie in a second. "Boston."

Now Guilfoyle leaned back and stretched his legs as if he were trying to buy time. "That is strange, indeed. Your accent is nowhere near Boston. I happen to have several good friends at West Point who grew up in Boston."

"Well, I didn't exactly grow up there," I hurried. "My parents traveled a lot."

"I see." For a moment, nobody spoke. The fires crackled in the distance as everyone was waiting for something exciting to happen. "And now you're traveling with an Indian squaw. Somehow I don't believe your story."

I stood frozen. Mumbles erupted among the soldiers. They were probably spoiling for entertainment. Maybe they'd arrest me.

To my relief Guilfoyle shook his head. "I shall not concern myself further with your background. There are more important matters to consider." Guilfoyle rested a forefinger against his temple. "You do realize that you travel right through the territory of the Warm Springs Apaches." Guilfoyle's gaze traveled to the Irish.

"As I said, we're taking the straight route to southern California." The Irish showed a toothy smile. From the corner of my eye, I saw Fred nervously wiggling from foot to foot. He was liable to give us away.

"Ask her how she got to Fort Sumner?" Guilfoyle said to the scout who nodded and unleashed another barrage of Apachian.

I was puzzled. Last time, the game had enabled me to understand and even speak foreign languages. My medieval German hadn't been perfect, but they all understood me. Somehow, the Indian language wasn't included. Maybe this was a glitch. Maybe Jimmy's father had programmed world languages and their dialects, but somehow forgotten to include Indian tongues? A shiver came over me. What if the game was not anticipating me to be here? Or did it even care? I still knew almost nothing about how the game's missions worked.

I nearly missed Ela's response. She'd turned away from the Indian scout and addressed Guilfoyle himself—in English.

"It is true. I'm Chíhéne Nde…Warm Springs Apache. The Mexican Army murdered my people at Tres Castillos. When all was lost, and our warriors killed, chief *Bidu-ya* took his own life." Here Ela glanced at the Indian scout. She might as well have thrown a knife. "I was taken by a Mexican soldier. His brother took me to Fort Sumner to work in his bathhouse."

"Bidu-ya is *Chief Victorio*," the scout said. Despite Ela's hate-filled stares, he sounded impassive. "The massacre killed many Chíhéne."

Guilfoyle nodded. He looked smart and clean among the squalor of the soldier camp. His men watched to catch every word of the conversation.

"It may be wise to have her go to the Mescalero Reservation.

Many families have settled there and should welcome her." He glanced at Ela as if he wanted to determine if she posed a threat.

"Sir, with all due respect," the Irish said. He still smiled but it looked forced. "We'll take good care of her. She's a member of our group and Max Nerds will certainly be responsible for her."

"Yes, I will," I hurried, feeling the Irish's warning glance on me. "Ela wants to come with us." I was pretty sure Ela preferred to go with me. But as with all Indian matters, they were never asked what they wanted. What the whites wanted always came first.

"What *do* you want?" Guilfoyle asked Ela.

"Go with Max," Ela said, her gaze finally shifting to my face. It was impossible to know what she was thinking, her eyes dark as usual, her mouth strong and unsmiling.

Guilfoyle retrieved his cup. "I shall think on the matter. Why don't you join us for supper? Make yourselves comfortable." Without waiting for a response, Guilfoyle signaled the men near the campfire to approach.

The Irish nodded. "Sir, we'd like to cross the Rio Grande before nightfall."

Guilfoyle frowned. It was obvious he was unused to being argued with. "You'll be free to go soon enough."

As we turned away, Ela hissed something to the scout.

"What did you say to him?" I whispered when we settled around the fire.

Ela's eyes flashed. "I called him apple. Red skin, white inside."

"Is he Apache?"

Ela nodded. "Mescalero."

Dinner consisted of greasy bean stew the color of mud, accompanied by a dry cracker that stuck to the roof of my mouth. We sat thirty feet away from the soldiers, avoiding eye contact with each other. I was dissecting a lump of gristle when I felt a hand clamp down on my shoulder.

The Irish's eyes burned brightly as he whispered. "We'll head out in a few minutes. No wrong moves, boy. Go with Wade to collect your horse." Wade stood waiting behind the Irish like a praying mantis. The evil grin was back on his face.

I nodded, watching Fred take hold of Ela's arm. They were obviously afraid I'd try to stay behind and rat them out. To them, everything was about their own gain. They had no clue how guilty I felt. That my guilt and whatever else was churning my insides would never allow me to leave Ela or put her in danger.

Ignoring Wade, I retrieved my horse. Near the tent, the Irish spoke with Guilfoyle, and then joined us. Apparently, the Lieutenant had relented, probably not wanting to deal with a hot Indian girl stirring up the men.

We headed downriver until the trees opened up to scrubs and bushes. The Rio Grande sparkled in the evening sun.

Not knowing what the horse would do in the water, a knot was forming in my stomach. I was a decent swimmer, but the river was at least fifty yards across and currents could be deadly. I noticed Ela rubbing the horse's neck and leaning forward to speak into its ears.

"Boss, you sure we can't find a ferry or some other way?" Fred had gotten off his horse and was staring at the watery expanse. The water looked brown as hot chocolate, impossible to tell depth.

"Get back in your saddle, Fred," the Irish barked. "Wade, you lead, then Max, Fred—I'll be last."

Was there a glimmer of worry on Wade's face, a tremor in his lips and jaw? I hoped so. Nonetheless, Wade headed into the stream, holding the reins tight to keep the horse's head above water. It started to snort as the water rose to its chest.

Our horse followed. Ela kept rubbing and speaking to it as the water rose. It was struggling. We'd all drown.

I slid off and began swimming alongside. The horse immediately did better, though its nostrils flared and its eyes were wide with fear.

Ela remained in the saddle. She shot me a look, but when she saw I stayed close, she relaxed and concentrated on the horse. Behind us things weren't going so well.

Fred was too heavy. When I turned to check, Fred's mare struggled to stay afloat. He was dragging them both down. Fred was refusing to leave the saddle and as the current got stronger, both went under. The horse reappeared, kicking and snorting, trying to overtake Ela and me. Fred was nowhere to be seen.

The Irish shouted something nasty and dived into the waves. I kept swimming on my back next to Ela watching the spectacle. Maybe my problems would be mostly solved if the Irish and Fred drowned.

But a moment later, the Irish broke the surface, holding a

sputtering and gurgling Fred at the neck. Fred churned the water, throwing his arm around the Irish who smacked him in the nose. Fred went temporarily limp. With his new weight, the Irish returned to his horse and fastened a lasso under Fred's arms. By the time they arrived on the other side, the horses were exhausted while Fred crawled on all fours out of the mud.

"Let's go," the Irish said. "We have an hour until nightfall."

Fred, who was covered in muck and heaved for air, climbed into the saddle. His nose had swollen to a bulb and bled. Nobody paid any attention, but I knew he was furious with the Irish.

The heat was still intense and I hoped my clothes would dry quickly. At night, temperatures sank near freezing and I knew I'd be miserable. I took off my shirt and wrung out the water before joining Ela. Thankfully, my hat still dangled from the saddle.

Funny. I no longer cared it was an old sombrero soaked with sweat. Without it, I would've fried. And in some way, deep down, it was as if a part of Billy the Kid was travelling along.

The ground stretched in front of us on a long plateau, cottonwoods giving way to grasses and shrubs, followed by rolling hills and in the distance…the Black Range.

We stopped near the overhang of a cliff and what appeared to be a shallow cave. While the men got busy collecting wood and settling down, I leaned against one of the boulders, watching Ela roll out our blanket.

I needed to find out what she was planning. With every hour and every mile I'd hoped to find a way to escape. But the men took turns watching, even at night, and my chance to get away never came. Now we were close to our imaginary claim.

Soon they'd know we'd lied and we'd die a miserable death. A new tremble took over my back as I watched Ela slide under the cover. Trying to hide my fear I crawled over to join her. The tension between the men was growing, especially after the encounter with the Army.

I knew it wouldn't take much to provoke them.

CHAPTER FOURTEEN

Ela scanned the steeply rising path. "We'll have to walk."

After a day traversing pretty even ground covered in hard grasses, we'd arrived in the foothills, the Black Range towering ahead. Everywhere I looked, the land rose or fell. Crevices and ravines stretched in all directions, forcing us to twist and turn and sometimes retrace our steps.

The path narrowed and disappeared between house-sized boulders. In some places there was no trail at all and visibility reached only a few feet to the next curve.

I'd grown up in the U.S. and knew Yellowstone and Colorado. But nothing prepared me for the wildness of this place. Trees and rocks expanded in front of me and no matter how hard I looked, I didn't see a single sign of a human. There were no houses, no huts, not even a fire pit or a fence. Just wilderness on a scale I'd never seen.

Something cold crept up my spine as I imagined being lost out here. An intense longing for home and my mom came over me.

"How much farther?" the Irish asked. He yanked the reins so hard that his horse whinnied and tried to rise.

"Two more days," Ela said. "The place is higher in the mountains."

"No tricks, Squaw." The Irish threw a suspicious glance at me. He was starting to squint at us like Wade. "I don't know why we even bother to take *you* along."

"I'm glad to shoot'em for you, Boss," Wade said as if he'd

heard my thoughts.

"I'll decide," The Irish said, his voice drowned by a hacking cough. I hoped it was Narsimha's legacy. I turned my head away so the Irish couldn't see my grim smile. "Let's head up. Ela, you lead the way with Max. Remember, we're right behind you."

The trail was so narrow that we had to walk single file. Ela led. I followed with our horse.

To my frustration the Irish and Wade were watching us even more closely. Especially at night I felt Wade's or Fred's eyes on me whenever I awoke. A waste of energy the way I saw it.

As if I could've gotten away. The terrain was treacherous under the best of circumstances. In the dark it'd take half a second to fall into a hole and break your neck. To my left a rock wall reached into the sky, on the right, the path crumpled into a void. One wrong step and I'd be flying off the mountain.

Maybe that wouldn't be so bad, the voice in my head whispered. It'd be quick and all your troubles would be solved. *But you've got to save the girl.* I chuckled grimly. It was crystal clear that Ela was saving me.

"Do you have a plan?" I whispered to Ela when the men lagged a few feet behind. I'd been staring at her backside, trying to stay focused. "They're watching us like lions on the hunt." Remembering Narsimha's name, I wanted to smack my forehead. Sometimes I was so stupid.

But Ela didn't seem to notice. "I'll find a way," she said under her breath. "Not much longer." I was still hoping we'd be rescued by her Indian friends, but there were no signs of life, not even a broken twig to indicate somebody had been up here.

What if Ela's friends acted like the Indians who'd killed Grace's parents? After all I was white like Wade and Fred. A shiver ran down my spine imagining being scalped.

I wondered what the game wanted me to do. I was still not completing a mission. Instead, I relied on an Indian girl to keep me going. *Really brave, Max.* What if I was failing the game's missions by getting too much help? I'd already lost two items I needed to return. And I was almost as clueless as when I'd landed in the Middle Ages. Truth was I was ashamed of being a useless burden. In present day life, guys were supposed to be strong and protect the girl.

What present day? I had about as much chance to go home as making my horse fly.

Climbing higher I started to pant. The lack of food and rest were getting to me, the uncertainty of our destiny adding the rest. By the sounds of it, the men had similar trouble. Ominous clouds brooded—ready to unleash more rain, a thick gray cushion ready to suffocate us. The air seemed electric with pending thunder.

When the weather broke, we were heading downhill into a narrow gorge. Thunder rumbled above us, followed by staccato flashes. With every minute the rain intensified until it felt like walking under water. The air was filled with it, turning everything gray and wet. The drops were huge and pounding on my hat so loudly that it drowned out all sound. The soil below was turning to mud, rivulets of water rushing past me.

The next flash came even faster, but the thunder was what made me cringe.

My ears rang. I'd never been out in the open in such a storm—especially not at high altitude. Sure I'd been caught in some lightning, but this was as if the Gods were throwing their wrath at the mountain. I felt exposed and uneasy, keeping my eyes on Ela's proud shoulders. With every minute I was more impressed.

Ela suddenly stopped and I almost ran into her. When I peered over her shoulder, I almost shrieked. Below us a lake had swallowed the path. And the water was rising—fast. Flashflood.

Ela shouted against the wind, "Turn back. Quickly."

The men behind us had stopped, but had not seen the watery assault. I pointed behind me to catch Fred's attention. Fred wasn't looking, picking something off his pants. I yelled, the wind and rain swallowing my words.

I finally caught the Irish's eye who immediately yelled something in Wade's ear. The water was lapping at my boots, moving up my ankles. It felt as if the ground was dissolving beneath my feet. *Slow idiots.*

There was no place to go, the men behind us clogging the only path. I patted the horse's nose, coaxing it to turn on the spot.

It whinnied, its hooves splashing as it tried to stay upright. The ground was relatively even for such a maneuver, but it also allowed the rising water to catch us faster. I clamped my fingers around the bridle, hoping the horse would keep me upright.

By the time the gang had turned around, I was up to my hips

in brownish water, sucking and pulling me backwards. If I let go, I'd be swept away.

Ela had moved in front of me again, holding on to the horse's saddle. She was a foot shorter than I, the water above her waist. Her dress billowed around her, pulling her down. I screamed at her to hurry, yet my voice was snuffed out by the pounding of the water and wind—as if someone had put a hand across my mouth.

The water sucked and pushed, rising higher still. Everything around me had turned into a giant lake that boiled and churned around us.

I wanted to move faster, but couldn't. Every step was agony. My thighs burned and my feet were numb in the icy water. The ground had been uneven before. The water made it treacherous. Ela pulled her dress tight around her waist. She leaned forward and I'd almost caught up to her when she slipped. In a split-second she was gone, gurgling water closing above her.

Before I could jump after her, she emerged a few feet to my right, sputtering and swiping at the hair plastered across her face. She recaptured her footing and moved toward me, eyes burning determination. Pushing sideways, I reached for her.

"Take my hand," I panted over the wind and rushing water. There was not enough air to move my body and speak at the same time.

She extended her arm until I was able to grab her wrist.

"I've got you." I pulled her closer until my arm fit around her back. She felt tiny against my shoulder. I smiled grimly. At last I was able to do something for her.

When I snapped the reins, the horse doubled its efforts. Every step was excruciating. But at last the water level subsided. Keeping my gaze on the tree line above us, I pushed and dragged Ela with me. To my surprise I was freezing despite the strenuous effort. Ela didn't look any better. Her lips were purplish and she was trembling against my side.

When we finally collapsed along a crumbling ledge above the trail, the Irish, Fred and Wade were right there. I ignored them, wishing they'd drowned.

"What now?" the Irish yelled to Ela.

"We must wait. The path is this way." She waved at the lake that was covering everything below us now, a whirling churning brown mass of water.

"Can't we go around?" Wade asked.

Ela shook her head. "There is a way, but horses won't climb."

I looked around. Though we were on higher ground, I saw nothing but sheets of gray as the sky melted into the air around us. That had to be one-hundred percent humidity. I was *breathing* water. At least it helped rinse my clothes. I took off my hat and let the rain wash my hair. Now that we'd stopped, shivers were taking over my body.

I moved to Ela and helped her up. "We must keep busy or we'll freeze."

She nodded and touched my hand. Her eyes were ringed by grayish shadows and I wanted nothing more than to take her away somewhere safe.

As quickly as the storm had begun, it stopped. Below us, the water gushed past, tearing at anything that stood in its way.

"Can we find a cave and make a fire?" I asked, suppressing the trembling in my voice.

Ela nodded. "I know a place, not far. But we have to wait until the water moves on." To my relief, the Irish nodded. He looked even worse than when I'd seen him in Fort Sumner. His skin had a sickly sheen and he seemed to have lost weight. The cough was getting more pronounced now that we were wet and cold. Despite my anger, a bit of sorry crept into my heart. I really didn't want it to, but there it was. Fred didn't look much better. His nose was bluish and he wheezed, trying to suck air through it.

Only Wade seemed unchanged. Most of the time I managed to ignore him. I couldn't concentrate when I did look because Wade's sneer was constant now. As if he were ready to blow me to pieces any second.

I realized I was on borrowed time. If the men even thought they'd found the gold, they'd kill us. I swallowed, but the dryness in my throat persisted. Though I hung out next to Ela, the men hovered, stifling my every breath. Too close to have a talk and find out what Ela was planning.

To her you're no different than the others. Maybe she'll get rid of you, too. I glanced at her from the side, but her eyes were far away.

The rain had long stopped before we were able to cross. A weak sun broke through the clouds in the west. Shadows crept up around us. Hurrying along, we reached another cave just as the sun disappeared behind the mountain and turned everything gray. The opening was a comfortable eight feet tall and several feet wide. It wasn't very deep, maybe like a small living room, but at least we were out of the wind.

The ground was covered in pine needles and twigs though not enough for a fire. The Irish ordered me to go with Fred to collect wood.

Everything was soaked, and our fire produced more smoke than heat. Still, I was thankful for the bit of warmth and dry space. I wrung out my shirt and socks, though it didn't do much good. As we went down for another uncomfortable night, I worried about the next day.

We'd have to get away soon or the Irish would figure out that there was no claim. No gold. I wondered why we had so little equipment. Did he think the gold was lying in the open to be picked up? Or was he going to get supplies once he knew the place. He still carried the nugget. I'd watched him one evening when he'd pulled out the gold and looked at it. It would certainly pay for equipment and plenty of food. Horror crept up in me then.

They'd get rid of us as soon as we arrived. We had to escape in the next twenty-four hours.

I awoke. It was nearly dark except for a trace of gray in the cave entrance. We'd drawn farther in, away from the wind, taking our horses along. I pulled up my knees and tried to drift back to sleep, but the cold made it impossible.

There.

Something rustled. I sat up listening, my mind on high alert. Surely, bears and wolves lived in these mountains. What if some grizzly waltzed in to snack on us?

Another sound too low to identify drifted in.

I carefully straightened and crept past Wade and the Irish who were sleeping to my right, their hats covering their faces. I froze. Ela was gone. So was Fred.

Alarmed, I dashed to the cave entrance.

And wished I carried a gun.

CHAPTER FIFTEEN

In the early morning light Fred towered above Ela, pinning her to the ground, his bulky upper body nearly drowning her. His chest was heaving, one hand around the girl's throat, the other tearing at her clothes. Fred's face was bright red as he kept fumbling with Ela's skirt.

Ela was powerless. She was fighting for breath, her eyes wide with fear, her arms flailing without effect—a mosquito scratching at an elephant. She tried to kick, but Fred weighed down her thighs with his legs. Except for some sticks crunching beneath them, they struggled in eerie silence. Ela's eyes were bulging. I knew the brute would choke her to death with his paw squeezing her throat. I needed a weapon. Grabbing the first thing I saw, I smashed it on Fred's head. The rock splintered over the gruesome scar, but to my horror, Fred didn't collapse.

Instead he roared like a mad bear and jumped off the girl to focus his energy on me. Which was fine because it was distracting him from Ela. But he got to his feet a lot quicker than I expected, his face a mask of furious crazy, blood dripping, eyes blazing, lips pulled back exposing his disgusting teeth.

Really quick. And I had nothing to fight with, not even a stick…or better yet a gun.

The only thing I had going for me was quickness. As Fred moved to seize me, I ducked and slipped to the right. But space in front of the cave was limited and there was no time to climb uphill or down.

I hurled another rock at Fred. It bounced off his arm, eliciting no more than a groan. Fred kept coming. From the corner of my eye, I saw Ela scramble up the slope and out of sight.

"Why did you attack the girl?" I yelled. It was the last thing I managed before I was picked up and thrown. I landed on my back. My lungs deflated. Struggling for breath, I watched Fred approach. He looked frightful, blood dripping from his forehead and jaw, his eyes wild with rage.

Still gasping I forced myself to roll sideways to get out of Fred's reach. I had to get to the cave. The Irish would stop Fred, I was sure of it.

I attempted to crawl inside when I felt Fred grab my feet and lift me off the ground, head down. The world turned. In a last show of strength, I curled upward to try to pry away Fred's hand from my ankles. But it was too late. Fred hurled me next to the cave's entrance, my head barely missing a soccer ball sized rock.

Pine needles and twigs, blown into a heap, softened my landing. Hearing voices behind me, I sighed with relief. I was lucky Fred hadn't flung me off the mountain and the Irish was finally waking up.

That's when I noticed a new sound: a soft rattle. Before I had time to move, the rattling intensified. Fred had stopped his attack and was staring to my right. Sudden dread made me turn my head.

It was a mistake.

The leaves shifted.

The rattlesnake's head dove with lightning speed, clamping down on my forearm. The snake was gray and yellow and no more than four feet long. But its fangs were needle-sharp, burying deep into my skin, releasing its terrible venom.

I screamed, shaking and waving my arm. When at last the snake let go and flew across the ground, I began to crawl…crawl away…crawl toward the cave. Nothing in my life had ever hurt this much.

I stared in shock at the two bite marks on my forearm right above the wrist, blood trickling from the punctures. Pain surged through my shoulder, down my chest and up my neck.

I couldn't think of anything else.

Fred hovered nearby, the wildness in his eyes replaced by something else: glee. I wanted to feel anger, but my body had other ideas. My heart raced, a whoosh that filled my ears. My vision blurred as if I were looking through fog.

The Irish and Wade came running. A shot rang out and the snake blew apart. I wanted to feel relief, but the poison was already making me dizzy.

"What happened?" the Irish asked.

"He got bitten by a rattler," Fred said, wiping blood from his chin with his sleeve.

As the ache oozed through my body, I heard the Irish say something like good riddance. I couldn't be sure—the throbbing was too great. My arm was swelling, my fingers turning to sausages ready to burst. I crawled and leaned against a rock. My right hand, the entire arm was going numb. Soon, the poison would reach my heart and I'd die.

Panic crept through me, a sense of doom.

I needed to do something, but I didn't know what. My hand pulsated and I knew that the poison was now spreading through every cell in my body. I hadn't been afraid earlier—the fight with Fred had been pure adrenalin. But now that I sat still, I began to shake. It was becoming harder by the second to move my fingers, not to mention my arm or body.

I was going to die for sure. No more game, no more going home. I'd never see my mother or Jimmy again.

Above me the bandits talked, their voices reaching me through a fog.

"What happened to you, Fred?" Wade asked. "Boss, he's bleeding like a damn pig."

From far away I heard Fred explaining how he'd been attacked by me.

"Where's the Indian?" the Irish yelled.

"Don't know, didn't see her," Fred said.

I wanted to scream *filthy liar*. You attacked her. Who could blame her for running away? Instead I was mute, the words stuck in my throat, my mouth and tongue frozen with poison and terror.

"We've got to find her," the Irish barked. "I'll hold you responsible. Let's track her."

"What about him?" Wade asked.

The Irish coughed. "Let's leave the kid. He's dead weight." Through the fog of pain, my ears perked up.

"Haha," Wade laughed. "Dead all right. The rattler is saving us a bullet."

I wanted to punch him, but I couldn't even lift my head. My eyelids drooped. I tried to listen to the thugs, but their sounds were muted in my ears because my blood was pounding in my neck as loud as a hammer.

Concentrate, my woozy mind urged. How do you treat snakebite? We had antidotes where I came from. In the wilderness in 1881 I had nothing. I didn't even have my knife to cut open the wound, if that was the right thing to do. My knife.

Wade had my knife.

"Can I get my knife back," I croaked, a voice that sounded like somebody else.

Nobody answered. My vision blurry, I dragged myself to the entrance of the cave. It was empty.

I was alone.

The men had gone…scattered…to find Ela. I hoped they wouldn't find her. She knew these mountains. The men did not. Even if I died now, at least I'd enabled her to get away. Ela, Wade, what was it that I was searching for?

I closed my eyes and saw nothing.

I dreamed. I was floating in liquid. Suspended. Was that what death felt like? I didn't mind. But the terrible pain was always there. A throbbing and burning that engulfed the right side of my body and blackened my soul. My stomach felt like a sack of bile, but my body was too tired to heave.

Shadows drifted in and out, strange voices spoke. They floated too—like mist. I can't understand you, I wanted to shout, but my throat was blocked and nothing came out. Not even a moan. Had I gone to heaven? Was God speaking to me?

A giant snake the size of a whale slithered around me, its body dry and cold, its eyes yellow slits. It lifted me off the ground and carried me away. My lids were glued shut. It was as dark as new moon.

I couldn't hear either. Only feel. Every inch of my left side seethed and throbbed. The snake was tugging at my arm. It burned worse and I tried pulling away but my arms were no longer attached. They floated in mid-air, the sleeves of my white shirt fluttering.

The snake turned into a wolf chewing my hand. Its mane was gray and white and beautiful, its golden eyes wise. The pain was so great.

I screamed, but it wasn't me, it was some other creature that made these animal sounds. I knew I was dying.

Smoke drifted into my nose. Had I rolled into the fire? The pain was still there but more tolerable, a dull throb. I opened my eyes and blinked. It was too bright for the cave, for death. Yet, not light like being outside.

I'd always imagined heaven to be bright and sunny—certainly not smoky. I tried to focus beyond the smoke. A fire burned a few feet away. Something moved in the shadows, but my eyes refused to focus. I began to tremble. The wolf was back to finish me off.

Something soft touched my skin—the wolf's fur. My fingers cramped as I pulled back. It would bite and then there would be nothing.

I waited for the pain, the snapping sound of my bones, yet nothing happened. My right arm was attached again, though it was feeling numb and foreign as if someone had taken it off and sewn it back on. Beneath me more softness.

My eyes flew open, my left hand touching the surface beneath me. I was laying on some kind of fur.

What?

I tried to sit, but only made it onto one elbow—the good arm. I was definitely not in the cave or in heaven.

I was…in some dome-shaped tent—except its poles were made of crisscrossed wood to support assorted grasses that formed the actual walls. The floor was covered with animal skins, one of which I was lying on.

I remembered my adventure in medieval Germany, when I'd found myself buck-naked in a huge bed. I fumbled below the cover. And sighed. I still wore boxers.

When I heard movement, I slumped back down and pretended to sleep. Peeking through one eyelid, I saw an old woman with long gray hair and strands of beads around her wrinkly neck tend the fire. Then my right hand was being lifted while the woman softly spoke in some strange language. She sang a bit, then she mumbled some more while her fingers pried my forearm. I was surprised that I didn't feel much pain.

"*Ha annsi?*" the woman said.

I peered through one eye and found the old woman staring at

me with something of a smile. Her cheeks were round and as reddish brown as ripe apples. Was she talking to me? Not a word fit through my throat.

"Grandmother is asking how you are?" A voice said from the shadows. "You can answer, *doo ansi*. It means *I'm fine*."

I stared in disbelief as Ela's face drifted into view. The old woman smiled, showing a few brownish teeth.

"What? I thought I was…" I stumbled.

"Dead?" Ela shook her head. "You are lucky. Ussen smiled on us and showed me the way to my people."

I blinked. Maybe I was still dreaming. I had to be as good as dead with a rattlesnake bite. "Where are we? How…" I knew I sounded like an imbecile.

Ela kneeled and took my good hand. "The bite is better?"

I grew aware of my arm, hidden under a layer of bark held in place by green fibers.

"It feels pretty good," I mumbled while opening and closing my fingers. They were still swollen, but moved just fine. "What is that?"

"Grandmother used snakeroot to treat the bite."

I nodded as I felt myself grin. I was going to live. To my surprise my throat tightened.

"You saved me," I choked. "What happened?"

Instead of answering Ela handed me a woven container smeared with tar.

"Drink."

I inspected the contents, carefully trying a few drops.

"It is clean water." She got up and rummaged inside a basket that looked like a roundish backpack. "You must eat," she said, handing me a beige-colored item resembling an oversized cookie. "Banana yucca. Try it."

I wasn't exactly hungry. But then how could I refuse her? The cake tasted slightly sweet and not like anything I'd ever eaten.

"I overheard the men… what happened with the snake," Ela began. "I hid above the cave. After the men left, I returned with aloe. Then I went to find help. I walked all day until I found them.

"Them?"

"My people. They brought you here. Grandmother took care of you. I helped."

Ela smiled. It was the first real smile, I'd seen. It transformed her face and I couldn't help but stare. Ela's eyes sparkled even in the greenish light of the hut. Her hair, braided into one thick long strand, made her high cheekbones more pronounced. She was hot. And I wanted to kiss her.

To distract myself, I took another nibble from the yucca cake.

"What is wrong?" Ela asked.

"Eh, nothing," I said, clearing my throat. "Where are my clothes?"

"By the door—I washed them." She straightened, lithe as a cat. "I will wait for you outside."

I looked after her. Had her cheeks turned pink or was it my imagination? I smiled. One could always hope.

It was my new motto. I crawled out of the furs, the cool air creating instant goose bumps. I wondered what day it was and how long I'd been sick. The way my pants fit, I'd not eaten in a while.

I crawled outside.

And stared.

CHAPTER SIXTEEN

Between the sheer walls of a two-hundred-fifty-foot cliff towering above and a chasm on the other side below, the land formed a plateau. Sprinkled around it sat a dozen or so huts to form a Native American village. Fires burned and in the windless air of the morning their smoke went up in straight lines like long white fingers extending into the sky. The air felt cool and crisp and smelled very clean.

I took a deep breath. I'd been given a new life and I felt thankful. Not only had I survived a rattlesnake bite, I stood in the middle of an authentic Indian village, a place few white people had ever seen. Certainly none in my generation. My classmates never in a million years experienced something like this. Because it didn't exist where I'd come from. Everything here had extinction written across it. The cruelty of the white man knew no bounds, he stole or destroyed everything Native Americans held dear.

I flinched when I heard screams. A handful of little boys played with toy bows, yelling and jumping when their stubby arrows hit the straw target. Women hunched over what looked like deer hides, scraping them with stones. Others were weaving baskets from long strands of fibers. More women and girls were unpacking and sorting various plants into piles. Others were cutting and preparing food. Everyone seemed to work until I took another step into the open.

Like the sounds of the wind, a whispering began as one by one the Indian women stopped their tasks and began to watch me.

I stopped. Where was Ela? Why wasn't she here to protect me? I felt my cheeks flame when three boys no older than six or seven darted within a few feet of me. They chattered and pointed, but I was unable to understand a word. Still the people gaped. I noticed there were few men and those present were old like my grandfather or young teenage boys.

"I will show you the village," Ela said, hurrying toward me. She was smiling again, her braided hair reaching down to her waist. She wore a short leather dress and high boots decorated with black and turquoise beads. I nodded, trying not to ogle. She looked amazing and I longed for her touch. "You must excuse them. They have not seen a white man in the village in a long time. Some of them have never seen one close."

"*Indaa łigá'í,*" some of them mumbled as I walked next to Ela.

"What are they saying?" I whispered.

"They call you *pale eyes*." Ela pointed at my face. "Your eyes are white."

I'd never noticed before, but her eyes didn't just have brown-black pupils. Where my eyes were white, hers were the color of milk coffee.

"I always thought they meant our skin," I mumbled.

Ela took my left hand and pointed at one of the huts. "This is Grandmother's place." Sitting on a blanket, the old woman nodded while she continued arranging roots and bark in the sun.

"Where is your grandfather?"

Ela hesitated. "She is not my real grandmother. We call our old people grandfather and grandmother. My family is dead. My parents were killed last year during the massacre. My brother, *Kuruk,* is getting ready for the warpath. Grandmother took him in. He's the last one after Narsimha..." She hastened forward, shouting something at a boy slightly younger than us.

Despite the crisp mountain air, he was bare-chested except for a necklace of vicious-looking claws. His hair was long and flowing and tied with the traditional Apache cloth headband. Even when Ela approached, he didn't smile. From the way he squinted, I recognized Narsimha's features.

"This is Kuruk," she said. "It means *bear*. Last year he fought a black bear with his knife."

Instead of greeting me, Kuruk fired back in Apachian and though I didn't understand what the boy said, I knew from the loathing look that it wasn't exactly a friendly comment. Ela hissed something at him, but Kuruk turned and walked off.

When Ela remained quiet I asked, "What did he say?"

"He's angry." She turned to face me, her eyes shining black pools, her shoulders quivering. That's when I knew it was best to shut up. "I'll show you the rest of the village."

As we walked around the field I felt her sadness like a dark cloud. She'd lost her parents in a massacre, her older brother to a white man's disease and alcohol. No wonder her younger brother loathed anything white. Maybe the entire village loathed me. But then why had they saved my life?

"How come you know so much English?" I hurried to distract her. "The Mexican brute sure didn't teach you all that in a few months."

"We had a white girl in the village. She'd been taken from a settlement and lived with us for many years. We were friends."

"Where's she now?"

"She died."

"Oh." I looked around. The busyness of the village had reluctantly resumed as we made our rounds, though I still felt eyes wander my way. I had a thousand questions. Where were all the men? Was this what was left of the Warm Springs Apaches? What did they think of me? Was I a prisoner?

"You must rest," Ela said after a few minutes. As soon as she said it, I realized how my legs dragged. I had the energy of an eighty-year old man. My arm throbbed again while the skin beneath the wrapping itched like crazy. I wanted to tear away the cover and rake my fingernails across, but I was afraid of what I'd find. My fingers were still swollen and appeared bruised as if I'd dipped them in beet juice.

"Don't Indians live in teepees?" I muttered as I crawled into the greenish gloom of my hut.

"It is called *kowa*...wikiup. Plains Indians live in teepees."

"Sorry, I guess I'm pretty ignorant how Indians live."

Ela paused and threw me a strange look. "Grandmother says that many years ago we lived in teepees. But hides have become sparse and too valuable."

"Because the white men killed all the buffalo and chased you off your land."

Ela nodded. Her face was calm and I wondered how she

could be so controlled. I'd scream and fume like a madman about the unfairness of it all. I remembered Kuruk. He was mad enough for the two of them. Maybe girls were different.

Weird that I'd never considered that Native American tribes, even the bands within each tribe, were as diverse as people from various different countries. In the movies, they were always the same: good white men fought bad Indians. Yet, here in the village, the atmosphere was harmonious like they were all part of a large family. They'd saved my life and taken me in.

Ela tended the fire as I slid beneath the furs. I fought to keep my eyes open. I really should figure out what I was going to do…and was asleep.

When I awoke, gray light filtered through the walls. I wondered how long I'd slept and if it was dinnertime. My bladder was bursting. I listened, but everything was quiet. Strange. I crept out of my cover and looked around. I was alone, the fire almost dead. My bladder urged and I crawled outside.

Nothing moved in the gray light. The wikiups stood silent. Behind my hut, a bird chirped. Then another. It had to be early morning. I'd obviously missed dinner and slept through the night.

Cool mist hit my face as I rushed off toward the bushes. Where did Indians do their business? I had no idea. Right now, I just needed a tree. Stumbling through some prickly bushes I stopped at a gnarled pine. The resin smelled wonderfully fresh. While I peed I remembered my last adventure when I'd used pine to disinfect Juliana's leg. Juliana. I shook my head. I hadn't thought of her in ages. What was happening to me?

Feeling relieved I decided to walk around. My stomach growled. Maybe I'd find something to eat. Even worse, my throat was dry. I needed water. Lichen covered the ground in colorful patches. The grass in-between was yellow and so dry that it crunched under my feet. Above me, more birds began their morning songs.

I looked over my shoulder, worried that I'd lose my way. I still saw a glimpse of the grassy field. Just a little farther. A new sound joined the birds: something gurgling—a stream. The sound of rushing water grew as I broke through a thicket.

My jaw dropped.

CHAPTER SEVENTEEN

Maybe thirty yards ahead, a fifty-foot rock face formed a ledge over which a small waterfall tumbled into a basin below. And in the middle of the pool, arms stretched toward the cascading water, stood Ela. She was naked and had her eyes closed as she rinsed her hair.

I knew I should leave or make some kind of noise to announce myself. But I couldn't. I stood rooted to the spot, my eyes glued to Ela's chest. Her breasts were small and partially hidden by her long hair. Everything on her was dark and beautiful. I felt my breath catch and heat rose to my cheeks. I wanted to jump in, fold her in my arms and kiss her.

Hide, my mind reeled. Don't let her see you gawking or she'll never be your girlfriend. What was I thinking? But it was true. I was a complete fool and yet, I couldn't help but be drawn to her. Maybe it was her dark hair, or her eyes, or her defiance against the nasty men. All I knew was that I wanted to make a move.

Now would be a mistake, the sane part of my brain commented. Reluctantly I slumped low and crawled back through the brush. Fighting the urge to take another peek, I forced myself to walk another twenty yards. I turned and began to whistle, making a point to stomp on branches and kick rocks. I sounded like a blustering idiot.

When I arrived at the stream a second time, Ela had slipped into her leather dress. She was dripping wet so I knew she'd hurried to cover up.

"Have you come to bathe?" she asked, walking toward me.

I looked at her, afraid my eyes would give away my secret, hoping my cheeks didn't redden again. Trying to chase away the vision of her naked body, I shrugged. My gaze fell on my forearm still wrapped in bark.

"Can I take it off?" I said, struggling to sound casual.

"I'll do it." Despite the cold, Ela's fingers nimbly removed the wrapping. A green paste, now brittle and flaking away covered the skin. Underneath, the bite marks were still visible, the surrounding tissue bruised in rainbow colors. But the swelling was mostly gone.

"I'll tell the others not to disturb you." The corners of Ela's mouth turned upward just the slightest bit. Was she mocking me? Silent as a shadow she disappeared into the woods.

I walked closer to the pool. Along the edge, large flat rocks formed a sort of table. After looking around one more time, I dropped my clothes and stepped into the water…and suppressed a yelp.

The stream was mind-numbingly cold. Icicles stabbed my toes and ankles. Goosebumps covered every inch of skin. Any excitement I'd felt earlier evaporated. What if she was watching? A wimp who couldn't even get into the water.

I took another step. The water lapped at my calves. One more. My knees turned to ice. How could Ela stand in here and not freeze to death? I kept going until my waist was submerged. Beneath the waterfall the water trickled and spewed. I drank my fill while rubbing myself furiously. My teeth were no longer my own— they chattered and rattled.

Clean and frozen to the bone, I hurried out. My fingers were stiff and uncooperative as I yanked on my pants. Frustrated I left my shoelaces open and jogged toward the village.

Shouts rang out just as I reached the open field. Women and children were running towards the far end where some villagers were already assembled. I followed as worry crept up inside me. I scanned the trees for impending attack. Nothing.

Instead I saw three young men, one of them Kuruk, talking excitedly. They had dumped a deer and two jackrabbits on the ground, though nobody seemed to pay any attention. Instead they were listening, some of them mumbling. *Grandmother* stood closest to the boys, apparently asking questions. Ela was with her and I pushed my way through the crowd.

"What's going on?" I asked.

"Kuruk and his friends went hunting and found a white man. He was dead. They want to know if we can come to see him."

I tried to hide my alarm. Wade, Fred and the Irish were pursuing Ela. They wouldn't think twice about mowing down the entire village, so they could get their dirty hands on her and the imaginary gold. As if Ela had heard me, she patted my still freezing hand.

"They'll not find us here."

I shook my head. She was in my brain sometimes. Are you sure, I wanted to say. But at that moment Kuruk waved at me. He looked just as grouchy as always, his eyes dark with anger and irritation.

"I told Kuruk you will go," Ela said. "He will show you the white man."

Why me, I wanted to say. He hates me.

Ela squeezed my fingers. "Do not worry, he will keep you safe."

Great. She thinks I need protection from a boy. And how am I going to communicate? I wanted *her* to come along. *Grow up*, I scolded. You're obviously older and had eleven years of school. You have a laptop and a cell phone. You play stupid stinking computer games.

I shook my head. *You're full of shit.* You can't shoot a gun, hunt or survive on your own out here.

Ela and her people walked off and Kuruk was already thirty yards ahead, jumping like an antelope across rocks and fallen trees.

The land fell way in rugged folds. Ravines lurked, trees fallen like toothpicks making descent difficult. Try as I might, I could not keep up. Every few minutes, I saw Kuruk slow down and wait. But the boy always kept his distance and stayed well ahead.

At last the ground leveled and I thought I recognized the overflowing creek we had crossed days before. It was hard to tell. Everything looked similar. Valleys and ridges, trees, caves and streams formed a wilderness maze.

When Kuruk finally stopped along a narrow creek, he didn't look the slightest bit out of breath. Lodged between two boulders, a man lay face down in the water.

The horrific stench of decomposition reached my nose. Flies swarmed. I tried to ignore the bloody shirt. I wanted to puke.

The man's head was submerged and hidden below driftwood. It looked like he'd been swept here by the water and gotten stuck.

Kuruk stood over the man, apparently unaffected by the gruesome stink. When I approached, the boy lifted the man's head from the water. I recoiled. Fred's bloated face looked greenish and distorted, but the scalped back of his head was unmistaken. A bullet hole was visible on his forehead.

"I know him," I managed before I turned away. "His name is…was Fred." Who cared if Kuruk didn't understand? I had to leave right now before I threw up. This game was a nightmare and I wanted to go home. See my mom and live a normal life. *Quit being a wimp, you've got to finish the game.*

Without so much as a grunt, Kuruk yanked the bloated corpse from the rocks. Fred continued his floating journey downstream. Kuruk quickly glanced at me before turning back the way we'd come. As before, he stayed well ahead. Several times, he climbed completely out of sight, unexpectedly reappearing next to some tree or rock formation.

I tried to keep a straight face despite the side stitch and my aching chest. The altitude was getting to me. I had a hard time forgetting Fred's sickening muck. Scenes of our fight replayed in my head: Fred on top of Ela forcing up her skirt, his wild eyes when the rock bounced off his arm, the blood running down his temples. Fred had been shot.

I vaguely remembered what the Irish said after I'd been bitten. He'd probably put two and two together and, after they couldn't find Ela, killed Fred. I wondered where they were now, but I was getting more and more miserable. My lungs burned from lack of oxygen. My thighs had turned to pudding and my ankles throbbed.

I'd admit the need to rest over my dead body.

That's when I remembered my knife. Wade had stolen it. My stomach lurched in panic. I'd have to find Wade or I'd never go home from the game. How in the heck was I going to find him? I'd always figured I'd somehow steal it back. The sheer magnitude of the task took the last of my breath. My lungs wheezed and I slowed down.

I hadn't seen Kuruk. Let him go ahead because I might as well be dead. I'd never go home. My mother's gentle eyes floated into my vision. It was too much. I didn't even wipe my cheeks as I crumpled to the ground.

Kuruk's voice reached through the fog. "Pale Eyes come along."

I looked up, angrily ripping at some dry grass to blow my nose. The Indian had no business to see me like this. Then I stared. Kuruk had spoken English. Not perfect, but not bad.

"So you *do* speak English," I said, coughing to clear my throat. I forced my legs to straighten. The boy was staring at me, his eyes black pools just like Ela's. Then I slumped back down. "Why don't you just leave me here to rot? I'm sure you wouldn't mind a bit."

Inside me, fury was overtaking self-pity. An anger like none I'd ever felt. So what, the Indians had been dealt a pile of dung. I wasn't any better off. I had no home anymore either and my family was as good as dead.

"Come now," Kuruk said.

"Or what? You're going to kill me?" I eyed the bow and metal-tipped arrows, the knife stuck in Kuruk's waistband.

Kuruk opened his mouth to answer when he suddenly froze. With the sweep of his arm, he shoved me off the rock and threw himself next to me on the ground. That's when I heard it, too: horse clatter.

I lay still, imagining the Irish and Wade hunting us down, Kuruk attempting to shoot them with his arrows. We'd be dead before we hit the ground.

The hooves thundered louder. Kuruk peered uphill. Against my better judgment I followed suit. The soil shifted beneath me, unleashing several rocks. Before I had time to act, the clip clop changed course. Someone was coming our way. I pressed myself down, my snake-bitten forearm rubbing painfully against the rocky ground.

With a shout Kuruk jumped from his hiding spot, his bow ready for attack. I followed slowly, wishing for the tenth time for a gun. On the hill a few feet above us towered a horse, the Indian on top motionless, his rifle trained on Kuruk. Then me. The warrior's eyes burned fiercely among the red paint on his face. He wore pale leather pants and breechcloths with a cotton shirt, his hair bound with a cloth headband.

He shouted something. Kuruk answered, his eyes swiveling back and forth between the Indian and the group of riders farther up the hill. There had to be fifteen of them. The rider close to us yelled to his friends and a second Indian approached. Fatigue and dread were making my legs tremble and I sank back on the boulder. Let them haggle it out. We'd be dead soon enough.

To my amazement, Kuruk lowered his bow when the approaching Indian said something. Kuruk nodded and pointed my way. Great, now he put the blame on me.

I tried standing again, but my legs refused. In frozen fascination I watched the second rider get off his horse and approach. He moved as quick and nimble as my old friend Bero.

"You Ela's friend," the man said in English.

My voice refused to cooperate so I nodded. This warrior, painted up like his mate, wore a blue and white headband. His eyes were more brown than black and very shiny as if looking at two pebbles submerged in water. He looked smart like he'd not miss a thing.

"You come with us."

I nodded again. To my amazement, the Indian with the sparkling eyes placed an arm around Kuruk's bony shoulders and led him uphill.

CHAPTER EIGHTEEN

The next second, I found myself yanked on top of a horse with the Indian riding behind me. I balanced on a blanket and had trouble staying upright. Whenever I began to slide I felt the warrior nudge me back into position.

My cheeks were hot with embarrassment, but inside I was steaming. I couldn't even ride a stupid horse without falling off. They were probably laughing about me. Why had Dr. Stuler forgotten to include Indian languages?

On the hilltop, words flew back and forth between Shiny Eyes and the other warriors. And warriors they were—faces painted red, some black, their long hair wrapped with cotton headbands. They wore breechclouts over leather pants and regular shirts like I'd seen the Mexicans wear in Fort Sumner. They had twenty or so extra horses and additional pack mules with them. Secretly I wondered if they had been stolen.

My mind was a blur. I was riding among a group of Apaches. It was like a movie scene and I was in it. Except this was real. At home nobody would believe me. The ache in my stomach returned. Somehow I had to get used to the idea that I'd never go home.

The village exploded into shouts as we rode onto the field. Horses were tethered while the women ran back and forth, offering water and food. Nobody was paying attention to me, so I wandered toward my wikiup. I was pooped and no matter how interesting life in this Indian village was, it couldn't make up for the terrible sadness, tearing a hole into my chest.

I felt out of place—a nobody—lacking even the most basic skills to survive. In the first game, I hadn't known what it took to return home. I'd simply tried to survive and by chance made it back to present day. I didn't really know this time either, at least regarding the missions, but I felt out of my element. I would never survive in this wild land. And my knife was irreparably gone.

Too depressed to move I dug under the cover and fell asleep.

"Max?" Ela's voice drifted into my consciousness. "Come and join the feast. There will be dancing."

I shook off the cobwebs and leaned on one elbow. Five feet away Ela kneeled in the gloom. She'd pulled her hair back and added a bead necklace to her dress.

"I'll be outside."

"Wait," I called after her.

"What is it?"

"Can you just sit and talk for a minute?"

Ela raised her eyebrows, but quickly lowered herself next to me.

"It was Fred," I said. Fred's disgusting muck, his bloated face and horrible scars danced in my vision.

"Kuruk told me." Ela grimaced. "He pretends he doesn't know, but he speaks the white man's language well enough. He's proud."

"Somebody killed Fred. You think the other two will find us?"

Ela shook her head. "They were lost in the mountains. *Mountain Spirit* is frowning on them. It is no place for white men." She placed her hand on my good arm, making my skin burn with longing. "Now will you come?"

"You think the others are dead?"

Ela shrugged. "Maybe. Many people die out here."

I grabbed her hand. "You think we'll find them like Fred. Wade had something of mine. I must get it back." I couldn't keep the urgency from my voice.

"I will ask the warriors. They have traveled far." Ela let go of my hand and straightened. "Now come. You must meet our most esteemed guest."

"Who is it?"

Her voice mysterious and low she said, "You shall see."

Around the open field fires burned, carrying the delicious smell of roasted meat. I swallowed. I hadn't eaten all day. Most of the warriors were sitting near Grandmother's wikiup, partying and chatting up a storm. Once in a while one of them hollered and gesticulated, probably to emphasize a point.

I was glad for Ela's firm grip when we walked into the middle of the feasting men. Because there, among the warriors, sat the oldest Indian, I'd ever seen. He was tiny and shrunken, his face scrunched into a thousand wrinkles. Pronounced cheekbones made his face look wide. Even now in the midst of the reveling, his lips pressed flat and he looked angry.

Ela kept holding on to me as she bowed and addressed the old man. "*Hadínyaa? Shiitsooyee.*

"This is Chief *Kas-tziden*. We call him *Nana*," Ela said to me, though she was still looking at the old man. "He's on a vengeance raid. He brought us horses and supplies."

I stared. Things were getting weirder by the minute. Now I was introduced to some mummy-lookalike Indian chief who acted as if he could barely move, let alone lead a bunch of warriors.

Behind us Kuruk could be heard chatting and laughing. I'd never seen him behave this happy or animated.

"Kuruk says Nana eluded the Army," Ela continued. "He led them on a chase. They have won many fights and lost no warriors."

Nana said something, his voice low and gravelly.

Ela smiled. "Ah, yes, Nana says they will never catch him." She said something else, grabbing my injured arm.

"*To-nuest-chee-shee-dah.*" Nana held out a wrinkly hand.

Ela pushed me forward and I sank on my knees in front of Nana. "Show him your arm. Nana has Power over rattlesnakes. He can avoid them and treat bites."

Nana raised both arms toward the sky and then placed a forefinger on my wrist. Even his finger was a bunch of wrinkles. Amazing I thought as I listened to the old man's mumbling. How can someone that old ride around New Mexico and not be caught? He had to be some amazing warrior.

Nana waved a dismissive hand. "*Haee'a.*"

"Very nice to meet you," I said, bowing several times while crawling backwards. "Can we eat?" I whispered under my breath, anxious to get away from the stern chief. "I'm starving."

Ela said something else and bowed before dragging me

toward one of the fires. Baskets with cactus fruit, raspberries, sunflower seeds and pine nuts sat on the ground. There were clay dishes with baked onions and some kind of pale roots and boiled meat. I selected a roasted leg of rabbit and picked from the various offerings. Nobody paid attention as everyone was listening to Nana and his warriors.

"His name is *Kaytennae*." Ela pointed at the man with the shiny eyes. "He helps Nana lead the warriors and takes care of him."

Kaytennae offered the old Indian a piece of brownish-red meat. It seemed raw and by the way it dripped, I figured it was liver. Yuck. Nana took a bite and handed it off to his neighbor.

To my dismay Ela moved away to a different mostly female group. She was talking to a woman dressed like a man in leather breeches, her eyes grave in the firelight. By the way, her face was painted she had come with the men.

How I wished I'd paid better attention to history. The game obviously hadn't included Apachian. I'd have to learn it word-by-word or be the clueless village idiot. I took another handful of pine nuts noticing with a pang that the dull ache in my arm was gone. I stared at Nana from a distance. Something magical was going on. The old chief sat quietly, listening to his men. His eyes were giving nothing away.

I didn't notice that Ela had returned until she whispered into my ear. "My heart is glad to see *Lozen*. She is one of the greatest warrior women. Her special Power makes her see the enemy."

I took another look at the warrior woman who'd rejoined Nana and Kaytennae. Among them she looked like a man, her hair, held by a headband, long and thick. "What exactly are they doing riding all over the place?"

"It is vengeance war. The Mexicans killed my parents, but they also killed chief Victorio who was Lozen's brother and Nana's nephew. They have been riding for weeks. They brought supplies for the village, but they won't stay. It is not done, Nana says."

I looked around me. These people had been hunted nearly to extinction. And amazingly, I sat right in the middle of the few who had escaped. So far.

"Did you ask them if they saw Wade and the Irish?" I said.

"They have not seen them. Dead or alive."

I felt Ela's hand on my forearm. "Lozen is telling a story."

"What story?"

"I'll explain. It tells how Coyote created fire."

I nodded dumbly, trying to figure out what coyotes had to do with fire.

"*Iłk'idą, kǫǫ yá'édįná'a,*" Lozen said. "*Ákoo Tł'ízhe hooghéí dá'áíná bikǫ' 'ólíná'a.*"

"*Long ago, there was no fire,*" Ela began to translate. "*Then only those who are called Flies had fire.*

"Then the Flies held a ceremony.
And Coyote came there. At that place where
they held the ceremony, Coyote danced around
and around at the edge of the fire. And he
continually poked his tail in the fire.

Then they spoke thus to him:
"Friend, your tail will burn,"
they said to him.

Then:
"Let it burn!"
he said to them.
And he put his tail in the fire.
The fire flared up under his tail.

Then many of them circled around him.
The Flies, they did so.
Then many of them circled around him but
that Coyote jumped over [and] away from
them with the fire.
He ran away from them with the fire.
They ran behind him.

Then, farther on, he gave fire to the Eagle.
At that place, now, he scattered the fire all over
among these mountains.
Fire was burning in every direction.

Then these Flies tried to put out the fire but
they tried in vain.

Then, that Coyote having been helped by the
blowing of the wind, the fire, becoming
impossible to control, burned on.
In this way, fire came into existence.

Then [the Flies] hated that Coyote.
And they spoke thus to him:
"The stones, the earth, the water: let them all
become hot for him!" they said to him.
That happened exactly so.

Then he was dashing around and around.
The Coyote did so.
All of these became hot for him.
Therefore he ran away in vain.
A [pond of] water lay there.

"This, also, used to be cool." he said.
And he jumped into the water that lay there.
A [hissing] noise was heard.
Right there, he was boiled.

At this time, anything that they said occurred
in exactly that way.
Anything of which one said:
"It is to happen so."
happened in just that way.
For that reason one did not say just anything
to someone.
If one spoke in that way to someone one
hated, it happened in exactly that way.
For that reason, one did not say just anything
to someone.
They spoke only in a very good way.

Then, it having happened so in this place, fire
came into existence. Because of Coyote, fire
came into existence, they say.
In this way, the old people have told them
about it."

As Lozen's voice faded, several warriors stood up and began to dance, their voices low at first, then rising and falling. Drums pounded. One by one, more men joined. I watched in fascination. The fires were low now, the stars and a half-moon providing most of the light.

My breath caught. Last time I'd seen a half moon had been a month ago walking with Grace in the desert. I'd been in the game over four weeks. How much longer would I be here?

What if it's forever?

Somewhere in the distance an owl hooted and my attention returned to the warriors, the crackling fires, the drums and song. Despite my heartache and longing to go home, it *was* magical.

How I wanted to put my arm around Ela. In *my* world, I would've shown her something cool on the computer. Or watched a movie together. Here I was out of my element—an awkward stranger too clumsy to keep up, too dumb to hunt and unable to support himself.

Why would Ela want anything to do with me? *Why not*, my mind argued. There aren't too many boys old enough to be her boyfriend. And the warriors are too busy fighting.

I stole a glance at my side. Like me Ela watched the men dance. She turned to look at me, a smile playing around her lips. My fingers twitched, wanting to grab hers.

Grandmother's voice wafted across and Ela jumped up.

I'd missed my chance.

Village life was quiet the next morning. I sat outside, catching a bit of sun while chewing leftover baked roots and berries. Near the overhanging cliff, the corral was overflowing with horses. Indian warriors were rifling through bags, the mules and horses had carried. Boxes of tools, assorted guns and equipment spread across the grass. Sacks of flour, sugar and coffee were stacked nearby, Indian girls sorting them into piles.

Nana emerged from his wikiup and limped towards the enclosure. He looked stiff and dragged a foot. I saw him nod at one of the little boys who, chased by his mother, disappeared naked and screaming into a wikiup. When Nana joined his men, they all stopped what they were doing and gathered around him. They nodded and spoke quietly.

Kaytennae walked over to Grandmother's hut and escorted her back to the corral while Ela hurried to my side. Within minutes every warrior was on horseback, Nana among them. His mare was the color of oatmeal and though much shorter than his men, he looked as regal as any war chief.

Nana nimbly led his warriors across the open field when the warrior woman, Lozen, got off her horse. Everyone had come to a stop as she turned east, her eyes closed. She raised her arms, palms out.

Nobody spoke. After a minute or two, Lozen addressed the men in a low voice.

"What is she saying?" I whispered.

"Lozen says the enemy is moving north near the Rio Grande," Ela said. Did she know about the Buffalo soldiers we'd seen? Without another word, Lozen mounted her horse and the men and lone woman rode off.

One by one the women and children began to whoop. I wondered what they thought: the warriors who may not live to see another day or their families and children who may never see their brothers, fathers and uncles again. My father and Dr. Stuler went to work every day and everybody expected them home at night. No sweat. What a cushy life they had.

As soon as the warriors were gone, Ela joined her grandmother who'd returned to her wikiups. One by one the villagers began carrying the contents of their huts into the open. It looked like housecleaning day as skins, furs, baskets and blankets were stacked on the ground. It was a beautiful sunny day, the sky a dark blue against the red of the cliff.

Near the corral, Kuruk was kicking up dust with his moccasin. He looked even angrier than usual if that was possible. I wanted to ask, but then thought better of it. The way the guy looked he was spoiling for a fight.

"You must hurry," Ela said, running towards me. "We leave this afternoon."

I stared. "Why? This is the coolest piece of land I've ever seen."

Ela smiled. "I know you won't understand, but we'll go to our summer camp. And to *Ojo Caliente* after that. It is never safe to stay too long. The forest has been picked over and now that we have enough horses, we can make the journey much quicker."

"What's Ojo Caliente?"

Ela's expression turned dreamy. "A holy place with warm waters and beautiful mountains. It is where we got our name from…Warm Springs Apache."

I nodded, imagining sitting naked in a hot tub with Ela. My gaze returned to Kuruk, bringing me back to earth. "What's wrong with him?"

"He wanted to go with the warriors. Nana said no. Before he can become an apprentice, he must learn to control his anger." Ela yelled something and Kuruk slinked off toward Grandmother's hut. "I must return and help," Ela said.

"What about me?" I asked.

Ela's eyes sparkled in the early morning sun. "What is it that you want?"

You, I wanted to say. I want to be near you, learn your ways and fit in. *And* I want to be at home like a normal kid. Like Jimmy and the girls in my class. I want to see mom… and dad.

I shook my head. Life in this game was impossible.

When I didn't answer, Ela said, "You can pack your wikiup. And if we work hard and finish early, I'll have a surprise."

Ela's naked body in the waterfall flashed through my mind. I hid my smile. Surely, she had something else in store.

Either way, I was excited to find out.

CHAPTER NINETEEN

By early afternoon, the contents of Grandmother's and my hut were packed and attached to several horses. Most of the supplies had been repackaged and spread across the mules. A few women were still working in the open, rolling up hides and folding blankets, strapping pots and baskets on more horses.

I sat in the shade of a pine tree, sipping from a water skin. My forearm felt amazing despite the morning work. Nana had the Power all right.

"You ready for your surprise?" Ela shielded her eyes from the glare with one hand, holding the other behind her back. I jumped up, trying to catch a glimpse of what she was hiding. She laughed as she revealed a rifle and six bullets.

"I will teach you to shoot. Nana brought ammunition, but we must save most of it for hunting and the white..." Her eyes grew darker. "I mean—"

"I know what you mean," I hurried. "I don't blame you a bit. It's okay to hate white people. They're stealing your world."

She nodded and touched her throat. "You are not like other pale eyes."

I didn't speak. I couldn't. *I know history and how it all ends.* Clearing my throat, I said, "So where do we go?"

"Come." Ela took my hand. We climbed downhill until we reached a narrow clearing. The ground was covered in rocks and grasses. Brush clung to the gravelly soil. Ela stopped at a shoulder-high boulder. She'd brought a piece of bark and, with the help of a small rock, draped it on top so that the bark hung over the side.

"Follow me," she said, stepping back thirty yards. "The first thing we do is shoot with our mind." She faced the boulder and closed her eyes. "Do this with me."

I joined her and stared at the bark.

"Close your eyes. Can you see the target in your mind? Imagine you are pointing a gun. Oh, here." Ela handed me the rifle. "Let's do this first. Hold it correctly or you can hurt yourself." She adjusted my right arm, so the butt rested against my shoulder, forefinger at the trigger. "The left hand supports underneath. Like this." She moved around me, her hands cool on my arm and hand, her chest leaning in.

I was trying to focus on the gun, her nearness taking my breath. *Concentrate*, I scolded. Why had I never shown any interest when my father had offered to teach me? I would've been able to impress her. Of course, I'd hated the Army business, our constant moves and my father's absences.

"Good. Now stand still and close your eyes. Feel the weight of the gun. How your arms and fingers hold onto it. Now think about the target. Point your rifle. Imagine the bullet inside, how it flies along the barrel... and finds its mark."

I stood, visualizing the bark bursting apart. Even after what Wade and the Irish had done I couldn't imagine shooting a person.

"One more thing."

I opened my eyes. Ela walked around me like a master drill sergeant. "Your legs and feet must be strong. Feel them rooted to the earth. I readjusted my weight and moved my feet to a wider stance.

"Good. Now do it again. Close your eyes. Feel the gun."

I stood, the rifle pressed into my shoulder. My forefinger twitched.

"Can I try it now?"

"Not yet. Let me show you." Ela reclaimed the gun and placed two bullets in the loading chamber. "This is a Winchester, so you can use multiple bullets. They load from the right."

Without missing a beat she stepped next to me, briefly closed her eyes and fired. My ears rang. Thirty yards away, the bark tore apart and stone chips exploded.

"Who taught you to shoot?" I asked, running toward the boulder. "Wow, you got it right through the middle." I reattached the shredded bark and hurried back to Ela.

"Your turn." She handed me the gun. "Father taught us when we were young. He always said, it was important to hunt food and more important to defend ourselves."

I adjusted the rifle and closed my eyes, trying to remember what Ela had told me. I tried to prepare for the noise and held my breath. The gun exploded. The recoil knocked my shoulder backwards, making my right arm buzz. The bark hadn't moved, the boulder stood untouched…mocking.

"Where did it go?"

Ela pointed into the distance. "The trees over there."

She walked around me as if she were looking for obvious signs of error. "Try it again without a bullet."

I aimed, trying to swallow my frustration. I closed my eyes, taking mental inventory of my body. I opened my eyes. The rifle clicked.

"It is your breath," Ela said. "Breathe deeply, let out half, hold, look where you're going to shoot. Then pull the trigger."

I tried again. Shoulder, feet, right hand, left hand, finger, breathe, hold. *Click.*

"That was better. Now you shoot." She loaded two more bullets.

Again, I took position and aimed. At the last moment, doubt crept into my mind and I lowered the Winchester.

"What?" Ela said. "Feel the way your feet stand on the ground, your body and the rifle. They are one." Her voice was soothing now, almost hypnotic.

I grabbed the rifle and closed my eyes, checking everything. It was becoming more natural to hold the gun.

"Now open your eyes. See the target. Breathe and shoot."

I listened and pulled the trigger. Stone chips blasted from the boulder.

"One more. Do it now." Ela's voice sounded triumphant.

I repeated and this time bark and rock exploded. I lowered the rifle, my shoulder aflame from the recoil, a grin spreading across my face. I'd hit the target and Ela was proud of me.

Ela smiled, her teeth white in the blazing sun. Without thinking, I pulled her close. My mouth found hers. I felt her body tense, her hands pushing against my chest. But then she yielded. We stood motionless. Blood rushed through my head as I felt her body press against mine. I remembered the waterfall and wondered if she was naked underneath the dress.

Time lost all meaning.

At last Ela leaned back. "We must return. The village is leaving."

"Just one more kiss?" I pulled her close again. "By the way, what does Ela mean?"

Ela looked dreamy. "It means *earth*."

"You're solid and warm like the earth," I breathed. "My earth." I placed a palm on her cheek. Somehow I couldn't stop smiling.

"*Nü nahii'maa at'e, ya nahiika'ee at'e*. It means *the earth is our Mother, the sky is our Father*." Ela threw her arms around my neck. "One more kiss."

I forgot everything but Ela pushing against me, her arms wrapped around my neck and her lips on mine. For a moment I was in heaven.

"Ela!" Kuruk's voice was venomous. A barrage of Apachian followed. It sounded rude even if I didn't understand a word.

Ela ducked her head and grabbed the rifle. "We must go," she muttered. "They are waiting."

I nodded, my mind foggy as I tried to control my feverish body. Kuruk was glaring at me. Great, now I'd thrown an extra barrel of oil on Kuruk's grouch fire. Still, I climbed uphill with a goofy grin on my face.

This time, Kuruk stayed close, his gaze remaining on me. He yelled something as soon as we reached the field. Only a few villagers were waiting and whatever he'd said, mumbling erupted while Ela's cheeks turned a shade darker. She hurried to grab the reins of her horse, nodding at me to take another.

Progress was slow. We walked in a line heading west, first downhill, then up, through valleys and canyons over peaks and up mountains. I kept my eyes on Ela, her hair flowing across her back, her proud shoulders and assured steps. I longed to stop and kiss her again, but the trek went on without break.

Though I took sips from my water skin several times, the Apaches neither drank nor ate.

My stomach ached with hunger and the memory of our kisses.

CHAPTER TWENTY

We camped in the open. Only a few fires burned and I rolled myself into one of the buffalo hides. I'd hoped Ela would be close, but Kuruk had made sure she was with Grandmother. The next day was the same. I barely had a chance to speak with Ela, Kuruk hanging out nearby and glowering at me every time we stopped. By evening we reached our new home near a small stream.

Like a well-oiled machine, the Indians began collecting saplings and grasses to build their huts. Others prepared the ground, unpacked horses and cooked. Ela was busy cutting wood to size for the wikiup frames.

"Can I help?" I asked.

"Pull these branches off. We'll need to—"

"Grandmother wants to talk to you both," Kuruk said, appearing out of nowhere. He'd spoken English so I'd understand. Something was up.

Grandmother was resting on a blanket, her face somber. To my frustration, Kuruk materialized by her side. She said something and patted the ground.

Ela bent her head in deference and sat down. I followed suit. This didn't look good. The old woman was going to punish us. I watched anxiously as Grandmother and Ela began to talk. When Kuruk threw in some comment, Grandmother cut him off with a raised hand. He shut up, but I knew from his reddened face he was fuming.

At last, Ela turned toward me. To my surprise her cheeks were flushed as well. "Grandmother asks whether you want to make life here with us…me. She says I've been ready for marriage for a while. And that it is not acceptable to…be indecent." Ela's cheeks flamed darker. "She says you must take me as your wife."

I opened my mouth and closed it, my throat closed with a mixture of shock and annoyance. History was repeating itself. Last time Bero had asked me about marrying Juliana. Since when was kissing reason to marry? I hadn't even made it to second base yet.

Kuruk said something. Again Grandmother raised her hand and he shut up.

"I…," I stumbled.

"Grandmother says you must follow our laws and put your horse in front of my hut tomorrow night for all to see."

"I don't have a horse and besides, what does a horse have to do with it?"

"It is a custom," Ela said. "A suitor will stake his horse in front of the girl's home. If she accepts his offer, she will feed and water the horse. She has four days to decide this."

I looked at her. She was beautiful, even now after our trek and working all morning. I wanted to hang out with her, kiss and touch her. But marriage? That was ridiculous. I couldn't marry. I was sixteen, a kid, with a year of high school left. *But you're not going back*, my mind whispered. *You're stuck here in the most brainless game of all time.*

I grew aware that Ela, Grandmother and Kuruk were staring at me. They were waiting for a response. I cleared my throat. "I must think about it. I'm sorry."

Without another word I jumped up and ran toward the river. Some of the villagers were looking at me curiously, but I didn't pay attention. I just walked until the riverbank narrowed. I sagged to the ground beneath a pine tree, kicking a few cones in the process.

My life was a nightmare. I'd finally managed to distract myself, have a bit of fun, find a girlfriend and the first thing they wanted to do is get me married. Impossible.

It was clear I had to do something about my situation. Ela would never understand. Not after what happened in the clearing two days ago. My mother's face drifted into view, my father's. Then Jimmy's. How I missed them, the convenient life I'd led in Bornhagen. How could Dr. Stuler call the game the best thing ever? Something people would want to play for fun?

The game was killing me.

You've got two choices. Either you stay here with Ela and marry her. Forget about going home and just accept the fact that you lost your family and your modern life. Become an Indian and live like *Kevin Costner* in *Dances with Wolves.* I'd have to learn to hunt and fight. Learn Apachian and forever remain here.

Or leave.

That was ludicrous. How was I going to find Wade? New Mexico was huge and I was alone without resources or the most basic knowledge about surviving in this place. I might search for years and never find him. *You might as well give up,* the voice in my head whispered. Stay here and become an Indian.

No, my mind screamed. That would mean the game had won. No way I'd accept that.

Not yet.

For a moment I became aware of the water. The stream was clear and probably ice-cold. Strange I'd never seen anybody fish. There had to be a bunch of trout in there. I licked my lips, suddenly craving my mom's lasagna, the best pasta in the world. I'd never eat it again.

Being near Ela had been a distraction. Now my old thoughts were back in full force and with it the feeling of utter helplessness. I was so depressed that I didn't want to move. Not now, not ever. Just sit here and turn into one of the boulders.

But that wasn't how it worked. My stomach churned with hunger, I was thirsty.

And I had to make a decision.

Now!

By the time I marched into the village, new frames of wikiups were going up in a long oval around the field. Ela was attaching saplings to the hut, her fingers deftly weaving in and out.

"Can I talk to you?" I said. "Alone?"

Ela nodded. Grandmother was busy unrolling a humungous buffalo skin and Kuruk was nowhere to be seen. I pulled Ela through a bunch of shrubs into the shade of a Ponderosa Pine.

"I'm sorry about Grandmother," she stammered. "And Kuruk is—"

"No, I'm sorry." I grabbed her hands. "It's all my fault for misunderstanding. I'm not very familiar with Native American culture. I never meant to put you in a bad situation. It's just…" I wanted to hug her so badly, but I was afraid now. Afraid to give her the wrong message. Afraid Grandmother would punish her.

Ela yanked her hands out of my embrace. "What is Native American?" she started. But then her gaze narrowed and she looked like the first time I'd seen her at the Mexican's washhouse. "You are going to leave."

"I've got no choice," I said lamely.

She shook her head ever so slightly as tears glistened in those beautiful eyes. I'd never seen her like this. Which only made it more obvious that I hadn't understood a thing about her or picked up on her willingness to be my wife.

What? It was absurd. I'd played the game from hell twice and got away with a would-be wife each time. Great going, Max.

"Listen, I want to explain. I…must return to my family or at least try. I really like you, but I'm not ready to marry."

A tear rolled down Ela's cheek, but she remained silent.

"Believe me, if I *were* ready, I'd marry you and no one else. You're amazing, smart and beautiful. But I just can't…" my voice stopped working.

"You said your family was dead."

"They're not, just far away. I must find them." Or die trying. "I told you Wade took something from me. Without it I can't go home. I have to find him first."

"How?"

"I don't have a clue."

"What is a clue?"

"It means I don't have any idea. I'll ride back the way we came and ask around."

"You can't go alone," Ela cried.

"Why not?"

"You will die. It is too dangerous for pale eyes."

"I have no choice."

Ela shook her head. "They will kill you."

"I've got to try. I've got to get back home." My voice faltered. The thought of going out into the wilderness alone *was* frightening. Enemies lurked everywhere. Nature was unpredictable. Chances were great, I'd never make it. Still I had to do it.

"I'm leaving tomorrow," I finally said. There, at last I'd made a decision. I should've felt good, relieved, but all I wanted was to crawl into my new wiki-up and forget about life.

Without another word, Ela turned on her heels and hurried off. I remained behind. That had gone exceptionally well. How I hated this game.

Visions of Dr. Stuler's face drifted into my mind, the smile he'd carried on his lips when he talked about the world's greatest game. More like the world's greatest nightmare. The cruelest most disastrous game ever invented. I wanted to beat the guy to a pulp.

The new fury about my situation was making it hard to stay still, so I stomped off a second time. I had to clear my head and make a plan. Develop a strategy where to go.

When I emerged in the clearing a while later, Ela, Kuruk and Grandmother were talking. Even from a distance, I knew that Kuruk seethed. He was jerking his head, his lips curled into a sneer. Ela ignored him and headed my way.

I kept my head low, embarrassed about having put her in a bad spot. Yet, with all the trouble I'd put her in, the heartache I'd caused her, she produced a soft smile, handing me something wrapped in leather. My heart tucked painfully as the voice in my head whispered...*you could've had her all to yourself.*

"Grandmother says you must have a proper weapon for your journey."

The rifle inside the hide was a Winchester, the same kind of gun I'd practiced with. A small leather pouch held fifteen bullets.

"Sorry, there are only a few shells. We must save ammunition for hunting and attacks."

"Oh, Ela, don't apologize giving me this," I cried. Gratefulness joined my already overflowing emotions.

"We will give you a horse and food." Ela's voice quivered as she hurried away. "I must help Grandmother."

I inspected the rifle, wondering if I'd be able to hunt. Or shoot someone. I loaded a couple of bullets and tied the pouch to my belt loop. Nobody was paying attention. The village was taking shape as the wikiups were being covered with grasses. It was slow painstaking work. Even the little kids were helping to cut grass and bind it together.

I knew I should help. Show my gratitude. I didn't even have anything to give back. These people had saved my life, shared food and shelter, offered to embrace me into their family.

And what did I do?

I said *no thanks*. Give me more stuff so I can leave. I was an ungrateful bastard. Deep in thought, I wandered back towards the creek.

I stopped in alarm when I noticed Kuruk leaning against the red bark of a pine tree, his arms crossed, his eyes squinting.

"Pale eyes leaves. Good!" he shouted. "Take virtue of my sister, take food and horse from the People."

"I'm sorry," I said. Despite my frustration I was in no mood to argue. "Ela is wonderful. I never meant—"

"Pale eyes like all of them." Kuruk spit and mumbled something else too low for me to understand. He pushed off the tree and disappeared into the bushes.

I sighed. At least the guy wasn't going to beat me up or worse. I slumped on a rock to study my gun when I heard a commotion beyond the thicket. Branches snapped, somebody yelled—a low guttural sound of terror. And something else: a purr, then hissing followed by Kuruk's blood-curdling cry.

I broke into a run.

CHAPTER TWENTY-ONE

Yanking the rifle to my chest, I charged through the undergrowth. My heart raced so hard it felt as if it was ready to break through my ribcage. But that was nothing in comparison to what happened next.

In the shadow of the pines a death scene was unfolding. A cougar the color of milk coffee was rolling on the ground with Kuruk trapped beneath. The cougar's corner teeth, an easy two inches long, gleamed as it lowered its jaw. To my great surprise the cougar purred like my neighbor's kitty.

The boy was frantically pushing his fist against the animal's throat to keep it from ripping off his face. Kuruk was strong, nearly fully grown with lean muscles and a life spent outdoors. Against the cougar he had no chance. In the recesses of my mind I realized Kuruk would die. Nobody won a fight with a killing machine of a hundred-fifty pounds of muscle.

I pointed the rifle, my palms so slick they felt greased. If I missed I'd kill Kuruk, but then he was going to be dead in a second anyway.

On the ground the animal jumped back only to change position. Its huge paws swiped at Kuruk's throat. Despite its size it was limber and quick. It leaped again, this time digging its claws into Kuruk's leather shirt. Kuruk tried to roll away. The cougar was playing for keeps.

Shoot, my mind urged. My forefinger squeezed the trigger— almost. *You have fired a total of two bullets in your life. You're going to miss.*

A scream rang out. Kuruk curled forward to push the cat away from his leg—face and neck a sickening red. The cougar had buried its jaw into the boy's thigh, just above the knee, yanking, tugging. Blood gushed through Kuruk's leather pants.

I stopped breathing. *Shoot.* I squeezed the trigger and the shot exploded in my ear. Kuruk and the cougar momentarily stopped what they were doing. I'd missed them both.

The cat seemed to hesitate as if it were deciding between continuing the attack and fleeing.

Then it focused on me.

Head bent low, it swiped a tongue across its teeth gleaming with Kuruk's blood. Its eyes were almost golden, its whiskers long and white—an equally beautiful and terrifying sight.

It walked silently, fluidly, its paws soft on the pine needles. Not even that fast as if it knew it was by far superior to the weak human standing there trembling in his boots.

Ten yards. I had one bullet left. My stomach dissolved, my legs turned liquid with terror. I was out of time. This was the moment I realized I was next. While Kuruk would bleed to death, I'd get my face bitten off or my neck broken or both…

Breathe Ela's voice instructed in my head. I checked my stance and aimed. Five yards. Now!

Breathing out I squeezed the trigger. The cougar stopped in its tracks as if it were shocked by the blast. Then it leaped into the air and crashed to the ground. Its great paws trembled as its golden chest bloomed red. Then it grew still. I took a careful step forward, my thighs almost too weak to support me, the air struggling through my lungs. The cat was dead.

Hands shaking I threw down the rifle and ran toward Kuruk. Blood gushed from the boy's leg, soaking the pine needles. Kuruk was trying to stem the flow, but his hands were torn and he had no strength to sit up.

I ripped a bunch of leaves from a bush and threw myself next to Kuruk. The leather pants were shredded, revealing ripped flesh and more blood. Everything was turning red. I shuddered.

Don't lose it now. Taking ragged breaths, I pushed the leaves on top of Kuruk's leg.

"Shsh, lie still. We'll have to stop the bleeding. I know it hurts."

Kuruk whimpered. The leather was soaked crimson several

inches below the knee and up to his hip. It was soaking the ground. Kuruk was losing blood like crazy. From what I could tell it wasn't pumping, so at least no major artery. But unless I kept the pressure on, Kuruk could bleed to death. There was no time to call for help. He needed a compression bandage. I twisted my neck looking for something suitable.

"Can you put your hand on your leg for a second? You've got to press hard or it won't work. I have to find a rope to slow the bleeding."

Kuruk mumbled incoherently and held out a shaky arm.

"Right here, press down." I guided Kuruk's fingers into place and let go. The gushing resumed. "Harder, like this."

I pushed down into the wound, ignoring Kuruk's scream, ignoring my own fear and disgust. Had Kuruk been white he'd have been as pale as the bark of a birch tree. Instead his skin was tinged gray, a sweaty sheen on his forehead. He looked as if he had no blood left. Still, with his shaky hand he applied more pressure. It had to be the bravest thing he'd ever done.

I tried a smile. "Good job. I'll be right back."

Jumping up I bolted toward the undergrowth. I needed some kind of tough grass that could be tied without breaking. Or…my gaze fell on a bush covered with white fragrant flowers. Honeysuckle. I could use the vines.

Ripping off handfuls, I raced back to Kuruk. To my relief the boy was still pushing down on his leg. I didn't want to think how badly that had to hurt. Kuruk's eyes were half-closed. He looked like he'd pass out any second. I went to work, roping the strands of vine around Kuruk's leg, pulling tight across the leaves. Not too tight, my mind whispered. I fashioned a knot. Then I picked up a log and propped up the lower leg. Good, the flow had slowed to a trickle.

Kuruk's eyes were closed now.

"I'll get help," I said. "Just be still."

I raced through the woods, my vision replaying the scene, Kuruk under the cougar, the cat's huge incisors, blood covering everything, the cougar's silent walk toward me. All of a sudden I felt faint. The trees grew blurry as I stumbled forward.

Ela's only relative couldn't die. Not as long as I had anything to say about it. I was surprised to hear myself scream. "Help! Kuruk is hurt."

Ela was the first to drop her sticks. She hollered something and several women, including Grandmother came running.

"We need a stretcher…something to carry him with," I panted. "A cougar attacked him."

Ela shouted at the women before turning around. "Where is he?"

I pointed toward the creek. Four of the younger women approached with a long piece of leather stretched between two sturdy tree limbs, the kind they transported gear on during the move.

They laid Kuruk down next to Grandmother's hut. I worried he'd died from the loss of blood, but a faint gurgle came from his chest. His eyelids were tinged purple. Grandmother mumbled and raised her arms to the sky.

"What're we going to do?" I said watching the old woman rummage through her pots. "He needs immediate help." The ER in Heiligenstadt was filled with doctors who knew what they were doing. Where such a wound was easy to fix. I'd been there once getting stitches after ripping my toe open in some half buried barbwire.

Grandmother bent over Kuruk. She held a knife and gently cut away what was left of the leather breeches.

"We need to clean the wound, disinfect it," I shouted, trying to calm my panic. Visions of Juliana in Bero's grimy hut returned. Once again I was stuck in a place with no help, no medical supplies and not much knowledge.

"Grandmother has medicine Power. She knows what to do," Ela said as if she'd heard my thoughts. With a curious glance toward me, the old woman fingered the vines around Kuruk's thigh. She said something to Ela and another young woman. Both hurried off.

"We need to clean his leg," I tried again. As I watched the girls scatter I noticed a couple of wooden boxes with English printed on them near the newly constructed horse corral. Nana and his warriors had to have brought them a few days ago. They were undoubtedly looted from white people. Ignoring the group of spectators assembled around Grandmother and Kuruk, I inspected the boxes.

One contained a tripod and what looked like measuring

equipment I didn't understand. The other was stuffed with a cast-iron pan, a coffee pot and assorted silverware. I grabbed the pan and coffee pot and dove into the crowd.

Ela was back, too. Several baskets and pouches stood aligned near the old woman. Kuruk's leg was exposed now. Blood trickled in thin rivulets from the wound which looked like it had been through a meat-grinder. Right above the knee, layers of skin and flesh hung loosely to one side. There were several deeper holes that looked like puncture wounds from the cougar's humongous incisors.

"Ela, listen," I panted, shoving my way through the bystanders. "The wound is open and maybe infected by the cat's paws or saliva. We need to clean it well so it doesn't go bad. I know what we can use to do this. And it needs to be sewn up or he'll have a huge hole in his leg muscle forever."

Ela shook her head. "Grandmother is the village healer."

"I know," I said. "But my mother is a healer where I come from and we know a lot of things."

"We saved your life from snakebite."

Ela was right. What did I know about Indian healing? Obviously they'd done the right thing for me.

What if they don't?

"I just want to help," I said aloud. "He may lose his leg if it's done wrong." Ela hesitated by the way she fidgeted. This was not the Ela I knew—her eyes darted, her breath fast and unsteady. "Come on, we need to do this fast."

At last Ela nodded. She said something to Grandmother who'd opened several of her baskets and was grinding green leaves into a pulp. A discussion ensued while I wiggled back and forth.

We were wasting time. The wound needed to be cleaned before the cougar's germs took hold of Kuruk's body. Without waiting for a decision, I stuck the cast-iron pan into a nearby fire, added water and headed toward the woods.

Doubt crept up the back of my spine like a slimy insect. I shivered remembering the huge beast taking aim at me. What if Kuruk died? Would the game consider it a failed mission? *How can you think of missions when somebody is suffering like this*, the voice in my head sneered. *But it may not work. Just because you helped Juliana doesn't mean it's going to work this time.*

Still I knew I had to try. I'd leave tomorrow anyway unless the villagers would take me first for killing Kuruk.

By the time I returned with an armful of pine boughs and bark, Ela and Grandmother were still talking while some of the villagers had also begun to whisper. They pointed at me and the pot, then Grandmother and Kuruk.

I was stuffing pine into the pan when Ela appeared next to me. "Grandmother says if you have Power of healing, she will help you."

I nodded as feelings of relief joined my anxiety. "I'll be right there."

Hoping the coffee pot was fairly clean, I rinsed it with a bit of precious pine water.

One look at Kuruk's leg made me doubt my sanity. What was I thinking? His leg looked horrific, a bloody mess a trained surgeon would take hours to fix. Flies swarmed ready to dive for a meal.

"Tell her, I'll be happy to learn from her, and that we can work together." I stared at the green pulp Grandmother had been working on. Maybe it was time to bow out. "What is that?"

"Sage to put on the wound."

"I'll watch her then," I said. To my surprise Ela squinted at me.

"You say you are a healer. Now you help Kuruk."

I swallowed because at that moment my throat was as dry as during my trek through the desert with Grace. The entire village was assembled around us now, everyone watching. As if she'd understood Ela's words, Grandmother waved a hand at me, pointing at Kuruk's terrible wound. I nodded. I'd asked for it and now I was going to finish.

Somewhere in the depth of my throat I found my voice. "Put some into this water. We'll use it to rinse the wound." I poured a bit of pine water over my hands, still covered in Kuruk's blood. The piney smell stung my nose.

"It will hurt terribly, so we need to make sure he lies still," I said. "Also ask Grandmother what she puts over the wound."

"Bark and the stem of prickly pear cactus," Ela translated.

"Have someone heat more water in the pan," I said, kneeling next to Kuruk.

I swallowed as I gripped the coffee pot. The liquid was still pretty warm, but I didn't want to wait any longer. Ever so carefully

I trickled pine solution over the boy's leg. He'd been semi-conscious, but now that the liquid burned into his open flesh, he began to scream.

"Hold him still," I shouted. Ela said something and three of Kuruk's friends took hold of his legs and arms, their dark eyes boring into me.

I imagined what they were thinking.

How they were going to kill me nice and slow if I failed.

I'd always loved the idea of cowboys and Indians and watched all sorts of movies. Everyone knew how Indians tortured their prisoners in the most outrageous ways. Right. Except with the Warm Springs Apaches I'd seen nothing but kindness and caring for each other. And they'd accepted me into their midst without knowing a thing about my past. I decided at that moment I'd never believe another Indian story unless it was written by a real historian.

Pushing all doubt away, I concentrated on the task of disinfecting the wound. Behind me the crowd watched in silence. I kept rinsing until most of the blood had cleared. Several dark areas showed where the cougar's teeth or claws had left deep punctures. They had clotted. I hoped the bleeding had been enough to clear these areas because it'd be impossible to dig that deep without opening things up. It was a risk I had to take.

"I need to close this," I said, inspecting the loose flesh on what used to be Kuruk's thigh. "What do you sew with?"

"Buffalo bone and sinew," Ela whispered over my shoulder. "Why?" I turned to face her. Beads of sweat clung to her forehead and her eyes shone too bright. She'd not left my side and looked as if she'd keel over any moment.

I wanted to crumple up beside her. "Show me."

Kuruk's face was distorted with pain. I'd emptied the entire contents of the coffee pot across his leg. Mr. Frankenstein at work, causing maximum agony. Grandmother had treated his face, neck and hands which luckily were only superficial scratches.

Though nobody had spoken, the villagers watched every move. Grandmother was humming as she prepared more of the green paste and strips of bark.

"Here," Ela said. On her palm lay a length of pale thread and a needle shaped from a sharply pointed bone splinter.

"Let's clean them before…" I got up, the world temporarily

spinning. Taking a deep breath, I waited for it to come back into focus. My stomach was acting weird, not exactly sick, but I didn't want the others to see my doubts.

I'd once sewn an apron in fifth grade and given it to my mother as a present. Why did I think I'd sew what took surgeons years to learn. My legs trembled and I took a few steps toward the fire to distract myself. Somehow I had to gather strength and finish this. Adding more pine and bark I stirred the mixture with a wooden spoon. It was boiling.

Placing the pan on the ground, I quickly dipped the bone and sinew. I didn't want to soften them or make the sinew disintegrate.

"Get me a clean piece of leather I can put these things on."

Now that the villagers couldn't see my face the worry returned. I was liable to screw this up big time. What if Kuruk got an infection? As nasty as the wound looked, it was a huge possibility. What if he died or lost his leg?

I imagined a one-legged Kuruk run from the white thugs like Wade. He wouldn't have a chance. Nor would he live a normal life. He wouldn't hunt or find a wife. He'd die a miserable lonely death. A ragged breath escaped me. It was so loud that Ela materialized next to me.

I forced my face back to confidence. *Finish the job.*

Finish so I could leave. Had that just been my plan an hour ago? It seemed like a year had passed since this morning.

I placed the bone and sinew on the leather, poured more pine water into the pot and washed my hands a second time. The idea of touching the lose flesh on Kuruk's leg made me tremble. On TV everything was easy. Once, the man on *Dual Survival* had sewn his own shoulder on the show. If they could do it, so could I.

The bystanders parted as I returned to Kuruk's side. The sinewy thread had softened in the hot water and was pliable. I carefully adjusted the lose flesh. Some parts were nearly severed. As I pushed them back in place, my stomach threatened to spill over. *Don't puke.* Not now while Kuruk's life was at stake and the villagers watched everything I did. Not while I had the life of Ela's only remaining brother in my hands.

I bent low, pushing everything aside. Nothing could matter now but the wound I had to fix.

The squeaky sound of the needle piercing flesh almost made me stop. I pushed the needle into the skin to make a loop, just like

I'd seen on TV and when the doctor had stitched up my toe. I wiped my sweaty temples with my forearm, worried I'd drip on my patient. Another loop, not too tight.

Pretend it's a piece of fabric.

Not a chance. I breathed shallowly. Below the top layer, Kuruk's skin was pink. I kept going loop after loop, counting thirty-three stitches, not the neat sutures of the ER doctor, but the work of Frankenstein. Still the skin lay in place where it belonged.

I poured another pot of pine water across and sat back, noticing with satisfaction that the flies had no stomach for the piney smell. My shirt was soaked with sweat and my hands had a mind of their own. I washed them again in cold water and nodded at Grandmother.

The old woman had watched every movement, everything I'd done. Now she placed the sage mush over Kuruk's leg and loosely covered it with bark. Then she folded a buffalo skin over him. Without another word, she collected her wares and returned to the half-finished wikiup. The other villagers trickled after her... except Ela.

"I didn't know you're a healer," she said. Her eyes were dark and beautiful and for the first time ever, full of admiration. I wanted to kiss her, just for a brief time escape this life of discomfort and stress, of uncertainty and likely death. The idea of leaving here tomorrow and never seeing her again was absurd.

"Can we just go somewhere? Alone?" I asked. To my relief she nodded and took my hand. Nobody was paying attention except for a young girl who'd taken up post next to Kuruk, obviously in charge of reporting any changes.

Now with his eyes closed, Kuruk looked more like a child than a teen. The anger had left and revealed a handsome face with high cheekbones and the same shaped mouth as Ela's. The grayish tinge seemed softer, but maybe that was my wishful thinking.

Just as we walked into the pine trees, several voices began to scream, "*Ndołkah.*"

More yells and shouts followed as a horde of kids came running into the open. One of them, a little boy of four or five with nothing but a loincloth, his face grungy with dust, made a beeline toward us. He rattled off something in Apachian, shouting and jumping for emphasis.

"They found the cougar," Ela said.

I sighed, having completely forgotten about it. Timing was lousy as usual.

Like wildfire, word spread around the village and within minutes, the animal was dragged into the middle of the field. One by one the Indians came to inspect the cat. They pointed and whispered and some of them nodded at me.

"Grandmother says we're supposed to see her," said Ela who'd picked up an armful of lunch items: dried berries, baked roots from last night and more agave cakes.

"Can't we have our picnic first?" I said.

Ela glanced at me with that knowing look that said, "You obey your elders—always."

How different things were in modern day. Teenagers did what they wanted. They argued with their parents and seemed always unhappy or complaining about something.

Despite their terrible defeats, despite the fact, the Indians had lost most of their land and were being hunted like animals, the Chíhéne Nde were a happy People. Everyone worked together—there wasn't the need to have lots of materialistic junk like the newest i-phone, laptop and designer clothes. Like Jimmy, the idiot. Now from a distance I wondered how we could ever have become friends. Sure, we were both American, sure we liked to game. But that's where the similarities ended.

Grabbing an agave cake, I sauntered after Ela who smiled and offered me her hand.

"It is not a bad thing to speak with Grandmother," she said with one of those rare grins. "She is just and wise. She has led the village well since the men left."

So Grandmother was the mayor. To my surprise, a new crowd gathered around the still incomplete wikiup where Grandmother and Ela would sleep. At this rate they'd never get it finished.

"*Da' nzho.*" Grandmother waved and pointed at the buffalo skin on the ground. More Apachian followed as Ela and I slumped in front of her.

I was confused. I'd already told them I wasn't going to marry and had to leave. What did she want with me now?

"Grandmother says you killed *ndołkah*—cougar. She says you saved Kuruk's life," Ela translated.

Grandmother kept talking.

"She says Ussen has been merciful to send a great *diyin*

shaman to help the People."

Grandmother nodded and her old face turned into a thousand wrinkly smiles. "There'll be a feast tonight to celebrate your journey."

Ela jumped up and helped Grandmother to her feet. "Now you must select the part of the animal you want to carry with you."

"What do you mean?"

Instead of giving me a straight answer, Grandmother and Ela straightened and walked through the parting crowd into the field. As Ela waived for me to follow, the Indians began patting me on the shoulder. I hurried after the two women and as soon as I arrived, someone handed me a huge hunting knife, the blade a foot long.

"I would take the claws," Ela said.

I stared at the dead cougar which seemed to have shrunken since this morning. It was beautiful even in death, its golden eyes dull now, its legs and tail relaxed. Its whiskers and mouth were still covered with Kuruk's blood, yet I felt sorry for having slain such a beautiful animal.

"What do you mean?" I asked dumbfounded.

"Or you could take the teeth." She smiled. "It is your right." Only when my eyes fell on one of the youths who wore a necklace of bear claws similar to Kuruk's, did I understand.

I grabbed one of the paws and began to dig out the nails. It was a messy job and I'd had just about enough dealing with bloody meat. I really had no use for claws or teeth, but the villagers looked expectant and excited. I couldn't let them down.

The little boys were squirming close, not to miss a thing. When I'd cut the ten claws from the front paws I stopped. My hands and forearms were sticky again attracting new flies. The claws were covered in more blood, gristle and bits of fur.

"I will clean them," Ela said, sweeping up the grisly claws. "You go and wash. We must prepare for the feast."

She announced something to the others and everyone vanished.

CHAPTER TWENTY-TWO

After taking an *ice* bath in the creek, I wandered back to the village. Someone had returned my rifle to my half-finished wikiup. I slumped to the ground, the excitement of this morning taking its toll demanding a nap. I unrolled my sleeping fur when I looked up and froze.

Indians formed a line in front of my makeshift bed. Nobody seemed to care that I wanted to be left alone. Instead they stepped forward, smiling and nodding. Mumbling Apachian they handed me small packets wrapped in leather, bits of bark and leaves.

"Thanks," I said over and over, wracking my brain for the Apachian word for thank you. "Eh, *Iheedn*."

In the silence that followed, after the villagers had resumed their work, I stared numbly at the pile: a small beaded pouch, a necklace of colorful beads, a piece of honey comb, a colorful stone—the villagers' way of thanking me for saving Kuruk.

My heart turned heavy. Just one more night and I'd go.

Renewed worry crept up inside me. Here in the village I'd had a sense of peace and security. Out there was another story. I'd face bandits, bears and cougars, soldiers and gold diggers, not to mention the harsh nature of this wild country.

With a sigh I straightened. *Better not dwell on that now.* In the end it was the only choice, no matter how little sense it made. Staying made even less sense. Better check on Kuruk.

The boy lay still and apparently asleep, so I quickly inspected the wound. I still detected the pine odor that mixed with the smell of blood and Grandmother's sage. I watched for swelling or a reddish line that indicated a blood infection. There was none. I sighed again. Kuruk was doing okay—for now. It was way too early to tell.

Too restless to sleep now, I wandered around the village. Whenever I approached one of the huts, the Indians stopped what they were doing, nodded and smiled at me. I grinned back, but I wasn't sure what to think. Kuruk could die as easily as a storm bringing thunderclouds. And if he did, my rescue operation would lose its appeal.

Besides, wasn't it my fault that Kuruk had been so mad that he stalked off without being careful? Under normal circumstances he would've been more alert when moving through new terrain.

Half embarrassed, half confused, I returned to my campsite. I knew I should rest for tomorrow, but relaxing was impossible. Instead I sorted through my gifts, trying to figure out how I was going to carry them all.

By dusk a large fire burned near Grandmother's hut. One by one the villagers delivered dishes to share.

"Time to eat," Ela said. She'd bound her long hair into two braids, the ends decorated with beads and feathers. I smiled, but my heart was heavy. "Kuruk is awake."

I jumped up. "How is he?"

"Better."

Kuruk lay gazing into the sky.

"Grandmother has changed the wrapping and given him *peyote* for the pain," Ela said.

I kneeled to take another look at the leg. Nothing had changed. "Do you have any burning sensation," I asked, my head filled with visions of infected oozing wounds. "Or throbbing?" I touched Kuruk's forehead.

Kuruk stared. He was far away, his mouth relaxed almost in a half-smile.

"What is that stuff you just mentioned…peyote?"

"A cactus. Medicine people use it for visions. We use it to treat pain."

I glanced at Kuruk, suppressing a grin. The boy was in a drug daze. Just as well. He'd be still and hopefully heal.

"Before I forget, in eight days you'll have to remove the stitches," I said. "Otherwise, they'll grow in and get infected." My memory was fuzzy how long my own stitches had remained. Hopefully, that was the right timeframe.

"Stitches?"

"Yeah, the thread I used to sew up Kuruk's leg."

"Oh." Ela tugged at her braids. "I don't know—"

"Look, it's easy. You cut each loop and pull out the pieces. Make sure your hands are really clean."

Ela nodded. "I will tell Grandmother." She looked up. "The feast is beginning."

Near the large fire and to the right of Grandmother, a bison skin lay prepared on the ground. I was told it was my place of honor. Here and there I overheard the word *ndołkah* as people nodded and smiled at me. As soon as I plopped down, Ela handed me a piece of meat.

"It is heart of the mountain lion," she said, nodding at me encouragingly. "Grandmother wanted you to have it." She smiled one of her rare smiles. "I cooked it for you first."

Trying to keep a straight face I nodded and took a nibble. Gross. The heart meat was tough and chewy, so I set it aside quietly, hoping that people would leave me alone.

Of course, that was wishful thinking.

Every few seconds they offered me some dish or other, yucca cakes, roasted jackrabbit, deer, berries and wild cactus fruit until I was ready to burst. The sky was filled with stars, a nearly full moon bathing everything in bluish light.

For the first time, I felt comfortable being here. I'd done something good, something important. And now that I was more at ease, I was going to leave. Could it get any more stupid?

Nobody forces you to go, my mind griped. *You may die tomorrow.* Yet, I couldn't stay. The memories of my modern-day life were too strong. I wanted to see my mother. Even my father was pretty okay if you ignored the girlfriend. There was Jimmy, school and…

The damn game! It was all Dr. Stuler's fault. Why did the man think this was a great invention when you just about died every time? It was ludicrous. I'd never play again. Not ever. *If* I made it back.

"I will miss you," Ela said through the haze of my thoughts.

"You've got no idea how much I'll miss *you*," I said. The fires were burning low, the few remaining villagers murmuring or humming quietly. I placed a hand on Ela's forearm, conscious how the others may react. Nobody seemed to notice. Finally, I squeezed her fingers. "I want to stay, I just can't."

"I understand," Ela said. "You need to find your People. Just like I did."

I looked into her dark eyes. Words were suddenly impossible to find. All I knew was that my heart felt as if it had been ripped apart, a piece permanently staying here with Ela and her People.

Out of the blue I began to giggle, a deep guttural sound that was close to crying. Life sucked.

I lay awake until the early morning hours. Some of the wikiups had been finished but mine wasn't one of them. I slept beneath the pelt of a bison, my body warm and my cheeks icy. Nothing moved, not even a twig snapped in the woods. I'd been scared before, but this was different. Tomorrow night, I'd be alone…lying in some chunk of wilderness among bears, wolves and cougars—not to mention the human sort of animal.

"You must wake," Ela said, jostling my shoulder.

I squinted to chase away the fog in my brain. The morning sky was a bright blue. Perfect travel weather, hah.

Clearing my throat I asked, "What time is it?"

"Time to begin your journey. Grandmother says it is best to face challenges early."

Reluctantly I crawled out of my furs. I felt grumpy. What did Grandmother know? Why couldn't she let me sleep in?

"I'll be ready in a few minutes."

I headed to the creek, peed behind a tree and washed my face. I caught my reflection on the pooling water near the stream's edge. My hair had grown. I looked older, thinner and very tanned. I'd been in the game at least…it had to be seven weeks. It seemed like a year.

Grandmother obviously knew a lot more about my worries even if she didn't understand me. My heart pounded with anxiety. I had no GPS, no compass, not even an old-fashioned paper map. I looked into the sky. I'd have to navigate with the help of the sun. But what if it was cloudy?

The village was already busy working to complete the remaining huts, clean, sew and cook. Chewing some leftovers, I strolled across the open field where Ela was strapping a woven basket, water skin and my new gun to a brown mare with a white chest.

"I guess I'm ready," I announced, taking in her long legs in the knee-length moccasins. The dreaded moment had arrived. I had to say good-bye.

Not trusting my voice I took her hand in mine. That seemed to be the signal because the entire village crowded around us. They all patted my shoulders and arms, some throwing me grave looks, others smiling.

"I'll miss you," I croaked, my throat refusing to let any other words come out.

"Where will you go?"

"Back to Fort Sumner. Might as well start there."

"I will miss you," Ela said. She rested her forehead against my chest. When she looked up again, her chocolate eyes were shiny with tears. "This is for you." I recognized the cougar's claws as she fastened the necklace around my throat. "It will keep you safe."

"But I have nothing for you," I said.

"You gave me my brother." Her smile was warm and enveloped me like a hug.

You've got it all wrong, I wanted to scream. Instead, I abruptly let go and bowed toward Grandmother, gripping the horse's reins. While I was trying to arrange myself on a saddle-less horse, I noticed two of Kuruk's hunting buddies mount up. Their movements were fluid and effortless. Compared to them I had to look like some crude joke.

I put some heel into the horse's flank and to my great relief it began to move.

"They will take you to the big river," Ela said, walking next to me. "It was Kuruk's idea."

Kuruk. I smacked my forehead. Without a word I slid off the horse and marched to Kuruk's bed. The young Indian was awake, his eyes focused.

"You feel better," I said.

"You saved me." Kuruk's voice was low, but clear. "We're brothers now."

Seeing the kid lying there all helpless made me swallow another lump. "Yeah, I'll miss your grumpy face." I thumped Kuruk's shoulder.

"May Ussen protect you."

"You take care of your sister, okay?" I cleared my throat. I'd better go before I lost it completely.

"I won't forget you," Kuruk yelled after me.

"I won't forget you either," I mumbled. Without looking at anyone, I climbed on the horse a second time, thankful she was docile.

As I rode off, the villagers watched, each of them shouting something. The two boys rode behind me until we reached the end of the clearing. I fought the urge to turn around.

Giving in, I twisted carefully. Falling off was not an option.

Ela stood near Grandmother's hut, one hand shading her eyes, the other one raised with an open palm. I was too far to see her face clearly, but I knew she was crying. I coughed to make the lump in my throat disappear, but it refused. Instead I angrily wiped my eyes and rammed my heels into the horse's flanks.

As the village disappeared from sight, the two boys took the lead.

CHAPTER TWENTY-THREE

The Rio Grande sparkled in the evening sun, the wind adding ripples. The river seemed higher and faster than when I'd crossed with Wade and the Irish.

We'd made it here in three days, following an invisible trail beneath sharp cliffs, across gravelly hillsides and plains, through pine forests and across dry streambeds. The Indian boys rarely spoke. One of them, a skinny guy with a long hooked nose, took off to hunt twice, returning each time with a jackrabbit. I was amazed how the kid knew where we were or what direction to travel. To me everything looked the same: an alien wilderness ready to swallow me.

With every mile I was more thankful for Kuruk's friends. Alone, I would've simply walked in a circle and died of hunger.

Twice we saw mining camps in the distance, but the Indians stayed away and I was not going to argue. I doubted Wade and the Irish would hang out in such a camp for long. Newcomers weren't welcome and the stolen gold had to be exchanged for dollars in a town. The question was which town.

I tried remembering when I'd arrived at Ela's village. The snakebite had put me in some coma, but I estimated I'd lived with them for at least two or three weeks. That made about six or seven weeks altogether. Wade and the Irish could feasibly be anywhere. My heart sank imagining me riding from town to town searching for the thugs and my knife. Without it I'd never go home.

I jerked back to reality when the two Indian boys said

something. As usual I didn't understand, though it was clear they were ready to turn back. Without me they'd be three times as fast. I nodded but before I mumbled thank you they'd disappeared silently as ghosts.

I was alone.

Glancing at the murky expanse of the river, I decided to take a break. I needed all my wits to make it across. Who knew what lurked below the surface?

Discouraged I walked the horse into the shade of an ancient cottonwood. Here I'd been on my own for five minutes and I already felt unfit for this place. In a way it was worse than the Middle Ages. At least then there'd been people to turn to. Bero, Juliana, Knight Werner, even Luanda had been close.

This place was different. The sheer expanse of the sky, the country so huge and empty were hard to comprehend. I was as insignificant as an ant. One wrong move and I'd hurt myself or get hurt. Dangers seemed to lurk everywhere and the feeling of dread grew steadily until I was sick to my stomach.

To distract myself I munched a piece of dry meat and a few pine nuts. I had to pull myself together before I'd lose it and turn back.

Back where?

With a pang I realized that I had no way of returning to Ela's place. I was a blind man in a vast land, totally unequipped for Wild West living.

"Quit your whining and get on with it," I mumbled, squinting across the glare of the water. The land was flat on the other side and then rose in a sequence of mountains. Fort Sumner was somewhere east and north. Hopefully the Mexican still had my sweater. If I didn't find the men I'd continue to Santa Fe. The two of them had to be somewhere.

Too bad I didn't have my phone to show around photos. Still, the men were hard to forget: Wade with his cruel eyes and matching mouth, the leather coat and nasty temper. The Irish, a head shorter with green eyes and a raspy voice. By now, he had to be coughing up a storm, courtesy of Narsimha. I smiled grimly.

Absentmindedly I fingered the tiny pouch that hung around my neck—a gift from Grandmother. A few small gold nuggets, pieces of dried cactus and sage hid inside. The plants were for protection, Ela had translated, to keep my vision clear and my heart strong. I sighed. I needed plenty of both. As I watched the river and listened to the chirps of some bird above me, the raw beauty of the place took my breath away.

I stood unmoving.

It was easier to do nothing, lose myself in this land and *avoid* failing at this incredibly stupid game than to get up and risk everything. It hit me that I'd just left everyone behind who was on my side. Just like I'd left my parents—they were on another planet.

I'd left them because I was mad over stupid stuff. My dad leaving us, my mom working too much. I still remember when my dad came to my room. We'd just moved to Germany with the Army, boxes were stacked everywhere.

"I've got to go away," he'd said.

"Away?" I'd thought he meant go on a mission with the Army. The way he did several times a year.

My dad nodded. "Your mom and I…" He cleared his throat. "It's difficult to explain. You'll be moving near your aunt."

I'd stayed in my room until the next morning when my mom showed up with breakfast. Her eyes were puffy and I knew she'd been crying. That was when I'd sworn never to forgive my dad.

Now all I wanted was to be near him…them. Gaming was a perfect escape, kind of like a dream. Kind of like wishing I'd get my home back…the way it used to be.

I sat frozen, my mind a black hole filled with desperation.

The sun stood low in the west when I straightened my aching legs. I wasn't used to riding for days on end and my thighs cramped painfully. Not to mention my butt which felt like I'd been sitting on a bed of nails.

I had to cross the river before nightfall. Checking that basket and rifle were secure, I led the horse toward the bank. The water rushed past uncaring. I mounted and stroked the mare's neck before squeezing its flanks to urge it forward.

I'd gotten much better at riding, but this was altogether different. The horse was afraid. It snorted and slobbered as the river got deeper. I leaned forward and made myself as light as possible.

"Come on. You can do it, Frank," I said aloud. Though it was a mare, it somehow seemed right it should have a name when we were venturing through this hellish country. "Just a little farther."

Frank swam with ears twitching. I held on. The river looked

black toward the middle—and fast with miniature white caps. My ears were filled with the sound of gurgling water, Frank's labored breathing and my own gasps. If anybody was watching from shore, I'd make an excellent target.

"Good job," I repeated over and over, rubbing the hairy tuft between Frank's ears.

Out of the corner of my eyes I saw a tree trunk barreling down on us. It was huge, roots still attached. To my horror it was tilting now, the tip moving into the stream as if it wanted to skewer Frank.

"Faster," I screamed. There was no way to go back.

The log was ten feet away. "Come on."

Just when it looked as if the log was going to spear us, the root got stuck on something and the tip of the trunk swung around, missing my head by a foot. It went so fast that I had no time to act or get out of the way.

The realization of having avoided sure death made me gasp. Frank was worse. I wondered if she'd sensed the log coming at us. She was wheezing and I worried we'd go under any second. The shore was getting closer way too slowly. How long had we been in the river?

Without warning, Frank rose from the water and dragged us onto the shore. Her eyes still rolled and she showed her teeth sucking air. We were more than two hundred yards downstream.

"Can you go on a few more feet? I don't like these tall grasses. They're probably full of snakes or Indians or Wade," I panted, patting Frank's neck.

We trudged on, a sodden mess of travelers.

At last the grasses thinned, giving way to a gently rising land of sagebrush, pasture and gnarly trees. I tied Frank to a thicket of bright green shrubs, what looked like a decent meal for the horse.

The sun had dipped below the mountain and it was turning immediately cool. My Indian guides had made small cook fires to fix the meat. Tonight there would be no fire. My matches were wet and though I'd seen every episode of *Dual Survival* and countless techniques of starting fires I wouldn't have a chance. *Cody Lundeen* had said during every show that fire making was an art. I believed him and I sure didn't have the energy. The way I felt I wouldn't have been able to start one with lighter fluid.

Instead I broke off a limb and brushed the sandy ground,

trying to warn off any creepy bugs. I'd seen scorpions in the desert. After the snake attack I was in no mood for another bite.

I rung out my wet pants and shirt, put them back on and crawled beneath the bush. The rolled-up buffalo hide Ela had sent along was nearly dry despite being half submerged in the river.

The light was fading quickly now. Over the din of a cricket concert, I heard rustling from the direction of the water. My hand patted the cold metal of the rifle. It meant to be reassuring, but all I felt was anxiety.

I awoke with a start. It was dawn. Frank stood nearby nibbling sagebrush.

"Time for breakfast?" I said, patting her on the rump. I rummaged through my supplies, selecting a banana yucca cake and a handful of dried blueberries. I thought ruefully about breakfasts at home: fresh roles with butter and blackberry jam or some of that delicious smoked ham—German butchers were amazing—and a big cup of coffee with cream.

Keep on dreaming. *You won't ever eat that again unless you find Wade.*

Chewing slowly, I unrolled the piece of deer leather, Kuruk's friends had prepared for me. It was a primitive map, showing the Black Range and its neighboring mountains, the Rio Grande and the landscape to the east: hills, mountains and a bunch of desert.

That's where it became tricky. There were no villages nearby and I'd easily ride past the town. For now I'd travel northeast and find a path between two mountain ranges. If all went well I'd be in Fort Sumner in three days.

Scanning the area one last time, I mounted and headed east. Cacti dotted the ground like huge spiky fingers. The heat intensified. I'd forgotten how hot and relentless the sun hammered this region. I pulled my hat low, keeping Frank at a slow trot. When the sun was overhead, we stopped in the shade of a boulder, the size of my house at home.

I drank only a few sips, well aware the water skin would not last much longer in this heat. Which was another problem because nobody lived long without water. I'd have to find some soon. I chewed a piece of honeycomb for energy and closed my eyes.

When I awoke I knew I'd slept too long. The air had a cool edge to it, the sun stood well in the west. Frank was busy munching some of the hard grass covering the ground.

"Damn," I said mounting Frank. "Why didn't you wake me?"

Frank hung her head low and trotted off. I heard and saw no one. It was just as well. Unless they were settlers, they were most likely thieves or bandits looking for an easy score. Every so often, I massaged the neck of the rifle. I should probably hunt something. My provisions were low and I'd be out by tomorrow.

But hunting was a skill and Ela had never had a chance to show me. Besides I wasn't sure how good she was in the first place. As far as I knew boys were taught to hunt while girls stayed in the village to do everything else. Heck, I couldn't even do a snare. Worse was that I needed water soon. For me and Frank. And there was no creek, river or lake in sight. Well, there were riverbeds, but they contained nothing but rocks.

During my hike with Grace we'd come within a hair's width of dying. It seemed like a hundred years ago. Behind me a bunch of grayish clouds towered on the horizon. I heard rumbling. Maybe I could collect rainwater. But the clouds remained stubbornly farther west.

And I was riding in the opposite direction.

Drinking the last of the water, I camped on a low-rising hill. From here, I had a good view of the surrounding land. To my right, another mountain towered high. According to the map, I'd pass it on the left and head somewhat northeast tomorrow.

A much taller range waited ahead. It'd be the last of the mountains before I'd hit flat country. As I got closer I realized that the mountain range was much taller and massive than I'd expected…or remembered. I licked my lips which had cracked and blistered in the heat. There had to be water up there.

Despite Wade and the Irish in the group, it had been easy to follow Ela. She knew where to go. Now I had to decide everything alone. What if I made the wrong decision, took a wrong turn?

At first I'd somewhat enjoyed being alone. The Indian settlement's constant companionship had been irritating at times. Especially after they'd seen me with Ela, every villager wanted to make sure Ela kept her virtue and one Indian or another hovered nearby. Now I was having trouble being alone. Frank was a great listener, but she was a mare of few words.

Ahead, the path hinted left and right, the ground rocky with pebbles strewn across.

"Which way should we go, Frank?" I asked, patting the horse on the neck. Both trails pointed higher and disappeared around the next bend. I chose left.

The trail grew steeper. A sheer wall towered to my right, a drop-off of a hundred fifty feet and growing on my left. Rocks crumbled as Frank searched for footing. At last, I dismounted and walked, pulling Frank behind me. My legs ached with fatigue, but my throat was worse. I'd need water very soon or I'd perish.

To my frustration, our progress was more than slow and no matter how I listened, I heard nothing that sounded like water, not even a drip or a gurgle. Instead the wind howled between the rocks like the first night in the game.

By early afternoon, I was desperate. I needed something to drink—nothing else mattered.

There was none. Just barren rocks, covered by scraggly plants. What looked like riverbeds or creeks was dry. I remembered the aloe, but up here I couldn't find any. There'd been some plants near the river, but of course I'd been too anxious to move ahead. Nightfall came even quicker, the sun not reaching into the narrow valley. I decided to try a fire beneath a shallow cliff overhang.

Rolled into the pelt, I sat chewing the last yucca cake. Tomorrow I'd have to find water or else. And I needed to hunt.

Despite my two-day journey, I hadn't seen anything but a few birds. I knew I was way noisier than the Indians. I'd grown up with grocery and convenience stores, bottled drinks and packaged meat. Why hadn't I asked Ela to teach me how to trap things? *Because you were too busy ogling her cute behind*, my mind sneered. Besides, I'd have taken years to learn.

Maybe Kuruk was dead by now and Ela hated me for killing her brother. I sighed.

The lack of water was making me dizzy. I fell into uneasy sleep, dreaming of wolves with glowing red eyes. They were howling up a storm. Frank whinnied, her hooves nervously treading along our path.

And suddenly I knew I wasn't in a dream at all.

A feeling of panic crept up my spine as I scrambled to sit. The wind had increased and the indentation in the rock face offered little protection. My meager fire was long gone. In the endless sky, heavy clouds rushed past a crescent moon. There: the howling again. It came from my right up the hill.

Tethered on a scraggly bush a few feet away, Frank answered with a bay.

"Shsh." I jumped up and gripped my rifle. Rocks dislodged and rumbled over the edge of the trail. The moon had moved behind a cloud, turning everything pitch black. Another howl. Closer.

A branch snapped, and with a terrifying bay, Frank disappeared down the path, the clip clop of his feet fading into the distance.

"Frank?" I screamed, but there was no time to worry about the horse. The next howl was so close that I jumped up and clutched my rifle to my chest. Had the stone ledge not been behind me, I would've fallen because my legs had turned to pudding.

Then came a second and third howl. The wolf pack was closing in. Trying to ignore my shaking hands I checked my rifle. But what good did it do if you couldn't see? The cloud cover remained thick. Nothing but inky blackness. The wolves just had to follow their noses to a tasty meal.

All I could do now was to keep my back against the rock. Why hadn't I kept the fire going? A few burning logs would've helped keep them away. I held a shaky arm out to see where the coals had been. There was still some heat. All I needed was more wood.

Haha, very funny, Max. *Why don't you go out there and collect some while the wolves are tearing you to pieces?*

I gripped my rifle tighter and waited, training my ears to shut out the wailing wind. I was in a nightmare. Except it was real.

The snarl came so sudden and close that I almost dropped the gun.

"Leave me alone," I yelled at the top of my lungs. I'd had no idea how shrill my voice could be.

More growling, this time from the left. Then another straight ahead. I was surrounded. I squeezed the rifle so tightly, it felt as if I could dent it. It was all different when you couldn't adjust your feet… aim at an invisible enemy. *Close your eyes and see the target*, Ela's voice whispered. *You can hear them.*

A snarl came directly from the front. A shot blasted. In the flash I saw the wolf's bared teeth before it leapt up and disappeared. Padded feet scattered.

The snarling had stopped.

I slid down the rock face and leaned back, welcoming the unyielding cold, almost glad that my shoulder throbbed from the backlash of the rifle. At least I was still here. But then I remembered Frank and realized that I'd likely never see her again. She'd either be eaten by wolves or run away fifty miles. Which left me to hike on foot across these mountains and through the desert. I'd never make it.

A wolf howled. Then another. They were close. Too close. It could only mean one thing. They were regrouping for another attack. I began to tremble all over again.

"I hate you," I screamed. "All of you. That goes for you Dr. Stuler and your brainless game."

I closed my eyes. Might as well, I couldn't see anything anyway. Ela's voice returned. *Listen to your body.* See the target in your mind. Be calm. I touched the pouch around my neck. My Chíhéne Nde friends were with me. I sighed, a rattling sound deep in my chest. Breathing right during a shot was the hardest thing.

The snarling resumed. They were coming. The soil shifted to my left… sniffing, then another growl. I pointed my gun, imagining the wolf I'd seen earlier, his shoulders at my eyelevel.

All I had to do was shoot straight. But the target was moving. It was light and limber and very hungry. It was cunning and patient. I felt my arms shake and pressed the rifle into my shoulder until it screamed.

Whether it was the pain or the terror, my mind cleared until there was nothing but the sounds in front of me. The soft tread straight ahead, a low growl to my right. Another snarl closer yet. I fired.

This time, the wolf yelped. His friends scattered. It grew quiet except for the wind. I wondered if the wolf was dead or lying close to me injured. Only the wind filled my ears. I dropped my rifle and felt around the ground. Nothing. The wolf was gone. Man, I was a lousy shot. Couldn't even kill something from three feet away.

I contemplated searching for wood, but the darkness was all engulfing. I'd more likely fall off the cliff. At least here I had the wall at my back in case the wolves returned again. Unless they'd eat their injured mate. I tried remembering wildlife shows about wolves. They'd never discussed human bait.

I was liable to use up all my bullets and after that…

Retrieving the rifle, I pulled the bison skin up to my neck and sat waiting. A few times I heard faint howling and what sounded like whinnying.

Frank.

They'd gotten my mare.

My chest tightened as I imagined the wolves jumping on Frank's back. They'd kill the only friend I had left. Without her I was doomed.

Exhaustion finally took over and I dozed off.

The first thing I noticed when I awoke was the quiet. The light of dawn barely reached across the mountain. For a moment I contemplated dozing longer when the nightmarish scenes of the wolves returned.

I jumped up. I had to find Frank. Only then did I remember that I had no water and only a handful of nuts left. Still, the horse was my friend. Without her I'd never make it. I owed it to her. Rolling up the buffalo hide, I threw it over my shoulder… and winced. The thing weighed a hundred pounds. I'd last five minutes.

Without it I'd freeze my butt off, but I had no choice. I rolled up the skin and stuffed it under the rock. Then I grabbed the rifle and headed down the path until I reached the part where the trail split.

Which way had Frank gone?

I imagined the horse racing through here in panic. She'd go straight the way we'd come. I kept walking, my steps less sure now, my head achy with dehydration. Around every bent I expected to find Frank, prepare myself for the bloody remains, the wolves had left. But each time a new vista opened up, there was nothing but wilderness. A few times I yelled for her.

All I got back was silence.

I'd read somewhere that silence can be loud when it is profound. Well, the quiet I heard screamed at me. It was total desolation and at that moment I was sure I'd never see home again. My body was giving out now, my steps staggering on the rocky ground.

I needed water…and Frank.

CHAPTER TWENTY-FOUR

To my frustration the clouds were thick, my only way to navigate thwarted. I looked up and licked my lips. Maybe it'd rain finally. I'd be lost but at least I'd have water.

"Come on, just a few drops," I whispered.

The water skin was attached to Frank's neck. Great. Even if it did rain, I'd have no way of collecting any. My wits were leaving me and I had trouble focusing my eyes. My headache morphed into a sledgehammer migraine.

It was impossible to think straight, my mind wandering as if it were a maze. I started one thought which flowed into another and another. Must find water... find Frank who carries the water skin...have to go where it rains...what if Frank has gone a different way...I'm going to die... wolves ate Frank.

Until I felt I was going crazy.

When I stumbled around a boulder, the land flattened into a grassy pasture. Not the green lawns we mow every week, but a yellowish expanse of dried grasses with an occasional shrub thrown in. I was pretty sure it was the way I'd come yesterday. I was going the wrong way... back to Ela. The mountains in the distance blurred and I no longer knew if my eyes were playing tricks or if the rain made them hazy.

Either way I'd not make it that far. Not now.

I felt sleepy and weak. I should find a bush to rest under. Maybe Frank would sniff her way to me if she was alive. I considered calling out again, but my throat had turned to dust, my eyelids heavy.

I staggered and banged my knees when I felt some strange vibration in the ground. My mind was playing tricks again. But then I swore there was movement some ways ahead. My tired brain scrambled to make my eyes focus.

Even from here I knew they were Indians. Memories of the terrible raid returned, Indians scalping and killing the settlers…the grotesque head of Grace's mother. I looked for a place to hide, but the open ground provided no cover. When I straightened and attempted to run, my legs had a mind of their own. They moved in slow motion, the Indians were on horseback.

By the sounds of it, they had discovered me anyway because the hoof pounding grew rapidly louder. I dropped to the ground so exhausted I was unable to move another step.

Remembering the rifle, I crawled behind a clump of sagebrush and attempted to aim. But by the time I trimmed the barrel, the Indians had almost reached me. Perhaps I'd squeeze off a few before they killed me. I definitely should shoot myself before they tore the skin off my head.

Instead my mind did nothing to make my limbs move. I watched the action like a visitor at a movie theater, a complete imbecile.

Two Indians rode in front, two more flanked the main body. It was a small band, no more than fifteen riders with thirty or forty extra horses. My hands trembled. Where should I start when they all moved so fast? The horses were easier but it wouldn't do me any good. Besides, I couldn't kill innocent animals.

I had ten bullets minus one for me.

Within seconds the two Indians upfront drew near. They slid off their mounts so fast that I didn't even have time to adjust my aim. Without a word, one of them grabbed my rifle while the other jumped on my back. I smelled the grease on their skin…and my fear. The knife came out of nowhere, pushing against my throat.

It was over.

"Please," I whimpered. Without knowing it, my right hand found the leather pouch on my neck.

One of the Indians shouted something. Then another spoke. I understood nothing, my attention focused on the cold metal on my neck. To my surprise the Indian straightened and pulled me to a stand, facing the riders. One of them said something and pointed at my chest.

I looked down, remembering the cougar necklace Ela had made. With shaky hands I took it off and held it high in the air.

"It's yours," I said, my voice pathetic and feeble.

Somewhere in the back of the horde, somebody chuckled. Another voice joined until the entire band of Indians was laughing. What was so funny? I stared at the warriors when I noticed something strange: a man with a brightly patterned headband, a long nose and very shiny eyes.

I knew that man. It was Kaytennae, Chief Nana's right hand.

I blinked and sure enough, Nana was right there toward the back. I lowered my necklace and stood waiting. The Indian next to me inspected the rifle. A sharp retort came from Kaytennae and the man dropped the gun.

I heard Nana say something in Apachian and Kaytennae climbed off his horse.

"You Max, Ela's friend," he said in English, walking slowly closer. He'd raised an arm, his palm open in greeting.

"Yes." I tried to figure out what was going on, but my mind was tired—the wolf attack, lack of sleep and water had taken the last bit of my brainpower.

"Ela's charm?" Kaytennae pointed at my chest again.

"Oh, this is from Grandmother."

Kaytennae said something to the group. "*Shiichoo, shiichoo*," they all yelled. I squeezed the leather pouch and nodded. I'd heard that word many times. It had to mean Grandmother.

"Why you here? Ela here?"

Why indeed. I shook my head, throwing a longing glance at the faraway mountains.

"I'm going to Fort Sumner to find someone. Last night wolves attacked me. My horse ran away. I've been looking for her and…water." I swallowed, my tongue thick in my mouth.

Kaytennae nodded and said something in Apachian.

A water skin flew my way. I grabbed it and drank greedily.

"Thanks," I managed, wiping my chin with a shirtsleeve that had seen better days.

The other two Indians had mounted their horses again except for Kaytennae who was still standing near me.

Unsure of proper etiquette, I asked "Where are you going?"

"Mescalero reservation," Kaytennae said as Nana shouted

something. "Nana says you need horse to go to Fort Sumner. We will give you horse."

Speechless I bowed toward the old chief. They'd saved my life, stitched me up, given me gifts, a horse and now Nana offered another?

"Thank you for your generosity. I don't know what to say."

"*Tł'iish.*" Nana pointed at my forearm.

I looked down and remembered the snake. "Yeah, right, the snake bite has healed well." I bowed again.

Nana nodded, his wide mouth hinting at a smile though his eyes remained grave.

"You come." Kaytennae waved at a warrior.

Where to I wanted to say, just as a horse was brought forward. It was small and looked young. I grabbed the reins and scrambled on top, trying to appear as if I'd ridden bareback lots of times.

Nana said something and Kaytennae jumped catlike on his horse.

"We find horse."

I nodded, feeling intensely grateful. Taking another sip of water, I realized that the Indians had saved my life a second time. Just because I was friends with Ela. I shook my head. I should've been dead by now. Instead I was riding with an Apache band through New Mexico. Life was crazier than an insane asylum.

Nana's warriors took off in full gallop. Within minutes they were a hundred yards ahead. Though Nana was ancient he was just as fast—unlike me who had trouble keeping up. Even with the saddle I hadn't been a good rider. But without I knew what a pathetic excuse I was, wiggling around, trying not to slide off, the horse trying to catch up and me clutching onto the reins too tightly. My insides churned from the movement, a miniature rollercoaster, jostling every bone in my body. I worried about falling, trying to adjust my butt to the constantly moving surface I was trying to cling to.

If I broke something, I'd be stuck here forever.

The Indians seemed fused to their horses. Two of them had left the group and disappeared into the foothills. Two more spread to the sides. They were now two-hundred yards ahead, entering the steepening slope, I had returned from.

Without warning the men stopped. As I hobbled closer, I caught a few curious stares from the younger warriors. They were probably thinking what a loser I was and that I rode worse than their great-grandmother.

But then I noticed one of the scouts was returning, holding a rope and behind him trotted Frank, the remains of a woven basket hanging from her neck.

"Frank." I slid off my *training* horse and hurried to take a closer look. Frank neighed, her eyes wide, dried snot around her nostrils. Patting her I mumbled, "Hey, old friend, glad you're okay." She'd had a bad night just like me.

As I handed the reins to the small horse back to a young warrior, a discussion ensued among the men. I didn't understand a word and I didn't care. I was just thrilled to have my horse back. After attaching the water skin, I slung the rifle around my back and mounted. I was starving, but I'd give it my best to keep up.

Meanwhile, Nana was quietly speaking to Kaytennae who in turn called the young warrior in charge of the horses. More talk followed and by the looks of it, the young guy didn't care for what he was told. He began to argue, but one look from Nana shut him up.

"*Goyathlay* will take you," Kaytennae said.

"Take me?" I asked.

"To the Fort Sumner."

"Why...I thought...," I started. Looking back and forth between Kaytennae and Nana, I tried ignoring Goyathlay's glares. Nana said something to Goyathlay who quickly lost the glare.

"You say you go to the Fort. Goyathlay take you so you find way," Kaytennae said, tossing a leather bag my way and holding out an arm. "*Da go Te'.*"

I nodded too shocked to answer. They were obviously not interested in taking me along, a dead weight who couldn't keep up. And instead of sending me on my greenhorn way, they were making sure I'd actually find the town. Obviously they knew a lot more about my accident-prone trip than I'd told.

I felt embarrassed, but hugely relieved at the same time. The main goal was to get to Fort Sumner in one piece. And thanks to Nana, my chances had risen considerably. I still couldn't smile but my heart was a bit lighter.

Before I had time to investigate what the bag contained, the band took off, leaving behind one sullen-looking Indian. He muttered something, shook his head and heeled his horse in the flanks. That obviously meant *keep up or I'll kick your butt.*

I strapped on the sack and took off after him. At least tried. Like with Kuruk I didn't have a chance, but Goyathlay obviously had strict instructions and waited every so often until I scrambled near.

I had a whole new appreciation for respecting your elders.

I quickly understood that I'd never have made it alone. The paths we took were hidden between boulders and thickets. Under the cloudy sky there was no way to figure out directions. I'd have died of thirst or been eaten by wolves. Deep within the mountain range, we stopped at a trickling waterfall and refilled our skins. Even that was hidden and I'd have passed straight by it. Frank drank his fill and seemed much happier to follow another animal.

By late afternoon we descended the eastern slopes and didn't stop until we were at the bottom. Goyathlay gestured for me to sit, whipped out a piece of dry meat and started chewing. I followed suit, having found jerky in my bag. It was tough and almost the consistently of leather, but it kept my gums occupied.

Without any ado, the Indian folded himself into his blanket and fell asleep. I sat, trying to decide how to sleep in freezing temperatures. I sorely missed my bison skin. Too bad, horses slept standing or I would've snuggled up to Frank.

The night was long and I woke every hour to reposition my freezing limps. It didn't help and I was wide awake before dawn. Teeth chattering, I walked behind a bush to relieve myself. When I returned, as the first light crept across the horizon, the Indian sat chewing another piece of leather and calmly watching me. The anger was gone from his face, but by the way he squinted it was clear he found me laughable and a waste of time.

On my first day in the game I'd landed in the middle of a bandit camp. Now I was about to return to the town where people had cheated and stolen from me.

"I'm ready." I nodded to the Indian and pointed at Frank. Goyathlay grumpily straightened and mounted his horse in one sweeping jump while I clambered onto mine.

As before, Goyathlay went ahead. But this time, on the flat ground, he fell into a full-out gallop. I followed the dust cloud, hoping I'd somehow get faster. The Indian was obviously quite tired of babysitting a white man. Who could blame him? I'd have felt the same, probably rolled my eyes and sworn a few choice words.

But Frank was tired and I didn't have the heart to push her harder nor did I want to fall off. Just when I'd lost sight of the Indian, I discovered him sitting on some boulder as if he belonged to the landscape.

In a way he did, of course. The Indians embraced this country, had lived with it and from it for centuries. We white intruders knew nothing of the sort, just to take and destroy.

Before us the ground slowly turned to gravel and desert. Scraggly brush and grasses took turns with reddish stone and sand. The sun was back, beating relentlessly and my water skin was shrinking fast.

The Indian didn't seem affected. He'd merely taken off his shirt and rode bare-chested.

We made it into Fort Sumner by evening. From a mile away the buildings looked fake like a bunch of randomly tossed shoeboxes.

The Indian pointed and turned his horse.

"Wait," I yelled. Goyathlay yanked his horse to a stop and looked over his shoulder. "Here, take this," I said, dangling the cougar necklace. The Indian leaned forward, his eyes on Ela's intricate beadwork. He wanted it, but something held him back. Maybe Nana wouldn't approve or Goyathlay thought he'd have to return the favor. If I remembered right, the receiver of a gift had to give a present himself. Except for certain white guys with the name Max who only received things.

The Indian shouted something and leaning low across his horse rode off. Within seconds he shrank into the distance, a tiny spec on the horizon.

Remembering my task ahead, I slowly trotted into town.

CHAPTER TWENTY-FIVE

"Come on, Frank," I said, tugging on the reins, "we better find you a place to stay. Let's see if Grace is still around."

Fort Sumner looked just as dusty and drab as last time. After leading Frank to the complimentary water trough in front of Beaver Smith's saloon, I tied her to a wooden post and went inside.

Things were just getting busy: occasional shouts erupted from a few gaming tables, here and there somebody laughed, but you could still make out the tinkling from the piano. Most tables were occupied and a few men hovered near the bar.

I hadn't exactly figured out what to do, so I slumped down at a table along the wall. Somehow I'd hoped to see Billy the Kid, but neither he nor Pete Maxwell were here tonight. I'd been gone from town more than six weeks. Maybe Grace had left and gone to San Francisco.

As if called by my thoughts, Grace appeared with a tray of dinner plates. After serving her customers, she scanned the room when her eyes lodged on me... and widened. Her mouth opened and closed. Then she marched to my table, her upper body stiff with rage.

"Hi," I said dryly.

"What're you doing here?" Grace yelled. "I thought you left me or you were dead. Now you show up weeks later like nothing happened? Go to hell."

She turned and steamrolled into the backroom before I managed to say a word. A few patrons looked at me curiously before they returned to their drinks.

"Nice to see you, too," I finally mumbled. Here I expected she'd be happy to see me. *Just goes to show your deep knowledge of girls,* the voice in my head commented. I kept sitting and waiting, but each time Grace returned she ignored me, serving drinks and plates of food and cleaning up dishes.

"I think the young man wants to order," a Mexican-looking guy with a humungous sombrero said as Grace cleared a nearby table.

"He needs to leave," she said without looking at me.

"I'm doing no such thing," I said. I'd been in a good mood when I got here, glad I'd made it this far. Now Grace was being an idiot and I was fresh out of patience.

I jumped up and grabbed her forearm.

"Leave me alone," she said, yanking in vein.

"You're going to listen first." I held onto the girl's arm. I didn't even care if it hurt a little. "Do you think you're the only one having been served a lousy deal? I left because I was kidnapped by a bunch of thugs. A snake almost killed me and I was attacked by a cougar. I've ridden hundreds of miles. It took me until now to return." I'd carefully left out the Indians.

"What seems to be the problem here?" Beaver Smith materialized next to me, fisting a revolver. "Grace?"

I let go of her, but she stayed put. "Everything is fine. I...I just had a misunderstanding with Max." She looked at me, her cheeks flushed.

"I see your friend is back." The bar owner eyeballed me through his gold-rimmed glasses.

"Yes, I'm back," I said. "And I'd love a beer and some dinner."

"I'll get it right away." Grace turned on her heels and almost sprinted into the kitchen as Beaver Smith slowly walked back to the bar mumbling and shaking his head.

I grinned. Let her feel guilty. She needed to after the way she'd acted.

"So, what happened?" she said, placing a mug of beer, water and a dinner plate in front of me a few minutes later. Then her eyes fell on my cougar necklace and the beaded leather pouch on my chest. "You have Indian company?"

"Can you take a break for a moment? I'll explain. It's a long story."

"I can't now. Tell me tonight."

I stared after her as she resumed serving the increasingly rowdy clientele. Was I supposed to go and sleep in her room? Somehow it seemed wrong now. I was older and more experienced.

I'd have to rent a place, which was probably for the best anyway. Now that I'd made it back I had to come up with a plan. And for that I needed a quiet place to think.

Unless he'd thrown it out, the Mexican had my sweater. Last time we'd met, he wanted to kill me. Now he probably wanted to kill me more because Ela had disappeared at the same time. Most likely somebody had seen us together. I'd get blamed no matter what.

And there was the not too minor problem of searching for Wade: *if* he could be found and *if* he still had the knife. It seemed ludicrous to search for a guy who was potentially hundreds of miles away in any direction. Besides, Wade wanted me dead as well.

My good mood fizzled into gloom. My odds were worse than ever.

I thought longingly of Ela and her village. Maybe I should've stayed with her. I'd finally been accepted and was learning Apachian. Ela liked me well enough to get married. Her clear dark eyes, her fierce strength had impressed me. A sigh escaped.

I'd given up the only good place to live… for what?

Around the bar the noise level had reached concert proportions. Men shouted and laughed, interrupted by the screams and giggles of the saloon's bar women. I blinked. The beer was turning my bones to lead and my mind sluggish. All I wanted to do was sleep.

I downed the water and fought my way through the bar crowd. Beaver Smith was washing glasses as I leaned over the counter.

"Can I get a room for a week or two?"

"You lost your welcome with Grace?" Smith wiped his hands on his apron, scanning a board where room keys usually hung. "Sorry, we're full. Got some miners coming through."

"Is there another place in town?"

The barman shook his head. "You might try Pete Maxwell's place. His farmhands live on site. You worked for him before, right?"

I swallowed a curse. Pete was surely pissed after waiting for me in vein. He'd had to restock all the goods I'd selected before the Irish took me prisoner. He'd gone to find the banker after hours so he could pay me. The man had to be furious.

Grace passed nearby, her cheeks flushed, her arms loaded with beer glasses and a bottle of whiskey. She threw me a curious glance and I found myself relieved she didn't stop. Asking Grace was not an option. Instead I paid the barman with one of the tiny nuggets I'd gotten from Grandmother, picked up the change, and dragged myself to the swinging door.

A few weeks ago Narsimha had sat out here, quietly drinking whiskey. As I untied Frank I wondered what they'd done with the Indian's body.

Trotting down the street, I threw an anxious glance at the bathhouse. The town was fuller than normal. Three or four rough-looking characters, their faces dark with months' beards, their clothes stained with sweat and dust, were lounging in front, apparently waiting their turn for some hot water. Though none of the men looked familiar, I pulled my hat low.

I'd only been back a few hours and was already regretting it. The Mexican wanted to shoot me, Pete was mad and surely the horse trader was angry as well. Worse, I was still no closer to getting home. I'd better come up with ideas fast, before my money and luck ran out.

The Maxwell's expansive ranch house glowed orange in the evening sun. In the adjacent orchard, a few last peaches glowed in the silvery green leaves. I wondered what to do. I'd seen the squat buildings near the river, but had no idea who lived there.

The main house looked impressive and rich with a wide entrance, dozens of windows and a white picket fence around it. I imagined being thrown from the porch. Maybe it was better to go straight to the cabins and see if some overseer would allow me to stay. I turned Frank toward the river. Despite the heat, the ground was covered in lush grasses. In the distance cattle and sheep grazed. Here and there a man could be seen walking, ropes or a pick ax on his shoulder.

One cabin stood slightly apart from the rest. It was bigger and looked well-cared for. I tied Frank to a pole and knocked.

A Latino-looking woman with a thick black braid and a broad

face opened the door.

"Yes?" she said.

"Eh, I'm looking for a place to stay," I said. "Do you—"

"Wait here." The woman disappeared. I heard her call someone inside and a man stepped onto the porch.

"Can I help you?" he asked.

I stared. It was Mr. Silva, the same guy who'd stopped by Pete's store ages ago. Apparently he'd recognized me as well. "Didn't you leave the area?" His eyes were impassive, but not unfriendly.

I decided to go for it. "I need a place to stay. Beaver Smith's place is full and I just returned after being kidnapped…anyway…"

"Kidnapped?"

I shrugged. "I'd been given a gold nugget and these gangsters figured I owned a claim."

"I heard a tale about a nugget."

"Yeah, it's true. The men stole it from me."

Silva shook his head, taking in my road-worn appearance. I had to be looking ghastly after days in the saddle and no bath.

"Looks like you're in a tight spot, kid." He moved farther onto the porch. "We only have rooms for workers. Peach picking is done, but we have some work mending fences. Also the camp cook could use an assistant."

I opened my mouth and closed it. I didn't exactly want to work all day. All I wanted was to get my stuff and leave. But how could I explain this in two minutes?

You can't ever explain where you're from. Not if you had a year to do it.

Silva had somehow interpreted my silence as a yes. "We pay a dollar a day plus room and board. Pay is once a week on Friday. I'll show you the room."

"Thank you." I scrambled after the man who wore the same blue coveralls he'd sported in the store weeks ago.

The cabin was square with a wooden plank floor and four bunk beds.

"Most of the pickers have left. You can choose any bed. Breakfast is at six a.m. The washhouse is the last building on the left." Silva turned to leave. "One more thing, no guns during work. Lose it or hide it." Silva's gaze stopped on my chest. "And get rid of those claws."

As soon as Silva left, I stuck my rifle under the mattress, hung the necklace on the bedpost and left in search for the bathhouse. The sun had disappeared and dusk was settling. Remembering Frank, I turned back toward Silva's house.

"Sorry, Frank," I mumbled unknotting the reins. "Looks like they have a nice corral over there." Frank nuzzled my ear as if she understood. "Haha, that tickles."

"You talking to horses now?" a voice said. I swiveled around. Billy the Kid, his hat dusty like his clothes, was climbing off his mount. "If it isn't the greenhorn. Didn't you leave?"

"I've got unfinished business."

"Unfinished business, eh? Sounds interesting." Billy's blue eyes looked gray in the veining light—and tired. "You staying here?"

I pointed. "In that cabin over there."

"I might stop by in a bit…if you care to tell me your tale. Got to see my sweetheart first." The careless smile was back. I wanted to ask if it was Paulita, but then I remembered the girl acting secretive at the store. Eyeing the two revolvers, I decided against it.

"Cool. I need some advice," I said instead. Now that I'd said it out loud, I knew that the Kid was just the right guy to help me deal with the bandits.

As Billy disappeared toward the orchard, I headed to the paddock and then the bathhouse. Inside were a few open stalls with drain holes. I discovered a water pump and wooden pails outside, filled two and carried them in. Then I washed myself and my clothes. Since the place was empty, I draped everything around me and snuck back to my cabin where I hung up my clothes on one of the bunks and crawled into bed. I was out in a minute.

"Hey, greenhorn."

I emerged from a fog and sat up.

"It's almost morning. I've got to leave soon." Billy slumped down on one of the beds, a coal lamp next to him. "You want to tell me what's biting you?"

"Why don't you stay?" I mumbled, rubbing his eyes.

"Isn't safe. Rumor has it Garrett is on to me."

Forgotten bits of Billy the Kid history returned to my sleep-heavy brain. Right, not Garcy, the sheriff's name was Garrett.

"Pat Garrett?" I said aloud.

A strange transformation happened on Billy's face. Like last time, the easy-go-lucky expression was replaced by an angry squint.

"You know him?"

"No, just heard of him?"

"What did you hear?"

I swallowed. I couldn't really say I knew for a fact that Pat Garrett was going to shoot Billy the Kid. It was well-recorded history though some conspiracy theorists claimed, Billy escaped and continued living in Texas under the assumed name of Brushy Bill.

"Look, if you know something, you've got to tell me." Billy sat up straighter, his right hand playing on the holster of his revolver.

"I'd heard about him earlier. Didn't he arrest you?"

Billy nodded. "I got away." The way he shifted on the bed and pulled up his legs, he didn't want to talk about it so I kept my mouth shut. "Did you get yourself in trouble?" he continued. "You don't look like a field hand or a cowboy…in fact you don't look like anyone I've ever met. Where're you from again?"

"East coast," I said, wishing I'd come up with something more authentic or at least more interesting. Somehow I liked this guy and wanted to impress him. Strange he was so unlike the descriptions I'd read.

"Right." Billy rubbed his eyes and yawned. "So you want to tell me about your adventure?"

"Yeah, you see, there are a couple of guys who stole something from me. Both have it in for me, if you know what I mean." I tried a grin which was quickly returned by the Kid.

"You kidding."

"One of them owns the bathhouse in town. I left my sweater…shirt in there, but if I go inside, he may blow me away. I helped his Indian slave girl escape."

"You've got a girl." The Kid's grin grew wider. "You sure don't seem the type."

Thanks a lot. Not that I'd ever achieve smooth operator coolness like Billy, but I'd at least kissed a few girls.

"She's far away," I said. Now that I mentioned Ela, my heart ached. "Anyway, I'm sort of screwed cause I can't go in and look for my stuff."

"Screwed?"

"Yeah, I mean I'm in a pickle…in trouble."

"Sounds like it."

"But there is something else. This bandit took my knife. He and his friend kidnapped me…us."

The smirk was back on Billy's face. "So buy a new knife."

"Impossible. I must have this one. Anyway, I was hoping you might be able to advise me on how to find them."

When Billy didn't answer, I continued. "Their names are Wade and Irish. Wade wears a leather coat, has really cold eyes and a nasty sneer on his face. The Irish has green eyes, is short and probably coughing a lot these days."

For a moment Billy closed his eyes. "Can't say I met them. But I'm not in town much. You might check with the sheriff's office. Chances are they have a warrant out—maybe even a poster. You could ask Beaver Smith. He sees a lot of folks and never forgets a face. And of course, the town stables are a good place to ask. Or the bathhouse. Though that doesn't sound like an option." Billy laughed. "You've got yourself in a bind all right. I don't quite understand why you're looking for an old shirt and can't buy yourself another knife."

"Sorry, it's personal."

The Kid stretched and headed for the door. "Well, I've got to go. It's been a busy night. How about this? You've got a gun, right?"

I nodded.

"Just march into the bathhouse and demand your shirt. That brute in there is a coward, beating up women. Show him who is boss. You might be surprised. Maybe I'll see you tonight, eh?"

"Thanks, man."

Billy shook his head. "You sure sound like nobody I know."

"Hey, Billy," I yelled after him. The Kid stopped at the door where a gray shimmer announced another day. "Be careful."

The door slammed. Billy was gone.

I closed my eyes, but sleep wouldn't come. A terrible dread was gripping me. Not about my own miserable life I was trying to figure out. No, I was sure it had to do with Billy. I tried recalling the shooting of Billy the Kid. If I remembered right, Billy had been unarmed when Garrett shot him. That was hard to believe when the Kid always wore two revolvers, not to mention carried a rifle.

I was reasonably sure it had happened here in Fort Sumner. But where and when? My ninth grade history book cover floated into my memory. The details were fuzzy. I tried remembering the movies with Billy the Kid. Of course, they were Hollywood creations, but Pete Maxwell was somehow involved.

What if I told Billy that I knew about Garrett's attack? That Garrett would shoot him like a dog. I shook my head. Billy would be suspicious. But then, didn't I have an obligation to warn him? *What if you change history*, my mind whispered. Was that a good thing? Was it even possible? I sure liked Billy who seemed popular around here. So what he was sleeping with Paulita. He was hurting no one.

I'd do the same if I had a chance. Pathetic, I hadn't even made it past kissing Ela. I sighed. This game was the worst ever. At least in the first game I'd had *some* privacy with Juliana. I sighed again, realizing that I missed both girls…and Bero.

Serves you right for making friends in a stinking computer game. But these are real people, my mind argued. Why couldn't I find cool friends like that in real life? I had Jimmy, of course, but Jimmy's dad…was another story. And none of the modern girls seemed nearly as interesting as Juliana and Ela.

I remembered what Billy had said about the Mexican. Maybe he was right. He'd been around rough guys a long time. He'd killed men. And the way he walked and talked you knew not to mess with him. I made up my mind to visit Billy and warn him.

I had to.

CHAPTER TWENTY-SIX

Sharp clangs sounded somewhere outside. That had to be the breakfast call. I leaped out of bed and yanked on my almost dry clothes. Much better. I was reasonably clean and had a place to sleep.

When I opened the door, the aroma of bacon wafted into my nose. Hurrying after it, I found ten or so men crowding around a cook fire. A burly looking guy was ladling beans onto plates as the first rays of sun washed across the camp. On a table nearby, cornbread, bacon and several pies waited. The men filed along, grabbing food and a mug of coffee. Nodding at no one in particular, I grabbed a tin plate and waited my turn.

The food was amazing, the best I'd eaten since landing in the game. I closed my eyes and chewed, going for seconds as soon as I swallowed the last bite.

Silva materialized next to me. "Ready for a busy day?"

I shoveled the remaining beans into my mouth. "Sure."

"You'll do fence repair with Rodriguez and Perez, the two fellows over there. Silva pointed at two stocky guys sitting on a bench slurping coffee. This afternoon, you'll come back and help the cook with dinner."

I nodded though I was squirming inside. Instead of finding my stuff and getting the heck out of this game, I was wasting more time. But if I walked off right now, I'd lose my room. Who knew how long I'd need it?

By afternoon I was drenched in sweat. We were rewiring and setting fence posts on the open field cross-fenced for cattle and sheep. The wires cut skin like knives and I wore heavy leather gloves, making me even hotter. The Mexicans by comparison were used to working in the heat. They chatted among themselves and though I noticed that I understood them well—no doubt courtesy of Dr. Stuler's Spanish language programming—I didn't let on that I knew what they were saying.

Not that I cared anyway. I was thinking about getting away to the bathhouse to retrieve my sweater and making inquiries about Wade. Only when I heard Billy's name come up did I tune in. I was unrolling wire from a humungous spool, first straightening the line, then cutting a piece.

"Billy wants to marry her," one of the workers said.

"Nah, Señor Pedro won't allow it," the second guy said, smashing a sledgehammer onto a fencepost.

"They say she's carrying Billy's child." The man crossed himself.

The second man halted his hammer and emphatically shook his head. "It won't happen."

"But she must get married."

"She'll marry someone else, you'll see."

"Billy won't like that." The second guy pulled out a red-checkered cloth and wiped his face.

"They won't ask him. They're rich and he's poor—like us."

I felt two pairs of eyes on me.

I'd forgotten what I was doing and hurried to retrieve the wire cutters. My mind was reeling. So it was true. Paulita was carrying Billy's child. Shreds of memory were coming back to me. They were going to get rid of Billy by tipping off Garrett.

Some friends Billy had. I shook my head. The rich always won. It was that way in the Middle Ages. It was that way in 1871 and in the twenty-first century.

In the early afternoon I stumbled back to camp. I was tired and soaked through. No matter how much water I'd sucked down I was still thirsty. The cook looked grumpy when I arrived. He had a barrel stomach, obviously tasting too much of his own food.

"You're late. Supper is in two hours. Cut up these peaches while I make the dough."

Nice to meet you, too. I eyed the basket where a hundred

yellow jackets competed for dinner. How do you cut up peaches that are half smashed with stinging insects swarming around your head? I smirked. Very carefully.

The foot long knife blade glinted as I struggled to cut and remove pits without getting stung. Then it was time to fry bacon. At least I was outside, the smoke from the fire keeping other bugs away. Frustration was making it hard to concentrate on the pan that was splattering all over the place. I'd wasted another day and though I had a bed and was going to get dinner, it seemed the least of my worries.

I wondered if the cook knew where Billy was hiding. Maybe. But the way the guy looked he wasn't going to be nice about it. When I saw Silva walking past the camp, I made up my mind and scrambled after him.

"Mr. Silva, wait a minute," I yelled.

"What can I do for you?" Silva threw a glance at my pants that were coated with a layer of dust, bacon fat and peach juice.

"I'm wondering if you know where I find Billy?" Before Silva could tell me off, I hurried on. "Billy and I talked last night and I've got to…he's helping me."

"I see."

"Please, it's really important."

Silva shot me another look as if to gauge if I posed a threat. Apparently not because he nodded over his shoulder. "Try Francisco Lobato's sheep camp down river."

The peach pie flavor from dinner still in my mouth, I hurried to my room, retrieved my rifle and saddled Frank.

"You and I are going on an adventure," I whispered. Obviously glad to do something, Frank snorted and nibbled at my collar. I mounted and headed along the Pecos River. I loved streams, but this river smelled rotten. Its water barely moved and appeared thick and slimy. Near the bank I made out a rough path.

"Hope this is right," I mumbled. "At least we won't get lost if we stay near."

Frank didn't answer and trotted on. The ranch and its outbuildings disappeared and gave way to the river and rolling hills with dried pastures and cottonwoods beyond. I wondered if I'd run into bandits out here. Maybe I should dismount and grab my rifle. Just in case.

You think you're going to survive if the likes of Wade are shooting at you, my brain mocked. I shrugged. I didn't even have a revolver. The path grew rougher, sagebrush and tough grasses dotted the darkening landscape.

It was impossible to tell how long I'd been riding. The rocky soil still retained the day's heat. I was sweating and had taken off my hat to swipe at the biting flies that swarmed us. What a miserable life this was with no showers, decent houses or refrigerators. Worse I still had no clue how the game worked and what it wanted from me. Heck, I was no longer sure if I needed my stuff back.

That was the assumption I'd made after returning from the Middle Ages because it made sense to me. But who knew what was really going on? What missions I still had to complete. Maybe I was supposed to slaughter a cow or kill a man.

Just then I heard a low whistle. It came from the hills to my right. Sure enough a few dozen sheep grazed contentedly, their wooly coats pale dots in the dusk. I left the trail and climbed toward the sheep. As I got closer I saw more sheep. A couple of burly longhaired dogs began to bark.

"You there," someone said behind me. "Raise your arms nice and slow. Ready to steal yourself some sheep?"

I lifted my hands, suddenly glad my rifle was tucked away.

"I'm looking for Billy," I shouted, wondering if I should turn around to face the man.

"What business do you have with him?"

"I'm…he and I talked last night. He's helping me."

"Helping you do what?"

Fresh fury rose up in my throat at the mocking voice. You couldn't even take a ride without being threatened.

"None of your business," I blurted.

"Let the Greenhorn go, Lobato," a familiar voice said. "What're you doing in these parts?" In the dancing light of a campfire, Billy's grin was unmistaken.

I found myself smile in return. "Wanted to see where you're hanging out."

"Hanging out?"

"Yeah, I mean…anyway I've got to talk to you."

"Sure, come and join us, we're just about to have dinner. Lobato here fixes the lousiest beans in New Mexico, but I've got something tastier."

Billy chuckled while Lobato grumbled something unintelligible. I guided Frank to follow Billy and Lobato whose face was entirely covered by a dark beard and matching curls, giving him the appearance of a shaggy bear.

"Never mind him," Billy said as I slumped down by the fire. Something smelled delicious and though I'd recently eaten, I was salivating. "Shot a couple rabbits today." He tore a piece from the roast and held it out to me.

"This is really good," I mumbled between bites of rabbit leg.

Billy shot me another grin, his face orange shadows in the glow of the fire. "So what's biting you that you have to track me down?"

My mind whirled. Here was my chance to come clean and tell Billy about the ambush. "You should get yourself a revolver, Greenhorn. Never know when you might need it."

"True, but then I'm in the company of a great outlaw who'll do the shooting for me."

Billy chuckled. "Not bad, Greenhorn. What if I turn out to be a fraud? You're way too trusting."

"That's because I'm not from around here. Where I come from people don't carry guns. Nobody shoots except the police and a few criminals."

Billy's eyes widened. "I didn't realize they don't have guns on the east coast."

"I'm not really from the east coast." I took a deep breath. "In fact, I'm not even living on this continent. I'm from Europe."

"How can you live in Europe and speak such good English."

Max sighed. "I was born in the U.S., my dad is in the Army, but I moved to Germany with my mother."

"Germany?"

"Yeah, that's where I live."

"Greenhorn, from what I can see, you're living right here in good old 1881 New Mexico. You sure you didn't get too much sun today?" There was the careless chuckle again.

"Actually no, I'm dead serious. Okay, can you try to have an open mind?"

Billy nodded, his eyes sparkling. Did it mean curiosity and mockery?

"You said yourself I sounded like nobody you knew. It's

because I'm from a different time. I was born in the late 1990's. And I know about you from history books. You're sort of a folk hero and that's why I know that Pat Garrett—"

"Now wait a minute." In a split second the Kid was on his feet. "You're telling me that you can travel through time? I'm in books?" He kicked the dirt, the air filling with dust.

I nodded. Billy looked like he was trying to work things out. Still, his right hand was on his pistol and the left wasn't far from the other gun.

At last he began to laugh, a deep belly laugh this time. "Greenhorn, I'm at sea. That's the biggest bunch of crock I've ever heard. Me in a book," he chuckled. "Billy the Kid in a book." He slumped back down and laughed some more.

I shook my head in frustration. What had the sea to do with anything? "It's really not funny," I muttered. *Get to the main point.* "The reason you're in the books is because you—"

"I'm what?" Billy's expression changed as sudden as the sting of a scorpion.

"Pat Garrett is going to kill you," I whispered.

For a moment it was quiet except for the fire crackling. In the shine of the flames the Kid's expression was grim.

"He's tried before," Billy said. "Now look, Greenhorn, I don't know what you intend, but I'm perfectly capable of taking care of myself." As if to make a point he pulled both pistols and swirled them around his forefingers before stuffing them back into their holsters.

The movement was so quick that I didn't have time to think up a reply. "You worry about your own business. In fact I think it's time you head back to town before you get lost. Did you find your shirt and knife?"

"Not yet," I said, getting up slowly.

I was irritated. Of course, Billy didn't believe me. Who in their right mind would? Still, I wanted more time. Explain it better. But there was Billy, stepping from one foot to another looking impatient. It wasn't a good idea to make him angry.

As I rode off I heard Billy mumbling, "…from a different time… in books, that's truly rich."

I shook my head. In my mind I still saw Billy's expression of incredulity as if I'd escaped from an insane asylum.

Still, I'd try again as soon as Billy was coming to see Paulita.

Beaver Smith's saloon was buzzing with activity. I pushed my way straight to the bar, not even stopping to see if Grace was there.

"I'd like a beer," I yelled in the general direction of the barkeep. When Beaver Smith placed a mug in front of me, I asked, "I'm looking for a couple of men. I think they were here about seven weeks ago. One guy is very short with green eyes and an Irish accent. They call him the Irish. Has a scar on his throat and likely coughs a lot. His friend is tall with a short leather coat. He looks really mean like he wants to kill you."

The bartender glanced at the ceiling as if Wade's foul muck was plastered up there.

"Mmmh, that sounds familiar." His gaze landed on me. "I do remember now. They asked about you. The next day they were gone. So were you."

"Any chance you've seen them since?" I asked, trying to keep my voice steady. This was it. Maybe I'd go home tonight.

The barkeeper shook his head. "Sorry, haven't seen them." He scanned the bar where a new group of cowboys had arrived. "I've got work to do."

"Just one more thing. Will you let me know if you see them? I'll pay you. I'm staying at Maxwell's camp."

Beaver Smith turned away, but I thought he'd nodded.

I took a sip of beer. Remembering how tired I'd felt yesterday, I pushed it away. I could wait here a hundred years and never see Wade again. My head low I walked out.

"Max, wait," Grace called after me.

"Oh, hi."

"Why didn't you stay last night?" She sounded breathless, her eyes more anxious than angry.

"I was too tired," I said. "And there were no rooms so I went to Maxwell's ranch."

"Oh." Grace's cheeks turned pink. She was working out the bit about me not coming to her room. "You want to meet sometime? I'm off tomorrow. We could take a walk."

I stared. Was this the same girl who'd wanted me thrown from the saloon yesterday? Who'd glared at me every chance she got. I'd never figure her out.

"Sure, except I've got a job and won't have time till evening."

She nodded, her eyes, much lighter than Ela's still on me. "I'll wait for you after dinner." Out came the first smile I'd ever seen. Sure she'd smiled at the men in the saloon. But never at me. What was the world coming to? I grinned back.

"Tomorrow then."

When I entered the town stables, the same million flies as last time greeted me, and an even more intense stink of dung. The stable owner who'd reminded me of Santa almost tripped when he recognized me.

"You lost, Boy? Last time I saw you, you reserved two horses and never picked them up. Don't have them anymore."

"I'm not looking for a horse," I said. "I wonder if you've seen two men, one short with an Irish accent and green eyes and the other tall and real mean looking. The short one should be coughing a lot."

Santa shook his head. "Never saw them. My memory isn't too good, though."

It was good enough to remember me. Somehow, by the way the man leered, I didn't trust him. Maybe he'd given away my secret about the gold nugget.

"Thanks, but no thanks," I mumbled, turning on my heels.

I mounted Frank and trotted down the street. I was back to square one—at least as far as Wade was concerned.

That left one other issue, the one I'd dreaded ever since talking to Billy last night.

CHAPTER TWENTY-SEVEN

Like last night, a few men hung around the entrance to the bathhouse, each in a state of filth and disrepair. When I approached, rifle tucked under my elbow, curious glances followed me. I was trying to imitate Clint Eastwood's walk in *Hang 'Em High*, sort of swinging in the knees and looking cool in his poncho. I was glad they didn't realize how my heart thumped in my chest and my lungs wanted to burst.

To my surprise a middle-aged woman stood behind the counter. She'd once been pretty, but her face showed the deep lines of a hard life. She was sweating in the dank room, her flushed cheeks matching her worn hands.

"Yes," she said, but when she looked up and saw my rifle, she shook her head. "We don't have anything worth stealing, young man."

"I'm not looking to steal," I said, trying to keep my voice low and forceful. If the Mexican showed up now, I'd have two people to keep in check. "I left a sweater here a few weeks ago. I'd like to pick it up."

Frowning, the woman ducked behind the counter. "This is all we have," she said, holding up several items fit for a scarecrow. "*Most* people take their clothes with them." It sounded like a reprimand. In fact, the woman reminded me of my sixth-grade math teacher who always complained how the kids nowadays acted rude.

My sweater wasn't among the pile of smelly rags. When Ela was here she'd kept everything spotless, even people's forgotten clothes. "Would it trouble you too much to check the backroom? The Mexican guy was here last time. He may know more."

"I can take care of business perfectly well, Mister." The woman sucked in her cheeks, her eyes traveling back to my rifle.

Now was the time to show strength. That's what Billy had talked about. I raised my rifle just a bit so the barrel peeked over the counter. "If you don't look, I will," I said. "Unless the Mexican is here to do it."

"He's at dinner," the woman said, her voice now a tad shrill. "And I don't have time for such nonsense."

"In that case I'll look myself."

"You can't do that." The woman threw up her arms. "Fine, I'll go."

I waited, my heart still beating wildly in my neck. Even though I wasn't robbing a bank, this was what it had to feel like. Any second, the Mexican could return. Any second, I might get shot.

Another minute passed. Then another. What if the woman had run out to get her boss? My palms were drenched as I kept clutching the gun. Laughable that I was holding up a bathhouse over an old stained sweater.

"I don't find anything that looks like a shirt," the woman said. She held a couple of raggedy towels and a vest.

"When will your boss be back?"

She shrugged and pulled out an old-fashioned watch on a silver chain. "Before ten thirty I hope."

"What time is it now?"

"Almost ten."

I turned without a word, too upset to exchange pleasantries. The game was getting the best of me. It was looking more and more like I'd be stuck for good. My talk with Billy had made me feel better. It'd been like a fresh breath of hope. I felt stronger and more daring when Billy was around.

Billy. Something just hit my memory. In front of the bathhouse a man had taken off his boots and was walking around on socks. Socks. Billy had been in socks when he'd gotten shot by Garrett.

I rushed back inside. "What day is it?"

The woman frowned again. "Why, the fourteenth."

"Fourteenth of what?"

"July, of course."

I turned on my heels, ignoring the woman's incredulous stare. The last light faded as I rode back to Maxwell's ranch. Something about that date bothered me. And there were the socks.

But my mind was whirling from dealing with the woman, threatening her like a common criminal. I'd sunken pretty low that I held up some worn-out housewife trying to make a living.

A few lights flickered in Silva's window. A horse was tethered nearby. It looked like Billy's. Had The Kid come looking for me? Probably not, especially after hearing such a tale from me. More likely he was in the orchard with Paulita. That's why he'd worn socks instead of shoes. Because he'd taken his clothes off. You didn't make love with pistols on your hips.

I smirked, wondering if I should enter the orchard to search for Billy. It was a dark night, almost no moon. I'd be liable to get shot.

"Let's go to bed," I said to Frank.

In my room I lit a lamp and was just about to hit the bathhouse for a quick rinse when the door was yanked open.

"I wondered when you'd be back," Silva said. He looked furious. "I'd kick your ass out tonight if we weren't short and if it weren't your first day."

"What happened?"

"You left without cleaning up after dinner. The assistant washes dishes and cleans the kitchen every night. The cook was ready to ring your scrawny neck."

"I didn't know," I said, not the least bit sorry I'd missed such an important duty. I casually slid my rifle under the mattress. "Honest, I had no idea. I thought—"

"Never mind what you thought. Don't let it happen again." Silva turned and slammed the door shut behind him.

What a bunch of crock. I felt mutinous. How was I supposed to know if the cook said nothing? He'd just wanted a scapegoat. Of course, I'd been distracted and tired. Obviously it meant I'd work even longer, scrubbing dishes and cleaning up the cook's pigsty, long *after* the other men had gone to the saloon.

Remembering my former task, I headed outside. I was sick of living in the Wild West. I wanted to go home so bad it hurt, angry tears running down my cheeks. I hated everything about this game.

Now and forever.

When I returned from the bathhouse, I noticed a shadow moving away from Silva's porch. "I'll be right back," someone said. It was Billy.

Maybe Billy was coming to see me which meant a chance to explain again. But the Kid disappeared around the corner, leaving his horse. I grinned. Billy was going to see his girl.

I'd just crawled into bed when I heard two booms. Sitting up straight, I immediately knew what it was. They'd shot Billy the Kid. I jumped up, fumbling for my clothes in the dark.

I'd failed him.

The anger I'd felt earlier turned to self-loathing as I hugged my knees. I'd been too much of a coward to tell Billy the whole story. Why hadn't I insisted?

Sweat began to trickle down my neck. What if that was the game's mission? I'd had ample time to warn Billy. Why hadn't I said that Garrett was going to shoot him at the Maxwell ranch? That it was best to leave.

But no, I'd been too preoccupied saving my own hide. Instead of slinking out of the sheep camp, I should've stayed my ground and explained more about the game. About my life, the way things were in the future. A sob escaped me, ringing loud in the stillness. If I'd only been a man…

By the time I made it outside, several lights dotted the camp. In front of me Silva was racing up the hill. For such a laid-back fellow he was pretty fast. I followed through the orchard, across the fence. Ahead were more lights.

In the semidarkness I made out several people on the porch, but before I got there, somebody screamed—a terrible bloodcurdling cry of sadness and fury.

"They killed my little boy," a woman cried. As I drew closer, I recognized the old Indian slave, Deluvina, jump at a tall man. "You piss-pot. You son-of-a-bitch." Tears ran down her face while several people restrained her from hitting the man.

I caught a glimpse of the bedroom beyond. On the floor lay Billy. He was in socks, a knife near his right hand. He was on his back, unmoving.

He was dead.

Silva and Pete stood on the porch, not with the relaxed stance of people talking, but the sort of frozen posture caused by shock.

Silva's eyes were shiny with tears. The short Indian woman was whimpering and glaring at the tall man whose face showed a mix of elation and pride. No doubt that this was Sheriff Pat Garrett. I'd stepped smack into the middle of one of the most famous executions of all time.

Contrary to what some reports said, Billy the Kid had no guns on him. He'd been mowed down without a chance of defending himself, a cowardly act.

"Take him to the carpenter's shop," Pete Maxwell was just saying.

"I'll watch over him." Silva wiped a tear from the corner of his eye.

"It's the Kid," someone else said. "Billy is dead. Pat Garrett shot the Kid."

I stared at the tall man with the dark mustache who stood talking to another man. I turned away, anger bubbling up my throat—anger at myself for being too chicken-shit to adequately warn Billy, anger at Garrett who'd shot Billy, and anger at Wade and the Mexican, who were keeping me from going home. Let's not forget Dr. Stuler.

I'd failed miserably at everything. It was a wonder I'd survived this long. I'd considered the Middle Ages challenging. Hah.

As I slinked back to my hut, I became more and more convinced that the game had wanted me to save Billy. Well, I'd screwed that up. Now Billy was dead. And to think that just a few hours ago I'd sat next to him in camp and told him about Pat Garrett. *Why didn't you tell him about the circumstances? Why didn't you insist? But you tried,* my mind argued. *Not hard enough.*

It was my fault. With the exception of Bero at Hanstein, Billy had been the closest to a guy friend I'd had. I'd failed him.

Other than the murderer and his helpers I was the only person in this place who'd known. My knees began to wobble so much, I had to sit down. I rubbed my thighs, but couldn't stop them from shaking.

After a while I crawled into bed and curled into a ball, hoping that sleep would stop the pain, even if just for a little while. Tomorrow I'd skip work and go straight to the Mexican. Then I'd leave town, maybe head to Santa Fe to look for Wade.

I'd never felt as lonely and lost in my life.

CHAPTER TWENTY-EIGHT

Nobody was paying attention to me at breakfast. Silva was nowhere to be seen and the men seemed subdued. I overheard one of them saying that Silva was staying with Billy for a wake and that Billy would be buried at noon today.

Even the cook had quit grumbling and silently ladled beans. They were mourning Billy. A new lump formed in my throat and I turned away quickly. What was the use of talking to anyone? What good did it do to hang around here? Pretending to use the outhouse, I slipped into my cabin to retrieve the gun. I donned the cougar necklace and patted Grandmother's pouch on my chest as I left.

Frank stood waiting and I stuck my face into her mane. "You're the only friend now."

It was way too early for the bathhouse, but I hadn't seen the sheriff yet. Billy had said the sheriff would have posters of criminals. Weird how the Kid was made out to be such a thug when in reality he was cool and friendly while Wade and the Irish were evil. At that moment I realized that Billy had reminded me of myself, a young guy, sort of lonely, trying to figure things out.

Everything was quiet as I rode onto Main Street. Not even a rooster moved as if Billy's death had laid a shroud of sorrow over the land. Fort Sumner's sheriff, a short round man with a shock of black hair, was sipping a mug of coffee when I entered.

"What can I do for you?" he asked, leaning back in search of a comfortable position.

"I'm looking for a couple of men, a short Irish guy with green eyes and a mean-looking tall man in a leather coat. Billy suggested…" my voice faltered. I cleared my throat. "I'm wondering if there is a reward out for them, because they stole my gold and kidnapped me. They probably killed people, too." Vivid images of Narsimha, bony and crumpled on his blanket, returned to me. "Maybe you've got wanted posters?"

"Stole your gold?" The sheriff put down his mug. "When was this?"

"A few weeks ago."

"Hmm, let me think." The man was annoyingly slow. I stepped from one foot to the other, rearranged my hat, moved it back and forth. "Yes, I do remember a couple of cowboys that fit the description. They were only in town for a day or two. Can't say I know them. We have no rewards out. Probably one of them rustlers living from hand to mouth."

My last shred of hope sank like an anchor in the ocean. "If you do see them again, could you leave word with Mr. Silva at the Maxwell ranch?" My gaze fell on a newspaper cutout from the *Las Vegas Gazette* that was pinned on the wall.

BILLY THE KID

$500 Reward

*I will pay $500 reward to any person or persons
who will capture William Bonny, alias The Kid, and
deliver him to any sheriff of New Mexico.
Satisfactory proofs of identity will be required.*

My eyes threatened to spill over so I quickly looked away and walked out. Garrett would be rewarded for murder. So much for justice.

"I'll be sure to let you know," the sheriff called after me.

I remounted and rode up and down Main Street which, according to the clock in Pete Maxwell's store, took me exactly three-and-a-half minutes. I rode back and forth, not really paying attention to the awakening town. I had to plan my next step, but my mind kept returning to the body on the floor.

There was nothing left of Billy the Kid. His liveliness, his strength and humor had leached away into the wooden boards. A sigh escaped me, the sound waking me from my thoughts.

I had to make things happen today because I'd surely lose my bed at the camp by this evening. Remembering Grace, I stopped in front of the saloon.

"Max." Grace waved a plate of half-eaten pancakes in front of her. "You aren't working." There was the smile again.

"Changed my mind. Actually I'm thinking of leaving today." Now that I'd said it out loud, I felt better. Doing nothing was not an option.

"Where are you going?" It sounded like a cry. "I expected…you came back…"

I looked at the girl who'd changed so much since the first time I'd seen her. I realized that she thought I'd returned for her.

"Look," I tried. "I've got to find these two men who kidnapped me. They took something I must have back."

Her eyes traveled to my chest. "Were they Indians?"

I shook my head, feeling her eyes burn into my necklace which hung like iron and chains from my neck. Its claws seemed to mock me, the memory of Ela like a sharp stitch in my side. Despite the snake bite it had been the only time I'd been reasonable happy. Grace wanted to believe all Indians were bad because her parents had been killed by Indians.

"Why didn't you warn me when Wade and the Irish arrived in town?" Grace looked at me, her eyes wide and growing. "You did know them. I was with them when the Indians attacked your wagons."

"I don't know what you're talking about."

"I'm talking about the day I disappeared. Surely, you saw the two thugs right here in the saloon."

Grace shrugged. "I was annoyed at you."

I stared. "Annoyed at me?" My voice rose. "Your anger just about cost me my life. What happened?"

"They came and asked for you, so I told them you were with that Indian girl and I—"

"Her name is Ela and she saved my life. In fact her people saved me several times over." I jumped up and smacked a fist on the table. Grace was impossible. I could've been safe and having a good time traveling with Ela *alone*. Instead I'd been set up. "I'm leaving." I straightened and smacked two dollar bills on the table. "I still owe you for the room."

"So, that's it?" she shouted. "Two dollars and you're leaving."

"That's right." She'd stabbed me in the back after I saved her life. They'd killed Billy and I'd lost my place to sleep. Life in this town was over. "I want to go home, I mean really home. For that I've got to find these men."

To my surprise Grace jumped up and headed for the stairs. "I hate you," she yelled.

I put my hat back on and walked out. Girls were impossible.

The general store's door stood ajar. Unlike last time the list in my head was short: food and ammunition.

Pete Maxwell stood behind the counter staring into space. He looked pale with gray pouches under his eyes as if he hadn't slept. He didn't move until I stopped three feet away.

"Max?" Pete cleared his throat. "Aren't you working for Silva?"

"I'm leaving town, so I need a few things." The man looked guilty and now that I thought about it, I remembered the cowboy rushing away from the store, the comments the workers had made yesterday.

It smelled a lot like Pete had tipped off Garrett just like the history book said. New fury made my throat tighten. Poor Billy hadn't fit the rich guy's plan. So they eliminated him. I wanted to punch the man. When Pete didn't answer, I fished the last two nuggets I had left from Grandmother and smacked them on the counter. "What's it worth?"

Pete grabbed the scale. "Seventy-seven dollars."

"I need ammunition for this rifle," I said in a cold voice. I knew I sounded rude, but I couldn't help myself. Strangely, Pete didn't seem to notice nor did he seem to expect an apology for having been stood up weeks ago. It was clear that Pete Maxwell was feeling guilty.

"Sure, sure, I'll get it." He rummaged beneath the counter, pulling out drawers.

I hurried through the store, collecting tins of biscuit, jerky, dry beans, salt, another water skin, a blanket and a bag to hold everything. Now that I was collecting stuff I wanted to leave as quickly as possible.

"Fifty-two dollars for the lot. Here's your change."

I nodded and stuffed the bills into my pocket. "I guess you got what you wanted," I mumbled as I turned on my heels.

Pete Maxwell didn't answer, the store quiet as a tomb when I slammed the door shut. I didn't want anything to do with this place ever again. To my frustration, I couldn't see straight, because my eyes were blurry with tears.

"Damn game," I shouted. Frank's ears twitched nervously. "Sorry buddy, I didn't mean to scare you." I loaded my goods and mounted. I had one more stop to make.

The first customers were entering the bathhouse. The haggard woman was running back and forth, filling tubs and heating water.

When she saw me approach with the rifle, she yelled, "I told you I don't have your shirt. What else do you want?"

"I need to speak with your boss."

"He's sleeping." One of the customers yelled for more water and she disappeared into one of the rooms.

I stood undecided. I was holding a nasty weapon but I sure wasn't prepared to use it. At least not shooting a person. *Nonsense,* Billy the Kid's voice mocked, *the man is a thug. Take what's yours.*

I grimaced. The Kid was right.

Just as the woman returned behind the counter, I marched past her. Yanking aside the curtain to the backroom, I was temporarily disoriented because the room was dark and stunk like old socks.

As my eyes adjusted I noticed a huge lump on a cot in the corner. The lump was snoring.

I froze. The Mexican was liable to have a weapon near him. Billy wouldn't hesitate one second. Swallowing hard, I marched to the bed and shoved the rifle barrel into the back of the sleeping man.

"Wake up."

Grunting and snorting emanated from the cot, followed by cussing. "I told you not to wake me, woman."

"I'm not your woman," I said, poking the man a second time. "I've got a question and expect you to answer. Unless you want a hole in your gut."

The threat was obviously enough to wake the man and he rolled onto his back, staring wild-eyed at me. "What do you want?" he said, his voice quivering.

"I left my sweater here a few weeks ago. It was brown and had a torn sleeve and Ela...Antonia cleaned it for me. I need it back."

"I don't have it," the Mexican said, wiping a sweaty palm

across his face.

"Where is it?"

The girl came to ask for you. She took it.

"What girl?"

"The one working at Beaver Smith's, Grace."

I stared. The fat guy appeared to tell the truth. He was breathing loudly, his eyes flitting between my hopefully stony face and the rifle.

"You sure?"

The Mexican nodded fervently. "Just ask her. You'll see."

Without comment I headed outside, ignoring the red-faced woman. Billy had been right. The guy was a wimp. That didn't stop my arms from shaking. I'd just mounted Frank when I realized I'd have to return to the saloon.

What the heck was Grace doing with my sweater? The girl was getting on my nerves. Weeks ago when I hadn't returned, she'd obviously gone to ask about me—and taken my sweater as a souvenir.

I returned to the saloon and leaped up the stairs, angry and relieved at the same time. At least I'd get one thing back and Grace wasn't nearly as dangerous to deal with as the Mexican.

Pounding on the door, I yelled, "Grace, open up, it's Max."

CHAPTER TWENTY-NINE

I heard shuffling through the closed door and just when I got the creepy feeling that something was wrong, the door flew open. Someone grabbed me by the neck and tossed me on the bed. The movement was so sudden that the rifle tore from my hand and skidded across the floor.

By the time I was able to breathe again, I was looking into the tip of a gun barrel. And at the other end stood none other than Wade. He wore a new hat and different leather coat, but the evil sneer was just the same.

"Aren't we lucky," he mocked. "Here, Gracey just told us you were on your way out of town." I glanced sideways and there was the girl lying next to me, her arms bound to the top rail. She looked ashen and her lower lip had a nasty gash.

"You're a hard man to catch," another voice said. I knew it was the Irish by the way he hunched over on the chair. That's where the similarities ended. His usually bright green eyes were fogged as if someone had pulled a curtain across them. He had lost weight and there were blood spots on his shirt. Sure enough, he started to cough. I turned the other way, my nose inches from Grace's chin.

"You going to get your claim without us?" Wade said, smacking the rifle butt into my stomach. I doubled over and fought for air. The pain was excruciating as it traveled to my feet and hands. Another shove to my back sent spasms up to my head.

Apparently, Wade was now in charge of such menial tasks as

extracting information.

"Talk kid, we don't have all day. Look Boss, he's wearing Injun jewels." Wade tucked the tip of his rifle under the cougar necklace and jerked. Beads and claws scattered across the bed. I swallowed an insult for destroying Ela's beautiful work. It was my good luck charm. Ela had said so.

My luck had obviously run out.

Billy's face drifted into my mind. *Never show them you're afraid.*

"Maybe if you wouldn't tickle me so much, I could explain things," I said aloud.

"The kid has a sense of humor," the Irish croaked. "Make it fast."

I tried to think of a good story. Obviously I didn't need to leave anymore since my objective was standing right in the room. Question was did he still have the knife? And what about the gold? If I told them the nugget had been a gift from Narsimha, they were liable to shoot me. If I said I had a claim they were going to force me to go along. No way I'd travel with them again. I had to buy time.

"You still have my knife?" I said, trying to look casual.

Wade frowned. But then he rummaged through his pocket. "You mean this? It's mine."

I sighed inwardly as I eyed my ticket home. It looked grimy, but the Swiss cross was clearly visible. That meant there was still a chance to leave this nightmare of a game. I'd have to figure out how. Quickly.

Things didn't exactly look promising. They had all the guns and I lay flat on my back. What would Billy the Kid do? Of course, The Kid would never be in a situation like this. Except that he'd just been shot, having forgotten to carry his guns. Either way Billy wouldn't be afraid.

"You looking for more gold. Wasn't that nugget enough?"

"Wade here has a nasty gambling habit." The Irish was overcome by another coughing fit. I held my breath and finally, when the coughing didn't stop, turned my face into the bed sheet.

What was *that?*

Beneath Grace's pillow lay... my sweater. She'd taken it to bed with her? What was that supposed to mean? I shot her a glance, but she was watching her tormenters. By the time I looked up again, the Irish was wiping blood from his hand.

There was still some justice in the world.

"Maybe I'll have me a piece of woman for a change," Wade said, his eyes roving over Grace, his grin more evil than ever. A tremble went through Grace. I quietly moved my hand to touch her shoulder.

"Actually, you might want to let Grace go," I said. "She's due downstairs any minute. If she doesn't show, Beaver Smith will come up here to investigate. He always carries a gun."

"But I—" Grace started. I squeezed her arm.

"He wouldn't really care what happens to me, but Grace is another matter. He'll get the sheriff."

Wade looked at the Irish who'd leaned back in his chair wheezing.

"What if she gets the sheriff once she's out?" Wade said.

"She won't do that, Grace, will you?" I winked at her, hoping she'd get the message. "After all, you could always wait for her."

"No, I promise to be quiet," Grace said. "I have to help serve lunch."

"Let her go," the Irish said. "He's the one we want."

Grumbling something, Wade untied the girl. She threw a wild-eyed glance at me and ran to the door.

"Oh, can you take care of my horse," I yelled after her. "She's in front, the one with the white patch on her chest."

Grace nodded and quickly closed the door as I took hold of the sweater. "Is it okay if I put this on? I'm cold."

"How can you be cold, boy?" Wade said. He stared out the window where the sun was baking the street below.

"I'm not feeling well." I wiped my forehead in apparent discomfort.

"Put it on." The Irish took a sip from a water skin. He looked like he'd fall off his chair any second.

I yanked on my sweater. Now I needed one more thing.

"Tell us about the gold." Wade poked the rifle into my stomach. "I'm running out of patience."

"I had some gold, but I spent it on the way. Ela and I found it near the cave like she said."

Wade and the Irish were leaning closer. "Where near the cave?" Wade said.

Just then I had an idea. "If you get me some paper I draw a map."

Only when I'd said it out loud did I realize that my plan had a terrible flaw. Once the men had the map there was no reason to let me live.

I swallowed, but the dryness in my throat spread to my tongue. Time was running out. *Think,* I scolded myself. *You've got to do something now.*

"I'll get the paper," the Irish said. "That doesn't mean we'll let you go." As he stood up, a new coughing fit overtook him. He opened the door with shaky fingers and disappeared.

"Only the two of us," Wade sneered. "Finally I can teach you a lesson."

"How about I show you another trick with the knife?" I said. I pointed at Wade's pocket. "I bet you don't know all the secret things this knife can do."

Suspicion and curiosity competed in Wade's expression. He tilted his head sideways, obviously trying to determine if I was telling the truth. I forced my face into my best innocent look. The one I used with my mom sometimes.

"Don't think you can play me, kid. I'll shoot holes into every part of your body until you look like a damn strainer."

I nodded and held out a palm. "I promise I won't do anything. You'll get it back."

Wade handed over the knife. To my horror nothing happened. I'd expected to feel the pull of the game taking me back to present day.

I massaged the knife. Still nothing. That could only mean one thing. I hadn't finished the game's missions. I started to sweat. I'd be dead within the hour.

"What're you waiting for? Show me." Wade still aimed the rifle at my stomach.

With shaking fingers I unfolded the first blade. *Come on, stupid game, why aren't you working?* I had the matchbox, wore the sweater and held the knife. What else was there? Panic crept up my spine. It was never clear what all I had to do. Stupid Dr. Stuler had refused to talk about specifics. Now I was screwed. Any minute the Irish would be back.

"That's nothing new." Wade pushed hard at my ribs. "Show me something I don't know."

"How about this one?" I unfolded the small knife. The rifle answered by drilling into my side. Gasping I unfolded the tiny file.

Wade stamped his feet. "You take me for an idiot? Give me back my knife."

"What about the scissors?"

Wade spit on the floor.

I unfolded the last tool. I was out of options. "And this?"

"I've seen that one, too." Wade stepped to the bed.

"You know what it's for?"

For the first time, Wade looked uncertain.

"Opening wine bottles." I turned the corkscrew in a twisting motion.

"What's that?" Wade said. The uncertainty in his features had turned to suspicion as the black shadow of rage was growing on his face.

When had they invented corkscrews?

"Give it back." His cheeks and forehead scarlet now, Wade swiped at the knife, but I managed to collapse the scissors and file and pulled my hand out of reach.

"How about I'll blow you to pieces right now," Wade hollered. His eyes were bulging, his evil face a mask of fury. I trembled.

Now, now. I want to go home.

The door opened as Wade threw himself on me. "Give me back my knife."

"Stop this bullshit," the Irish wheezed. His voice didn't carry and Wade continued pushing me into the mattress. He was heavy and tall and I was stuck. In desperation, I swiped at Wade's face with the open knife, the larger blade cutting into the man's cheek. Wade grunted, ramming one knee into my pubic bone. I screamed and pulled my arms overhead to smack his face. I was ready to die fighting.

"Give it to me," Wade huffed. Out of nowhere the one-foot blade of a hunting knife appeared at my throat. I froze. Wade laughed crazily. "That's a knife, kid."

The knife tip traveled along my collarbone. "What's this?" Wade yanked at the leather string of my pouch. "Got more gold in there?" With a vicious tug, he ripped the pouch from my neck.

"Get off. We'll finish him later," the Irish said just as I felt a terrible squeeze on my chest.

I was thinking that Wade had crushed my ribcage with his other knee when the room turned fuzzy. I was struggling for air, but my lungs refused to rise. Wade, blood running from his right cheek, was shouting something as the Irish's emaciated face came into view, yelling and waving a piece of paper.

I couldn't understand them, like my ears were filled with fluid, a gurgling sound mixed with the rushing of a storm. I tried moving, but the pain intensified and I lay still, a paralyzed blob ready for slaughter.

I was passing out. Wade had finally gotten the best of me.

I closed my eyes as the room dissolved into blackness.

CHAPTER THIRTY

I blinked. Light shone behind my eyelids. I wasn't dead after all. The Irish probably wanted his map first. When I opened my eyes I gasped. Outside my window a lawn mower droned. Birds sang and the smells of barbecued meat hung in the air. I sat up. I was lying on my bed, still holding the knife with the two open blades stained with blood. Disgusted I wiped them on my sweater.

I was home!

I swallowed against the tightening lump in my throat as the realization of having escaped Wade and certain death hit me.

A knock on the door made me jump. "You ready for dinner? We can talk some more." Even muffled through the door, I detected the concern in my mom's voice. I swallowed away another lump. All I wanted was to rip open the door and hug her.

Right now that would be a mistake.

"Will be there in a minute," I said, surprised how normal my voice sounded. It was the only normal thing about me because when I sat up I almost shouted.

The reflection in the mirror across the room was frightening. Blood splattered my face. My skin was smudged with grime, my clothes in tatters. A red welt bloomed on my neck where Wade had ripped away Ela's necklace.

Better get in the shower or my mother will have a heart attack.

I carefully opened the door and scanned the hallway—empty. Dishes rattled in the kitchen and the delicious smell made my stomach growl. I tiptoed into the bathroom and locked the door.

Tearing off my clothes, I stepped into the shower. Even after the Middle Ages I hadn't felt this good. Hot water and as much soap as I wanted.

The mirror was foggy and I wiped it dry. A pair of green-blue eyes stared back. They were older and filled with something new. My face was much more tanned than I remembered and somewhat thinner.

Back in my room I stuffed my clothes in an old plastic sack under the bed. They stunk worse than the sewage plant near Heiligenstadt. I'd throw them out as soon as I had a chance. My mother would be curious so I'd have to do it after she went to work.

Putting on a collared polo shirt and jeans I stepped into the kitchen. My mother stood by the window, her eyes far away.

"Mom?"

"I was thinking maybe we could book…" The smile on her face froze as she focused on me.

"What's wrong?" I asked.

My mother shook her head. "What happened to your face?"

"My face."

"Yes, I can't remember you being so tanned." My mom stepped closer and I fought the urge to hug her. "You aren't going to one of those tanning salons to ruin your skin?"

"No way," I said, trying to look innocent. "What were you saying about booking?"

My mom turned back to the stove, swiping a hand over her eyes. "Oh, I meant one of those last-minute trips." She paused. "You sure you're telling me everything?"

There was uncertainty in her voice like she wasn't trusting her own senses. I wanted nothing more than to fill her in, tell her she wasn't imagining things or not remembering her own son's looks. But I couldn't do it. At least not yet. She'd never believe me anyway.

"I don't mind staying home," I said aloud, trying to recall my last conversation with her. More than seven weeks had passed and my head was filled with memories of Ela and Wade and Billy.

To my surprise my face refused to smile. Instead I felt tears in my eyes. And it had nothing to do with vacation. In fact, right now, I didn't care if I ever went on a trip again.

"But you're crying." My mother hurried in for a hug. "We'll

find something nice to do."

I shook my head against her shoulder, drinking in her nearness and the feeling that I was safe at last. "It's fine."

"You know I don't like disappointing you," she mumbled into my collarbone.

When I didn't answer, she scanned my face. "What's wrong? You lost weight again, I can see it in your..."

I shrugged.

"Your hair is getting so long. And you've grown, too. Your tan...I swear this job makes me a terrible mother. Why don't I notice these things?" She turned toward the table.

"You're a great mom," I said, reluctantly letting her go. How could I explain that I'd just spent seven weeks in 1881? Better forget about it. "Mmmh, is that bean soup?"

My mom threw me a curious glance. "I didn't realize you liked it that well."

"Love it." I hurried to help dish up and bit into a slice of fresh bread. German bread was my favorite.

The room sank into silence while I inhaled dinner. I couldn't help but close my eyes because the flavor of the smoked brats and bacon were out of this world. Bacon. The memories of Maxwell's camp returned. Billy was dead and I'd never see Ela again. When I opened my eyes, my mother was staring at me, her forehead scrunched with worry.

"What is happening to you? Maybe we need to get a counselor."

I vehemently shook my head. "I'm all right. It's been a hard day and I'm pretty tired."

She nodded, but I knew she didn't believe me. "I'll speak with your father this weekend."

"Did you know he's getting married?"

She nodded again.

"And you're okay with that?"

"Your father is a grown man and he can do what he wants." She abruptly stood and carried her bowl to the sink.

"I know but he's marrying some stupid chick half his age. I mean she—"

"How about we move in the living room and talk about another trip? What do you think about Croatia or Italy? Or we could go to France." She turned to face me.

"Can I have more soup?"

"Of course." She hurried to refill my plate. I followed her movements, the realization that I was safe hitting me fully. Something warm flowed through my middle and it wasn't the hot soup. How could I explain to her that I didn't want to travel, only sit here in the kitchen and enjoy her company?

"Leave room for dessert. I bought your favorite chocolate ice cream?" The smile was back, the forced kind that didn't reach the eyes.

Settling in the living room, a humungous bowl of chocolate ice cream in front of me, we discussed trips and fall schedules. Mom looked tired. To my frustration, she poured herself a glass of whiskey. I wanted to ask her why she drank all the time. I couldn't. Not now.

"Did you ever travel to New Mexico?" I said instead. "You know where Billy the Kid ran around?"

"Isn't that the outlaw who killed lots of people? Your father and I went once before you were born."

"I'm not sure how many he killed, but he was a nice guy, really." I thought how Billy had been friendly and helped me. Even more so, he'd transferred some of his strength to me. I smiled.

"You talk like you met the boy," my mother said.

I quickly inspected my bowl, trying to hide my face. "I feel like I did," I said when I was able to speak again. "Just studied it in school."

"Oh, weren't you doing World War Two?"

"We are. It's a pet project of *Herr* Hubelmann."

"I see." The room turned quiet. My mother took a sip of whiskey. "Max?"

"Yeah."

"You would tell me if something is wrong..." Her eyes met mine. "I mean seriously wrong. If you have suicidal thoughts or make yourself throw up..."

I placed my bowl on the glass end table. "Are you worried I'd kill myself?"

She nodded, her eyes shiny.

"Oh Mom, nothing could be farther from the truth. I'm actually really happy to be here—and alive." This time my smile was open.

And when I said it aloud I realized how true it was. If the

game had taught me one thing then it was how lucky I could count myself to be alive in the twenty-first century. How good I had it.

Even if Jimmy lived in a mansion and had tons of money, I didn't care. I shuddered thinking about the grimy conditions in Fort Sumner, the heat, the terrible track into the mountains, the trigger-happy men who knew no morals.

"You're acting so strangely. I can't quite put my finger on it." My mother took another sip.

I gave her my best innocent look. "How about we'll watch TV?"

"What, no gaming tonight?"

I shook my head. I'd not go near a computer any time soon.

CHAPTER THIRTY-ONE

I heard a buzzing noise. Wade was going after me. My eyes flew open as the memory of last night returned and relief flooded me. I was home…and safe.

The buzzing continued. I leaned out of bed to dig through my backpack. Jimmy had texted three times. Once last night—I'd passed out on the couch by a pathetic nine o'clock—and twice this morning.

Call me, it said. Then again, *where are you? Call me!*

I punched in a note and sauntered to the bathroom. I whistled as I peed and threw a few handfuls of water on my face. There, my phone again. This time it rang.

"Why aren't you answering?" Jimmy sounded exasperated. "I'm leaving this afternoon and my best friend is ignoring me."

"I'm not ignoring you. I was mad yesterday because my mom canceled our vacation and my dad is getting married to some twenty year-old."

"Want to talk? Come over. Father isn't back from the office yet. We probably won't even leave till evening."

I shook my head. Jimmy's parents kept strange hours. They were up when others slept and vice versa. Of course, Dr. Stuler just about never slept. At least that's what Jimmy said.

"I'll be there in thirty. Got to eat first."

My mother had left fresh baked rolls, butter and blackberry jam on the table. Right, it was Saturday and she was working until noon. I poured myself a huge glass of orange juice, stuffed my face and headed out the door with a smile.

The air smelled fresh and full of promise. I looked down the orderly street with its rock gardens and well-kept flowerbeds. No thugs lurked in the alley. I had a full belly and cold drinks any time I wanted. I began to whistle.

Jimmy grinned as he opened the door. "What happened?"

I thumped him in the shoulder and wandered down the hall. "I was busy."

"Doing what?" Jimmy slumped into his super-ergonomic gamer chair while I threw myself onto the couch. "You don't seem upset."

"Not anymore."

Jimmy stared. "I'd be livid if father canceled our vacation. Not to mention the dad thing…"

I shrugged, feeling annoyed. Everything was about Jimmy and how he could get maximum fun out of everything. "I *was* stinking mad, but that was a long time ago."

"I don't get it. You only found out last night and now…"

I shook my head and watched with glee as Jimmy's eyes grew larger.

"You played again."

I nodded.

"Your hair looks weirdly long this morning. And you've got a tan." Jimmy jumped off his chair and sagged next to me. "Tell me! You went back to see that girl…Juliana and the pig herder…what was his name—Bero? Did you meet that knight again, too?"

"None of the above. That's where I tried to go, but I ended up in 1881 New Mexico."

"You're kidding. Can't you select where you go?"

"That's what I thought. But everything went really fast… I was too pissed to pay attention. Anyway, I ended up meeting Billy the Kid."

"The outlaw? For real?"

"Yep. He was awesome and super friendly. A bit twitchy maybe, but no way he killed all those people. He helped me quite a bit." I chewed my lower lip, remembering how Billy's voice had stayed with me when I'd confronted the Mexican. How he'd whispered strength into my mind when Wade had me pinned. "He was shot right before I got away."

"Too bad you couldn't warn him." Jimmy's remark twisted

like a knife.

I remembered the dead body that looked nothing like the full-of-life Billy and my half-hearted attempts to warn him…because I'd been too chicken to insist and explain better. Just because my memory had been fuzzy didn't mean I couldn't have said more.

"… you there?" Jimmy said.

I drifted back to present day. "What?"

"What's the matter with you? I asked how long you played."

"Not sure. At least six weeks, probably seven. I got bitten by a rattlesnake and lived in an Indian village for a while. Oh, and I shot a cougar."

Jimmy leaned back and pursed his lips. "You sure you did all that?"

"I know how it sounds. But it's true. I met an Native American girl."

"Wait a minute. You had the hots for Juliana."

"I do…I did. But Ela was really cool and she looked amazing." The memory of Ela standing proud and defiant in front of the Irish and Wade made me smile.

"Did you…do it with her?"

"I would have except that the villagers watched us like hawks. Her brother about killed me when he saw us kiss."

"Not even second base?" Jimmy sounded disappointed.

I shook my head. Jimmy didn't understand a thing. "It didn't matter. It was the most amazing thing living with the Indians. I met a great Apache chief. They called him Nana. He was a thousand years old, but rode horses like a maniac. That about sums it up."

Not really. But how could I explain the terror, the heat and discomfort I'd experienced? How could I explain how it felt when you lay dying from a rattlesnake bite in some forgotten cave? Or staring into Wade's hate-filled eyes, losing the nugget and seeing Narsimha get shot.

Jimmy got up and paced the floor. "I can't believe you did all that. I mean it sounds like fun and all, but it can't be true. I mean, you've got no proof. Nothing but fantastic stories…"

I froze. Jimmy was right. I'd brought nothing back. Now that I thought about it, I hadn't traveled back until Wade ripped the cougar necklace and Grandmother's pouch off my neck. I had nothing but my own body and the items I'd brought with me into the game. Suddenly I remembered something and pulled down the collar of my shirt.

"The thug that stole my gold did this to me."

Jimmy bent low, his eyes squinting. "Wow, a couple of bruises, big deal. Still sounds more like you read a cool book. Or maybe you should go to the doctor."

"What about this?" I stuck out my hand. My forearm showed the outlines of two narrow scars. "That's the rattle snake bite. Chief Nana had the Power to heal it completely."

Jimmy's eyes narrowed. "Listen to yourself, man. That's plain crazy."

I stood up, anger heating my insides. "Fine. You don't have to believe me. Nobody will. It's in my head."

"I'm just saying—"

"Jimmy, are you packed?" Jimmy's mother's voice drifted up the hall. "Your father returned."

"Yes, Mother," Jimmy shouted at the door. And to me, "I guess we'll leave early for once."

"I'm gone already." I marched to the door, surprised I felt no envy, only a dull fury that even Jimmy didn't believe me.

"What're you going to do all this time in good old Bornhagen?" Jimmy couldn't keep the sarcasm from his voice.

I bit back a nasty comment and headed for the door. "Rest and enjoy living in a peaceful place. By the way, when you get back I'd like to talk to your father."

"I doubt he'll want to see you." Jimmy pulled his suitcase onto its rollers. "You know how he is. Always working and no time for us."

For you. Too angry to wait I hurried downstairs. Jimmy was an idiot.

"Hello Max," Dr. Stuler said when I entered the courtyard. He was stuffing *Louis Vuitton* suitcases into the trunk of his S-class Mercedes.

"Hi Dr. Stuler." I hesitated. Should I tell the man about my newest adventure? Why the heck not. "I played the game again."

Dr. Stuler's back froze above the cavernous hole of the trunk. When he turned his marble-like eyes gave nothing away. "You did?"

I nodded.

"Expert...Level Two?"

I nodded again. Amazing how the man's pupils were so tiny—

like pin pricks. "I'd like to hear about it. In my office." Producing a business card, his voice sounded forceful all of the sudden, kind of demanding. "Call my secretary—she knows my schedule." Stuler looked weirdly flushed, sort of seething like a volcano. I abruptly turned. Better leave before the man blew up.

"And Max," Dr. Stuler called after me. "I'd appreciate absolute confidentiality. Even with Jimmy."

"What about me?" Jimmy said from the front door.

"Nothing, Son. Hand me your bag." Jimmy made a face but obediently walked to the car.

I strolled down the expansive driveway. Something felt off. I couldn't put my finger on it. Stuler acted all surprised, yet to me he seemed to put up a show. And Stuler hadn't even considered asking whether I *wanted* to talk or if it was convenient to commute to Kassel. He assumed people jumped when he spoke. Jerk. *But you wanted to talk to him anyway.* Still, I had the feeling Stuler knew about my games already.

And there was Jimmy. Strange that Jimmy hadn't even played. Why not? Why was Stuler protecting his son, ignoring him…worse, talking down to him?

And why was I feeling so worried when it came to Dr. Stuler and the game? Hadn't I just lived among gunslingers and wild Indians? What could a man in a fancy suit and an expensive Mercedes do to me? Somehow I didn't care to find out.

Across the street stood a man, I'd never seen before, but I was too worked up to pay attention.

CHAPTER THIRTY-TWO

"Is something wrong with your computer?" My mom leaned against the doorframe to my room. I was lying on my bed, reading a book about Billy the Kid I'd found at the library.

"No, why?"

"I haven't seen you play all week." The worry wrinkle on her forehead was back. I mean not that I don't like you reading. You're just…different."

I jumped off the bed and embraced her. "I'm fine, Mom. What's for dinner?"

She shook her head against my shoulder. "I don't know, buddy. You don't seem to be yourself." She sighed and stepped back. "Let's make these pizza breads you like. Turn on the oven and set the table. I'll be there in a minute."

I wandered into the kitchen and fiddled with the oven knobs. Opening one of the kitchen cabinets I glanced across the window when I saw movement. On the sidewalk in front of our fenced-in yard stood the same man, I'd seen near Jimmy's house. That wasn't the weird part. What was weird was that he faced my house and stared straight into the window. I leaned over the sink for a better look.

The man's hair was dark and fell over his face. He wore a short beard and looked like his clothes were hanging in folds over his bony frame.

When I opened the window, the man quickly turned and limped off. He was definitely not well.

"Mom?"

"What is it? You were going to set the table—"

"I think you have a creep stalking you."

"What?"

"Yeah, I just saw some guy staring into our window."

My mom tugged at the freezer door. "Who would stalk a forty-year old woman?"

"Don't know, for a mom you still look pretty cute."

She shook her head. "Haha, you're too funny, Max."

"No, really. You should be careful. Predators live everywhere, even in Bornhagen." I went back to the window, but the man was nowhere to be seen. While my mom assembled a salad, I checked the entrance and back door locks. I lowered the shades in his mother's bedroom, though her window was facing the garden.

I remembered my rifle. Too bad I didn't have it close. Wade had probably stolen it. I sighed. With a pang of guilt I remembered Frank, fervently hoping Grace was going to take care of her.

Strange that nobody even knew I'd lived in the Wild West among ruthless men and Apaches. I'd thought back and forth all week whether I should tell my mom. In the end I'd concluded there was no way. As much as I loved her, I just couldn't. Like Jimmy, she'd declare me a mental case. Probably worry like crazy and send me to the doctor. No, she had enough going on.

Around ten o'clock the following day I decided to take the bus to Heiligenstadt. It was a beautiful morning with an intensely blue sky, perfect for swimming. Though the town's pool was really a spa and I was neither interested in beauty wraps, saunas nor Roman steam baths, the outside pool was a nice size with plenty of room to stretch out on the green.

Besides, I hoped to run into a few of my classmates. I surely couldn't be the only guy stuck home during summer break.

The bus stop was five minutes away—well, everything in Bornhagen was within a five-minute walk—and I was going over the contents of my sports bag when my neck began to tingle. Somebody was watching me. I quickly turned, but the street was empty except for a couple of women with shopping baskets heading my way.

I shook my head and continued to the bus stop. I was losing it. After two hair-raising adventures, small wonder I was imagining things. I showed my pass to the bus driver and headed to the back. The rear seats were perfect if you wanted to watch girls or anyone else interesting entering the bus.

Plopping down I suddenly froze. The man who'd stared at our house last night was coming around a house corner and took position near the bus stop…and waited. His head was hidden behind a sign, but I was sure it was him.

Even watching him through the window last night, I was reasonably sure I didn't know the man. Yet, there was something that struck a chord, something familiar. Heat rose to my cheeks. What if he was going after my mother once I was gone to the pool? He'd have free reign. But then why was he at the bus stop? *Maybe he wants to make sure you're gone.*

The heat in my face intensified and I pulled out my cell phone.

"Mom?"

"You know you're not supposed to call me at work unless it's an emergency," my mom said in a low tone, her business voice.

"Well, it is because…" The bus rolled forward past the sign and I spun around to get another look. The man's face was deeply lined and his eyes were staring right at me. Had I imagined it or did the guy nod? The bus gathered speed and left the village.

"Max, are you there?" My mom sounded irritated.

"Eh, yes. Remember that guy from last night? The one watching our window? I just saw him at the bus stop. I'm going to the pool. I'm worried he'll wait for you now. I'm gone and you know…"

"Oh, Max. I'll be fine. Enjoy yourself."

"I can get out at the next stop and walk back."

"Don't. I'll visit my sister this afternoon. Have a great day and I'll see you at dinnertime."

"Promise me to be careful," I said.

"I've got to go."

I swam and lazed near the pool. I saw two girls from my class and hung out with them for a while. Ordinarily I would've been shy, but after New Mexico everything seemed so easy. Still, the man's face kept appearing in my mind. I was tempted to call my mom again to check up on her.

I grimaced. Strange how the tables turned. I felt older and

more mature than a week ago. *Because you are*, the voice in my head reminded me.

"Mom?" I yelled as I unlocked the front door. It was early evening and the air was thick with grilled meats my neighbors were fixing. I raced through the house and sighed heavily when I found her in the garden, pulling weeds. "Did you see him?"

"Who?"

"The stalker." I threw down my swim bag and slumped into one of the lawn chairs.

"I didn't see anyone. Are you sure you're not imagining things. One too many computer games, perhaps?" Pulling off her gloves, my mom winked at me.

I shook my head in frustration.

"Why don't you start the grill? We'll have steaks tonight."

The following week flew by and Dr. Stuler's business card still burned in my jeans pocket. I knew he was due back any day. While Jimmy would head to some adventure camp, his father would return to his lab.

Somehow I dreaded to go, yet my anger about the game and what I'd gone through simmered constantly. I was having nightmares and though the dreams about sinister Ott had diminished, they'd been replaced by visions of Wade and a blood-sputtering Irish.

But on Thursday all that changed.

After riding my bike to *Witzenhausen* to buy groceries, a black sedan was parked around the curve from my house. Normally, I wouldn't have noticed, but the car had a *Kassel* license plate and somebody sat in the driver's seat waiting behind tinted windows. Waiting for what, I wondered. My neighbors all had driveways and garages and a strange car in the village was highly unusual. I pulled my bike around back and stuck the groceries inside, contemplating whether I should take another look when the doorbell rang.

As I tore it open I almost fell over. The thin man with the beard and the wrinkled face stood there. So close he looked even bonier. Only his brown eyes glowed brightly as if a fire smoldered inside.

For a moment I was speechless while the man obviously had similar trouble. He finally cleared his throat. "Max Anderson?"

"Who *are* you?" I closed the door to the width of a foot,

ramming my left leg against it from the inside, in case the weirdo was going to try to rush in. But the man stood there unmoving. "Look, I don't appreciate your stalking. Leave us alone or we'll call the police," I yelled, shutting the door further.

"Please, hear me out."

"Look man, I can't help you." I was about to close the door altogether, when the man said something that made me yank it wide open.

"You played the game," he mumbled. It was not a question.

"Do I know you?"

The man shook his head. "You may have seen me once, but I'm not sure now. My memory isn't what it used to be. It's… I know *you*."

I frowned. "I don't get it."

"From the game. You played *Earthrider.*"

On the street, the black sedan drove by. The thin man abruptly turned to look over his shoulder.

"Yeah, you mean the game Dr. Stuler invented?"

The man nodded, throwing another glance along the street. The vehicle had disappeared around the curve.

"It's just that…how can I explain this? Is it possible to come in?"

I hesitated. My mother's voice echoed through my head: *never talk to strangers, don't open the door and never let anyone in.*

"Sorry, I can't."

The black sedan returned from the other direction. This time it drove very slowly.

The man ducked his head. "I'm afraid I must go. Watch yourself."

"Why…"

But the man had already walked off. The black sedan stopped fifty feet down the street. Nobody got out. Remembering my groceries, I hurried back to the kitchen. If I recognized one thing, it was fear. And that man was afraid. Why had he asked me about the game? What did the guy know about it? Was the black car following him? He didn't look dangerous, more like beaten-up and sick.

I'd talk to him next time I saw him.

CHAPTER THIRTY-THREE

But the man had vanished. No matter how often I walked outside or rode the bus or my bike, the mysterious stranger was nowhere to be found. I'd fallen into a routine of going to the pool most days and spending the rest of the time at the library.

My coolest find was a book about Chief Nana, the ancient Apache, a dissertation about Nana's raid in 1881 when he'd led fifteen or so warriors on a more than three-thousand mile vengeance war across New Mexico. And the U.S. Army never managed to catch him or even capture one of the wounded—because Nana had never left anyone behind.

Not that it did him any good. He eventually ended up at the San Carlos reservation after being hunted down by Indian scouts. In one last act of defiance he fled the reservation with Geronimo in 1885 only to end up in Fort Marion, Florida and later Fort Sill. He died a very old man, feeble and nearly blind.

I was there. I was right in the middle of it. I wondered what had become of Ela. The book said the Chíhéne Nde never recovered their homeland. They were killed and scattered across reservations and military prisons. If Ela lived she'd probably gone to a reservation. I pulled up my legs on the bed and stared into nothing.

The phone startled me.

"Max Anderson?"

"Yes?"

"This is *Frau* Keitel, Dr. Stuler's assistant. He has asked to see you as soon as possible. Would tomorrow at ten o'clock be convenient?" The woman sounded like one of those digital voices void of emotion.

"Um, I guess."

"*Marbachshöhe, Johanna Wäscher Straße 108.* Tell the guard you're to see Dr. Stuler. He'll give you a pass. *Auf Wiederhören.*" The phone clicked.

I closed my mouth and tossed the phone on the bed. So much for asking questions. During the only meeting I'd had after I first played the game, Dr. Stuler had been tight-lipped and seemed only marginally interested. Something had obviously changed…to the point that Stuler had tracked me down. I wondered how Stuler knew my cell phone number.

Maybe I shouldn't go. Yet, I was curious. Despite my ordeal in both games and maybe because of it I wanted to know how things worked. How the game determined when the missions were complete? Why you landed in some random year?

I remembered the wrinkled skinny man. How could he know me from the game when I remembered none of it? Obviously the guy had to have played. Or he was crazy.

The bus to *Kassel* was crowded with people commuting to work. I sat squeezed between a gray-skinned man in a crumpled suit and a young woman with immaculate make-up, her lipstick bright red in the dullness of the morning. I wished I'd stayed in bed.

To my frustration I'd woken way early, unable to get back to sleep. The gray-skinned man left, then the young woman. I jerked out of my contemplation when somebody tapped me on the shoulder and slid into the seat next to me.

I blinked. The wrinkled man with the beard looked even worse in the bluish light of the bus. "I need to talk to you," he muttered. He was out of breath as if he'd run fast. "You're going to see Dr. Stuler."

I nodded, too shocked to say anything.

"Listen to me." The man's hands fluttered in the air. "You've got to be careful. Stuler is obsessed and will do anything—"

"Wait a minute," I shouted, "can we start from the beginning? What's your name and how do you know me?"

The man grimaced as if what he was going to say was painful. "Karl Schmidt. The reason I know you," his brown eyes bored into mine, "you saved me from certain death." The man's Adams apple bopped as he swallowed.

"How can that be? I don't remember ever seeing you."

"You'll *play* again."

"No way I'll play that evil game ever again," I yelled and jumped up. "You must be out of your mind." Some of the passengers turned to watch. I ignored them.

"Sit down before we draw more attention," Karl hissed. "Don't you understand it's dangerous?"

"Yeah, the game is dangerous all right." I squinted out the window, but didn't see anything.

Karl bent forward until his nose nearly touched my shoulder. "I don't just mean the game," he whispered. "I'm being watched. They don't want me talking to anyone who's played, especially you."

"How many players are there?"

"A dozen give or take. Many of them are dead. Well, we don't know, but they went missing."

"How do you know? You mean, Stuler killed them?"

"No." Karl impatiently shook his head. "They don't return from the game. You understand? I wouldn't have, if it hadn't been for you."

"How do you know that?"

"Think about it. You return the same second you leave to the same room where you started the game. And if you don't show, it means you're dead. You may have lived whenever wherever in the past, but the fact remains you aren't coming back to present day. Anyone watching you play would know within seconds."

Both times when I'd returned from the game, I'd landed on the bed in my room. I hadn't paid much attention to the timeframe except that my watch had stopped the first time I went to the Middle Ages. That confirmed I'd disappeared and reappeared nearly seamlessly no matter how long I stayed in the past.

"But I don't remember you," I said more quietly this time.

For a moment Karl didn't speak.

"Look, all I know is that you'll play again."

"What if I refuse?"

"It won't matter. Fact is, I wouldn't be here otherwise."

"But why me? What does Stuler want with *me*?"

Karl bent even lower, his voice a whisper. "Don't you

understand? You're a beta, a test player. Stuler selected you specifically because you're a fine gamer. He likes using Americans because he'll launch the game in the U.S. first."

"But that's crazy. You said yourself barely anyone made it back. Besides, I insisted to play. Stuler wasn't even near me."

Karl chuckled. It sounded bitter. "You think he didn't know that his son would loan you the game. He knows everything that goes on…in his house and the company. Stuler has cameras everywhere."

"You mean he planted the game with Jimmy, knowing full and well I'd…" I shook my head. It seemed preposterous, but then…Stuler knew how Jimmy and me played all the time, how we shared stuff. "That's crazy," I mumbled.

"Stuler *is* crazy," Karl said. "But you're special to him. Right now, as far as I know, you're the only one who finished level two."

"How do you know?" I was starting to sweat. "That can't be true."

"Oh, I know," Karl said, taking a deep breath. It rattled in his chest. "I worked for Stuler, in fact I *volunteered* to play. I wanted fame then. My face on Forbes magazine. Millions in the bank. That was a long time ago." He sighed.

"How can he sell a game where people die? He'd get arrested in five seconds."

"He'll make changes to the game based on your input."

"You said there were others. How many returned."

"As far as I know only five or six. One was shot full of bullets when he arrived. He died within hours. I was almost dead."

"But don't the families find out. What about all the others?"

"Remember, you simply disappear?" Karl said. "There is no body, no remains, nothing but a computer screen and some blank-looking disk. It's a case of missing persons."

I leaned back to catch my breath. The air in the bus was thick and stale. Or maybe it was the panic I felt. "What should I do?"

Karl shook his head. "You've got to be careful. I don't know what Stuler has in mind for you. Except that you're his prime test specimen. So, be on your toes."

"What if I don't go?"

"He'll *convince* you. Be sure of it."

What if Stuler was going to hurt my mother? I swallowed the worry lump away. "Can't we go to the police? I mean we tell them what happened. About Stuler's involvement, about the game and how it makes you travel to dangerous places."

"You think the police will believe us?"

I looked at the man who might as well have escaped from a mental institution or from under a bridge. And myself? I was a sixteen-year old kid from the States who'd played one too many computer games and lost his marbles. Time travel was nothing but science fiction. Great. I was screwed.

"What now?" I finally said.

"You go in there and play along," Karl said. "I'll see you in the past." Without another word he straightened and walked to the front of the bus.

"What's that supposed to mean?" I mumbled to myself.

We had reached the outskirts of Kassel. I watched Karl leave the bus and walk off, his head low, his upper body slouched forward as if leaning into a strong wind.

So Stuler was nuts and he'd used me as a guinea pig. And according to Karl Schmidt, I'd play again. That left the question where and when in the past. Why hadn't I asked? I didn't know anything about Karl and there were a million Schmidts in Germany. Not to mention Schmit, Schmitt and Schmid. I was starting to sweat again. Why was I always so stupid?

I should've asked for a phone number or Karl's address.

Industriepark Marbachshöhe sounded from the loudspeaker. I abruptly straightened and lined up behind a man in a McDonald's uniform. If it was true and I'd play again, I mused as I exited the bus, there was only one explanation.

I'd either be forced or blackmailed.

CHAPTER THIRTY-FOUR

With shaky fingers I pulled my phone from my pocket to check the GPS. My formerly clean shirt was drenched and I smelled my own sweat. The closer I got to Stuler's company, the more panicked I felt. And no matter how slowly I walked, the house numbers were counting down. My phone said 9:45. Maybe I should call my mom and tell her where I was going. If anything happened to me she'd at least know where to search.

But somehow I couldn't. She had no idea about the game and I'd need a week to explain it all. There was no time. I wanted to scream, realizing I was envious of the people walking the street. They were safe from Dr. Stuler, the maniac.

I could just not show up. Turn around and go home. But now that Stuler knew about me playing a second time he'd continue to harass me, I was sure of that. And I wanted it to be over, once and for all. No more games, no more discussions.

Do this one thing, I urged myself. After that you're free. I sighed, trying to believe it.

Ahead, the sidewalk broadened. Rosebushes bloomed in concrete planters, a stark contrast to the barbwire fence looming eight feet high. Behind it a water fountain bubbled, but the sound didn't calm my nerves. I stared at the expanse of glass and stainless steel, a six-story building where people died. Okay, technically they died somewhere in the past.

Seeing nobody behind the fence, I approached the guardhouse. I'd made up my mind, vowing I wouldn't play again.

Karl was surely mad. He looked crazy and acted all twitchy.

"I'm here to see Dr. Stuler," I said, wishing my voice would stop quaking.

"Name?" The man in the glass enclosure checked a computer screen. I noticed he wore a gun on his hip. Not too many people in Germany even owned guns. It wasn't like in the U.S. where the people were gun-crazy.

"Max Anderson."

"ID please."

I fumbled with my wallet and showed my German id. Because my mom was German and I'd been born in the States, I was automatically a dual citizen. I loved the fact I owned two passports.

"Wait here." The man made a phone call and within a minute, a second guard marched from the entrance of the building to meet me. A door buzzed and I entered the courtyard. I couldn't shake the feeling that I was locked in.

At least the woman in the lobby appeared friendlier. She shot me a smile and nodded at the guard who walked with me every step. "Sixth floor."

By the time the elevator halted, I was hyperventilating. I stuck my nose into my shirt to calm myself. No way I'd pass out in this place. *Get a grip. What would Billy the Kid do?*

The executive lobby was decked in more glass and teak. Halogen lights stretched along the ceiling, reflecting in a blinding glare on the reception desk. As the guard silently disappeared into the elevator, a woman materialized from behind the desk. She was beautiful in an artificial way. I wondered how she could breathe under all that makeup, the tight black silky blouse and an equally taut skirt.

"Willkommen bei *HisTech*, Herr Anderson," she beamed. "May I offer you a refreshment—coffee, tea, soft drink?"

"Coke, thanks," I croaked.

"Right away. Make yourself comfortable." Bubbly laughter escaped the glossed-over lips, which reminded me of Paulita's friend in Pete Maxwell's general store a thousand years ago.

"Max, glad you could make it." A man of about thirty, his hand outstretched, walked toward me. I jumped up, almost upsetting the fancy mini-coke can and shook hands. The man looked like a model with dark cropped hair and a complexion any teenager would kill for. "Please come with me. Dr. Stuler has requested a bit of paperwork. Nothing to worry about."

The door closed behind us and I found myself in a square room with gray-paneled walls and a mirror across one entire wall. A plain table and chair were the only furniture. It seemed weird to have such a tiny space in this fancy huge building…a glorified prison cell.

"Take a seat," Handsome said.

When I slid into the chair, the man produced a folder and placed it in front of me. He nodded at the wall. "Once you're done, press the button."

The door snapped shut with a measured click.

I turned to look at the call button on the doorframe. And something else high on the wall: tiny cameras on all four corners. I stared at my own reflection. Chances were that was a one-way observation mirror. Had Karl and the other test gamers been in here playing while people were watching?

I'm the guinea pig now. Wonder if the door is locked. I was tempted to go and try it, but then my curiosity about what was hidden in the folder won out. I'd check later.

Two identical sets of questionnaires waited inside, one for each game. They wanted to know where I'd been day-by-day, every detail about the people I'd met, languages spoken, what I'd done and the skills I'd used.

My stomach growled by the time I finished. I checked my cell phone. It was almost two o'clock—I'd been here nearly four hours. My phone showed no bars indicating that satellites were blocked.

The creepy feeling from earlier returned, a tingling that worked up my spine and spread through my gut. I stared at my image in the mirror, wondering if people watched from the other side. I was still tanned, my cheekbones more pronounced than I remembered. I'd definitely lost weight. But my skin was clear and my eyes shone brightly.

I jumped up and pressed the button. Nothing happened, at least as far as I could tell. I tried the door…locked. My mind began to reel. Would they shut me in here and force me to play? But seconds later the bubbly woman opened the door, a brilliant smile on her plump lips. She led me down another corridor to a teakwood entrance, the size of a garage door. She pressed a keyed lock pad and the door swung silently open.

"Dr. Stuler will be with you shortly."

I ambled into the expanse of the most modern office I'd ever seen. A dozen large monitors covered one wall. In front of it sat a table with a single screen and a fancy hard drive, the captain's chair reminding me of Captain Kirk's power seat. Two additional supersized screens occupied a fifteen-foot side table in the corner.

But the main focus was the glass desk the size of a dining table for ten. Nothing was on it except for a phone. And behind it was a floor-to-ceiling window with views of the city. More glass.

The guy sure needed a lot of light. I wondered if he had a medical issue or if there was some other reason for Stuler's need for bright rooms. Maybe he's afraid of the dark. Before I could smile I felt Stuler's pinprick pupils zoom into my face.

"Good of you to visit."

I nodded, feeling my mouth go dry. It hadn't exactly been my choice. According to Karl I'd been set up all along. And now I was stuck in the trap like a fly on sticky paper.

Suppressing a shudder I said, "I'm sort of in a hurry. My mom is—"

"Have a seat," Stuler said, waving at an arrangement of black leather. "It won't take long." I sagged into the couch while Stuler chose a single recliner. "So, you played the game a couple of times." It sounded dismissive as if Stuler were surprised that I succeeded in both games.

I nodded again.

"How did you like it?"

What a bozo question. How was I supposed to answer that? "I only played the second time because I wanted to return to see some people I'd met in the first round."

"And?"

"I ended up in an entirely different place and time. Actually that's exactly what I want to know." I leaned forward, for a moment forgetting that I was the one being interviewed. "Is there a way to select a particular year? Let's say I want to go to 1471 Bornhagen again. Could I do it?"

"We're working on it," Stuler said. "The code now is set for random years and locations."

I frowned. "What does that mean?"

"Imagine numbers from 0 through 2,000, each reflecting one of the past 2,000 years, except the order is scrambled. The numbers rotate at the rate of two per second in a pre-determined sequence. So, in theory you could pick the same year if you know when the given year ticks by."

"I still don't understand."

"Let me show you." Stuler moved to the captain's chair and punched the keyboard. On the wall the back-to-back monitors came to life. I dug deeper into the cushions. What if this was the trap Karl had talked about? Stuler wanted me to sit down. Had he set up the game to suck me away as soon as I drew near. "You won't be able to see it from a distance," Stuler said interrupting my thoughts.

I straightened and took a few steps toward the table. "I don't want to play again."

"The game transport system is disabled," Stuler said without emotion. On the giant screen, the globe was rotating slowly. "The first time around, the player always begins in his hometown. Of course, it could be ten years into the past or a thousand." He smiled. "Or in your case 1471."

I nodded, but my gaze was drawn to a pop-up window in the top right corner I'd never seen on my computer. It showed random numbers flitting by.

"These are the years," Stuler said. "And the moment you click on the globe, the year is determined by those numbers. It's brilliant."

Says who? The man was impossible. "So if I knew what order the numbers came in I'd be able to actually select the year?" I said aloud.

"In theory, yes. But as you can see, the randomization and speed make it rather difficult. And the globe goes faster with each level, which alters the location you're landing in. We're working on a simpler version.

"For players who want to return to the same place. Imagine all the historians and adventurers going back to experience any place anywhere in the world. Can you imagine what that will do for historical research?" The crazy look was back in Stuler's eyes.

"Do you have any idea how dangerous this game is?" I carefully backed up toward my couch.

"Sure it's challenging."

"Not challenging, life-threatening." My chest tightened with anger. "You have no idea. I almost died. Not just once, but a bunch of times."

"Almost, but you didn't."

"Right, because I was lucky."

"We expect many adults will be playing. That's why your experience is so important. To determine what age level is appropriate."

"That's why I'm a beta?" I couldn't keep the sarcasm from my voice.

Stuler's face turned into a mask. "Who told you that?"

"Nobody," I said, furious with myself for revealing Karl's information.

"I see." Stuler moved to his desk and punched a button on his phone. "I believe this meeting is over."

"What about the markers? How does the game determine missions?" I hurried. "Could I change history? Or can you? And why can't you take anything from the past with you?"

Ignoring me, Stuler turned off the computer and sat down behind his glass desk.

The office door opened. "You called," the plasticky receptionist said.

"Elke, please escort Mr. Anderson to the elevator."

"At once."

I followed the woman down the hall. I was half relieved when I walked past the fountain to the guard booth, but the other half was still fuming about Stuler. The man was a certified maniac. And he'd obviously flipped out when I mentioned the beta.

That was fine with me. Let Stuler know he was not going to pull any more tricks without me knowing about it. I grimaced and scanned the building.

High above on the sixth floor a man stood watching. He had green eyes hard as marbles.

CHAPTER THIRTY-FIVE

I slumped in front of my PC. It was nearly five in the afternoon and my mom would arrive soon. All the way home on the bus I'd thought about Karl. He was the key to many of my questions. My stomach cramped as I recalled my conversation with Stuler. Why had I mentioned the beta? Now Stuler knew for sure that Karl had talked.

I had put him in danger.

With shaky fingers I punched in Karl's name into the online phone book. There were seventeen private Karl Schmidt and forty-eight Karl Schmitt in Kassel. With a sigh I created an excel list and began dialing.

Most of them didn't pick up, so I left messages. "Hi, this is Max. Call me asap." I left my phone number. The ones I reached didn't sound like the Karl I knew. What if he had an unlisted number? Or lived outside Kassel?

"Your father wants to know if you need money for horseback riding this fall." My mom stood in the door to my room.

"I don't think so." Remembering my time in the saddle, I smirked. "I'm actually pretty good now."

"Maybe you should call him some time."

"Who?"

My mother sounded exasperated. "Are you even listening? I'm talking about your father."

I shrugged. I'd called my dad once after I returned from New Mexico. But even then, when I'd been so happy to be home, it had been hard to maintain a conversation.

"Dinner will be ready in fifteen minutes." I heard my mom walking off. Maybe I was turning as loony as Karl.

My phone rang. "This is Max."

"You got away." Karl sounded like he'd just run a 5K.

"Yeah, actually all they wanted was information."

"Did you see Stuler?"

"Yes, he showed me the trick with the years." Unconsciously, I rubbed my stomach where the old ache was growing. I had to come clean. "Eh, I may have said something about the beta," I stammered. "I mean, he made me so mad with his talk about the game…"

The line on the other end was silent.

"Karl?"

"I'm here. What did you say?"

"Just that I knew I was a beta." I remembered Stuler's reaction. "He broke up the meeting and refused to answer any of my questions."

"That was secret information. He'll know I told you," Karl said, his voice a quiver. "He'll want to shut me up."

"I'm sorry," I cried. "What can I do? I have so many questions." The line went quiet again. "You still there?"

"Shsh," Karl whispered. "Somebody is at the door."

"I'm *not* going to play again. Never."

"Then I wouldn't be here. I've got to—"

"Where do you live?" In the background something splintered with a crack. "Tell me your address."

"*Habichtstraße sieben*," The line went dead.

I rushed to the kitchen, trying to hide my shaking hands. Stuler had gotten Karl.

"What's the matter?" my mom asked.

"Can't eat right now. I've got to do something," I panted, checking for my wallet and phone on the way out the door. If I ran I'd still make the bus to Kassel.

Compared to this morning, the bus was nearly empty. I reviewed the GPS on my phone. Karl's place was near downtown.

It was a high-rise, well not exactly, but for German cities anything over three stories qualified. I punched the call button for K. Schmidt and waited. Nothing. According to the order of doorbells he lived on the fourth floor. When an elderly woman opened the door from the inside, I slipped into the foyer and climbed upstairs.

The hairs on the back of my neck rose when I noticed the camera along the ceiling. Karl's door was ajar. "Hello?"

I would've felt much better having my Winchester, but I had no choice. The hallway was dark, but there was light shining from under a door. I knocked. So much for a surprise. When nothing happened I opened the door. Karl's living room was sparsely furnished with an expensive-looking couch, a large oak desk and flat-screen. Papers lay strewn across the wool rug, but the place was empty. I scanned the other rooms: a single oversized bed in one, a bath and kitchen. There was no sign of Karl.

So, Stuler had caught him. Karl had been right all along.

I jumped when my phone rang.

"Where are you?" My mom sounded exasperated.

"I'll tell you when I get home. Don't worry." Remembering the meager bus service at night, I turned off my phone. I had to hurry before I'd get stuck in town and mom would kill me. Maybe Karl had left something behind, some kind of sign.

I opened the desk drawers and rifled through assorted bills. Obviously, Karl was old-fashioned and still received paper copies. I checked the bookshelf covering one entire wall. There were hundreds of volumes of science-related books, math, programming and computer technology. Nothing looked familiar or suspicious. I returned to the desk.

A photo frame showed Karl with a woman and a girl of maybe ten. He had his arm around them and looked like a different person: young, energetic and very happy. The Karl, I knew, looked twenty years older and washed-out. A two-by-three foot monthly planner covered the oak surface. Here and there appointments or notes were written in. There was nothing for today or yesterday. Later this week, Karl had made an appointment with an attorney. I wondered why.

"What are you doing here?"

I almost jumped out of my skin. A girl stood in the doorframe to Karl's living room, her arms crossed in front of her chest. She looked cute in an annoying way, her hair the color of ripe carrots, her eyes green. Right now they were spitting fire.

"Who are you?" I managed, stretching to make myself look taller.

"I should ask you the same, except I already know who you are." A shadow of smugness crossed her face. "Max Anderson, right?"

I nodded, annoyed that I couldn't think of something smart to say.

"I'm Emma."

Something clicked in the back of my brain. The girl on the photo next to Karl. Emma was his daughter.

"So how do you know me?" I said, moving away from the desk.

"Dad talked about you in great detail. After he returned he…"

To my surprise she blushed.

"I'm not playing again."

"But you will."

"No way."

Ever so quickly, Emma moved into the room and planted herself in front of me. She wasn't much of a threat because she was several inches shorter and actually pretty hot, except right now her face scrunched up with fury.

"If you didn't go back *again*, my dad wouldn't be here."

"There's got to be a mistake. I think you should worry where your dad is now."

"No mistake." Emma stubbornly chewed her upper lip. "You're going." It sounded like an order.

"You're hardly in a position to tell me what to do." I was getting furious, too. Cuteness was hardly an excuse for being a dictator.

To my surprise she shrugged. "Whatever. You're going whether I'm saying it or not." She glanced around the room. "Where *is* Dad?"

"Stuler got him."

"What makes you say that?" The angry voice was back, except now it included a tinge of fear.

"We were on the phone when Karl heard somebody at the door."

"Why would Stuler do that? Hasn't he hurt him enough?" Emma slumped into one of the leather chairs.

"Karl had been to visit me. He—"

"Why would Stuler care?" She glanced out the window where the evening sun turned everything orange.

"Stuler doesn't want Karl to talk to other players."

"You."

"Yeah."

"Because you'll rescue him."

I shook my head. Getting ready for round two. "I've played twice and nearly died a dozen times. Why in the heck would I do it again?"

Mumbling something unintelligible, Emma got up and marched to the door as if she hadn't heard me.

"Hello, anyone listening," I yelled at her back.

She turned to face me. "You of all people should know better. I don't care why you're going. Fact is you're going back and rescuing my father."

With that she hurried off and slammed the door. That had gone exceptionally well. The girl was as nuts as her father.

CHAPTER THIRTY-SIX

I lay awake daydreaming. It was after ten in the morning and though the sun blazed and the air was filled with the smells of fresh-cut grass and roses, I couldn't make myself go to the pool. I was just about to roll out of bed to grab a soda when the doorbell rang.

Still in my PJs I sauntered to the front door. UPS was supposed to drop off something for mom. Ever since she'd been working for slimy Parker she ordered her clothes online to save time.

I was about to open the door when the bell rang again. This time it continued buzzing like the visitor kept his thumb on the button. Annoying!

As soon as I cracked the door, it was pushed open with such force that I stumbled backwards, hitting my right foot on the coat rack.

"Damn you, Max." Emma burst into the hallway, her voice at a fever pitch as if she'd worked up to it all the way here.

"You want to tell me what you're doing here?" I managed, balancing on one foot, rubbing the other. That's when I noticed that I didn't have any real clothes on. "You can't come in here like that."

She shot me a glance, her lips pursed. "You think you've got anything I haven't seen. I don't care if you wear a flour sack."

"What do you want?"

"The truth."

"About what?" I was getting annoyed again. The girl was pushy *and* crazy.

"Why Stuler took Dad. You must have done something, said something…"

I shrugged recalling my meeting with Stuler when I'd told him I knew I was a beta. Stuler knew it had been Karl. *She'll kill you on the spot.*

"I may have mentioned something about a beta." *Where did that come from? Why couldn't I keep my mouth shut whenever a girl showed up?*

"So?"

"Stuler doesn't want your Dad talking to people. I told Stuler that I knew I was a beta….And the only reason I knew was because Karl told me."

"So, it *is* your fault. I knew it." Emma put herself in front of me, stabbing a forefinger into my chest. "If you don't know already, my father is ill."

"Why aren't you living with him?" I said, stepping back to get out of reach.

Emma sighed. "After he returned he was different. My mom…she couldn't deal with his anxiety, his panic attacks. He'd wake up screaming. They decided to separate."

For the first time I felt the need to put an arm around her. *Stop it, Max. She's the most annoying girl you've ever met.* Instead I waved her through to the kitchen.

"Want something to drink?"

"No, I want you to go to Stuler and get my Dad out."

"What? You nuts?"

"Somebody has to and you're the only person I could think of."

"Why don't *you* go and ask?"

"They'll turn me away. It's happened before when I wanted answers. Wanted to see Stuler to ask why my dad was in the hospital more dead than alive with a finger missing."

"What happened?"

"The guard escorted me out. I didn't even get within 50 yards of Stuler's office."

I sagged across from Emma and sipped my warm drink, asking myself why I didn't just send her away. But something about the way she sat hunched forward stopped me. Her eyes were filled with sadness and a bit too shiny.

"That place is a fortress."

"I know, but Stuler must like you as a gamer."

"What if it's a trap?"

Emma shrugged. "I know you'll find a way."

It was hard to resist the hope in her voice. Max to the rescue once again. Was I ever going to learn to say no?

Truth was I felt guilty. If I hadn't opened my big mouth, Stuler may have left Karl alone.

I would have to come up with a dumb excuse to return to Stuler's office and snoop around. *You are his number one gamer.* He'll be happy to get you back in his claws. For the first time, I wanted to stop Stuler. He'd nearly killed Karl and if the game were released, thousands maybe millions of people would be in danger. Not to mention the question if they were able to change history. The ramifications could be insanely dangerous.

I couldn't let that happen.

CHAPTER THIRTY-SEVEN

I paced. It was exactly three and one half steps between the door and the window of my room and I wanted to talk to someone. But Jimmy was still on vacation and besides, he was the wrong guy when it came to discussing Dr. Stuler. In fact, I didn't really care to see Jimmy any time soon.

I stopped abruptly. What if Jimmy was involved? What if he'd deliberately showed me the game, put up an act. I tried remembering our meeting when he'd given me the disc. My mind whirled. I'd watch him closely next time we met. In the meantime I'd find out what I could. Emma had left much more subdued than when she'd arrived.

Deep in thought I changed clothes and headed outside. As the bus was making its way toward Kassel, my mind continued to go in circles. What if Karl wasn't there? What if Stuler forced me to play? *He hadn't done it yesterday so why would he today.* Still I couldn't relax, sitting rigid and staring blindly out the window.

Approaching the fenced-in property of Histech, I swallowed the stubborn lump that kept popping up in my throat. Still my feet propelled me forward.

"May I help you?" The guard from yesterday didn't let on that he'd seen me before.

"I want to see Dr. Stuler," I blurted.

"Do you have an appointment?"

"Not really, but I forgot some important information yesterday when…"

The guard abruptly disappeared inside the glassed-in booth and picked up the phone. He nodded and threw several glances my way. It was impossible to tell what he was saying.

Without warning, a second guard materialized next to me. "Follow me."

This time I watched everything around me: how many steps it took to enter the building, how sloppily the guard entered the code on the entrance door: 192573, the cameras behind the reception desk, the smiling woman, the two elevators, each with a code pad. Nothing was done in this place without somebody else knowing about it.

Stuler is going to lock you in one of the little rooms. This is a fortress and you are way out of your league. By the time the elevator halted on the sixth floor, I was short of breath. My carefully laid out story had dissolved into thin air.

"Dr. Stuler is in a meeting," the Blonde said. Today the woman's lips were purple, reminding me of a plum.

"I…forgot a few things," I said, taking in the set of cameras along the ceiling.

"I've called his assistant." The Blonde's smile showed bleached teeth. Sure enough Handsome was making his way down the corridor.

"Hello Max," he said. "Why don't you come with me and I'll take your information to Dr. Stuler later."

"Eh, sure." From the looks of it, Handsome's considerably smaller office was next to Stuler's.

"Have a seat. You don't mind if I tape this?"

"No, sure, I mean…" my mind spun with bits and pieces of made-up stories, shreds of memories of New Mexico and the Middle Ages. "I wonder if you could tell me…" I paused. "I think I met someone from present day, another player. Is that possible?"

Handsome's face remained impassive, but he leaned slightly forward. "I suppose."

"I'm wondering how many people are playing right now. Wouldn't it screw up the missions if we hung out in the same place?"

Handsome nodded encouragingly, so I continued. "I mean if we're in the same place and we interact, isn't that messing up the markers? What's going to happen once you've got thousands or millions playing?"

For a moment, the room turned quiet. I'd gone too far.

Handsome's chiseled features scrunched into a frown. "I'll have to discuss it with Dr. Stuler. I think we have about half a dozen players right now. Who did you see?"

"That's the weird thing," I said, watching Handsome's face. "I never talked to him, but he had dark hair and was older, like in his forties. He just appeared… modern." I wondered what Karl had actually looked like when he'd entered the game."

"When was this?"

"My first try, level one."

"We did have an older player. He's no longer affiliated with the company."

I nodded. That had to be Karl. "I'm worried I'd screw things up. I mean if I ever play again. You think I could talk to this guy? If he's no longer with the program, that shouldn't be a problem, right?"

A shadow crept across Handsome's face. "I'm not sure that's protocol. I'll have to consult with Dr. Stuler before giving permission."

I nodded innocently. So Handsome didn't know about Karl being watched and possibly abducted. Dead end.

"I need to use the restroom," I said, abruptly jumping to my feet.

"Past the lobby, third door on your left."

I inwardly sighed with relief when Handsome stayed seated and picked up the phone.

"I'll be back in a second," I said rushing out.

I carefully looked around the corner into the lobby. The Blonde was rummaging through a cabinet and had her back turned. If I remembered right I'd been at the far end of the hallway yesterday. Judging by the mirror, there had to be an observation room next to it. I hurried on, glad nobody was coming my way. Sure enough, there was another door—the observation room? As my hand touched the knob, somebody was opening it from the inside.

"…so you see we monitor at all times…"

I would've recognized Dr. Stuler's voice anywhere. I jumped three feet to the only room without a keypad and found myself inside a supply closet. The shelves were wide and no matter how I squeezed the door remained ajar. Through the open slit I watched

Dr. Stuler and an Asian man with cropped black hair and a fancy suit walk down the hall.

My heart thumped madly against my ribcage. I had to leave this place. Handsome was probably searching for me already.

I shot to the door Stuler had just left, but I was too slow. It was locked. I eyed the keypad. What were the chances? I keyed in 192573. The door slid open and I was instantly bathed in greenish light.

But that wasn't the weird thing.

Along three sides, the walls were made of huge windows. And through them I saw into six small rooms, the kind I'd spent four hours in yesterday. Three were empty, one contained a woman with long dark hair who looked like a student, one a man in his twenties with a full beard and curly hair and... there was Karl. While the woman and the man were staring into a computer screen, Karl leaned forward in his chair, hands in his lap as if he were asleep.

I scanned the table in front of me, which looked like an oversized cockpit with a thousand buttons of different sizes and colors. My fingers shook. Any moment somebody could enter the room. They'd probably left because Stuler was giving a tour. *Calm down*. Pretend you got lost.

Bending lower I noticed that many of the buttons were marked with tiny labels. The rooms were numbered. Karl was in five. I kept searching: lights, computer, heart rate, blood pressure, cameras, audio, door...wait a minute.

I pressed the audio button and leaned over the microphone. "Hey Karl, can you hear me?"

The transformation was immediate as Karl almost leaped from his chair. "Max, is that you?"

"Yeah, I'll open the door. Meet me in the hall. We need to get out of here."

Nodding, Karl ran for the entrance that clicked open instantly when I pushed the button.

Just then the bearded man disappeared and almost instantly reappeared. It was as if a frame was missing from a film, a slight skip. But there was the guy again and he was now wearing a tie-die shirt in rainbow colors. He still wore the beard but his hair was long and stringy and he looked much thinner with rings under this eyes.

Run. But my legs felt heavy and slow. Instead of going down the hall the way I'd come, I ran around the corner and almost crashed into Karl.

"There is only one way out," Karl hissed, "walk."

We turned and headed back toward the lobby. I'd forgotten Handsome, but there he was coming out of the washroom just as I passed by.

"Here you are," Handsome said, forcing a smile.

"I got lost," I said slowing down a bit. "Can I come back tomorrow? I've got terrible diarrhea." I patted my middle and scrunched up my face for effect, "something I ate."

Handsome looked doubtful, his gaze temporarily following Karl who walked on as if he were heading somewhere else. I held my breath, wondering if Handsome would start screaming or blowing a whistle. To my relief he nodded which could only mean that he didn't know Karl at all. "Be here at ten. Oh, I need to call a guard to accompany you."

"No need, I know the way down," I hurried, struggling to keep my voice even. Karl was obviously not waiting because when I turned around, he was already at the elevator. Every step seemed to take an hour as I scurried down the hall. My heart was pounding, my ears filled with rushing blood.

"Let's go," I managed when I reached Karl.

The elevator halted, the doors slid open with precision and there was one of the guards. I cringed but forced my mouth into a smile. To my relief the guard looked down the hall where Dr. Stuler and his guest in the fancy suit were heading our way.

Panic and adrenalin were competing in my legs as I leaped into the elevator. I wanted to run. Instead I had to wait for the doors to shut. Hammering the close button, I heard Dr. Stuler's voice.

"The guard will accompany you to the gate," Stuler said when he noticed me in the elevator. Our eyes met. The green pinpricks stung. I nodded while pushing Karl into the blind corner next to the elevator panel. The doors slid closed.

I heaved a sigh. Chances were we'd be discovered anyway. The elevator had at least two cameras, maybe other hidden ones.

"Was that Stuler?" Karl said. He sounded out of breath again.

"Listen," I whispered. "Is there another exit? Some other way we can get out?"

"The garage," Karl said. "Press the button to the basement."

I wanted to swear. The doors would open on ground level and we'd be apprehended. Still I pushed the garage button.

"As soon as the door opens, we'll push the close button."

Somewhere in the building an alarm sounded. It was as shrill as a World War Two siren.

"They found out I'm gone," Karl said.

"Or they're looking for me." My forefinger hovered on the elevator. My eye fell on another button. "What if we push the fire alarm?"

Karl shook his head. "That will stop the elevator."

"What did they want from you anyway?"

"Stuler's been using scare tactics. He doesn't want me talking to players, said he'd find a way to get his money back."

I shot Karl a curious glance. "What money?"

"Stuler paid me off… a couple million." Karl sighed. "I know what you think. I'm too young to retire, but you've got to understand I went from being a top programmer to being in terrible shape, closer to death than life. I couldn't work anymore." Karl rubbed his forehead.

"Maybe you should stay with us," I said. I wondered what my mom would say. I'd figure it out later. I had too many questions and Karl was liable to walk under a bus.

"I don't know."

"Come on, my mom is pretty cool for a mother and you can tell me what happened…how I saved you in the game. Besides, if Stuler shows up again, we're together.

"Another time. I'll be all right." He patted me on the shoulder.

The doors abruptly opened. To my great surprise, nobody stormed in. From where I stood, nobody was even near the elevator.

"We could go to the police," I offered, watching the doors close again.

"And say what?" Karl's voice was full of sarcasm. "That Stuler is a mad scientist, killing people? Everyone here respects him. He's known for all sorts of inventions. He's rich and donates millions to charity and the arts." Karl paused to catch his breath. "Look at us. A washed-out sicko and a teenager making outrageous accusations of time travel." He began to cough.

The thought occurred to me that I should tell him about his

daughter. "I met Emma."

Karl jerked to attention.

"She asked me to find you."

Karl shook his head. "That girl…"

He never finished his thought because loud banging reverberated through the elevator shaft. The door slid open. My eyes widened.

We were trapped.

CHAPTER THIRTY-EIGHT

Four guards rushed us. I was pushed against the stainless steel walls, my left cheek smashed flat, my hands forced behind me. I was cuffed in seconds. The way these guys acted they reminded me of Schwarzburg's henchmen. Karl didn't fare any better.

"Come with us," one of the men barked. I recognized him from the guard booth out front.

My heart was beating in my neck as the elevator whisked us back to the sixth floor. With every second I felt more scared, so scared that I couldn't get air, my throat tight as if somebody were choking me.

Just like entering the game, my mind sneered.

When the elevator doors opened, my legs wanted to remain in place. The shove from behind made me stumble forward. As I caught myself I looked up. At the end of the corridor, Dr. Stuler stood waiting, his eyes unmoving, sending icy shivers down my spine.

Without a word the guards marched us into Stuler's office where we came to a stop at his desk. Calmly, as if he were holding a business meeting, Stuler sat down.

I was hoping the guards would release us, but no such luck. They stood a foot away on each side.

"Max. I don't recall that we had a meeting today. Nor do I recall inviting you to my company." Stuler's voice was cold. Colder than I'd ever heard it. His marble eyes had crazy written all over them. "Karl. You surprise me. I thought we were going to have a talk. Instead you run off like a common criminal."

I stole a glance at Karl whose upper body slouched and shook like a wind-worn pine in the Black Range. He stood quietly, a rabbit waiting for the fox to strike. In a way watching Karl so obviously afraid made my own terror worse. Karl knew this man, a guy he'd worked with for over ten years.

Did he know what Stuler was really up to? What he wanted from us? I felt helpless and furious at the same time. Like an idiot I'd been deceived into thinking I was trying out a cool new game.

I wanted to destroy the game.

You're in handcuffs.

"My mom is waiting for me," I blurted.

Stuler raised an eyebrow, one manicured forefinger tapping his lips. "Really?" He abruptly bent forward and punched something into his phone.

"Elke, get me Max Anderson's mother. She lives in Bornhagen."

"At once," came the disembodied voice of the receptionist.

I held my breath. Would he reach Mom? Of course, it was after five and she'd be home, probably worried about me.

The phone buzzed.

"Anderson," my mom said.

"Dr. Stuler here, *guten Abend Frau Anderson*....yes, yes, it's been a while." I wanted to gag, my mother making small talk with a psychopath. "Say, would you mind if Max spends the night. Jimmy just returned and the boys...," he chuckled, "you know how it is, they want to spend time....yes, or course." Stuler's eyes met mine. "We'll take good care of him."

I swallowed the lump that was growing into a boulder. Something evil emanated from Stuler and I shuddered. Karl next to me wasn't doing any better, his shoulders slumped and his head hanging. When I tried moving my arms, the handcuffs bit into my wrists. With the guards next to us escape was impossible.

Stuler's lab was secure as a prison. It'd take a bomb...Wait a minute. If I wanted to destroy the game, I'd have to wipe out the lab, maybe the entire building. Even if it happened at night when the building was empty that was destruction of property. It was illegal and dangerous. I'd go to jail.

You are in jail. Stuler's jail.

I stood brooding when from the corner of my eye I noticed

something moving on the wall monitors. A tiny earth, no bigger than a thumbnail, rotated in slow motion. It pulsated like a beating heart.

The back of my neck began to tingle.

This thing looked like the globe I'd seen before entering the game. A feeling of dread began to grow in my stomach, spreading to my legs and making them heavy.

I remembered Juliana, the girl I'd fallen in love with during the first game in the Middle Ages, quickly overshadowed by the girl who'd bulldozed her way into my house. Emma. She wanted her dad back, but instead I'd gotten Karl and me into horrible danger.

According to both of them I'd play again. What had they said? Karl wouldn't be alive without me. That I'd helped him escape.

Question was, would Stuler force me somehow or would I choose freely? Not freely, not with me standing in Stuler's office in handcuffs and Stuler having paved the way for some uninterrupted time.

That's when it hit me.

The realization that while Karl was safe because I'd gotten him out of the game there was no knowing how the game would end for me.

Chances were I'd never see present day again.

Stuler nodded toward the screen. "Shall we?"

CHAPTER THIRTY-NINE

"Where are we going?" I croaked, wondering what Billy the Kid would do. I imagined him standing there with that easy grin, whirling his revolver and telling Stuler to go to hell. Then he'd blow the man straight through his fancy glass windows.

"The test rooms." My smile vanished as Stuler waved at the guards to lead the way. I realized I was more scared now than when I'd fought Wade. It took a ton of energy and strength and I was in no shape to play again.

A scream rang out.

Commotion broke out in the hallway. Handsome burst into Stuler's office followed by Elke who looked as if she'd seen a ghost. Handsome was white-faced, his chiseled cheekbones stretched tight.

"You better come at once," Handsome said. "There's been an incident. I've called the ambulance."

"Now?" Stuler barked, obviously annoyed about somebody interrupting his plans.

Handsome rushed to Stuler's side, whispering, "The medical student, something happened to her. She's…" He leaned in closer so I couldn't hear.

Since the doors were left open, I craned my neck. Six or seven people were running down the hall and on the far end, the entrance to the mirrored rooms was clogged with onlookers.

"This is not a good time," Stuler hissed.

"Please, Sir, I implore you." Handsome seemed to be beside

himself.

"It better be important." Stuler headed into the hall when he seemed to remember Karl and me. "Let them go. We'll deal with it later."

The guards opened our handcuffs and we found ourselves escorted to the elevator. Two EMTs spilled from the opening door and hurried toward the lab rooms.

"This way," Handsome yelled over the din of the crowd as the elevator doors closed. I looked at Karl who leaned against the wall.

"You okay?"

He nodded, his Adams apple bopping furiously.

As soon as we entered the street my phone rang.

"How did it go?" Emma's voice was breathless.

"Just got out."

"How's Dad?"

"He's with me. We're going home."

"What happened?"

"Stuler wanted me to play, but something happened with one of the other gamers. Didn't see what, though."

"So, you're not going to do it then?"

"Not any time soon if I can help it."

"Why not?"

"Emma, I'm tired, no exhausted. I want to sleep. Leave me alone." Truth was I had too many questions. I'd rushed into the game and landed in New Mexico. Chances were I'd land somewhere else entirely again. If I wanted to save Karl I'd better be absolutely sure to get to the right year and place.

"I'm coming over," Emma said.

"No, you're not. Talk to your Dad." I handed the phone to Karl. "Talk some sense into your daughter. She wants me to play the game so I can save you."

Karl took the phone and apparently listened to an onslaught because he held the phone three inches away and said nothing for a long time.

"Listen to me. Let him be for now." He clicked off and handed me my phone. "I'm sorry. She's a bit headstrong."

I shook my head. Emma was an idiot.

"I thought you were spending the night," my mother said as soon as I opened the door.

"Change of plans."

"Dinner is in the fridge."

"I'm not hungry." I headed for my room. My stomach growled but I was too tired to eat. I needed time alone. Time to think.

Karl had slinked off without saying much and I'd dozed on the bus. He knew what it took to play and how it drained every last ounce of energy.

After tossing and turning for two hours I got back up. It was after midnight, the house quiet. The events of today had shaken me more than I'd expected. The feelings of safety and comfort I'd experienced after my return had evaporated. Instead I felt dread, no a sort of terror I'd never felt in the game. There I'd been busy figuring things out. I'd learned stuff, helped people.

This was different. Stuler wasn't finished with me. I had to play again, whether I wanted to or not. Karl had said I was going back. He'd seen me in medieval Bornhagen.

And right now it looked as if Stuler would force me. He'd appeared positively crazy today.

The larger issue was, of course, that he had to be stopped. The game destroyed. He'd go down eventually, but not before injuring or killing thousands, maybe millions of gamers. Guys like me and Jimmy.

Jimmy! I wanted to talk to him. Find out if he knew about his father. Test him somehow.

Grabbing my phone I turned on my PC. I'd check messages to take my mind of. As I texted Jimmy I noticed movement on the computer monitor.

At the bottom right corner an earth slowly rotated, the blue and green pulsing like a beating heart.

The End

AUTHOR'S NOTE

Though this book is a work of fiction, it takes us to an actual and tumultuous period of U.S. history.

The early 1880s were a busy time in New Mexico. Settlers created homesteads and because silver and gold had been discovered, mining camps flourished. Outlaws and rustlers did whatever they pleased—most of the time. Money and lives were easily lost in gambling halls and on the range.

In the summer of 1881, Henry McCarty alias Billy the Kid was hiding from his longtime nemesis, Sheriff Pat Garrett, near Fort Sumner. Billy had many friends in the area and wanted to settle down, which seemed only possible if he could get a pardon from Governor Wallace. Billy was in love with Paulita Maxwell, heir to one of the largest estates in the country. Despite a promise, the pardon never came. Wallace ignored Billy's letters and announced a reward of $500 for his head. Pat Garrett, tipped off by Paulita's brother, Pete, showed up in Fort Sumner on July 14, 1881. He assassinated the unarmed Billy in the dark in Pete Maxwell's bedroom. Paulita married Jose Jamarillo in early 1882. It was rumored she was pregnant with Billy's child, though this was never proven.

Not far to the south and west, most of the Chíhéne Nde (Warm Springs Apaches) who'd lived for centuries in the Black Range Mountains (part of the Gila Wilderness) had been reduced to living at the Mescalero Indian Reservation. The rest were hunted by Mexican and U.S. Armies and despised by miners and settlers.

In the fall of 1880, the Mexican Army in the battle of *Tres Castillos* had killed Chief Victorio and many of his warriors along with women and children. Most survivors were made slaves and dragged off to Mexico.

Chief Nana Kas-tziden (Broken Foot)

Two who got away were Nana and Lozen, Victorio's uncle and sister. In June of 1881, Nana, in his late seventies and lame in one foot, collected a handful of warriors and went on a vengeance war. He and his men rode over 3,000 miles across New Mexico, attacking white settlements, Army posts and trains. They stole horses and supplies. To the chagrin and embarrassment of the U.S. Army, Nana was not only never caught, not a single warrior was ever taken—alive or dead.

After the raid, Nana teamed up with Geronimo and a few remaining Indian chiefs. Together they spent a few more years on the run. But as with all Native Americans, the reign of the Chíhéne Nde Apaches was over. Nana died in 1896 at Fort Sill, Oklahoma at the age of 89.

They were never able to return to their homeland in the Black Range of New Mexico.

ABOUT THE AUTHOR

Thank you for reading *Escape from the Past: The Kid (Book 2)*. My sincere hope is that you derived as much entertainment from reading this story as I enjoyed in creating it. If you have a few moments, please feel free to add your review of the book at your favorite online site for feedback (Amazon, Apple iTunes Store, Barnes & Noble, Kobo, Goodreads, etc.). Also, if you would like to connect with previous or upcoming books, please visit my website for information and to sign up for e-news: http://www.annetteoppenlander.com.

All the best, Annette

CONTACT ME

I always appreciate hearing from readers. Please contact me via the following social media channels:

Website: www.annetteoppenlander.com
Facebook: www.facebook.com/annetteoppenlanderauthor
Twitter: @aoppenlander
Pinterest: @annoppenlander

ABOUT THE AUTHOR

Annette Oppenlander is an award-winning writer, literary coach and educator. As a bestselling historical novelist, Oppenlander is known for her authentic characters and stories based on true events, coming alive in well-researched settings. Having lived in Germany the first half of her life and the second half in various parts of the U.S., Oppenlander inspires readers by illuminating story questions as relevant today as they were in the past.

Oppenlander's bestselling true WWII story, Surviving the Fatherland, has received multiple honors, including the 2017 National Indie Excellence Awards, the Indie B.R.A.G. awards and the Readers' Favorite Book Awards. It was also finalist in the 2017 Kindle Book Awards. Her historical time-travel trilogy, Escape from the Past, takes readers to the German Middle Ages and the Wild West. Uniquely, Oppenlander weaves actual historical figures and events into her plots, giving readers a flavor of true history while enjoying a good story. Oppenlander shares her knowledge through writing workshops at colleges, libraries and schools. She also offers vivid presentations and author visits. The mother of fraternal twins and a son, she recently moved with her husband and old mutt, Mocha, to Solingen, Germany.

"Nearly every place holds some kind of secret, something that makes history come alive. When we scrutinize people and places closely, history is no longer a date or number, it turns into a story."

If you enjoyed *Escape From the Past: The Kid* (Book 2), you may also enjoy the last installment of Max's adventure, *At Witches' End*, when Max returns to the Middle Ages and Castle Hanstein.

Read a sample below.

PREVIEW
ESCAPE FROM THE PAST
AT WITCHES' END (BOOK 3)

CHAPTER ONE

I was riding the bus home from school when my cellphone buzzed. *Text from unknown.* After the argument with Dr. Stuler I'd changed phones. Not even Jimmy knew my number.

Actually, other than driving to school together, Jimmy and me hadn't hung out for months. He'd tried a few times after he returned from all his fancy trips, but I'd blown him off. He acted all mad and hurt, but who knew what was an act and what was his father talking.

"You about ready? Fall break starts tomorrow."

"Who's this? Ready for what?" I answered. Some jerk had the wrong number.

"Emma. Need to see you."

I rolled my eyes. Stupid idiot of a girl. Why didn't she leave me alone? I hadn't talked to her since the day Karl and I had made it out of Histech.

I stuck the phone back in my pocket. I wasn't going to see anybody related to the game. My insides churned as the memories of summer returned, barely making it out of New Mexico alive, only to be abducted by Jimmy's father, Dr. Stuler.

261

As I unlocked the front door, a shadow rushed up to me.

"Why aren't you answering?" Emma's red hair glowed like the setting sun.

"The fact you're already waiting here tells me you really didn't want an answer."

"Hah."

I stepped inside, contemplating to shut the door in her face. *Don't be a douche.* She'd only keep pestering and I sort of was…curious.

"Coming in?"

She marched past me into the living room and plopped on the couch. I followed slowly, just to show I wasn't going to do her bidding. How could a girl be so annoying and so hot at the same time? If anything she'd gotten cuter. I never thought I'd go for freckles, but the way they sprinkled across her face I—.

"Hello. You listening?"

"What?" I sagged into the single chair, the coffee table as a safety zone between us.

"I said it's time you finish the game. Dad didn't want to bother you yet, but I think you're ready."

"I told you I'm not playing again."

Emma looked like she was going to pole vault across the table to wring my neck. Apparently she thought better of it and leaned forward instead.

"If you weren't playing any more, my father would be dead."

This time-travel thing was screwy. You could go back to any point in the past, but returned to the same exact second you left.

If you returned.

Karl had played long ago, even before my first game. He'd barely made it back alive. And supposedly I'd been the one to get him out.

"I can't handle it right now."

"How long are you going to wait?"

I shrugged. Till I'm ready I wanted to say. Assessing the angry squint on Emma's face I said nothing.

Emma pursed her lips. "You know he saved your life. You would've rotted in Schwarzburg's dungeon, had it not been for my dad."

"What are you saying?"

"I'm saying my father got a guy to spring you from the

dungeon."

"No way."

"No?" Emma jumped up. "I'm calling my dad right now."

"Why?" Secretly I was trying to remember who I'd told about the escape from Schwarzburg's cell in the first game. She was obviously trying to lay a guilt trip on me.

It wasn't going to work.

"Dad, yeah, I'm with Max. Tell him what you told me about helping him escape."

Emma listened to the phone. Obviously Karl wasn't too happy about her being here. Good!

Maybe he'd refuse to speak to me, but she handed over the phone.

"Hi Karl."

"How are you, Max?"

"Okay."

"Em wants me to tell you about the escape." Karl hesitated. It was obvious he didn't want to talk about it.

"How did you know? I mean my time at Rusteberg."

"I was staying in Marth, the little village nearby. Word got around that a strange character had been caught. I suspected it was somebody from the game…because I'd seen you once before."

"When?" Karl was hallucinating.

"In Hanstein's forest, I'd been on the run, they…cut off my middle finger. You were watching from the bushes. You wore that T-shirt with nerds printed on it." A bitter chuckle came across the phone.

In the recesses of my mind the scene from my first game returned. Landing in the woods, my panic being lost, Bero flinging pinecones at my head. My first night at Bero's hut…

"…and when Schwarzburg accused you to be Werner von Hanstein's spy, I knew I had to get you out."

The line went quiet for a moment as my mind took me back to the darkest time in my life.

I'd pushed it away, the horrific place no human should endure, feeling like a madman as I grew weaker and weaker.

"I convinced a peasant farmer who'd been wronged by Schwarzburg to help. He knew the area and took you to Hanstein. You know the rest."

I blindly stared out the back doors into the garden. I'd always wondered who had saved me and why. Later I stopped caring, just being glad to have escaped the game.

"I owe you one," I said quietly.

Karl let out a rattled sigh. "I know you don't want to play again. I don't blame you. But I wouldn't be talking to you right now, had you not saved me. I'm fine if we wait."

"I've got to think about it."

"Tell Em to leave you alone. You call me when you're ready."

I handed the phone to Emma and slumped back into the chair. "He says you should leave."

To my surprise Emma nodded and headed for the door.

That night I lay awake. It was clear I owed Karl. And truthfully I wasn't so worried to return to Hanstein. I had friends there. Knew my way around.

The unsettling part was that the game could send you anywhere. I'd tried to get to Hanstein last time and ended up in 1881 New Mexico. I could land in Normandy during World War II. Or I'd go to the American Civil War. Anything was possible.

I also wanted to destroy Stuler's game though I had no clue how to go about it. If I played again he'd find out. Which would draw new attention to me.

For the last two months I'd managed to forget the uneasy feeling I'd had when I escaped from New Mexico only to be forced into Stuler's office. At first I'd looked over my shoulder all the time, expecting the man to abduct me again. I'd slept fitfully having nightmares about my computer.

It had always been my favorite possession, but after discovering the game embedded on it, I hadn't felt safe. I even contemplated getting rid of the thing.

I turned on my back and stared at the ceiling. The house was silent, but not silent enough to calm my jittering nerves.

Playing the game contained a million risks. I was out of my league. Alone, one nerd against all of history, against Stuler's madness.

I needed help and there was only one guy capable of providing it.

CHAPTER TWO

Karl opened the door. He seemed better than the last time we'd met, his cheeks a bit fuller, his eyes brighter.

"I need to talk to you," I blurted, pushing past him into the kitchen.

"Of course."

"I lay awake all night, thinking how I'd handle this," I said. Karl nodded, holding my gaze. "If I do this game again, you're going to help me get to the right place and time."

"I don't know—"

"You said you were his top programmer. You know this game inside out. If I land anywhere else or at a different time, I'm screwed." I glanced at Karl across the table. "I can't handle another mistake like New Mexico."

Karl blinked rapidly. "I suppose I could…"

"Can you come to my place tomorrow? For some reason I've got a copy on my hard drive so I'm not using the PC. Doing all my work on the laptop now."

"I'll have to write new code, make sure the timer stops at the right moment."

I nodded. "How long?"

Karl tapped a finger on his lower lip. "Not long. A day should be fine. It's just…"

"What?"

"We have no way of testing it."

My mouth turned to sand. If Karl made a mistake, I'd end up

on the Western Front during WWI, being gassed in a trench.

"See you in the morning," I croaked. Heading for the front door I added, "Oh, and I want to stop Stuler. I need your help with that."

"Wait a minute." Karl rushed after me and pushed the door closed once more. "You're out of your mind. The man is crazy. You saw what he's capable of."

"That's exactly why we need to stop him."

Karl shook his head. "I'm not going to burn down his place."

"You don't have to." I grabbed onto Karl's forearm. "You know the company. He's got a server room, some place where all the game technology is kept."

"The third and fourth floors."

"Yeah."

"They're secured. Not even the elevator stops there." Karl leaned back against the wall.

"If you created a computer virus that infected everything…"

"I don't know."

"Can you do it?"

Karl finally nodded. "I'll give it some thought. Now let me get to work."

The screen buzzed, showing the familiar stone gate. I slid back until my butt leaned firmly against the chair. This time I'd pay attention to the way my body twisted when my room dissolved. Karl had installed a bunch of code on my computer. He'd explained it all, but compared to him my programming skills were mediocre.

The screen sizzled. The stone gate fell away and the outline of a castle appeared in the distance. Just like the first time. I expected to see Lord Werner and his brother, Lame Hans, in the woods, but the path in front of me was empty.

The button flashed. Upgrade to master level?

With a sigh I took mental inventory of my outfit, the items I'd prepped and stuck into my pants. *You may not return this time.* Just because I saved Karl didn't mean I'd be able to get back. *You're nuts.*

It was like the chicken and the egg. Which came first, Karl being there and being rescued by me or me going because I'd rescue Karl.

My forefinger's hover turned into a tremble. In fact my entire body had a mind of its own. The game had taught me respect for historical environments. Modern guys like me just didn't fit in. How many times could I be lucky?

If you want to survive you're going to have to make your own luck. What if it wasn't enough? Still, all I'd do is postpone the inevitable. I was going to play so why not now. Get it over with.

I clicked.

The monitor hovered and then receded, pulling the room with it. The walls moved out of proportion as if pulsating in and out of focus. Pressure engulfed me, took hold of my arms and legs. My chest stopped moving, my breath caught. Boulder-like weights crushed me. I forgot where I was, who I was.

All I wanted was to breathe.

Nothing mattered, except find a way to make my ribs rise and my lungs fill with air. I couldn't. I stared yet I saw nothing but stars—bright exploding lights that took over my vision until I thought I was going blind.

As quickly as the heaviness came, it disappeared. I blinked away the fuzziness.

Ever so slowly I looked down, recognizing my feet in the chocolate brown boots I'd bought last winter. They were fur-lined with rubber soles strong enough to withstand the harshest middle-age winter. I was prepared this time.

Beyond my feet a path stretched into the distance. I shielded my eyes against the orange glow of the sun and sniffed. The air was filled with the aroma of hay and dust, the heat shifting and shimmering above the brownish fields. I turned in a circle.

My room was definitely gone.

In that moment panic rose and my throat filled with bile. The feeling of complete loneliness was paralyzing. The only thing that came close had to be astronauts in space, knowing that millions of miles were between them and their families and that death lurked around the corner.

In the distance I made out a castle. Karl had gotten the location right. With a sigh, I yanked off the cape I'd been wearing. It had to be ninety degrees.

What day and time of year was it? Judging by the sun's vicious blaze, late afternoon and definitely not winter. I remembered the first time I'd been here when I'd not even known the year until a couple of weeks into the game. Of course, back then I hadn't known about time-travel. Now I wouldn't wait to ask. No matter how stupid I looked. What if Karl's calculations were wrong?

I turned toward the castle and followed the path until the first shacks of Bornhagen came into view. They were even shabbier than I remembered, especially in the harsh light of the afternoon. Worse was the smell that reached my nostrils—like a thick cocoon of a garbage dump.

It was so easy to forget the horrific stink of the Middle Ages when you lived in a clean home with plumbing. I held my breath, but soon sucked in air to keep going. The dust trail was littered with remnants of onion peels, rotting bones and what appeared like human waste. Some villagers simply tossed their excrement into the street for everyone to enjoy.

I carefully stepped across the stench, ignoring the scattering feet of my old friends, the rats. I stripped to a plain brown T-shirt and tucked my cape, a sort of oversized hooded sweater I'd bought at an online medieval clothing store, under my arm. My pants, made of thick wool, stuck to my skin and I wanted nothing more than to take them off—and the ridiculous, fur-lined boots. At home it was October and I'd frozen so badly last time that I'd never even considered it might be summer and I might be overdressed.

I wiped my dripping forehead when my feet forgot to move. Bero's hut was straight ahead, the door open as usual.

Of course, Bero wouldn't be here. He was a squire and likely sitting in the shade of the castle walls, stuffing his face and drinking wine.

I hesitated. Why not go straight to the castle, organize a cooler outfit and get reacquainted with Werner, Bero and Juliana. On the other hand, why not say hello to Juliana's mother.

I stopped at the outer gate to the barnyard when a girl rushed from the front door. She was carrying a bucket and had nearly reached me before she looked up. And froze. I was too stunned to say anything. The girl looked like Juliana, the same doe-brown eyes, short nose and skinny waist. But something was different about her. It had to be the hair, which was several shades lighter. Maybe I didn't remember it right.

"Oh heaven protect me," the girl screamed. She tossed down her bucket and raced back into the hut, slamming the door behind her.

I stood unmoving, raking my brain about the details of Juliana's face. My memory was playing tricks. Had I returned earlier and Juliana didn't know me yet? Could I potentially run into myself playing the game? I rubbed the back of my neck as if to inspire a new idea when I noticed movement behind the crud-covered windowpanes.

Still contemplating whether to move on or knock, the front door squeaked open a couple of inches. I couldn't tell who stood in the gloom so I took a couple of steps toward the hut.

"Juliana?" For a second the door remained still. Then it opened wide enough to reveal the girl's face. "Don't be afraid," I offered.

"I'm Adela," the girl said, her eyes filled with something like fear and annoyance.

Scenes from the past flashed through my mind. A twelve-year old Adela setting the table, Adela ogling at my every move.

"You remember me?"

"Of course. Max." To my surprise her voice was sharp with anger. "You just startled me."

"I...didn't recognize you."

When I took another step toward the door, she yelled, "Stay there. Mother will be back any moment and she'll whip me till the end of time if I let you in."

"What happened?"

"You ask *me* what happened?" Against her own advice, the door opened wider. I marveled at how much alike the two sisters were. By the looks of it, years had passed because the skinny girl I remembered had turned into a hottie. So much for Karl getting it right. What year had I returned?

Adela didn't seem to care or notice. Instead she kept glancing up and down the path as if hoping for help. I wanted to say, hey, it's me, your friend, but her eyes refused to meet mine. Instead, I followed her gaze and noticed that some of the huts were deserted, their doors ajar or missing, some lying broken in weed-covered front yards.

Adela's voice quivered. "You must go at once."

"Why? I'll explain it to your mother."

As an answer Adela slammed shut the door. What was the matter with the girl? She'd been shy, but quite friendly last time I'd been here.

With a shrug, I turned and walked up the trail toward the Klausenhof inn. Several visitors sat in the shade of the patio drinking from pewter mugs. Some wore the colorful linen of merchants, and some were dressed in chainmail. I glanced back and forth to find the familiar Hanstein crest of the three moons, but these men had blue and yellow on their breastplates, Schwarzburg's colors.

I lowered my head and rushed past. No need for them to recognize me.

Horses stomped in front of the barn, their chests covered in armored plates. Blankets with yellow lions on bright blue backgrounds covered them despite the heat. A lone carriage sat under the wide arms of the oak tree. I decided to move on before the knights got suspicious. Despite my medieval dress-up I had to look pretty weird, my hair two inches at most, my face too clean.

Of course, that would change within a day. I smirked. The Middle Ages should've been named the gross Ages. Anything you touched was covered in grime.

Like last time I had no money to pay someone for information or get a drink. It was impossible to get old coins. They were either in museums and private collections.

The path turned and rose toward the castle. Dripping with sweat, I rounded the corner toward the tiny village of Rimbach and the castle gates. I was looking forward to a refreshing beer in the coolness of the walls, hanging out with Bero and catching up.

And I wanted to see Juliana. My stomach lurched just thinking about her. I couldn't believe that I'd meet her in a few minutes, hug her close. I'd tried to remember her voice, her face but with every month it had been harder. Meeting Adela had brought it all back.

She had definitely changed, but medieval women matured much faster. I was only fifteen months older than last time and though I'd grown a bunch, my chin sprouted about seven hairs.

I'd try to get to the next level with Juliana. Many of my friends were doing it already and had been whispering of all-nighters and family packs of condoms. Even Jimmy had a girlfriend and recently gone all the way. I only knew because one of his "new" friends had talked about it.

"You lost?" A guard marched down from the gate, his arm heavy with a drawn sword. "You can't linger here. Scatter." He waved, making the blade slice the air.

I didn't recognize the man. I'd hoped to meet the old guard. Why hadn't I bothered to learn his name?

"I'm here to visit Lord Werner."

The guard squinted in obvious suspicion and shook his head. "Then you must not know much. The Lord is away. You can't wait hither."

"But I've been inside before."

The guard still held out his blade. "Many people visit Castle Hanstein. That doesn't mean you're allowed to loiter."

"Is he going to be back tonight?"

"Nay."

I half turned before I remembered Bero. "Then I'd like to see Bero, the squire."

The guard had begun walking uphill toward his hideout. "Squires don't receive visitors," he yelled over his shoulder.

"But he's my friend," I shouted after the man.

"Go away before I arrest you."

I discovered a second unfamiliar face in the shadow of the guard hold. The first guard was grumbling something and the other guy shook his head.

For a moment I stood unmoving. This wasn't at all what I'd expected. I'd thought the man would welcome me with open arms, slap me on the back, and invite me inside.

Instead the walls towered above, cold...indifferent and the gates remained closed. Beyond waited archers able to hit their target hundreds of yards away and well-trained knights ready to cut off heads with a single sweep of their long sword.

What was I supposed to do now?

End of Sample